Early Reviews

"A multitalented, bisexual, teenage slave becomes a symbol of freedom in this debut sci-fi saga… with energetic action scenes and sharply drawn characters, and the result is a vigorous tale." — **Kirkus Reviews**

"A riveting story with a powerful underlying political narrative—*The Chronicles of Spartak* will have an appeal across generations." — **David Kirp**, *New York Times Contributing Writer*

"Steven has this new genre ('new' because it avoids all the usual trappings of sci-fi novels and focuses on striving to make the future a better place rather than simply a rubble pile filled with odd creatures) down pat. If he continues this direction of writing he will be not only entertaining us with creative stories brilliantly written but also creating superheroes of substance – and very fine attributes!" — **Grady Harp**, Amazo*n (Top 100 Reviewer)*

"If you love *The Hunger Games*, and you want a bit more of a gritty and adult feel, you may love **Rising Son**." — **B.A. Brock**, *Queer SciFi*

"The treacherous world of 22nd century San Francisco as imagined by Steve Coulter would be a challenge to anyone but to 16-year-old Spartak Jones it becomes the stone on which he hones his athletic skills and his bravery. Coulter's writing can make us feel both at home and uneasy at the same time as he skillfully reveals a future we must fight against at all costs." — **Jewelle Gomez**, *Author of The Gilda Stories*

"Highly imaginative and creative, action packed, with a fascinating young protagonist who combines the physical and moral attributes of both Spiderman and Superman in his remarkable body and psyche. The pace never flags, the story holds suspense and tension in every scene. With its extrapolation of the politics and extremism of today, religious and political, *The Chronicles of Spartak* is a thoughtful and thoroughly entertaining achievement." — **Katherine V Forrest**, *Author of the Kate Delafield mystery series*

"This is a riveting political saga. The rich/poor divide is similar to the themes in the Presidential Election. I encourage you to read it. You will do it long into the night." — **Dr. Barbara O'Connor**, *Institute of Politics & Media, California State University, Sacramento*

"*The Chronicles of Spartak* is really intellectual, fast paced, has a lot of action, good characters, and I really appreciated the way a young queer athlete and a slave becomes a symbol for a revolution." — **Vigilantereads**

"The protagonist is a young and renowned athlete in a society that tolerates him for its entertainment. The writing is literate, direct, and a pleasure to read. There is a fascinating plot point—the return of slavery to the United States of America." — **Dennis Myers**, *Reno News & Review*

"We are so lucky to have writers that are producing books for the young and especially with this superhero, we have someone that everyone can be proud of and with whom sexuality is a non-issue… I found *The Chronicles of Spartak* to be totally absorbing and entertaining—so much so that I stopped everything else and read the book to completion in one sitting." — **Amos Lassen**, *Blogger*

Readers on Amazon:
"An excellent gripping read…an ending that couldn't have been imagined by the reader." — **Patricia**

"We are all Spartak!" — **Justarius**

"There are still heroes, and this story inspires – making me want to be more." — **Eric**

"A fast paced, page turning adventure I would recommend to science fiction readers." — **Casey**

"The next *Hunger Games* is here!" — **Julia**

Goodreads:
"Ever since I finished the book, on too many occasions - sadly - when reading/listening to the news, I've thought to myself: This is the beginning of Spartak's world - just as the author has presciently described it." — **Marina**

the chronicles of SPARTAK
Rising Son

Steven A. Coulter

No Apocalypse. No Zombies. No Vampires. No Magic Wands. No Dragons. Just an extraordinary teenager fighting for survival, freedom and love in a 22nd century America twisting out of control.

The Chronicles of Spartak – Rising Son

This is a work of fiction. Names, characters, places and incidents either are the product of the author's imagination or are used fictitiously. Any resemblance to real individuals—either living or dead—is strictly coincidental.

Published by Jubilation Media
P.O. Box 14664
4304 18th Street
San Francisco, CA 94114-0664

978-0-9966473-0-4 paperback
978-0-9966473-1-1 e-book
978-0-9966473-2-8 hard cover

Credits:
Cover by Melanie Rose Illustration and Sparkie Cathart, Kiaro Creative Approaches, Ltd.
Interior book design and formatting by Debbi Stocco, MyBookDesigner.com
Content editing by Katherine V. Forrest
Copy editing by Ruth Stanley
Web design by Kegan Quimby
Photo of the author by Steven Underhill

To Greg and Kirby, always there for me.

PROLOGUE

June 27, 2115
Ronald Reagan Arena
San Diego, California

BEING SHOT OUT OF A CANNON is not how I expected to spend my sixteenth birthday. "The audience will love it," gushed adults who didn't have to climb inside. This seemed like something ancient Romans might have wished to use on Christians when the lions weren't hungry. The vertical black cylinder, forty feet at the muzzle, nine feet in diameter, has a tiny door on the side, just above the breech, giving access through the chamber and into the round projectile inside.

This is supposed to be a showy and theatrical arrival for the awards ceremony. I grin and rush toward the door, looking thrilled for this new experience. Drama is one of my best high school classes. Downer boys like me know how to survive in this America.

To get into the giant sphere—giant being a relative term for a cannonball—I squat and waddle, not very dignified, four of us in a space that shouldn't hold one. I plop my gluteus maximus on the designated indent on a shelf that circles the inside.

"Keep arms at your sides," a mechanical female voice orders. A dozen wooly steel fingers thrust out from each side and wrap around my biceps, chest and thighs, python tight. A furry helmet, attached to the end of a metal column and wriggling like it's alive, drops from the ceiling and swallows the top of my head before it stretches to my ears, pushing scratchy fingers inside. The seat begins to heat and vibrate before contouring intimately into my butt. A metal arm unfolds from the wall and swings a horseshoe-shaped, undulating, disgusting white pad to my lips. "Open your mouth wide," the voice demands.

It pushes against my lips with increasing intensity before I surrender and it invades, enveloping my teeth. The arm detaches and folds back into its hiding place. I feel like meat in an enchilada. I close my eyes, waiting for liftoff, the least of my worries.

Being "the hope of my people" and "a hero" isn't easy—more like a joke. Neither is acting dignified when I'm strapped to a bench that's feeling up my tail end or in public when teenagers are screaming for me to take off my clothes. Not that it happens all the time, but Coach Johanson says people in my social strata believe in me, that I'm a symbol and need to make them proud, not act like a kid. A strange thing to say; acting like a kid isn't a luxury most kids have anymore but I still have my breakout moments.

"Att-en-tion boys!" the pilot bellows, inches from my face, "lean into your harness, bite your bit and enjoy the ride!" Our luminous silver aero-pod begins to vibrate and twirl inside the launch chamber. Everything goes black except a floating control panel. We stare straight ahead, not that there's an alternative, as the centrifugal force pins us back and whips our cheeks sideways.

An explosion below and we are airborne, my guts in my butt, eardrums squealing, a thousand feet over Reagan Arena, the pod glittering to those below like a mirrored dance ball. Before we lose our lunch, the spinning slows and we descend, circling the field twice, our faces red and slobbery but otherwise normal as we hover over the winner's platform. An odd hyena shriek from the pilot as his restraints withdraw; the man never offered his name, his brown head shaved except for a massive kinked topknot and a zigzag gelled beard.

We all yawn until our ears pop and stare into individual floating Z-ether screens to see what's happening below. It's a circus, twenty thousand teenagers, frenzied, howling and jumping up and down. The San Diego Youth Orchestra looks near exhaustion blasting out our welcome, pounding drums, endless violin tremolos, a female chorus reaching celestial peaks. It's both ridiculous and a total snort. In the lower stands I see hundreds of hand-lettered signs with my name and assorted suggestions on what I should do, mostly about displaying my anatomy, some more graphic than others.

The metal straps and helmet retract. I can breathe again and stretch my arms. I remove the bit, my tongue still intact, and wipe spit from my face with my shirt.

"Please, Spartak, keep your clothes on," Matt Dowell, on my left, teases me. He's from Philadelphia's Golden Heights High School and a sweetheart African American; a near-normal guy for a barronial.

"Yeah, blondie, your pretty face is skin enough," Hinkins Martinez says with a giggle, grabbing my head and giving me a knuckle grind. He's also a barronial, a swarthy Hispanic with Manzanita hair running down his back, from Marbush High in Seattle. They're both members of the top tier of the richest families and I'm a lowly scholarship guy from Ogden Academy in San Francisco and so far down the social ladder I'm called a downer. But on the mats, rings and bars, we're equals. I shove Hinkins away with a laugh, shaking my head, and finger-comb my long blond hair behind my ears. He's always a tease.

The lower two-thirds of the arena is packed with public school kids, all downer-brats like me, all sitting on hard benches. Above, divided from my kind by a wall and potted palms, are cushioned chairs, canopies, and tuxedoed butlers serving drinks in long-stemmed frosted glasses and hors d'oeuvres on silver trays to barronial teens, parents, celebrities and politicians. Lots of lace, high-collared coats, electric colors, diamond chokers, twirling, twisted hair and hats ready to orbit. The event's a prime draw on all nets and a fetish in upnose society, kind of like Ascot only the horses are muscular teens and there's lots of popping male sweat.

Being here is glory I could do without. I didn't see this coming, being recruited to compete in a sport controlled by the elites, winning, people taking notice, allowed to advance, winning again, dominating. And now a national title at sixteen, maybe. Catcalls about my physique are a poke but I hope I'm more than my body. If they knew what my life was about, just trying to survive, to keep my family safe, they might be disillusioned. Of course, I could be sitting in a jail cell right now given the things I've done. I zoom in on individual faces, the kids shouting my name, like I'm somebody. For this day, maybe I need to be.

"Land-ing," pilot no-name squeals. "Stay inside till I give the sig-nal."

The pod descends the last fifty feet, rotating slowly, and so silent inside it's like the earth is moving to us. Outside orchestra drums are pounding, violins screaming, singers trilling, the audience howling, all over-the-top, manufactured theatrics for a national audience. The door folds into a ramp as we land.

"Ladies and gentlemen," a rich-throated man announces to the stadium, "the United States Gymnastic Federation and the National Sport Reporters Guild are pleased to present the three male finalists for the title, America's Top Gymnast!"

We bound down the plank, lips stretched max, teeth gleaming, arms waving, and line up on preselected spots. The sky is cloudless, the sun hot for late June. As my friends' names are announced, there's a roar from everywhere. When my name's called the upper stands are muted, the lower erupts like I'm a World Cup soccer star.

A podium is below and dignitaries are in their seats, a row of multidimensional lumins tethered on each side. Judging by the green shape of the cylinders these are the latest model, DIMM4s, fully four-dimensional, capturing images so intimate that they can project the tiniest zit in excruciating detail. As if I need more worries. Around each of our necks are the team medals awarded our schools less than an hour ago for the National High School Gymnastics Faceoff and I'm wearing gold. Now it's for the individual title based on points throughout the season. Coach says oddsmakers rate me a hundred-to-one long shot and won't win even with my numbers, given the politics. I'm fine with that. I deserve to win but just being here's important.

"Spartak! Take off your shirt!" A female voice in the crowd.

I smile, embarrassed but excited. I'm the first downer to ever make it this far. My parents sacrificed to give me this opportunity and they had great genes to make me what I am. They're watching now, my friends too. I wish they could afford to be here. I focus on the podium, trying to act regal as the Federation insists, but turn my head just enough to connect faces with the high decibel voices in the cheap seats.

I see one girl crying as she stares at me. I can't ignore her and the others; this is their day too. They need to know I'm with them, one of them. Grinning, I break the mannequin rule and point at her, then someone else screams my name, then another, I'm doing rapid-fire pointing as the bottom crowd explodes, on its feet, thousands of fingers held high, a mass chant: *"Spartak, Spartak, Number One! Number One!"* I tear up like I always do and push my palms against my eyes to slow any gusher, wishing I'd brought a handkerchief.

"You sure milk it," Matt barks into my ear.

"Maybe a little," I admit.

"Will you marry me?" It's a man's voice in the left front row, part of a knot of muscle guys wearing UC Santa Barbara jerseys. I laugh and feel heat, blushing.

"A friend of yours?" Hinkins asks.

"Not yet."

My rooting section leaves me thrilled and anxious. I love the attention but know that those who see gymnasts as racehorses are angry that I'm here. I'm no thoroughbred. Coach said there were threats if I win. I don't need more complications in my life.

Hinkins leans into my ear. "Groupies mean you get laid a lot, right?" He's grinning, wanting details. I punch his shoulder. They're both seventeen and each has bested me once or twice in individual events but not this year.

A blast of trumpets.

We stiffen; Federation President Gerard Oswald is approaching the podium. I see a jostling, roped off row of reporters doing commentary, a hundred special guests sitting in fancy seats behind them. I'm the highest ranked gymnast in California and Coach says after today I'm a near certainty for the 2116 Olympics in Vancouver—four perfect scores and cinching Ogden Academy's win as national champion. Hinkins' team came in second today and Matt's was number three.

"Smile, Spartak!" I look up at a female reporter, middle-aged and ponytailed, who directs me to her lumin. Gymnastics outdraws football and sometimes rivals soccer in total audience. I give her my best high wattage dimpled boy smile.

"You're a media whore," Matt says with a snort.

"Nobody can resist that face," Hinkins teases.

Mr. Oswald, a dark-skinned man in his nineties with a pointed white goatee, wearing tight white trousers and a white smock that drapes around him like a toga, steps to the podium. On his head is a matching wide-brimmed hat impaled with an impossibly long purple feather. He makes a short statement I'm too nervous to hear, and begins the countdown. I wait for my name.

"Please honor…Matt Dowell, Number Three in America."

The audience is silent at first. I'm stunned. This was supposed to be my slot. But the crowd responds with an ovation and clinking crystal.

"At the number two ranking, please honor…Hinkins Martinez."

My friend looks shocked but recovers quickly and steps forward, arms high. Another two beat delay from the crowd, then it offers him an even louder ovation.

My head spins. How could this happen? Downers don't win. Did somebody do this? Am I a token to assuage barronial guilt for the way they treat us? Of course, I did have the most points. Both of them look at me and beam, offering thumbs-up, and rush to embrace me.

"You deserve this," Matt says.

"Beauty wins." Hinkins tugs my hair and giggles, sounding genuinely happy.

"And now, the top-ranked male gymnast in America…Spartak Jones of Ogden Academy!"

The guys move to the side as I step forward and thrust my arms toward heaven. There is silence, disbelief as people process one of my kind beating barronials. Then the lower stands ignite, arms skyward, the colorful fabrics of their clothes moving in sync, back and forth, like tentacles from thousands of delirious sea anemones swaying in the tide as one, screaming: *"Spartak, Number One, Number One, Number One!"*

More trumpets. Everyone is still.

Mr. Oswald walks up the steps with a laurel wreath on a pillow, all designed for media hype, right out of Greco-Roman times and unique to our ancient sport. My kneecaps twitching, I bite my lower lip and bend forward, my hands curled, arms at my side, wishing desperately that I'd peed when I had the chance, trying to look relaxed even as sweat soaks my tank top and drips into my warm-ups. The wreath is placed just above my ears. I steady it with both hands, feeling a little foolish, and straighten up. Too bad money doesn't come with the title, just leaves and honor. I'd rather have cash.

"Spartak Number One!" The shouts detonate from the bleachers.

In the upper sections, handfuls applaud but most of the spectators are in motion, like a herd of zebras retreating in silence toward the exits. An unexpected breeze lifts the American flag and school pennants around the awards grandstand, cooling my damp skin.

"We love you, Spartak!" a red-haired girl shouts just as Matt and Hinkins move up tight and we wrap our arms around each other, friends and competitors, rich and poor, facing the world.

Members of the three school teams bound onto the field, up the platform steps and gather around us. Matt accidently bumps my wreath onto my forehead and Hinkins pushes it back. I imagine Julius Caesar, unaware of what will happen to him next March but knowing he's vulnerable and with time to uncover any plot against him. Except he was a general with an army; I'm just a guy with leaves in my hair, dreaming of next year's Olympics and someday playing Chopin in concert with my dad. I had the points to win today but the unwritten rule should have put me in third. Yet it didn't. What about the threatened violence?

"Spartak! Spartak! Spartak!" My Ogden teammates begin to chant, all except one. Connor McClain, second son of the richest family in America, turns away. He nearly cost us the title when he'd slipped on the pommel horse and had a lousy landing on the high bar. I ignore him and grin at my friends, grateful for their support, pumping my arm skyward, shouting:

"Og-den! Og-den! Og-den!"

Everyone is forced to stop and take up the chant, honoring the top prep school in America founded by Barron Ogden, one of the wealthiest barronial men and the greatest philanthropist who ever lived. Even Connor has to cheer for his grandfather. Whoops and applause vibrate the arena as I beam, pretending it's for me. Nobody will spoil my birthday. The college boys shout suggestions so deviant I can't comprehend. God bless them!

CHAPTER 1

"Mr. Chief Justice and my distinguished colleagues...let the record be clear...the Supreme Court of the United States has just legalized slavery in America. This is not a clarification on contract law as posited by the majority. It sanctions the owning of one human being by another. And it is shameful."

Justice William O. Washington, his craggy black face encircled with a cascade of white dreadlocks and short trimmed beard, looked directly into the DIMM4 lumin as he spoke, and it captured the crinkled skin around his eyes. His nostrils flared once, lips pinched bloodless, voice like a bass drum, each syllable rolling out slow and sonorous.

"A fifteen-year-old girl is now the property of a man who loaned her destitute family money and she was used as collateral. That this could happen is a national disgrace. It is the most repugnant vote by this court in over two centuries, matching two other odious decisions: three years ago in *Temple Emanu-El v United States*, upholding Christianity as the official state religion and the *Dred Scott* decision of 1857 preceding the Civil War."

Someone coughed in the court chamber. A second lumin captured all nine justices, black-robed droids in tall leather seats, all men, stern-faced, surveying the audience below. The only movement was the rippling purple drapes hanging from the ceiling behind each jurist, the air conditioning turned high to combat the 115-degree heat outside in the nation's capital.

Justice Washington removed his old-fashioned wire-rimmed glasses and leaned back in his chair. Chief Justice Ashley Wilkins listened with steepled fingers touching his ski-slope nose, an eyebrow raised.

He was a round-faced fifty, soft and boyish with fashionable tawny and chocolate striped hair parted in the middle and draped to his shoulders with a slight flip. "Thank you, Justice Washington, for your provocative and inappropriate editorial," he said in a reedy voice, leaning forward on his elbows. His pale blue eyes were translucent in the light, a forced smile softening the snarl in his tone.

"This case simply affirms a lower court ruling expanding the definition of chattel in a financial transaction. You can't buy a house, use credit, or take a loan and walk away from the obligation. There are ramifications. Lenders must be protected. If poor families without assets choose, of their own free will, to use their children as collateral on loans, like taking an item to a pawnshop…so be it. It is now legal."

Chief Justice Wilkins paused, lips turning up into a self-satisfied smile, hands now folded on the dark oak dais. He turned toward Justice Washington. "The financial community is safe," he said, sounding like a teacher lecturing an obtuse student, "and that is our first obligation. It acknowledges a practice that has existed for decades, giving common law legal sanction, form, and protections. It is free enterprise efficiently providing a solution for the less fortunate and obviates the need for a new government program or new taxes. Indeed, it extends the freedom to borrow to more Americans. We are *expanding opportunity*." He lifted his head as if acknowledging applause in the silent courtroom.

"Amazing," Justice Washington said in a mocking tone. "I wonder if an African, brought here in chains centuries ago, saw the trip as an opportunity to travel. Now thousands of Americans, caught up in the black market of this latest abomination of the ruling elite, are just property. This decision is light years beyond the mere clarification of adoption procedure, it's about *selling* human beings and awarding clear title; unstated but implied is the right to *resell*. With due respect, Mr. Chief Justice, the protections you speak of are for the buyers not the poor nor those in bondage. If a slave were granted freedom, he or she, under this ruling, would have the legal status of a piece of furniture abandoned on a sidewalk and available to anyone who comes by. And God forbid we raise taxes to end slavery or help the poor."

The Chief Justice snapped, his face red, "You are twisting the implications of areas not yet addressed by this—"

"Even if granted freedom by their owner," Justice Washington growled, interrupting his colleague, "a member of this new subhuman class enters a legal twilight, no rights yet established, vulnerable to the predatory rich, no standing in court, no protections, and perhaps no longer even a citizen. No longer *human.*" His nostrils flared, his voice a trumpet blast of disgust. "A whole new dynamic is now in place both by what we have done and what we have not addressed. It is a horror and anathema to American values and the Constitution."

"Sir! You are out of order to debase the actions and motives of this court," Wilkins snarled. "I will not permit it!"

"As a justice of this court, I have the freedom to warn my countrymen watching this proceeding," Washington thundered. "For my six colleagues in the majority, perhaps your vote makes sense in an age when most Americans are so desperate that selling their children seems like their only option, when genes can be patented, corporations are people, and Americans pledge allegiance to a Christian flag."

"Justice Washington," Wilkins bellowed, "be wary of injecting blasphemy into our discussion of the law. Disagree but do not disparage our Creator. The End Times are here, we all know that, the world is convulsing in environmental catastrophes prophesied in the Bible. And our Savior, crucified, risen, and returning again next year, offers life and liberty for all who believe."

There was a long silence. Another judge, younger and with red hair, leaned forward to assess the delay. He saw Washington staring in his direction and snapped back, rigid in his seat.

Washington shook his head and exhaled loudly enough to be picked up on the mike. "Actually, Mr. Chief Justice, *WE* don't all have the chutzpah to announce God's intentions." He turned back to the lumin, his head high, wearing a bulldog grin, voice righteous.

"Blasphemy is ignoring the Constitution and groveling at the feet of the barronial class, sending a downer girl into a lifetime of involuntary servitude, no limits on how she can be used. Frankly, I care nothing about religious divination. It has no place here."

"You, a barronial, denounce your own class," roared Wilkins. "Being rich is a sign of God's blessing."

"Then God's blessing was funneled though eliminating estate taxes and manipulation of the tax code."

"You are being impertinent and disrespectful!"

"The downer class is poor because we keep it there. It has nothing to do with Jesus. Mark my word! In our obsession to protect the financial elite, we have created a market for slaves. Haute society will go shopping for human gewgaws to flaunt and prove their superiority. Why be a patron of the arts when you can own the artist and brag to your friends? Own the Rembrandt of our age and wrap yourself in his or her glory. Or buy a great musician, inventor, athlete…anyone appropriately beguiling? At the gates of heaven, I suspect St. Peter will offer a special greeting to those who sanction human bondage."

"Do not impugn our character and faith or misuse this public platform," Wilkins roared, his upper lip twisted in a snarl. "When six of us speak in unison—that is the law. You must accept it."

"Six votes shredding our Constitution and our obligations to our fellow human beings. This is madness. This is unacceptable."

"Enough," the Chief Justice declared. "We have announced our decision in *Sasser v Peabody*. By a vote of six to three, the lower court decision is affirmed." He slammed down his gavel. "We are adjourned."

* * *

"They actually did it. And one judge talked about downers." I started to cough and realized I'd stopped breathing partway through their argument. I touched the school symbol on the side of my class ring and the poster-sized Z-ether screen dissolved. A quick squeeze inside my right ear and the receiver went mute. I turned to my two best friends at the library table. "I think the judge really knew how to goad the Chief Justice." I looked around us to make sure no one else was listening. "And make him look the fool."

"Slavery…" Billy Eagle whispered and folded his arms over his head to hide the tremor in his hands. I could tell. He knew children in his tribe who'd been sold. Now it was legal. He'd been my closest male friend since the first day of school and longtime dorm-mate.

"Unbelievable," Rhonda Van Deen said, wiping her eyes.

We all heard stories or knew kids who'd disappeared, their parents silent, looking away, eyes glazed, when we passed on the street. After all, we were downers. But we were also students at Ogden Academy, recruited because of special talents, given scholarships, room and board, and our families awarded stipends.

I'd never seen this kind of anger out of anyone on the Supreme Court, not that I watched its proceedings much. Our civics teacher, Mr. Bonas, wanted our personal opinions in a paper due Monday, which meant Sunday. So we had the weekend, sort of.

Nine downers and eleven barronials in the class, a tough mix. Would we have to read aloud? I looked at Rhonda. Her tornado of pink hair and pink eye shadow almost matched the power of her soaring lyric soprano. That was why she was at the Academy. And we slept together sometimes. We had no secrets. She reached over and rubbed my bicep. I flexed and her fingers pressed deep in the muscle. She liked it; I did too.

Billy was a full-blooded Apache who shaved half his head bald, the other half tall black spikes of twisted hair. He did it mostly to upset his parents. He always had a silver feather dangling from his right ear, a gift from his late grandfather. And he was an old-world style master painter, fawned over by his art teachers as the greatest talent in a generation.

I reached back and untied the black ribbon holding my hair behind my head, a nervous habit. It fell to my shoulders and I finger combed it behind my ears as I gazed at my classmates.

"Leave your hair alone," Rhonda admonished as she often did, then reached over and pulled on it, making me grin.

My coaches said I was a certainty for next year's Olympics. I breathed the sport, part of my being, just as I did classical piano and math, my other scholarships. And all because my parents poured their dreams into me and molded me into someone the barronials would value and give me and my family a chance to escape the downer life. When I contacted them after winning the national title, they were sobbing.

"My cousin Malina was sold," Billy said, moving his elbows to the table and cradling his face in his hands, "just like in this case." He was breathing erratically. Rhonda stood and moved between us, using her arms to pull us together, our foreheads touching.

"It's okay," she murmured. "Spartak and I know."

We needed time for this decision to seep through our brains. Not that this was recent. On the black market, families had been selling kids to barronials, hoping they'd have a better life, since the collapse of the middle class forty years ago. It was contemptible that parents would do this and yet I understood it, understood desperation. An article I read said it was like in Haiti; sold children there were called *restaveks*. Of course it was illegal there and had been for three hundred years. Now it was here and official, with the force of law behind it.

The three of us held a unique status as gifted students, a temporarily privileged one, positioned between two worlds, two Americas. I looked around Ogden Library where we were sitting, a seven-story structure with columns twisting around like flames, pointed skyward, sheathed in titanium. It was nicknamed the Burning Bush.

The place was a magical anachronism, our refuge from the world. The architecture was whimsical and modern. Inside, the central reading room was 18th century, the ceiling held up by a series of giant stone umbrellas on columns and each four-story wall crammed with books, globes, green-shaded reading lamps, walkways, ladders, and staircases. It was theater. In the open stacks in the basement were over three million more books from past centuries. Electronically it had in storage everything ever published in any language.

"I thought Justice Washington was righteous," I said, still holding my friends, enjoying the connection, remembering his weathered face, like a black, well-manicured Moses. "He actually cares about downers." It was a revelation, someone so powerful worrying about people like us.

"I've seen him speak before and he seems genuine," Rhonda said, standing up, rubbing the back of our necks. We both sat up. Her massages were heaven.

"This isn't a spa, guys," she said after a few minutes of sweet manipulation, and moved back to her chair.

"Thanks, Rhonda. That felt so good." She often gave me a back rub after sex, doing *uh-ahs* over my muscles. I pulled up the mental image of the Chief Justice to regain my focus. "I think we should be honest," I said, "and write about our experiences. One or two barronials might laugh but most will be surprised, I think. They don't know much about our lives."

"Or care," Billy added.

"But we need to be political and not criticize the decision," I said.

Scholarship students were an awkward fit in an elite school and needed to suffocate personal opinions and pretend the world was good. As someone who'd done more than my share of street fighting, I sometimes wanted to pound the prissy rich boys when they acted like hyenas. But that was dangerous even if they started it.

"Why not say what we think?" Billy asked.

"We're two years from graduation."

"Spartak, you're already a famous athlete. Put some muscle in your words." Billy raised an eyebrow and cocked his head, daring me to disagree.

Rhonda picked up my hand before I could respond and interlaced our fingers. She did the same with Billy. "I love you both," she said. "I need to rehearse for tonight. So do you, Spartak. Let's get lunch and stare 'em down. They'll be watching."

CHAPTER 2

"Shadows in the dark, yearning to be free
Waiting for the sun, desperate to be part of day...
Phantoms on the outside, wanting more, wanting in
Searching for life, Searching for freedom
Freedom to love, freedom to live
Freedom, a wish you make with your heart
Shadows in the dark, yearning to be free
Open the door, my love, let me inside
Let me share your warmth, Let me stroke your passion...
Let me find love...Let me be free..."

RHONDA LIFTED BOTH ARMS OVERHEAD AS she belted the final words to her own musical composition, her dazzling voice rising higher and higher, the audience sitting up, leaning forward, mouths open, transfixed. It was a Bowie knife song, a secret anthem, subversive to those who understood the meaning; to others an operatic tour-de-force overhanging the vague lyrics that had something to do with unrequited love. She had courage. A goose bump, damp eyes performance, not what you expect from a sixteen-year-old schoolgirl. Her figure tastefully overwhelmed the tight pink cling wrap she wore from the middle of her spectacular breasts to just above her knees, her pink hair ethereal in the lights.

"Yes! Yes!" some guy shouted. The audience bounced to its feet, applauding and whistling. The 200-seat student performance minitheater at the academy was packed. It had perfect acoustics because of new reflective paneling and the vaulted ceiling.

"Rhonda! Rhonda! Rhonda!" I screamed from behind a side curtain, hoping others would do the same. And they did. She turned her head and pointed at me, her wagging finger saying "Bad boy," her grin saying, "Wow, I'm glad that's over."

And I was up next. It wasn't good to follow Rhonda Van Deen. There were six performers tonight and I was the final one. Girls could wear what they wanted to in these recitals. Boys had to don the official Ogden uniform: blue blazer with the gold academy crest on the breast pocket, red tie, white button-down shirt and khaki pants, an old- fashioned rich boy costume from another century.

Backstage, I bent over and stretched, wiggling my shoulders, arms, and fingers. I exhaled just as my teacher, Miss Hedwick, announced: "...and for our final performance, I am pleased to present sophomore Spartak Jones playing Chopin's *'Heroic' Polonaise in A-flat major, Opus 53."*

Maisey Hedwick was like a metronome come to life, tiny and precise, with tight brown curls, always proper and relentless. I was five-foot-nine plus a quarter and I towered over her as she gave me a peck on the cheek. I sat down on the leather bench.

The audience was mostly students and teachers. In the back I saw Sonia Washington, a senior from a famous barronial family, black and elegant, her hair pulled tight into a bun with a gardenia tucked behind an ear. I'd never talked to her but she was a regular at music department performances, gymnastic meets too. Next to her was another senior, Zinc McClain, her constant companion. He was the eldest son of the McClains, the clan that led the Twelve Families controlling just about everything. He had an odd face as if his nose were broken, and his brown skin was lightly mottled, strange to see in an age of easy physical perfection. Whispers said his father wouldn't allow cosmetics, calling it unmanly. If so, it was ironic that I thought he looked very manly and more interesting than the soft perfection so popular with rich kids. Students gossiped about him but kept their distance. He seemed dour and rarely spoke; speculation was he could be vicious, an untouchable.

I moved my hands above the keys and cleared my head, ignoring everything but the music. I loved this piece, an old standard, fast and joyous, played with fingers flashing, hands bouncing. I didn't really need the music; I had it memorized. Miss Hedwick was demanding.

I glanced at the audience and noticed Zinc glaring at me. I snapped my eyes back to the keyboard. His brother Connor was an arrogant jerk, trying to pick fights with me, knowing I didn't dare hit him. And now Zinc seemed angry for no reason. Had Connor said something? His botched scores at the Faceoff had knocked us into second place until I aced four events. I concentrated on my playing.

At the end, the audience rose up with serious applause, almost as good as for Rhonda. There were a few whistles and Rhonda screaming my name from behind the drape. Sonia Washington offered a wide smile with animated but delicate clapping. She caught my eye and nodded, blowing me a kiss. I grinned and waved, thrilled by this kind of recognition from someone like her. I noticed the multiple ropes of pearls tight around her neck like a collar—all real, no doubt. She nudged Zinc to get more enthusiastic with his clapping. He did. The man—he was nearly eighteen—was tall and slender, dressed in a flattering trim gray jacket, edged in blue with black military epaulets and high vertical collar. But he glowered before turning his head away.

* * *

After the concert I had to reenter my other world, the real one, to make a delivery, pick up a package, and go see my family at our apartment. It'd been three months since my last visit and I'd spend the weekend. Getting away was tough for scholarship kids. We were expected to be perfect and for me that meant endless hours in gymnastics, piano, and math. I was also on the fencing team, a useless sport but diverting since I didn't have to win.

On the side I did tutoring for barronial classmates but only for cash. It was inconvenient for them but no downer trusted banks and used them only when necessary. Mostly it was fun and the students really wanted to do better. Sometimes, often with younger girls, they just looked at me or found reasons to touch me. No big deal and a little embarrassing but I still got paid. I just made sure some adult was in the room with us if I was suspicious. And it was obvious that great wealth and intelligence were unrelated. I also did some sideways stuff, lucrative, but I couldn't discuss it with my parents so that they could claim ignorance if I got caught.

My first stop was to visit the Tabor family on Chester Alley. After that I'd go to a smelly, dark street to meet Dalix at midnight. We called it a business meeting, one best done in private away from the face rec lumins on every corner. He picked the location. The bruises on my shoulder and thigh were gone now, mementos from our last meeting.

Only a few people were out at this hour as I stood at the exit of the PT underground, short for pneumatic train tube. It moved you fast to some locations. Other trains were ancient, all part of a vast network.

"Congratulations, Spartak," a young woman said to me, holding her baby. "My name is Thista and this is my daughter, Lia."

"Nice to meet you," I said, surprised by her approach, and rubbed the back of a finger down the soft brown baby face. "She's beautiful."

"I can't wait to tell my husband we met. He's such a fan."

"Ahhhhm, thanks—"

A buzzing sound punched around us and the air swirled a dirt tornado. We raced back inside just as I caught a glimpse of a glowing red triangle disappearing in the distance. Buzzards we called them, low-flying aircarts popular with young male barronials, known for speed, triple air cannons, vertical takeoff, and the ability to make life miserable for people on the ground if it dropped out of its air corridor.

When the dirt settled, I said goodbye to Thista, kissed the baby at her insistence, and stepped to the curb. The road seemed clear. Of course it was. Poor people walked, rode bicycles, or took the PT so barronials could get where they needed to faster on empty streets. Or, swishing overhead. It cost money for a road or air use permit, part of congestion pricing. And it worked. Only barronials in high-performance buzzards, gyros, delivery pods, panzers, or other military and luxury crafts used the roads and air lanes. But few of us could afford vehicles of any kind so it didn't matter. The rich rarely came to this part of the city unless they were out to buy art from our community of artisans, or, more likely, make trouble.

I tried to act casual or as casual as one might at this hour in my school costume. I had a heavy bag over a shoulder and a small pack on my hip. Across the street was a looped projection of me completing the quadruple twist dismount and landing on my feet, arms extended, face beaming, and the crowd screaming. It was pure luck. I failed it most of the time in practice but took the risk; we needed the extra points to win. An elegant hand-lettered blue sign was next to it:

"SPARTAK #1 IN AMERICA!"

There was also a smaller one, not as finished, more childlike, leaning against the wall.

"Spartak lives in Castlemont!"

On the ground sat dozens of small bottles and cups filled with flowers, most still fresh. I rubbed my eyes and stood there, disbelieving. To my social class maybe I was a hero and here was where it counted, in our village, to people like Thista, not in a sports arena. It made me weird, embarrassed, and thrilled. My eyes watered. Time to move on.

It was a brisk ten-minute walk through a warren of narrow, meandering streets, nothing quite parallel, no corners at ninety degrees. Dad swore a drunken city architect had designed it over a generation ago when the last remnants of the middle class disintegrated. The buildings were made of syn-stone slabs and bolted into place. Most were flat-sided with peaked terra-cotta tile roofs, but a few had turrets and tall arches with baby angels or gargoyles over the main entrances. Like our building. There were even a half dozen drawbridges over drainage gullies. Some speculated the architectural pieces were remnants of a dismantled barronial amusement park. Others, like my dad, said it was an insider joke, a put-down on downers living in castles.

But, no matter, I loved the complex: thousands of tiny apartments, dozens of miniature parks and a massive community hothouse garden where we grew much of our food. Angry cherubs were scowling from overhead every time I left our building. Lots of trees, many planted by residents, fruit trees like lemon and pear, Southern Magnolias with huge fragrant flowers, even better were the Angel Trumpet Trees, elegant, sweet, pure white, and poisonous. Sidewalks were rarely repaired but always colorful. I stopped and admired a new painting kids had done, crack-art we called it, green alien spaceships on broken pieces of concrete attacking the red Space Elevator which was set to open next year. This was as close as any of us would get to it.

I ignored a small black box attached to a building as I passed. The lumins were watching. Even the new *Sniffers*, as we called them, identified people by smell. Kind of rude. So we had to be entrepreneurial, including where we got together.

Chester Alley was a tiny dead-end road with an abandoned apartment house set for demolition because of damage in the last earthquake. The Tabors lived in and around the basement unit. Two left turns and I was there. No lights anywhere but plenty of moonbeam. The lumins were broken and no Sniffers were yet installed. I moved slowly down five steps to the entrance holding onto a broken pipe banister. There was no door.

"Mr. Tabor, Mrs. Tabor, Amy," I called into the blackness. The place smelled like rotting wood with a whiff of sewer. "It's Spartak Jones. I'm sorry it's so late."

"Spartak," Mrs. Tabor said in a soft voice, emerging from the darkness, wrapping her arms around me and squeezing tight. Her hair was neatly combed, her clothes worn and soiled. I needed to bring perfume next time. "So wonderful of you to come."

"Of course, you're special to me."

"Thank you for saying that and being our friend. We're so proud of your victory...our victory."

I just looked at the ground. She was so innocent. As my eyes adjusted to the dim light, Mr. Tabor came up, a tall man, dark-skinned with even darker eyes. Amy was holding his hand. She was eight years old, tiny, a little younger than my brother. She grinned, exposing spaces of several missing teeth. I shook Tabor's hand and squatted down for a girl hug.

"Thank you," I said, standing and lifting the pack from my shoulder. "It's cosmic seeing you all." They were in worse shape than my last visit. "Here's some bread, milk, protein bars, vitamins, and other stuff I got from the school cafeteria with the help of my friend Tessie. Also some clothes I managed to procure from lost and found. It's amazing what rich kids abandon."

He took it all. I think he was crying. I was hopeless when emotional. I had to be strong; that's what people expected.

I reached into my pocket and took out a small roll of bills. "I got this from my tutoring work yesterday. Please take it." They were proud and seemed embarrassed. I stepped up to Mrs. Tabor and slipped it into her hand. "Please let me help."

"We're so lucky to have you in our lives," she said. Then they were all on me, holding, sniffling, and spreading lots of wet. Eventually I disentangled, wiped my eyes and wished for a handkerchief.

"I'll always be your friend and help when I can." My voice was a croak. I gave a pathetic little smile and dashed up the steps to the street, my next stop just a few blocks away.

The Tabors used to live in an apartment near us and got evicted for lack of payment. He got mouthy with a business owner, a barronial, and they were now unemployable even though there were lots of jobs.

Reapers. That's what they were now. Barronials, downers, and reapers—wealth beyond dreaming, just getting by, and abandoned. Downers were the new middle class. That was a popular joke. And reapers tended to disappear if they wandered into barronial neighborhoods and it was never clear what happened to them.

Sometimes people like me, someone slightly better off, harassed them. It was disgusting but a few downers thrived on being cruel, finding those who were weaker that they could put down and humiliate. I guess it made them feel superior and distracted them from their own precarious existence. I was used to the streets and few would challenge me but the Tabors' destitution twisted my gut. Would they survive?

But I could only do so much. My family had needs too and government did little to help poor people except telling them to get training and find a job. That didn't work if you were blacklisted, sick, or old.

Ogden Academy labeled me a math prodigy and I used my talent to sweet talk robots. Probably not what OA expected. Androids ran all the warehouses—no more human workers—and I mastered the coded language. We never took too much, to not draw attention, just enough that might seem like an error in their records. No one could live on downer wages. Jobs, mostly part-time, were plentiful, my parents both worked hard, but for survival pay. Our families needed us and I'd helped since boyhood but I didn't want to be a thief forever.

Dalix, Onzi, Mark, Jason and me. We'd been friends since we were toddlers, growing up here and attending the same elementary school. I didn't want to abandon my pack forever or squeeze them out of my life. Once in, no exit, that was the blood oath we'd made as boys. They were scared of being left behind, of being losers and tried to hold me down; kids above me at school, at least a few, tried to push me back.

I reached Boehner Lane on time, just at midnight. It was a black canyon running through the backside of an army of six-story apartments with peeling beige paint and rusting fire escapes. I saw a red splash of geraniums on a windowsill and a small flag with my name on it. Then it hit. Sniffer hell. I covered my nose and breathed through my mouth but the stench of disinfectant and mulch was liquid. So was the night. I couldn't see five feet because the fog was thick this close to the Pacific Ocean at the end of June on the edge of San Francisco.

I stepped into the alley, holding my head up, trying to look confident while I held my nose. Chopin filled my head. I wanted more of that, not this. But for people like me, what you want is always at the bottom of the possible. You do what you must to survive.

"I'm not here to fight," I yelled, hoping that would show good faith and avoid a fist in the mist. I stopped and waited for the breeze to open a window. A baby cried above me and I saw a light go on in an apartment.

"Spartak! Over here."

A figure stepped from behind a green compost bin nearby and waved, backlit by the nearly full moon now peeking through the swirling fog. There was no mistaking the bass drum voice with the Slavic accent. It was Dalix. Right on time. I could see the white of his grin, glistening off a security light, still missing part of a front tooth from our last encounter. He looked unchanged, big, smug, muscular, and dark; his long, black, curly hair swirled into a Samurai style topknot.

He was seventeen, our leader, strong, a good fighter and a gentle man when he wasn't angry or desperate.

"Truce," I said, raising my arms overhead as I walked to him. "Please don't hit me."

"America's top gymnast. I'm proud of you and us. You make downers look important," Dalix said as he slapped a hand behind my neck and pulled me between two bins, hiding us from view of the lumins.

"We're brothers. I don't want to hurt you!" He howled like a wolf, his favorite greeting, always good for a laugh, enfolding me in a tight squeeze, kissing my cheek, then pushing me to arm's length. "Or have you pound me!" He touched his broken tooth with an index finger.

"Sorry about that. I didn't mean to hit your face."

"We were fighting. I was trying to hurt you."

"But you never hit my face."

"Your face is way too pretty. We all agree."

I had to laugh. I really did care for him. The fight, weeks ago, had been brutal and stopped when enforcers arrived and we scattered. I'd hoped that would be the end of it. But we still had a business to run. "Here're new codes for the Latimer warehouse in Brisbane," I said, handing him a micro-cube from my hip pack.

"Perfect." He slipped it in the pocket of his old knee-length black morning coat. He loved the 18th century gentlemen fashion popular with barronials, and this one, taken two years ago in a heist, was a bit frayed. I preferred denim trousers and loose shirts.

"You look precious," Dalix said with a smirk, "Mr. Virgin." He pulled my tie from my coat and flipped it over my shoulder.

"Hey, you knew I had a concert."

Turning and bending down, he picked up a canvas shoulder bag.

"Here's your share from the last one. Robots love your magic coding, Math Boy."

"It's not just me Mr. Net Picker. You're a genius and the other guys know the players and have special talents." I poured it on thick, hoping to make a connection. I wasn't lying. He was amazing.

An aw-shucks smile suggested I scored. He was almost blushing. Dalix had a rotten life, living with friends or camping in abandoned buildings, his parents dead. I was family to him. Sometimes he stayed with us, a night here and there. And as boys we experimented together and were lovers as we entered our teens, but no longer.

I took the bag and swung it over my shoulder. It was heavier than normal, twenty pounds and thick.

"Some nice jackets inside, kids stuff, a few blouses…and some jewelry we couldn't sell." He shifted his weight, looking shy, wanting to please me, like the friends we used to be. "Maybe your mom will like it." He pulled out a wad of bills. "And here's your cash share from what we could unload."

"Thanks." I slipped it into my pants pocket. At least two months rent for my parents, judging by the heft.

"Dalix?"

"Don't say it."

"Nothing has changed. I…I want to stay friends with you and the others, I love you and the guys, but I need to slow down, do fewer jobs. My life is crazy. I need to succeed at the academy. I owe it to my family."

"No! Your family needs more than downer wages. We all do. You know that."

"Yes."

"So?"

"I'll still do the codes but not as often and I can't run with you guys anymore. Please give me a chance at this new life."

"I SAID NO!" His handsome face warped into a snarl, eyes desperate. "You're just too good for us! We're just street slugs!" He slammed my chest, putting his weight behind it, knocking me into a compost bin, then stomped off into the fog.

He was an important part of my life. I didn't want to lose him. But I was trying to move on. Being famous was complicated. I picked up the pack and jogged through the honeycomb of back alleys toward my parents' apartment, picking the path least traveled.

CHAPTER 3

I MISSED MY BROTHER GEO, NINE years old with the same mop of long blond hair and pale skin we all had. We were close and I worried about him being too sheltered by my parents trying to protect him from the life I led in the streets. They went with him and my sister whenever the two went out; even going to school was always with a group of students and parents. It kept them safe but unprepared. And friends told me it was getting more dangerous.

I stopped at Glory Lane, a ridiculous name for a narrow street. But it was my street. I turned left and heard footsteps as I neared an alley. A dozen people in *Liteon* hoods exploded onto the street just in front of me. I stopped, unsure what to do and tried not to look at them. They were almost surreal in their dark clothes with shimmering heads. They wore AR2 armbands, making a risky political statement. And two had holsters on their belts with old-fashioned lead bullet guns. I'd never seen them here before, but I supported their message. Bring back democracy; join the Second American Revolution, AR2. Somehow they'd hacked into every com system and drove the baronials crazy. Rich kids screamed at school when Nocturne hit their zans. Downers sucked in their cheeks to keep from laughing. We can't figure out the meaning of Nocturne or who it is, but we like the message. The government labeled AR2 terrorists. I assumed it was because that's what the Twelve Families wanted.

Two stopped beside me as the others ran past and seemed to be staring; hard to tell with the hoods. Maybe we were neighbors, even friends. I kept walking; best not to know. The sound of their footsteps disappeared behind me. I lifted the collar of my school jacket. I should have worn an overcoat.

A security panzer turned the corner two blocks ahead in the fog coming my way. All black glass on the outside, running on a single rubberized track in the middle, capable of lightning speeds and packing grade five weapons, all hidden. I tried to avoid them and, even more, the officers inside, charged with enforcing the law, at least for people like me. Rotten luck. I ignored it, staring at the sidewalk, keeping a steady pace and pretending I didn't see it or care. To run guaranteed getting hassled. It passed, moving slowly, likely confirming my identity. The street lumins and sniffers told them that too.

Six blocks to home; I could see the turret in the distance above the mist. I thought about my paper on the Supreme Court. Billy was right; be honest. The decision was a horror and we should speak out. But carefully. We couldn't change what the judges did and it wasn't worth getting punished just to make a point in school.

I jerked my head up. Shouting ahead, some kind of demonstration. Normally the neighborhood was silent this late. I looked behind me and saw the panzer had stopped. No sign of AR2. I couldn't go back or I'd get hassled by the enforcers. So I kept moving as the noise amped up, ricocheting off the syn-stone apartment buildings. Hundreds of voices were chanting. Half a block ahead they turned the corner, six abreast, men and women, shouting to a nonexistent crowd of spectators.

It was End Timers, hardcore Dominionists. Fuck. They wanted to take over the government and rule by divine right. Supposedly Jesus was set to return next year. End Timers hated AR2, a tool of Satan, they said, and a distraction from the Rapture. Good people would ascend to heaven or something like that if we gave ministers all the power. You bet. They must have held a rally to recruit angry downers. Things had changed in my neighborhood since my last visit.

I'd nowhere to hide so I pressed my back against the recessed doorway of a shop, locked for the night, selling secondhand furniture. A cloth doll resting in a wooden rocking chair with red yarn hair and lips stared at me. It was Raggedy Ann. My sister had one. It belonged to our great-grandmother. And I still had Raggedy Andy at home. His mouth and a button eye disappeared years ago. And I loved him anyway.

"Prepare to Meet Jesus," a banner demanded, black letters on white canvas, spread on poles fifteen feet apart.

"End Times October 2116," another proclaimed right behind.

"True Christians must rule... True Christians must rule...
...for Jes-us to return...! ...A-men! A-men..."

I stopped listening. They couldn't even rhyme. Don't these thumpers ever sleep? A sad, young woman, covered by a black lace shawl, smiled at me. An old couple, bent and tired, wearing matching purple plaid jackets, nodded as they passed. I waved. A hot-looking guy in his twenties offered a dimpled grin as he reached over to me.

"Brother, Earth is dying, prepare for Jesus, join Bishop Perry..."

We shook hands.

"You bet," I said, amazed at his green eyes and the sharp citrus tang of his cologne. I didn't shave much but liked to sniff my options.

"Jes-us! Jes-us!"

A pride of young people, *Jesusistas* we called them, hundreds, mostly in their twenties, marched in step and chanted, like some kind of military unit, right arms slamming their chests on the *Jes* of Jesus. Bizarre.

"Jes-us! Jes-us!"

Like foot soldiers at the Crusades, they wore black hooded shirts with huge gold crosses embroidered on the front and back. Several glared at me like I was Satan's fart. I lowered my head to avoid eye contact and held my palms together. Maybe they'd think I was praying and leave me alone. Two men jumped out, wrapping their hands over mine. A triple prayer.

"Huh?"

"Do you accept the divine truth of Bishop Perry?" a swarthy-looking guy shouted in my face. "Do you accept him as Earth's leader?" He needed to brush his teeth.

"Do you?" the other one, a redhead, demanded. Garlic breath. This was the most important question in the world. To them. I sensed they'd take offense if I answered no. And they were still holding me.

"Absolutely," I responded, my voice rising to ecstasy. *"October 2116! Bishop Perry! Hallelujah! Hallelujah!"* My dramatic skills from the academy paid off in so many ways. I stared hopefully into swarthy guy's eyes. I couldn't remember Perry's first name. Or care.

He ran a finger from my forehead to my chin and from ear to ear. "See you in heaven, brother." He kissed my cheek. His stubble scratched my chin. They rejoined the group. My performance worked.

Hallelujah.

A gunshot behind me. The hiss of solar pistols and the loud peeps when they recharged. Another shot. The Jesusistas surged forward screaming, *"Die for Jesus and eternal life!"*

My apartment building was three blocks ahead. I sprinted.

* * *

Out of breath and relieved to be home, I turned the corner to the entrance, skipped across the faux drawbridge and spotted my favorite stone cherub with the evil grin on the overhead arch. A sign pasted beside the door in wide red letters read:

SPARTAK LIVES HERE. #1.

HE'S MY BROTHER.

"Quasar!" I gasped, my emotions ripped; my brother did this, bragging to his friends, proud of me. I barely got my hand to my eyes in time. Why was I always so sentimental? Never a handkerchief when I needed one, so I rubbed it onto my shirtsleeve. I had to wash it anyway.

Someone dressed in dark clothing was sitting in shadows to my right. The face was down, hidden by a helmet. As I put my finger up to the door coder, the person stood and green neon stripes instantly glowed around the collar, epaulets and a corporate logo on the helmet—a circle with an X in the middle.

Holy Fuck! No!

"Hello, Spartak. Imagine running into you tonight." She smiled as she stood, lifting her visor and slipping a silver glove onto her right hand.

Please no!

"Hello Officer Rango. What are you doing here?"

She was one of my neighborhood enforcers, an employee of

Harmony Enforcement, Inc., the private company contracted by local government to maintain public order and was likely in the panzer I just saw. She faced me, moving within inches of my nose. Rango was in her forties, older than my mother, stout, dark-skinned, maybe Indian or Pakistani. That was certainly her accent. But her name wasn't. Imogene Rango. She smelled like fermenting sauerkraut, worse than Boehner Lane. Her uniform was immaculate as always, a bright orange-red solar pistol on her belt. My eyes focused on the glove, like medieval chainmail. She'd used it before on me. It could knock you senseless with a touch.

"I heard you'd be coming back late tonight. Your mom mentioned it. Such a nice lady and I try to look after her and your little brother and sister." She watched me, a smug expression, letting her words and threat sink in. She smiled, confident of success. "I knew you'd want to see me. What's in the shoulder bags, Apollo boy?"

"Just stuff from school." I tried to control my breathing. Not this again. "Beautiful fog tonight, don't you think?"

She extended her hand. I slumped and handed her the pouch and pack. She opened them and pulled out a woman's jacket. The price tag was still attached.

"This coat would take a month's wages for your dad. Let's go to the station."

"Please, ma'am, I beg you, don't do this. Not tonight."

She grabbed my arm with the glove. The jolt knocked me to the concrete sidewalk. I was on my side, curled into a fetal position, wheezing, my mouth open, the electrical punch snapping every cell in my body. She held the glove just above my face. "Don't resist. Facedown." I rolled to my stomach and put my hands behind my back. I felt the cold metallic mesh snake around my wrists and heard the buzz of the lock.

"Up, beautiful!"

I obeyed. She pushed me around a corner and up the stairs into a panzer. Another enforcer was inside, a younger woman, no helmet, burgundy hair, surly looking.

"This is Officer O'Reilly. I'm training her."

"Hello, ma'am."

I was shoved into the middle of the backseat, a canvas strap pulled tight across my lap; a metal collar clamped around my neck. The top closed and sealed.

"Activate the leash," Rango instructed her partner. A moment later green tractor beams shot from the collar to the walls of the panzer. It pulled me forward and stretched my neck. I couldn't move and hoped the transport didn't hit a rut in the road.

O'Reilly turned around to inspect my face. "Sweet choice," she said.

"Yes, indeed," Rango replied. "Yes, indeed."

At the substation, the desk sergeant, a gray-haired guy with a short beard and bulbous nose, smiled as we walked past him, shaking his head. O'Reilly disappeared into an office. Officer Rango took me to a small room in the back. There was a table and two chairs. The four walls were gray concrete; two had extensive water stains. A panel of harsh lights glowered above.

"Sit."

I did. She opened a small metal panel by the doorframe and flipped a switch.

"No lumins tonight, pretty boy, or any type of surveillance. Just the two of us. Nice and private."

I closed my eyes, feeling faint.

"Breathe, boy."

I needed to calm myself. Concentrate. Survive. She emptied the bag from Dalix on the table, separating the jackets, blouses, a couple of toys and the jewelry, mostly earrings and a few necklaces. There was no way I could talk my way out of this. She had me. Officer Rango shoved everything back into the bag and set it on the floor. She placed my hip pack next to it, uninterested. Stepping close, her chest towered above my eyes. She touched my chin and lifted my face to hers.

"You're such a delicious hunk." She ran her fingers through my hair. "So blond." She kissed the top of my head. "You smell so clean." Her hand slipped inside my jacket and squeezed my pectorals. "Great tits. Gymnastics has done you wonders. America's top gymnast." She laughed, almost a snicker. "Do you know what you do to women? And men, too, I'd guess."

"I'll do whatever you want. No record. Just let me go afterward. Please."

"I know." She stepped back, unhooked her solar pistol and unbuckled her belt, setting them on the empty chair. "Stand. Nose against the wall. Now!" I did as she demanded. One cuff slid open with a buzz. "Take off your clothes."

I kicked off my shoes and carefully folded the pants, still looking at the wall, not wanting her to see the bulge of money. Luckily I was not carrying any weapons or contraband. I turned and faced her, putting my pants on the chair seat and jacket over the back.

"Shorts and socks too."

I felt foolish standing there naked and helpless. But she seemed pleased, my not very private parts a good distraction from the money. She slipped off her glove so she could use both hands. No need to zap me again. I'd cooperate. I had before.

"Lie on the table. On your back, boy! Arms overhead."

I did. She pulled my hands to a corner, slipped the metal restraint around a table leg then recuffed my free hand. It was uncomfortable and humiliating but no point in complaining. She was the law.

Officer Rango moved to the other end of the interrogation table. I couldn't see her but I heard buckles flipping open. She must be taking off body armor. Snaps popped next, one by one, as she unfastened her shirt, then the zipper and her boots hitting the floor. She walked up to me. Her heavy breasts and dark nipples hung low above my face. Her hands roamed, pushed, and squeezed my chest, my abs, rubbed my legs, slipped between them, exploring. She cupped my balls and teased my cock, her mouth moved lower, enveloping it. Her tongue licked my throat, slimed my chin, pushed between my lips. She climbed on top of me. Rubbing. "You taste so good." She nibbled the top of my ear.

I breathed through my mouth to avoid the smell. If I could analyze and bottle her odor it would be a best seller on the black market, a sure way to plug Sniffers. Sex fantasies, I forced them into my head. I was somewhere else, with anyone else...searching. There was Dalix's dark face, my first lover, as boys, rubbing. Rhonda, oh yes, Rhonda, her sweet tongue and scent of roses. I had to perform. Rango beat me the first time when I couldn't.

She growled and lifted up. "Get it ready boy."

An hour later she dressed, watching me on the table, a satisfied grin spreading across her face. Uncuffing me, she nodded toward my clothes. As I dressed, I was numb, degraded. She picked up the bag and took some of the jewelry and one of the blouses, pushing back the rest.

"I'll let you keep some stuff. You did good tonight."

So far she hadn't checked my trouser pocket. I tried to hide the bulge with my jacket, folding it over my arm. This was not a real arrest but it would be if I didn't obey.

"You're free to go and…congratulations on the title."

I picked up the pack and bag in slow motion, not wanting her to have the satisfaction of knowing how humiliated and violated I felt. She relished her power over me, the famous downer athlete. I quick stepped from the room. The same sergeant was at the desk.

"Have a good time?" He laughed.

I went to the men's room by the front entrance. The door was locked. No way would I go searching for another. Not in this place. I ran outside, my heart pounding. Nothing was open at this hour, so I went to the PT underground. It was deserted. I started crying. Damn, not now. I hated losing control. My stomach heaved. I made it to a trash can nearby and emptied my gut.

The bathroom doors were locked. Always on PT at night. Didn't people have to piss after dark? I looked into a smudged pane of glass over a poster on a wall. My face was a blur. I straightened my hair and wiped off what appeared to be lipstick on my cheek and vomit on my chin. A schedule said three hours to the next train to my neighborhood. I could walk. No I couldn't. Not after that. I was weak, angry, and fucking helpless. My head was spinning. One dry heave after another.

"DAMN!" I pounded a brick wall with my fist.

Sometime later I found myself on a bench in a corner, my head in a fog. I heard someone clearing his throat, almost a growl, and looked up, rubbing my chapped lips. A man was standing over me, middle-aged, wearing a black suit and a red clerical collar. He was one of the

End Timers. Red for the color of Christ's blood; some kind of priest.

"Young man, do you need help?" He sat next to me. "Can I pray with you?"

"I just want to be alone." My mouth was so sticky I could barely talk.

"I can make things better," he said, touching my thigh and squeezing.

"NO!" I bolted across the platform, up the stairs, down a dozen streets to another PT station and bounded back down. An eternity passed. The train came. No one was on it, just automation and me. I thought about different stories I could tell my parents. None made sense. I discovered a mint in my pocket, the last one and I savored it. There were miracles. But I could taste her on my tongue, my clothes were swampy with her smell.

It was nearly dawn when I reached the apartment door; shaking, trying to be quiet, hoping everyone was asleep.

"Spartak's home!"

Geo shouted before the door lock finished clicking. My family was up early, sitting at the kitchen table, eating breakfast. My brother was in pajamas. I squatted down for hugs and kisses. I felt warm and safe, stinky and exposed.

"Geo, you look handsome and so grown up," I said, "and I've got presents." He squealed. "For each of you."

"Just in time for breakfast," Mom said, standing, offering a full tooth grin. "My son, the best in America."

To me she was the most beautiful woman in the world, her skin flawless, even with a few wrinkles around the eyes. Her long blond hair, thick and curly, seemed glamorous even if it was just a casual finger comb. I looked at her, embarrassed and confused, nodded and shoved the cash into my shoulder bag as I stood. With Geo's arm clamped around my waist, we walked to the table. I placed the pouch on the counter and gave Mom and Dad a hug, hoping they couldn't smell her. If they asked, I'd disintegrate. Mom was staring at my neck. Oh God! Did I have hickies? They were eating muesli, always good. I looked over to my sister and started toward her until she turned her head away.

"Hi, Kimber."

She mumbled something, clearly upset with me.

Dad pointed to the empty chair. "We were expecting you last night, son," he said with a mischievous grin, maybe hinting that young men like me need to sow their wild oats. He'd told me that once. Yeah. If only. He looked a little drawn, not sure why. "What kept you?"

"Can I wash up first?"

CHAPTER 4

"I am Nocturne," a boy's exuberant voice
announced on the all-zan blast.
"America the beautiful, what happened to the dream?
Of equality and freedom,
Till selfish gain no longer stain, the banner of the free!
Reclaim our birthright!
Join the Second American Revolution, AR2!"

BREAKFAST WAS OVER AND I LAUGHED when I watched the hack, popping up on millions of zans and implants around the country, imagining the barronials screaming. I turned off the Z-ether in my ring and the speaker in my ear, then looked around and remembered good times in this room, all 480 square feet of it, plenty of space for a family of five. Our apartment was better than most. I tried to see the bright side of things and that could be a challenge at times. Depending on how you counted, we had three rooms: a bedroom, a bathroom and everything else. We hung drapes around the beds for us kids.

The concrete floor was special, painted by Mom in intricate swirling patterns, an arithmetic progression she called it, mostly reds, browns, and greens with occasional flashes of blue and yellow. She was an artist and mathematician, a scholarship girl, a model, on her way up before they pushed her back down. As a hobby and sideline business, she did oil Monet-like paintings, mostly of flowers, and consigned them in a local shop. We had a few throw rugs, not much to look at but heaven when barefoot on a cold morning. The pale yellow walls were supposed to make the place seem larger and lend a sense of calm. The seven-foot ceiling was ivory to give the illusion of height. Good thing we weren't any taller.

There were images of all of us on the side of the kitchen cabinets. I noticed a print of me with the laurel wreath. I'd thought about bringing the wreath home but it was already falling apart. Part of one wall was covered with a quilt Mom sewed, adding patches to it every year. It was made of squares of our old clothes and artifacts like broken toys. She could look at each piece and give its history. It was colorful, ugly and so magical. She was a seamstress by trade and much in demand. And as a side gig the painting brought in some money. Everyone did more than one thing.

"Spartak..." Mom said.

I popped out of my daydream. "Sorry. Just a minute." I opened my hip pack and pulled out the rolled up tank top I wore at the Faceoff, sweat stained and in need of a wash. She took it and opened it up.

"Perfect."

"Can I try it on?" Geo squeaked, jumping up and down. "Can I?"

She handed it to him and we all laughed as he slipped it over his head.

Being naturally blond with light complexions made us unusual in a brown-skinned world. But different was good at least some of the time. My other life was so divergent. And I wanted it for all of us. Ogden Academy, catering to seventh to twelfth graders, barronial children and the brightest downers, scholarship kids.

Headhunters had recruited me in the sixth grade, offering full tuition, room and board starting the following year. I was a National Merit Scholar in math, won the California Rachmaninoff Competition in piano for my age group and was rated in the top ten nationally in gymnastics for boys twelve and under. I bawled like a five-year-old after they told me. Once I was selected, Mom and Dad got a stipend each month that saved us. We kept it as long as I did well. Barronials knew how to get what they wanted and keep it.

* * *

"You three, out of the house," Mom ordered late Saturday morning, pointing to the door. "Go to the park."

I was playing chess with Geo at the kitchen table, his face scrunched up in concentration, still wearing my impossibly big tank top over his shirt.

"Checkmate!" he screeched, slamming down the queen. He'd won without my help. And that pleased me.

Kimber was studying the Revolutionary War for school, sitting by the small front window with a view of the next building. We all grumbled and grabbed our jackets hanging on hooks at the door. It was mild out but this was San Francisco. Most of my clothes were still here because they didn't fit the dress code at the academy and would eventually go to Geo.

I looked at my little brother as we walked, draping my arm over his shoulder. People said we both resembled Dad and I always thanked them. I thought my father was handsome with a strong chin and straight nose but with some softer features like his full lips. He could have been an actor. Some said he looked a bit like a masculine version of the blond, blue-eyed Jesus paintings popular in some churches. I thought it was a weird comparison but…I could see the resemblance if he had a beard. I hoped I looked like him. He was also a top-rated soccer player at my age, muscular, with prospects for going professional. Mom was elegant and physically powerful yet feminine. She'd been on the women's swim team in school. I loved being seen with her and how people glanced; how people looked at both of them. Kimber was a ringer for Mom at the same age.

Glory Avenue was crowded; many were headed toward Cedar Park three blocks away, a treeless spot with a playground and flowers.

"Let's see if we can find a swing," I suggested. The three of us used to play for hours, seeing who could get highest. I was the official pusher.

The sandbox was packed with little kids. Bored parents visited nearby. The swing set was empty. I gestured with a bow and grin toward two canvas seats attached to chains.

"Yeow!" Geo leaped between the chains, plopped his butt on the canvas and swung high.

Kimber put a hand on each chain and sat. She seemed mechanical, indifferent. She flipped her long hair over her shoulders. "Let's do this." She didn't sound happy.

I stood behind them, pushing their shoulders when they came back.

"Michael!" Geo spotted his best friend just entering the park, jumped off the swing and ran to him. "Lookit my shirt!"

I was alone with my sister. There would be no better time. "Have I done something wrong?"

She kicked her feet hard to gain height, swung high and remained silent.

"Please tell me. I love you."

She dropped her heels into the sand, stopped the swing and jumped to her feet. She turned and faced me, arms stretched tight to her sides, hands clenched into fists.

"How could you ever do anything wrong?" It was more a growl than a shout. "You're mister perfect."

I stared for a moment, feeling like I'd been punched. "Can we sit and talk?" I headed to a log bench nearby and sat, trying to catch my breath from the assault. She followed and did the same. We both looked ahead.

"I'm not perfect, Kimber. I'm really something of a mess."

"Not to Mom and Dad. You get everything. Private lessons, a fancy rich-boy school. A national title. Look at your body, all big muscles. And your skin is so flawless it almost glows. They must feed you really well."

I flinched. A direct hit. Mom and Dad *were* playing favorites, a calculated gamble. When I got more, everyone else got less.

"Convenient you're here on another weekend we aren't scheduled for FoodCon." Her arms were crossed. I'd never seen her this angry. "Are you still embarrassed to have your rich friends see you asking for a handout? I can do it but you're too good."

FoodCon gave out groceries to poor families. Barronial kids stood behind a counter on weekends and took your list of items and some downer boy in the next room filled it. It was all a publicity stunt for them, posing for photos, showing how much they cared. The fashionably dressed rich teenagers were generally pleasant but it made me feel like a beggar. Of course it gave us a half dozen extra bags of groceries every month, two per visit.

Kimber and I had gone last year when I was home. Two of my schoolmates had been behind the counter. I'd turned away, horrified at standing in front of them. Kimber did it for me.

"Please don't be angry with me. My life's a little surreal..."

"Did you hear I had to stand in front of my science class and apologize for disagreeing with the teacher's claim about dinosaurs being on the earth at the same time with people?" Her voice was hard.

"Oh, no!" I knew they were in a new private voucher academy after the lone public school closed. "I'm sorry. That's awful."

"Easy for you. Geo and I have no alternatives. You get Ogden where they actually teach science."

I didn't know how to respond. How could schools ignore reality? "Kimber..."

"And so nice you could come and visit," she said, interrupting. "First time in three months. What is it, four miles?"

I put my arm out to touch her. She slid farther down the bench. I couldn't lose her. "I'm sorry. I didn't know about it. I thought your school would be better. And you're right. I'm a selfish, spoiled jerk. I knew what Mom and Dad spent on me meant less for you and Geo. I'm sorry."

I glanced at her and she turned her head.

"I...I'm really scared, Kimber." I leaned forward, elbows on my knees. "I might get expelled from the academy and that ends the stipend and my future. Then what do I do?"

"How could someone so perfect get expelled? They recruited you. You're in sports DIMMs all the time...the powerful, the oh-so-handsome all-natural gymnast, Spartak Jones! Some sportscasters just use your first name and swoon."

The sarcasm was painful, a tongue filet because it was true. I didn't know she was holding all this inside.

"Are you going to answer me?" She sounded indignant.

I turned to her, folding my legs under me, not wanting to invade her space by moving closer. "It's not fair to you. You're completely right. You have been short-changed. I didn't realize it at first, I was so self-absorbed." I stopped for a moment, afraid I might tear up. "Mom and Dad knew what was out there and wanted it for us. All of us." She was looking at me now, listening. "I was their boy-bot to shape into something barronials would value. Dad pushed me into weight training so I could defend myself on the street. Then he saw I could tumble and jump, and suddenly I was in gymnastics. The same with math and music. If I showed any aptitude, it became their unrelenting focus. And I wanted so bad to please them."

She was staring at me. The frowns were gone from her face, leaving just the contempt.

"I know the stipend and secret money you bring in saves us. Obviously I benefit. But I wonder what Geo and I might be now if we'd had the same attention you got."

"You'd be fantastic. But I was born first and they invested what little they had. If it'd been you, they'd have done the same. And maybe you'd be further ahead than I am."

She just watched. It made me nervous and I babbled.

"Sometimes my body and my hands were so sore from practicing that I cried at night."

"I heard you. When you have drapes for walls not much is secret."

"Sorry."

"I remember the first time I saw you do floor exercises," Kimber said, looking at me then away. "I thought you were a monkey."

"A monkey?"

"Only a monkey could do summersaults like you did."

"A monkey?"

She was focused on me now.

"Please don't hate me." My voice was raw.

She moved next to me. "I could never hate you, Spartak. I know what's happening. When you're here, everything seems better." She kissed my cheek. "And I am proud of you."

I put my arm around her and kissed the top of her head. I had to keep my family. "I'll do better. I promise."

Somehow.

* * *

It was a relaxing twenty-minute after dinner stroll to Mr. Jona's grocery with Geo. I figured it should be safe despite last night's AR2 fight with the Dominionists. No mention of it on the news flashes and not likely to happen again. My stomach turned thinking about Officer Rango, but she was a rare horror and only came at me late at night when I was alone. We really didn't need anything but Geo had said something he shouldn't have in front of Mom and I wanted to talk about it in private, something impossible at home. And I needed to spend some quiet time with my brother, my blood.

I began, "Some people use words to hurt people..."

"All I said was we were *downers,"* Geo interrupted, sounding defensive. "But we are, aren't we? That's what people call us."

"Yes they do. The *barronials* call people like us *downers* as a way of saying we're below them, that we're inferior because we're poor." I stopped and turned him toward me. "Maybe it makes them feel more important. In my view, if you're called an ugly name, own it and suck out the sting. That's what I do. But for Mom and Dad it's different. I think you know they once had better times. For me, it's just a word. Your statement's accurate but it hurts their feelings. Please don't use it in front of them."

"Okay."

I squeezed his shoulder. "Thanks, big guy." Shops were closed and few people were out because this was the final week of the International Soccer Championships in Madrid, the US against Mexico. Flickering lights and cheers burst from apartments above. I reached down to take Geo's hand but he pushed it away. I wasn't too old for that but he was.

"The name that matters most to me is my own. I can define it. Spartak Jones. I want to do great things."

"Dad says Spartak is Russian for Spartacus. You don't look like a gladiator."

"That was low." I faked a punch. "No, I look like a dopey scholarship kid."

A cold mist whipped around the corner into our faces. I told him,

"Button your coat, please." We were both wearing black stretcher pants and boots, a popular look. We each had on blue and gold lettermen's jackets from OA. Coach helped me get a small size at a discount and I gave it to Geo for Christmas. He always wore it. My tank top was underneath, still unwashed.

"What does *Geo* mean?" He looked up at me, a little boy again.

"A very important Greek name. It has to do with the earth. Like *geo*-graphy or *geo*-logy. Maybe you'll be a scientist."

"Did I tell you I got an A on my *GEO*-metry test?" He giggled so hard he could hardly get it out.

"See, what'd I tell you! That's sonic!" I licked my palm and slammed it against his in our secret ritual.

I heard the crunch of gravel behind us.

"Keep walking!" I put my arm around his shoulder. "Don't look back."

"What?" he asked, confused.

"Maybe nothing. I'm just being my cautious self."

A sleek black electro-cruiser sped down the street and slowed beside us. It was a bullet shaped Kiron66, two wheels at the back, the front cantilevered off the ground, impossible to see inside. But I knew. It was barronials on the hunt. The cruiser stopped and let us walk ahead before moving forward, pacing us about fifty feet to the rear.

"Don't slow down."

I quickened our pace. The cruiser disappeared in a fog swirl then punched out, moved closer and held the distance.

"Whoever's inside wants to hurt us. We need to ditch it but not panic." I tried to sound like an adult so he'd take me seriously. "There could be more than one cruiser. Act natural, two brothers on a walk. Can you do it?"

"Who are they?"

"Rich guys looking for sport."

We reached the next cross street, Euphoria Place, and turned the corner. At the end of this block I paused, using peripheral vision as I pretended to adjust Geo's collar. The vehicle was stopped. I pretended to laugh at something he said, like I hadn't seen them or wasn't concerned, and put a hand behind his neck as a thick fog blanket surged in our direction. We casually crossed the next street as it engulfed us.

"Run!" I pulled him around the corner and back to the sidewalk.

We scrambled past several apartment entrances and squeezed into a narrow trash nook, crouching behind a mulch bin that smelled like rotting food.

The cruiser came into view, paused and moved on as we watched its reflection on a broken piece of mirror behind the metal boxes. If they had a heat scope, they knew we were here. Lumins on the streets would identify them if they got out but they'd likely use blockers. And going to the enforcers wasn't an option. Harmony Enforcers weren't here to protect people like us. We were on our own and avoiding a fight was always best if you could.

Geo was chewing his lower lip. "Come here." I wrapped him in my arms. We waited ten minutes before I inched to the edge of our hiding place and peeked around the corner. It seemed clear. I motioned to my brother and we raced down a series of alleys until we reached Freedom Place and the only grocery store in our area that sold quality food downers could afford. It was mid-block, a glass front behind steel bars. A small neat sign in the window by the door read:

SPARTAK SHOPS HERE.

AMERICA'S TOP GYMNAST!

Mr. Jona, the owner, was a friendly old man and nearly deaf. His face bristled with gray whiskers. As we entered, he opened his arms and held us both. He didn't say anything and didn't have to.

"Thanks," I said. We looked at each other then pulled away as I struggled to contain my emotions. This hero gig was hard to handle. "Get some milk, Geo." I walked down the produce aisle in the back. "How about rainbow kale?" I yelled.

"No! Broccolini. It's crunchy."

"Okay, I'll pick a bunch." We were the only customers in the store so hollering back and forth was fun and helped lower the adrenaline level. Mr. Jona just smiled.

"I gotta pee," Geo yelled.

He had a small bladder. I laughed as I pulled the locator clip from my belt, synced with Geo's. He was already in the head.

At the counter I set the vegetables next to the milk. I picked up several free packages of government-issued *Fillos* that convinced your stomach you weren't hungry and provided essential vitamins and proteins. I put my index finger on his zan-cube, heard the familiar beep and my account was charged. I put the items in my shoulder pouch, slung it over my head and walked down the hallway.

"Hurry up, Geo." I knocked on the door. No response. I tried the knob and it opened. Empty. His locator clip was in the toilet.

"Geo!" There was an outside door in the hall. I stepped through it into a service alley as acid swabbed my throat.

"Geo! *GEO!*"

"Spartak…!" His voice was panicked and distant.

I sprinted toward his sound, around a corner into a dead-end street. Two men were lifting him into the backseat of the cruiser, the top up, the front leg balancing the twin tires in the rear, riding just a few inches off the ground. Geo's hands were cuffed behind his back. He was kicking and biting as best he could.

"STOP!" I screamed as I yanked a man's ponytail, punched his chest and slammed him into a wall. *"Bastards!"* I swung a fist at the other as he jumped back, just clipping the end of his chin. I lifted my brother out and pulled him to me.

"Are you okay?" His pants were undone.

"Yeah."

Ponytail man rubbed the back of his head and glared, his lips pulled back in a tight grin. This was blood sport, what they wanted. He was mid-twenties, clean-shaven and wearing a stylish high-neck blue Napoleonic jacket. His friend was big, about the same age, swarthy with a short beard. Dressed in a similar red one. I'd never seen them before. They were just rich thugs trolling.

I quick-stepped backward with Geo in my arms as the men watched. They weren't going to leave. We were just a couple of downer boys to use for entertainment. I knew their mindset—we'd submit, not resist because no court would accept our testimony.

Not this time. No one hurts Geo.

I set him on his feet. I needed to be free to fight.

"Stay behind me," I whispered. "Keep moving back. When I give the signal, run and find Mr. Jona."

"No!"

"Please don't argue." I lifted the shoulder bag over my head and set it on the ground.

"He's ours, downer boy." It was the one with the beard.

"Do your mamas know you beat up children?" I scoffed. Angry people were easier to defeat. "That's a crime even for you."

"Don't be so cocky, blond boy," beard-man taunted. "Is he your brother? Two pretty blond downers. And such white skin. Might be fun."

They weren't showing any weapons so it would be a street brawl. To my advantage. They moved in an arrogant saunter that was also helpful. They weren't in any kind of fighting mode. If I could keep them talking, we could put more distance between us. We were backing up faster than they were coming forward. I'd run if we could but either way I needed room.

"Raping a nine-year-old is illegal," I warned.

"We weren't going to rape him," hair-face said with a curled lip. "Just make sure he was prime all over." They both laughed. "Lots of uses for a pretty slave boy."

With each step backward I tensed my leg muscles, one knee bent, the other close to the street like I was in the blocks for the start of a race, just waiting for the signal. Surprise was crucial and they didn't know about my strength or that I'd been winning street fights since I was ten.

"But we could rape *you,*" red-coat taunted, "...just so you'll understand your place." They glanced at each other and laughed like it was funny.

"NOW!" I sprinted forward. I jumped, airborne, slamming my left boot tip hard into shave-guy's nuts and landed a fist directly into the shocked mouth of hairy-man, knocking him into a wall. I needed to take him out fast and delivered three more hits to his mouth. I heard a crunch, his eyes rolled up in his head and he collapsed. I stepped backward and turned, ready for round two. Clean-cut guy regained his balance, looking dumbfounded and rubbed his crotch.

I waited, ready for him, and grinned. "Not so tough, are ya?" Make him snort fire.

"Scum!" He charged like an enraged football tackle and I side-stepped, shoved him facedown to the pavement and dropped my knee onto his spine with a crack. I whipped my arm around his neck and wrenched his head back nearly ninety degrees—any more and I'd crush his vertebra. I squeezed, collapsing his windpipe. He thrashed, unable to lift his arms. I knuckle-punched his kidneys. He stopped struggling.

I kept up the pressure on his throat for another half minute then removed my arm. His head smacked the pavement. I pulled it back by his ponytail and dangled it until satisfied he was unconscious and let go.

I jumped up, panicked I'd ignored beard-man. But he hadn't moved. I kicked his leg. Nothing. His mouth was bloody with a few teeth bulging out his lips. I swiveled around to Geo. He stared at me, pale-faced, afraid like I was a stranger. I ran up to him, kneeled and wrapped my arms around him.

"Are you all right? Did they hurt you?"

He seemed in shock. I felt the cuffs on his wrists and stood, pushing him back. "Wait here."

I moved to the swarthy one and patted him down. No luck. The clean-shaven guy had a zan-stick in a pants pocket and a second set of restraints. I swiped the key over Geo's wrists and the cuffs buzzed, dropping to the pavement. I needed to keep them from coming after us, maybe raise some questions they'd have a hard time explaining. "Time for street justice," I mumbled, disgusted, ready for payback, as I dragged both men to the prow of the Kiron, handcuffed one, pulled the chain through a metal loop on the steel leg, and cuffed the second guy. I took the second restraint and repeated the process, both arms overhead for the perverts. I ripped open the shirts and pulled down the pants and shorts of both men, making the case for enforcers when they arrived.

I removed a small *Obscura* mister from my ankle strap and sprayed anything we'd touched, eliminating any finger, gene or odor prints. It was an equalizer, pricy on the black market but worth it. It also changed your scent, confusing the Sniffers. As I jogged back to Geo, I retrieved the canvas bag and lifted it over my head. Mom expected groceries. I pulled two *Cosmo* pins from my pocket and fastened one on Geo's collar behind his neck and one on mine. They'd do a subtle distort on our faces for the lumins without raising alarms.

"Close your eyes." I sprayed the rest of the *Obscura* over us before slipping the bottle back into its holster. I didn't want any of their scent on us if we were stopped.

I picked him up with both arms and kissed his forehead. He stared at me, his face ashen, and wrapped his arms tight around my neck. I fast-stepped toward our apartment, zigzagging through different alleys.

I went to a favorite small park and put him down on a bench. I sat next to him, wiped his tears with my thumbs and cradled his head in my shoulder to stop his shaking. He cried. I began to tremble, realizing if I'd delayed even another minute in the store I'd have lost him.

"It's okay, Geo, they can't hurt you now." I rubbed the back of his scalp. I tried to keep my own tears from becoming a river. After several minutes he regained his calm. I struggled to find mine.

In my experience, most barronials were pleasant, if condescending, maybe because they were ignorant of how others lived, or didn't care. Only a few were rabid wolves, using downers for sport. And they paid no price. Geo pushed me back to arm's length and stared.

"Who are you?" he asked, then grinned and wrapped me in a bear hug. "My hero! That was astronomical!"

His choice of words was sometimes slightly off. One of many things I loved about him. "Let's go home."

"How'd you learn to fight like that? When? Will you teach me?"

I put a finger to his lips. "Of course." I looked up at a bank of lumins and sniffers on posts. The thugs were cowards. Of course they'd have disabled them. No proof of their attack and no record of what I did to them. Their egos would take a hit when their security team or family found them. Otherwise it would be the enforcers. Delicious. Maybe they'd learn to stay away. Street justice was better than no justice.

"Take my hand."

Geo offered his with a grin. I squeezed it and we ran until we reached Glory Lane, then walked casually home. At the front door I turned him toward me and kneeled. He seemed normal now but I knew he was sensitive and would be haunted by what had been in store for him. He had a right to be.

"I'm proud of the way you had them screaming with your kicks."

"Really?"

"Really. We'll start some of your training tomorrow. You need to learn some street tactics. But…a favor to protect the family…can we keep all that just happened a secret for now, just between us? Lock it away in a corner of your brain. It's hard but it's what I do. If you tell Mom, Dad, or Kimber, they'll want to report it to the enforcers. They don't know what they're really like. We don't want those thugs to learn who we are." I thought of my sister, just thirteen, a dangerous age. "The enforcers won't protect us. They are not our friends."

His eyes widened. I hugged him. "I love you, Geo. Please be brave. Please trust me."

He pushed out his lower lip. I was asking a lot.

"Deal?" I licked my palm and held it toward him.

"I'll try," he said, pushing his hand into mine.

CHAPTER 5

"I am Nocturne," a man's deep, reassuring
voice announced on the all-zan blast.
"What happened to America, everyone equal and free?
Let our country be the dream it used to be.
Join the Second American Revolution, AR2!"

ANOTHER ZAN-HACK ON A SUNDAY MORNING. It was shirtsleeve weather and sunny, no fog, at least for a few hours. Mom and I walked through Cedar Park to the Castlemont Community Gardens. That was the name of our apartment complex: Castlemont. And it was mean-funny, as Dad said, but I liked it. We watched a group of boys play dodgeball and a mother nursing her baby under an arbor covered in white roses and purple trumpet vine with gardenias at the base. It smelled like perfume. A black bumblebee worked the blooms.

"Thank you for the money, son. You've saved us again."

"I'm glad I could help."

"I don't suppose you want to tell me where the clothes and jewelry came from or the cash?"

"Side jobs, Mom. Can we leave it at that?"

"Please be careful."

She pressed her index finger into a small hole on the lock. There was a buzz and a multipaned glass door swung open. Inside were ten acres of farmland covered with frosted glass. The walls were vertical gardens, the ground had neatly spaced plots of rich dirt with a dozen levels of rotating hydroponic trays suspended above, grow lights powered by solar panels on the roof. It was highly productive and a cooperative, honor system effort of most residents in Castlemont. Our plot was near the front and just a short walk.

"Hi Spartak! Congratulations. Hello Barbel, you must be so proud of your son," Mrs. Semrau said, a thin, elderly woman with rosy cheeks, on her knees loosening dirt around a row of tomatoes. We waved back.

Community gardens were popular across the country for downers. The produce was perfect for sustenance and bartering, a major part of the black economy. Locally produced vegetables were what most Californians used in the decades since the big agri-conglomerates and water districts destroyed the groundwater system in the Central Valley and left millions of acres parched and poisoned. Imported produce was often tainted since inspections were underfunded or left to private companies. As a result, few trusted any food where you didn't know the farm. That included barronials. Their food workers often stopped by and paid good money, always cash, sometimes bidding up the price and proving that capitalism could work. Private foundations had set up this garden and many others to stabilize the food source and pacify the population, to give us some sense of hope and, unintentionally, income.

"The squash is doing well," I said, stooping down to feel the smooth green surface. I revolved the hydroponic trays to check on different levels. "The spinach is about ready for picking."

"Yes, and we'll have some for dinner tonight."

"Great. How's Dad?" I stood next to her. "Please be honest." He didn't look like his energetic self and something was wrong.

"He's had some shortness of breath and gets dizzy sometimes, based on our home diagnostics, maybe his heart. We're saving up to visit the doctor. He's worried because they're cutting back his hours at the jewelry store. That means…well, you know. And his artwork is not selling as well as it once did. Rich folks always want something newer."

I tightened my fists and held my breath. Not news I wanted to hear. Is that why he looked gaunt? I wasn't imagining it. He was always so athletic, so vital. Like nearly all downers, Dad pieced together an income from many sources. Besides his jewelry skills, he created fanciful woodcarvings, often purchased by lower barronials or their entourages as gifts when they stopped by for fresh produce. Several shops in Castlemont specialized in downer art and occasionally it was picked up in barronial art galleries. Since full-time employment evaporated decades ago, a genuine artisans' community developed—intellectuals called it the Post-Work Age, total bullshit. Downers were entrepreneurial, finding jobs where they could, never any benefits or security, and experimented in art or things like I did with Dalix. Such a precarious life had taken a toll on my dad's heart. He was such a good man. The man I admired most in the world.

We sat on a nearby bench.

"Are Geo and Kimber doing well in school?"

"Yes. They're very bright. But the voucher school…I wish there was a public school nearby."

"That doesn't teach that dinosaurs and humans—"

"So you heard? I was furious and went down and argued with the teacher and principal but they quoted the Bible and threatened to kick her out. There are no other options." My mother looked pained, like she was a bad mother. She put her fingertips to her eyes, holding back tears.

"Oh Mom…"

"I do what I can. The best I came up with was to tutor her on what to ignore. Lie to the teachers. Other classes aren't so bad. She's smart."

I needed to find a way to help but the only solution I could think of was risky. Was Kimber too angry to keep a secret? Others could be at risk if she couldn't. And Mom looked so miserable. "Mom, I am going to make sure you get some books for her to read, and maybe you and dad too, that will help her understand issues without the religious and political screen. She needs an education on the real world but there are complications as you know with anything that does not fit official policy. They may be too adult for Geo. You must promise, you all must promise not to tell anyone or people will be hurt."

"What are you talking about?"

"Promise?"

"Yes, for you."

"I have access to certain books that give a different perspective on issues taught in public schools. Real history, real politics, real science. They are not on an electronic directory but delivered one person to another. She can study and learn the real world in as much detail as she wants, then pretend to believe the junk in her school. But no one outside the family can know. Others could be in trouble. I could be in trouble."

"Thank you, Spartak. That would be lovely. We know how to keep secrets."

"And your job, Mom?"

"Fashions change. Fabrics change. But old-fashioned seamstresses are forever. And I sell a few paintings."

I put my arm around her and hugged. I knew the academy stipend accounted for about a third of their income. They were doing better than many of our neighbors. But this was horrific news about Dad.

"How's rent?" There were no government subsidies or protections, even for the poor. No safety nets. No such thing as renter's rights.

"Going up again." She looked down. Her lower lip seemed to quiver. She was holding something back.

"Mom, talk to me."

She was silent. I sensed embarrassment.

"Please."

"You're sixteen now and certainly an adult given all that happens. You have a right to know—"

"Know what?"

"Please control your temper on what I'm about to say. Promise?"

How could I promise? I knew this was bad. She looked into my eyes. There was no choice. "Okay Mom, I promise."

"The landlord knows we get money from the academy…so our rent is raised to take most of it."

I jumped up. *"What?* That can't be legal. My God, I thought the stipend made you more comfortable. He's already so rich." I twisted around looking away from her, pushing my fist to my mouth. I wanted to punch the guy. I turned back. This was so unfair.

"Please calm down. We do keep some of it and that is so, so helpful," she said, looking up at me. "You are a lifesaver for us. Believe that. You're our salvation. And I assume it's legal. Everyone is on month-to-month rent, no leases for downers."

"Why? Why does he do it?"

"Because he can." She shrugged. "He's just greedy and *maximizing shareowner value* as they teach in Economics 101 and he's the sole shareowner. Social responsibility is no longer taught in business school, too uneconomic and distracting. He has no obligation to us."

My heart was pounding. Why did we have to be so helpless? Can't we ever get ahead? I was shaking with anger and had to get it under control.

"You're such an amazing son. We're so proud of you." Her hand touched my cheek as I sat next to her. "I know about your demerits at school. So unfair." I took her hand and squeezed. She didn't need my worries too. Mom began to cry softly. I held her. I couldn't handle Mom in tears. I felt like screaming. She leaned her head on my shoulder. "I sometimes don't know what to do…we don't want to be…to be *reapers*." It seemed like her energy faded and she was limp.

"No! Mom! Please don't use the R word. No way! We're not!" I pictured my family in the streets, like the Tabors, castoffs with no hope. "Mom, it won't happen. I won't let it."

Everything was going well for me and yet nothing was. I felt helpless and exhausted. Big biceps, flashing fingers on a keyboard, being intimate with grad school mathematics and a successful part-time thief weren't enough.

* * *

Sunday afternoon I took the Q Line to Sea Cliff across town to tutor another barronial kid from the academy. Cedric Rand was cordial but never let me forget my status or his. Even though Cedric was a senior and I was a lowly tenth grader, the math department chairman said I was the best tutor at the academy.

There were dozens of mansions on the bluff overlooking the Pacific Ocean as it flowed into San Francisco Bay under the Golden Gate Bridge. Some were titanium-clad marvels, others Victorian castles or twisted jumbles from a bad dream or a drunken architect. Cedric lived in what looked like a giant white marble flying saucer cantilevered halfway over the cliff edge with a panoramic view.

A uniformed guard met me at the side door—I'd never been invited to use the front one—and he took me through the servants quarters to the butler, a tall, elegant man in a black suit and white gloves. He led me to the reception area outside Cedric's suite of rooms and left me standing there as he went inside. A few minutes later he returned and escorted me into a small study.

The walls were painted like the lunar landscape; the ceiling was a starry night, the floor like regolith, all disturbing in its faux-realism. And the furniture looked like it was moonstone but was comfortable and soft, like the rug. I'd met him here before for tutoring. The room was as big as my parents' apartment.

"Spartak, come in," Cedric said, stepping out of his bedroom. He was taller than me, over six feet, and had one of the most muscular bodies at school, displayed to perfection by a pair of trim workout shorts. He was a fanatic about exercise and had his own fully equipped gym next to his bedroom. His forehead was beaded with sweat, long black hair clung to his shoulders and he was using a small towel to dry off. He hated math, particularly calculus, but his dad insisted he had to pass it. For me, the money was good. I liked looking at him, his handsome face, green eyes and perfect teeth. And smelling him: woodsy citrus with a little sweat.

I headed to a chair by his desk that overlooked the entrance to San Francisco Bay, where we normally sat. I could see the Golden Gate Bridge to my right and the Pacific Ocean to my left. It was intoxicating, like I was floating, watching the fog race inland, the ships below.

"No, in here," he said, pointing to his bedroom door. I followed him, curious to see if it was also astronomy obsessed. It was. He pointed to a couch that looked like a stone bench. The décor was like a planetarium, asteroids moving in the black void, his round bed floating like it was a ring around Saturn, the planet somehow projected over and under. It left me unsettled. And confirmed that taste and money were not connected.

I sat, the pretend-rock surprisingly comfortable, and he plopped beside me, his knee touching mine. I scooted away and he moved closer.

"Sit by me. I want to talk." He looked at my face, examining me for a moment before continuing. "I'm told I have the *second* best natural body of any guy at the academy. After you."

I felt my mouth lock and neck tense.

"You know I'm blunt. I don't want to do calculus. When I get my inheritance and I need that kind of talent, I'll hire it. You're the most beautiful boy at school, maybe anywhere, everyone comments on it, men and women, and all natural. That's what drives everybody crazy."

I wanted to look away from him but couldn't. He put a hand on my shoulder. "I fuck girls every week, sometimes every day. Mostly downers. I never wanted to try a guy until I met you and saw you at gymnastics practice. Even your skin is flawless. I'll make it worth your while."

My hands seemed to be self-destructing in my lap, my fingers clenching them together as if they'd fallen into a black hole. Somebody like him could easily ruin me. I never thought he would try this or I would have insisted someone sit with us. With no witnesses, he could charge me with trying to rape or assault him. Or he could make me a joke at school. If I walked away, he'd get insulted and hurt my family or me. I'd slept with several guys and enjoyed it. And I liked sex with girls too, particularly Rhonda, but only if it was consensual. Cedric was striking but very self-absorbed and a close friend of Connor. I wondered if this was another of Connor's games.

"What is it you want to do?"

"I want us both to take off our clothes and go to my bed and see where it goes. And I'll pay you double what you get for tutoring."

"I came here to teach. I like you Cedric and respect you but I'm not a whore." I felt my knees twitch, knowing the risks.

"I never said you were." His expression hinted that he was surprised at the pushback. "I'm sorry if that's what you think. But I heard you go both ways. I suspect you do it for free because you like it, not for money. I'll pay you five times the rate for tutoring. And you strip and go to my bed for free. Because you want to."

I thought of my conversation about money this morning with my mother. My tutoring income was important for my family and I could ruin it if I had a reputation as an easy mark for sex. There was no way out and he knew it.

I asked, "You're dom or sub?"

"Dominant." He stared at me without expression for what seemed like forever, then the edge of his lip curled upward.

I glanced down, feeling cornered again. I was tired of it. He was convinced he could force me to submit and ruin me if I didn't. No. Downer girls may be hungry to go to bed with him but…

Then I understood. I could work this. The escalating money was the key to his head. He wanted me, "the most beautiful boy at school." As ridiculous as that sounded. Not any guy. Me. And he'd had to humiliate himself to ask, even if he was hiding it. I lifted my head, confident, looking straight into his eyes. I'd win this round.

"I top. Ten times my tutorial rate. In cash and we tell no one."

"Agreed."

* * *

I finished my paper for Mr. Bonas—the Supreme Court decision did not concern some esoteric libertarian blather about contracts but legalizing slavery outlawed in the Constitution. I decided to be tough, no weaseling on this. I thought of Marcia Heller when we were both ten years old. Her family lost their apartment and she disappeared. And the Tabors. I owed it to them and Billy to be honest even on a silly class paper. Justice Washington's written statement was inspiring and I read several of his past opinions, mostly in dissent, and he was a champion. It gave me a sense of hope. With a sigh of relief and a little foreboding, I zanned my essay to Mr. Bonas.

The meal at dinner was a favorite: mac and cheese with kale. It was like a special occasion dinner and I was starved. Mom carried the baking dish from the stove and started with me. I picked up the spoon and did the math. There wasn't enough. I ate well at school and took half a spoonful.

"Coach will kill me if I gain any weight." I dipped in the dish again and put a big portion on Geo's plate.

Kimber stared. I couldn't read her face.

After dinner, we all started chanting: "Vio-lin! Vio-lin!"

Dad grinned, tugging on the long hair at his neck as he often did when he was happy. He picked up the old black case and took out his instrument. He once had a soaring career as a concert violinist, played with the San Francisco Symphony, a scholarship boy himself. Then he made fun of an uncommonly ridiculous US Senator in a private message to a few friends. Within a week, he was unemployed. His career evaporated. The privacy promises of the carriers were secondary when rooting out criminals or anyone not sucking up to the elite. So talking in code or silence was now standard downer procedure.

"Any requests?"

"It's been a long time since I heard you play Beethoven's *Romance Number 2 in F Major*." I delighted watching him play and knew this was a favorite.

"Oh, yes," Mom said. "Lovely."

"Only if Spartak accompanies me on the keyboard."

With Geo's help, I pulled the old plastic keyboard from its hiding place under my bed, attached the legs and plugged in the power. They'd bought it for me when I was four and it cost Dad two weeks wages. He was determined I would love music. I checked the keys. The E-flat still stuck, as always, so I needed to play around it.

Dad placed the violin to his chin, lifted the bow and closed his eyes. He looked energized, young again; so did Mom. I got misty as I played. Kimber and Geo nodded their heads to the rhythm. With limited access to paid media, we were on our own for evening entertainment but had all manner of books and chess and family. And we all loved live music.

Tradition called for a family song led by Dad. He had the greatest baritone with amazing volume. Not a trait I inherited. I played and he sang "Love is Forever," a show tune from an old Broadway musical from 2080. Afterward we all applauded, on our feet. Dad bowed.

At his insistence, I played his favorite Chopin, the *Fantasie Impromptu*. It was at once soothing and inspiring, it made me tingle and as I played, the music seemed to wrap around my family, protecting us. As long as I played, we were safe. Everyone looked at me, except Kimber. At the end she smiled. For a change, the neighbors didn't complain. I guess we were getting better or they were being generous.

CHAPTER 6

"A PERFECT BUSINESS ENVIRONMENT," SOME POLITICIAN announced on our Z-ether, an old 2095 model, talking about America, as we sat around the table on Monday before dawn. Oatmeal. It was the kind where kernels popped as you chewed. My favorite.

"How nice," Dad said. "The Chamber of Commerce just claimed victory—wages around the world have finally *democratized.* Such a PR man's work of art. We can all make the same take-home as some guy in Hanoi or Manila. Sweet. It gives a new meaning to the term minimum wage." His voice was more resigned than bitter. I knew this was the kind of criticism that had gotten him into trouble before. My father was maestro in more than music.

"What?" he said, looking into my face.

I just smiled. "I love you, Dad."

After breakfast, I slipped the Cedric money into Mom's purse and we did a group hug as I left with individual kisses.

"I love you," Kimber said. "Sorry about givin' you bird dung."

"Thank you, more than you know. I deserved it. And I love you."

I jogged into the alley behind the apartment, taking my usual route to the PT and school, wiping tears. Slowing to a fast-walk, I pulled a knitted red tie from my canvas messenger bag, tucked it under my collar and knotted it. I didn't want to be late meeting Rhonda at the academy. It was almost umbrella weather. I stuck out my tongue, as I did as a boy, tasting the thick San Francisco fog. July 4th fireworks would be lousy again this year. Not that it mattered when everything America had once stood for had been betrayed and besmirched by its highest symbol of justice, the Supreme Court. No, not entirely true. Lots of other things had gone wrong too and no heroes had emerged to make them right.

"SPARTAK!"

I stopped midway down Boehner Lane, not far from the spot I'd met Dalix last Friday night, a less odiferous section, where it widens for a compactor truck turnaround.

"We warned you, pretty boy!"

The hazy sun was at his back leaving his face in partial shadow, his hair haloed red. Footsteps behind me. Three figures ran up from the opposite end of the curved alleyway, spreading out, blocking any escape.

I turned and stepped back, lifting the strap of my bag over my head and securing it on my shoulder so I wouldn't lose it if I had a chance to run. I tucked my tie into the shirt so they couldn't grab it. I knew what was coming. They were afraid of losing what little they had and I was part of their world. I kept an eye on the three on my right and focused on Dalix to my left. One-on-one was acceptable. But four-to-one were bad odds and I couldn't afford to replace my school jacket.

Jason slapped his hands together as a distraction. I knew the tactic. We called him Horse, all muscle with pumped up legs, short, brown skin, long black hair tied back behind his head. Mark was thin; his tan face had a permanent snarl, but that was for show. Onzi's orange hair was a ridiculous steel wool disaster.

"Aren't we good enough?" Onzi said, eyes hard, aching to beat me senseless. I could tell by the metallic whine in his voice. He was drunk; likely they all were.

"Guys, please don't do this."

Two feet closer.

"Why? You're my friends!" I deepened my voice, trying to mask any fear, providing plenty of volume. Not really a question, more like a time killer so I could figure my strategy. I understood their anguish and felt it too for different reasons.

"I don't want to fight."

The three to my right were fifteen feet away and closing in quick quarter-steps, cautious but relentless. They understood what I could do. Dalix was about the same distance, facing me, crouched, waiting to tackle, inching forward. Their play never changed—surround and pound—and I knew they were confident that I'd slug it out. Not this time.

"You like kissing barronial assholes?" It was Mark.

I noticed that Jason, in the middle, the fat–faced muscle man, had a baseball bat at his side. That upped the ante. Why would they want to hurt me like that? So this meant I had to be tough. Fuck. If retreat wasn't an option, Coach taught me, take the offense and do the unexpected at turbo-speed. And fly.

"Please don't hurt me," I pleaded and feigned right.

As the three guys scrambled to cut me off, in a gymnastic move I leaped forward, one step, then a second for momentum and kicked my leather boot high, airborne, right into Dalix's jaw. He crumpled backward.

The others hesitated as I swiveled and vaulted high, legs wide, right into Horse's neck, crotch to larynx, wrapping my legs around his throat. He staggered back, dropping his club, colliding into Onzi while my thighs tightened, collapsing his airway. Riding high on my mount, hoping Horse wouldn't stumble, I seized Mark's long hair in the chaos, yanking him off-balance and forcing his head down. I held him while I twisted my legs, forcing Jason to turn. If he fell, I was finished. I only had seconds to maneuver or they'd overwhelm me.

"What're you afraid of, punk?" I taunted Onzi, needing him closer. He raced forward and swung just as I pitched backward and pulled Mark's head up, the blow connecting with Mark's jaw.

I snapped my heel upward, smashing Onzi hard in the face. He collapsed. I looked away. Mark was screaming, arms flailing, a pissed bull, still off-balance, grabbing at my forearm. I slammed a heel into Jason's kidney causing him to flail backward while I leaned forward and yanked Mark's hair with both hands. The two skulls collided with a crack. With a piercing, high-pitched cry, Mark fell, curling into a fetal position, arms around his head.

Jason collapsed to his knees, choking, thrashing at me. It was easy to block the sideways punches with open palms. I waited until his arms went limp, till he was close to blacking out, and then unwrapped my legs from his neck and stood. Horse had lived up to his name, a dependable mount, and fell onto the pavement on his back, next to his baseball bat. I watched him gasp and wheeze, hands cradling his throat. I stepped toward Onzi, ready to fight. The guy's face was bloody.

"I don't want to hurt you. But I will."

Onzi lurched to his feet and wobbled down the alley, looking back once before he disappeared around the corner. I stood, surveying the damage, remembering good times. Now this. Dalix was on his knees, head down, hands on his chin. Jason on his back, wheezing. Mark still curled, wailing.

"Please…I'm not your enemy!" My voice broke. I felt ashamed. "I'm sorry I had to do this." I started to tear; not very manly. These were my friends.

I turned and hustled out of the alley, across the street and down a stairway to the PT station. In a true wonder, a bathroom was open. I undid my shirt, found a paper towel to wipe my sweaty pits, and washed my face.

"This isn't your private lavatory," an old man griped.

"Sorry," I said, stepping back from the sink. Looking over his shoulder into the mirror, I rebuttoned my shirt, straightened my blazer, finger-combed my hair. It'd have to do. Five minutes later, I was on an express train to Ogden Academy four miles, ninety seconds and a world distant.

* * *

Exiting at the school PT station in Golden Gate Park, I spotted Rhonda across the street, standing beside the fifty-foot, black twisted wrought-iron gates. Hundreds of students, dressed like me, were hurrying past.

"Spartak, you're dripping!"

I shrugged as I approached her, a point of serenity in my mad life.

Rhonda pulled a lace handkerchief from between her breasts. She was nearly my height, into music and weight training, believing the stronger her body, the more powerful the voice. It worked.

"I'm amazed what you keep down there," I said, offering what I hoped was an appreciative grin. I took the cloth, sniffed, nodded approval and dabbed my face. "Hmmmm. Smells like Eau de Rhonda!"

She pushed a finger against my nose. "Watch your smart mouth, blondie. It's my signature scent—pink roses. And yours is boy sweat. You're late. What happened?"

"Oh, some career disagreements." I glanced down again at her chest, remembering past good times. "Do you want me to put this back?"

"Honey-boy, you've seen 'em, stroked 'em, and tasted 'em before. I'm not your flavor." She pulled me to her; it felt so good. "But I wish I was. Be careful out there." She pushed me back and took her handkerchief. "Yuck, you're still wet."

"We've only got ten minutes," I said, taking her hand, merging into the crowd of students and teachers hurrying down a cobblestone road, each side lined with dozens of dark, waxy-leafed ficus trees. They glowed in the dark, like a lighted pathway, all by splicing in the DNA of luminescent jellyfish and fireflies. The trees led to a row of five-story brick and stone buildings, fitted tight, reflecting the eclectic tastes of its founder, Barron Ogden two generations ago—Gothic, Renaissance, Art Nouveau, American colonial, and the neoclassical Beaux-Arts style used at City Hall. An odd ten-story Venetian-style clock tower was on the left. Weird and wonderful, all of it, nestled on two hundred acres in Golden Gate Park, surrounded by a twelve-foot sandstone wall and guard towers every three hundred yards to keep the rich kids safe. At the end of the cobblestones a neatly printed banner hung on the wall:

OA: AMERICA'S #1 GYMNASTIC TEAM!

We pushed through the three-story stone entryway, zigzagging toward the music department for an hour of solo practice.

"Hola, Spartak. ¿Estas listo para la prueba española?"

"Buenos días, señorita Veressa. Eso espero." I shrugged, hoping I got it right, this being my third language.

"Hi, Spartak. Ready to bare it all again in gymnastics?"

"Hey, Mitch. I hope not."

"Congratulations," chirped two girls in a four-arm embrace as we passed.

"My popular downer-boy," Rhonda teased.

For society to prosper, Barron Ogden had decreed, it needed more than the bored, often lazy and sometimes talentless children of the rich. The best thinkers, artists, musicians, dancers, scientists, athletes, mathematicians, philosophers—those with potential for greatness, no matter their class—had to be found early and educated. And he paid for it. All male students, regardless of status, had to wear identical uniforms provided by the academy, just like mine. Girls had more options, which pleased the boys, and many wore scooped-neck white blouses or thin shells, sometimes exposing ample cleavage under the jackets. And short tan skirts. A red scarf around a girl's neck or a pocket-square tucked into her jacket pocket was an acceptable alternative to the boys' red tie. Everyone looked equal, the rich and regular kids alike. That was the goal. But everyone knew.

Guys ogled Rhonda; she demanded it, a star to be. Her sassy runway walk, come-taste-me pout, few-secrets neckline and pink hair explosion were irresistible. I slipped my hand behind her waist, knowing it made guys jealous and girls keep their distance. We skipped together for a few yards until it got too crowded again. She was such fun. There was shouting as we turned a corner adjacent to the music department.

"Damn! It's him!" Rhonda snarled as she pointed at Connor McClain with a half dozen barronial thugs in the midst of a throng of excited students.

"Fight, fight, fight…"

Duncan Spike, a junior and member of Connor's posse, was pummeling a seventh-grade Latino boy against the sandstone wall.

"Please don't…" he cried just before a fist hammered his gut. The kid, maybe thirteen, dropped to his knees. Duncan, twice his size, gloated. "Pussy!"

I stepped toward him. Rhonda gripped my neck.

"NO!" her voice shouted in my ear, making me wince. "You have two demerits already. He wants you to try to be a hero. That's why he's here."

Connor was an untouchable, a McClain, likely pissed off because he nearly cost us the championship and it took me, a downer, to rescue him. But his hatred had started long before. Rhonda shoved me toward the stone archway of the music department a dozen feet away, bracing her feet and using all her weight to move me. I pictured my mother in the park and stopped resisting. I was a coward, letting the guy get thrashed. Like Connor and Duncan used to do to me my first year, and I'd just stand there, nowhere to run, knowing no one would interfere, holding up my arms to block the punches.

I felt my skin fry because I could beat any kid in school. But I could only fight selectively; defend yourself against the wrong boy and you get expelled. And I never touched anyone from the Twelve Families, like Connor. It was smartest just to take your beating. And that's what they counted on.

"SPARTAK JONES!" Connor shouted and the crowd parted for the Moses of punks.

Fuck! I thought. *Not again.* There was no winning this one.

McClain strutted toward me, long, black, wavy hair swaying, a satisfied grin revealing perfect teeth. "Did you want to protect this downer-brat?" He almost cackled.

We were the same age, in tenth grade. I thought he was a psycho. In classes we shared, he buckled down and did well. But afterward, he and his buddies thrived on violence, a kind of sport, intimidating poor kids. And I was certainly one of them. He seemed fixated on me, determined to mock me, hurt me, bring me down, make my life miserable, get me expelled. For entertainment, I assumed, just because he could. Nothing else made sense.

"Ya gonna do anything?" Connor looked smug and folded his arms. "I heard you made a pass at Cedric."

"You a coward?" Duncan taunted and laughed with his pack-mates. He held the boy by his hair then shoved him to the floor when the kid began to vomit. "What the fuck!"

"What's this guy done to you, Connor?" I moved toward him. Rhonda elbowed me hard in the gut, then bent low, pushing me back.

"That's what I thought." Connor stepped closer, hocked his throat and spat, a major wad splattering on my left eye.

"Aaagh…!" I staggered back, wiping the socket and flipped away milkish phlegm. "You asshole!" I lunged. Time to beat the jerk senseless. Rhonda slapped my face then slammed into me with her shoulder to my abs, using everything she had. I gasped, stunned and distracted. She shoved me under the archway.

"No, Spartak, he's not worth it!"

Damn, she was strong. And wise. I ceased resisting. I was humiliated by him, probably not the last time, but I was still in school.

Connor and his friends guffawed just as Headmaster Thragman stepped through the crowd and students backed away for the courtly, always syrupy gentleman with gray hair, ironed straight, neatly parted and hanging to his shoulders. His sandstone face had once been handsome and now stretched two times too many.

"What's going on here?" Thragman glanced at the wailing student on the floor with a bloody nose, puke down his shirt and then at Duncan and Connor before turning to me. His pale blue eyes were a calculator, adding up the risks.

"Are you creating trouble again, Spartak? One more demerit and you get suspended."

"No sir, I—"

"Yeah, he was," Connor said, sounding like he was ready to cry.

Everyone, maybe fifty students, were silent. No heroes here.

"Get to class and don't let this happen again."

Inside the music room Rhonda wiped my face with the handkerchief. "The headmaster probably pissed his pants. He knows but he's scared. You can't fight a McClain. You're lucky he let you go."

"HE SPIT ON ME!" My muscles ached for just one delicious, delirious, epochal punch into Connor's mouth.

"You told me about Coach Johanson's advice," she said, holding my shoulders, her nose an inch from my face. "*Suck it up and survive.* You're more than halfway to graduation. Be NUMB if you have to. That's life for people like us."

Eyes welling, humiliated, wanting to hide, I clenched my fists. A kid gets pounded senseless by rich thugs and I can do nothing. "The poor guy was probably picked at random because he was small, just to get at me." And I just stood there. No. Not true. I ran away.

"Thank you." I held her, feeling safe, enjoying her warmth, softness, and loyalty. "You're amazing. Who else would beat me up to save me?"

"I'll go check on the little guy," she said. "Make sure he's okay. Maybe we can take him out for ice cream sometime. Be his friend. You stay in here away from Connor."

"Yeah. Good idea. I love you." We kissed cheeks, touched foreheads, and parted. In the bathroom I washed my face—this seemed familiar—and rubbed my eyes. They were still blue but a little bloodshot. I felt defeated, a loser. Would I always have to live in fear of barronials and cops?

No way.

"Compartmentalize," I demanded, feeling defiant. Like I told Geo. The face in the mirror didn't look convinced. I did my best impression of an attack dog. I laughed. Better now. I pulled a black ribbon from my pocket and tied my hair at the nape of my neck, just like Thomas Jefferson. The height of fashion. Rhonda was right. I tried to kick the shame aside and lock up my pride. Or pretend to for a couple of hours.

In a small, padded music practice room, I hung up my coat, grateful to cool down, and began my standard stretching routine, bending over, flexing my back, shoulders, arms, hands, and fingers. I sat down and turned the knob on the side of the bench. The piano still intimidated me. It was a massive, luminous black concert grand with an adjustable seat. Adjustable tufted leather! Unreal. Miss Hedwick had laughed at me the first day, when I was afraid to touch it, worried about breaking something. I placed my thumb over the silver zan-cube, a giant three-inch model sitting on a nearby shelf, letting it read my print. A tiny screen projected above the com device. I used my hands to enlarge it to book size, moved it over the keyboard and gave an order.

"Display. Sheet Music. Frederick Chopin, *Etude Opus 10, Number One in C Major.*"

This was practice, not that I needed the score. In fact I hated the way the new Z-ethers displayed in DIMM4, notes floating, almost jumping out at me but it was required backup in case I blanked on the score. I held my fingers above the keyboard running specifics through my mind, lining them up, then began to play, hands dancing up and down, intricate fingering, one of the toughest pieces of its era.

"Not so hard, Spartak. Make love to the ivories, don't beat them to death."

I jumped. "Yes, Miss Hedwick."

Yes, she was right. It did sound better.

"Your mastery and technique are obvious, Spartak. It's the subtlety and texture you must focus on. Now, move on, Chopin *Etude Ten Number Two,* then *Three.*"

"Yes, Miss Hedwick."

The faster my fingers moved the more Chopin consumed me and Connor faded, a sour note delayed until fifth-period civics or in gymnastics after school.

CHAPTER 7

"THERE SEEMED TO BE MIXED VIEWS in the class papers on the *Sasser v Peabody* decision by the Supreme Court," Mr. Bonas announced at the start of civics class. He was middle-aged, a little thick in the middle, with a droopy brown mustache that melded into his mutton-chop sideburns and lion mane head of reddish hair. He wore a cinnamon swirl high-collar coat that was dreadful. Despite his questionable taste, I liked him, found him really earnest and friendly.

"My question to the class...is it *moral* to use human beings to guarantee contracts? Connor, your view was strongly stated. Legitimate?"

Connor sat across from me in the next row, our last names uncomfortably close in the alphabet, and seemed irritated. Watching him, I had to admit the guy was handsome. Swarthy, black hair to his shoulders, full lips. And yet the outside was just a distraction. A teenager who had everything mocking and physically abusing those who had little. The definition of a bully.

"Yeah, I think so," Connor replied, sounding like he was doing us a favor in responding. "It has nothing to do with morality. That's political nonsense. Like the chief judge said, if you put up something to guarantee payment and you default, you lose the collateral. The lender has a right to their money and needs to be protected by law."

"Billy, do you agree? Your views were heartfelt." Everyone in the class turned around at once. He was in the back row and sat up in his chair, lifted his chin high, seeming pleased.

"Human beings are *not* property," he said with force and a tinge of anger. "America fought a war to end slavery and now banks and rich people who want downer babies and wealthy, horny old men are using a national economic tragedy to circumvent the Constitution. It's like debtors' prisons in Charles Dickens, only worse."

"Strong words, Mr. Eagle. Thank you. Spartak. Your paper was also passionate."

Damn! I didn't want to talk about this. I hoped just being honest in a paper only the teacher would read was sufficient. But Billy had set a high bar for honesty and Connor already hated me.

"I agree with Billy Eagle. How can people use their children as collateral or sell them? Hopelessness. That is the only reason. Desperation and sometimes outright extortion. And this Supreme Court stood with the rich, not the poor; a tiny minority, not the majority." I started to get worked up as I verbalized it, my own words stoking my anger. "This began decades ago, outside of adoption laws, with poor families selling their children and rich families wanting to make sure their adoption was untouchable. Then that wasn't enough. Babies became a commodity, something to own. And it has morphed into buying people for other uses, like Ginny Sasser, the fifteen-year-old in the case. In the paper I said Justice Washington's written dissent captured the national affliction this case addressed. From what I've read, this is not what America used to be like—"

"Connor. Go ahead," Mr. Bonas said, interrupting me, anxious to stir debate. "You look anxious to cut in."

"Why are people so desperate? Because they're lazy." Connor sounded exasperated, like we were too dumb to get it. "If you work hard in America you get ahead. If you don't, you're a downer. We should not subsidize them. Like the Chief Justice said, this expands opportunity." He turned back to me in his seat looking smug.

"I guess I should've been born rich," I said.

Not the most endearing comment to make in front of a room full of barronial kids who thought they'd earned their position. But it was sweet. Connor snapped his head toward me, snarling, and there was a gasp in the class. I held Connor's gaze until he looked down and slapped his desktop, clearly pissed off. The canine school of intimidation won: the dog that looks away first loses.

"I'll post all your papers so you can read them," Mr. Bonas said after a short pause. "Some good work. Now, let's talk about S.B. 112 in the United States Senate on voter registration and the implications."

I didn't listen to anything else he said, just stared out the window, wondering how I would pay for having a big mouth.

* * *

"Spartak, take your shirt off, you have admirers."

"Please, no, Coach. Not again. It's embarrassing."

"There are barronials in the bleachers, even a Twelver. They're here to see you."

"Spartak!" someone shouted in the stands. A girl.

"Hey, hot stuff, want a date?" A guy.

I closed my eyes. Life was weird, often mortifying.

"Looks like maybe thirty today," Coach said. "Take it off, wave, let 'em have a good look, have fun with it and smile. Enjoy. It's a compliment. And it builds support for gymnastics."

I understood. I was a scholarship boy. And ever since the school poster and a DIMM4 came out showing me shirtless and popping sweat on the high bar in full multidimensional glory, I seemed to have acquired groupies.

We were in Ogden Stadium, built in the style of a Roman arena with 15,000 seats, a half-mile from the main school, used for statewide high school competitions as well as practice for all sports. For me, gymnastics was ethereal, body music, Chopin with sweat—flying, twisting, challenging every muscle, craving perfection for my team and parents. Coach always gave me special attention, saying I could be among the greatest in a century.

Condar Johanson was one of the few men who wore a crew cut, left over from his days as a marine combat instructor. Most men had long hair in the manner of Jesus. The churches, fashion designers and media pushed the look as proof of piety. For me, it saved the cost of a haircut or the horror of having my mom do it. Coach was forty, lanky with big hands, kind of a narrow face, intense, a scar below his left ear. and a tiger tattoo on his right shoulder. Nobody did tattoos. He was always there for me like a second father. Beginning in my freshman year when he took me aside and began instructing me on marine combat techniques and how to marry them with gymnastics and street brawling. He thought it might prove useful.

I did extensive publicity and news interviews at coach's insistence and felt embarrassed when I watched sports reporters speculate about me. Women journalists, there seemed to be a lot of them, liked to tape me at practice. It was motivating to hear the flattery even if I didn't believe it. And practice was relentless, even brutal. There were no excuses if I failed. Scholarship students must maximize their potential as a matter of return on investment.

I turned my back to the crowd and pulled off my shirt, tossing it on the bench. There were whistles, some suggestive. My pecs were massive, it seemed to me, too big, just like my arms, almost freakish, and my abs too ripped. But it was the body it took to own the rings, parallel bars and floor exercises. And people seemed to like it.

Coach pointed toward the fans in the bleachers. I swiveled around, lifting both arms overhead, turning on my best high-wattage smile, stepping forward a few steps, pointing at faces I recognized, even those I didn't, and bowing twice to applause. There were a few adults in the group; that was unusual. I didn't recognize them. Girls shrieked. I felt really stupid.

I spotted Zinc McClain and Sonia Washington in the middle of the group. She put two fingers in her mouth and whistled like a dock-worker. I laughed, shocked that that kind of noise could come from her delicate throat. The second time she applauded me in a week. I felt flattered and blew her a kiss. She pretended like she caught it.

Then I noticed Zinc watching me, an eyebrow raised, his lips scrunched up in kind of an odd way, maybe a snarl. Hard to tell. His hand was in the way. Was he upset because Sonia whistled? Because of the kiss? When our eyes met, he turned his head. Fuck. What now? I twisted back to my teammates and slipped on my tank top. Connor was glaring at me.

"Today we'll continue high bar dismounts," Coach announced. "And each of you will exceed your previous best."

A communal groan; this was pure misery on joints and hands.

"Spartak, you were reckless and lucky on the quadruple twist at the Faceoff. Do it again and again until you own it, like breathing."

I chalked my hands and stood under the bar. Coach grabbed my legs as I jumped, lifting me higher. I seized it, pulled up, scissoring my legs, and swung vertical. I then began rotations, faster and faster, flipping forward and back to gain speed, hands burning, then airborne, eighteen feet off the floor. Arms across my chest, body stiff, whirling, one, two, three, four, tuck and land. I stumbled, falling to the mat on one knee but jumped to my feet, arms raised, smiling as if in triumph, as was expected. The audience cheered.

"Close," Coach said. "But no points for almost. A faster count next time, a couple of more loops for height, increase your speed. Connor, up next. A double forward dismount."

Connor walked over to Coach, put an arm over his shoulder and whispered. "I *never* follow Spartak. Understood?"

I read his lips.

"My mistake," Coach said. "Matthew, to the bar. A double twist. Move it."

I watched Connor saunter to the warm-up mats looking satisfied. Even Coach was afraid of him.

CHAPTER 8

"Spartak," Mr. Hayabusa, my advanced calculus teacher announced in class, "go to the headmaster's office immediately." He was staring into the implant in his palm.

"Why?"

"No idea, just do as he asks."

People stared as I slipped my bag over my shoulder and left. I mentally scanned the possibilities. This wasn't encouraging but I hadn't done anything wrong that school could know about.

The hallway was deserted and my boots squeaked and echoed, kind of like being in a narrow cathedral. The ceiling was probably thirty feet high and painted with butterflies and birds. Billy could have done better. I wished they'd spent some of this money on schools Geo and Kimber attended.

Mr. Thragman's office was also grand, something I imagined to be like the antechamber to Napoleon's meeting room with his generals. Blue wallpaper with golden tigers and other carnivores, Ionian columns in corners and the doorways. Elaborately carved and gilded antique furniture, gilt-framed paintings of ancient battle scenes and naked nymphs.

I walked up to Mrs. Buttersworth, a plump, bubble-haired woman chewing gum and wearing a scarlet muumuu accented with white flowers and green parrots. Her fingernails were over an inch long and painted in undulating zebra stripes, kind of hypnotic. Through a window I saw the back of an enforcer's uniform.

"Oh, may I please run to the bathroom first?" I held my crotch, bobbing up and down, gritting my teeth.

"Make it fast," she said, barely looking up.

In the bathroom, a dozen stalls, chairs, even a couch. Insane. I sat on the sofa and grabbed a pillow, unzipping a side. I crossed my legs and pulled the *Obscura* mister and its strap from around my ankle. In my pocket was a *Cosmo* pin. I sprayed both to hide any prints or odor and stuffed them into the cushion and pulled up the zipper. I stood and put the cushion back, fluffed it, decided it looked normal. I checked my pockets for anything I shouldn't have. I was clean.

Back in the office, Thragman waved at me to enter. I hated the man, a weasel, but he didn't expel me when he could have. Maybe because Connor was a thug and he knew it, violating even his low standard of ethics. The cop was the physical opposite. One was a rodent and the cop more like a rodent eater, bear-like, with black hair climbing out of his collar, giant furry hands and a short-cropped beard. And he held his mouth like he was ready to bite. Not someone I wanted to be alone with in a cell.

"Spartak, take a seat. This is Lieutenant Mosser. He is investigating a murder and has questions."

"What? *Murder?*" I sat and examined the cop, having no trust of anyone in a blue uniform. Lieutenant Mosser turned his chair to face me directly. His mane of black hair was plastered down tight and tied behind his head, like a wrestler.

"You were with Cedric Rand Sunday afternoon, correct?"

"Uh, yeah. I tutor him in math once a week and have for months. *My God, was he killed?*" I felt overwhelmed, a DIMM4 picture of him naked in bed flashing in my head. I could still smell his scent.

"Please stand."

I did and he did the same, towering over me by several inches. He held up a slim black rod and a beam shot out, covering me in a green light. "If you have any contraband, this will detect it." He turned off the light. "Come closer." I walked up to him, pleased about my emergency trip to the men's room. "Hold out both hands, palms up." He used the same device but with a different code and a sapphire light covered my palms. "Return to your seat."

"Why won't you tell me? Did something happen to Cedric?"

"Normally your tutoring session lasts an hour," the cop said as he sat, his no-nonsense expression set in stone. "But the butler said you were there for over two. And Cedric asked his man for ten times the normal amount of cash he pays you."

"Why are you playing games? Did something happen to Cedric?"

"Answer the lieutenant's question, Spartak." Thragman sounded impatient.

"Your answer is being recorded and is admissible in court," the enforcer said, pointing to black dot in his eye. "Take responsibility for what you're about to say."

I struggled to remain composed. Another enforcer threatening me. Cedric must have been killed after we had sex. He'd gotten a Z-ether when we were getting dressed. I'd heard a little. He was really upset. I had to lie.

"Well?" the lieutenant said.

"After we were done discussing the calculus lesson, he asked about my family and what was happening with me and the Olympics. He said he heard my parents were having a hard time financially and wanted to help. So he offered me some money as a gift for all I'd done to help his grades. I was stunned at his graciousness and generosity."

"The butler said based on the condition of the sheets after you and Cedric left, you had sex."

"Yeah, there was that. He was working out in his private gym when I arrived and invited me in with his shirt off, just wearing trunks. He said he'd seen me in gymnastics practice and admired my all-natural physique, particularly my abs. I was flattered. He asked if he could see them and talk about my workout techniques. So I took off my shirt and he ran his hands over my stomach. And, well, we both got a little horny. No big deal."

"Are you a prostitute, Mr. Jones?" Thragman snapped, his lips pinched, the fingers on one hand silently doing pushups on his desktop.

"What! No! That's insulting! Can't two guys or girls or whatever combination have sex just because they want to?"

"A downer doing it for money with a barronial might be seen differently." The officer stared at me.

I just looked at him like I was affronted, not breaking my gaze. After a minute, he rubbed his mouth and glanced down ready to move on.

"You know the Dominionists demand proof of virginity before marriage," Thragman snarled.

"Guys don't have vaginas and don't make babies." I regretted it even as it exited my mouth. Being flippant was not smart, particularly to the headmaster.

"Don't be impertinent," Thragman said, slapping his palm on the desk.

"Dominonist dogma isn't the issue today, Mr. Thragman," the lieutenant said with a touch of irritation. But I noticed the corner of his lips turning upward just a bit. "He gave you money and you had sex. The butler said Cedric was extremely upset when you left."

"He was but not because of the sex. We had a good time. Exceptional, actually. He told the butler to bring the money, just like we always do. Cedric never handles cash. After we finished and were getting dressed, he got a Z-ether. He said he couldn't figure out the caller. Only a few people had his number and his line was super encrypted. He moved away from the bed as he talked. He placed another call and then came back to me. I was dressed by this time and sitting on the edge of his bed. He was red-faced, breathing fast, anxious, and seemed scared. I went up to him and put my hands on his shoulders, asking if I could help. He said no, a family emergency had come up, something bad, and I needed to go. At the door to his suite, the butler met us and gave me the money. Cedric kissed me, not on my cheek, and I left. Ask the butler."

"Did he say what he was upset about?"

"I heard a voice as he moved away from me, mentioning Joshua Rand. That's his uncle I think, the Mayor of San Francisco."

The lieutenant studied me for a long time before he exchanged glances with the headmaster, like they were hiding something. "Where did you go after?"

"I went home with my family and had dinner and stayed up late talking. I don't get home much. I gave my mom the money. Please tell me if something happened to Cedric."

"He was murdered a few hours after you were with him."

"Oh, God!" I jumped up, covering my mouth and turned around, my eyes wet. I did deep breathing, held it. "Why would anyone hurt him?"

"Sit," the cop said. I felt like a yo-yo.

"He went out to the Palladium afterward, meeting Connor McClain. Do you know the dance bar?"

"Yes, I was there once. I don't like it."

"Why?"

"It's a massive, gaudy pickup bar for rich kids to exploit poor ones. Downer girls stand around, near naked in see-through dresses, ready to run giddy to any barronial male who points at them. They hope a tryst might offer an easy way to change worlds. It happens with rich girls and poor boys as well. I find it revolting."

"Or boys on boys, I suspect," the cop said. "Why were you there?"

"Celebrating the birthday of a friend. If you're cute enough, you get in for free. We had no problem. A group of us went to see it. The place is stunning. Just not the purpose of it. We didn't stay long."

"And school gives you a more elegant way of finding rich boys."

I felt my mouth drop at the lieutenant's accusation. I tossed my arms up as I stood again. "You are insulting me! Why? I'm a scholarship student and work never-ending hours to be the best in my sport, my music and in math. I want to bring pride to my school and family. Cedric hit on *me*!"

"Thank you, Mr. Jones. Keep your voice down and please be seated and stay there. Your response seems genuine. And you have no contraband on you or traces of laser residue on your hands. I do not now consider you a suspect although that could change as new details emerge."

I rubbed my face as I sat. "Thank you, sir."

A Z-ether projected above the lieutenant's wrist and he expanded it with his fingers. It was Cedric astride his Raptor98 outside the Palladium nightclub, the image floating like a ghost. A tall, exotic black woman was standing next to him, the image hanging in the room. "Do you know her?"

"No, sir. I do not."

"Check out this edited DIMM4, the top quality, from security at the club. They keep close tabs when Twelvers enter." He slid his finger across his wrist. Immediately there was a shot from high in the ceiling down next to the dance floor. Cedric and Connor were talking, pointing to a woman approaching. A second lumin cut to her.

She was taller then Cedric, lithe, ebony skin, hair cut in short rows like undulating waves over her head, giant hoop earrings hanging close to her bare shoulders, changing from gold to blue to red. I found myself staring. She moved with attitude, high cheekbones, big golden eyes with glittering light-shifting lavender eye shadow, her head tilted slightly back, a leopard skin collar around her neck. She was dressed in a purple flow, diagonally cut from ankles to thigh, wrapping around her back to the center of each breast before plunging to her navel. Totally solar! A close-up of the two boys. The woman swept past Cedric like he didn't exist.

"Hey," Cedric snapped, lunged and grabbed her arm, knocking her offstride. "I'm waiting for you."

She swiveled and slapped his face, knocking him back. Her nostrils flared, her jaw set. "*You do not touch a woman without permission! Do you understand*?" Her voice was angry, her speech style exaggerated, slow and precise, her voice sexy deep.

"How dare you hit me," Cedric barked, rubbing his cheek.

"Bitch!" Connor screamed in her face.

She grabbed Connor by the throat and squeezed, lifting him off the ground.

"Boys do not tell me what to do." She shoved him into a group of open-mouthed onlookers.

Cedric looked stunned, shaken. Downers don't push back. I liked her immediately.

"Well?" she said, morphing the word into more a command than a question. She watched him, her lower lip pushed out in anger.

"I'm...I'm sorry. I thought you were the person I was to meet."

"Yes, you should be sorry. And I may be the person you want to meet, depending on what you want."

I noticed Connor rubbing his neck and keeping his distance. Three security guards rushed up. Cedric waved them away. I suspected she could've taken all of them. Too bad.

"I thought you were a downer girl," Cedric said, clarifying his mistake.

"And why would *that* make a difference in how you treat a woman?" She put her hands on her hips, appraising him.

"Downer girls want barronials—" he started to explain.

"And that is what you think I am, a poor girl desperate for your attention?" She shook her head. "You have much to learn."

"I'm Cedric Rand," he said, extending his hand. "I apologize."

She crossed her arms, making him look foolish. People were staring. "Adequate face," she said, lifting her chin, like royalty. She had that kind of confidence. And arrogance. "Why are you still wearing your shirt?"

"What?"

"Your shirt. I do not answer questions nor dance with men who wear shirts. It impedes the movement and the view." She pursed her lips and raised an eyebrow.

It took a moment before he understood. He immediately slipped off his sleeveless tee and tossed it on a chair. He flexed a bicep and inched out his chest. Around his neck was a two-inch wide band of emeralds set in illuminated gold-mesh. Below his belt were tight black stretch pants and knee-high boots.

She walked around him, an inspection. He started to turn.

"No! Do not move!"

Connor grabbed a steaming bottle of blue Gredon from a passing waitress wearing only lit-glo collar, pasties, and a sissy patch.

Cedric stood frozen until she faced him again and took his hand. "I am Kinuba Steele." Based on Cedric's expression, I figured the grip must have been intense. "I will dance with you and…I…am the woman you are looking for," she said. "You have a muscular body. Fine definition. It is good you don't listen to the religious monsters. Bodies are beautiful. Sex is to be celebrated. And all women are equal. Or better." She smirked. "I will teach you manners, then we will talk." She took his hand and they walked onto the dance floor. The image on the Z-ether ended.

"My goodness," I said. "That was stunning. I'd no idea surveillance was that sophisticated. And that woman is…a sizzle. No, that doesn't adequately describe her."

"Her name is Kinuba Steele as you heard," the lieutenant stated. "He left with her on his Raptor. And he was found dead three hours later in an abandoned apartment complex in Oakland scheduled to be torn down."

"I don't know her, Lieutenant," I said. "And the name is not familiar. She has lethality, like a soldier. And amazing legs. I'll ask around school."

Both men watched me, like I was still a suspect.

"May I ask how he died?"

"He was shot twice with a military grade solar pistol set to narrow band, once in the face. He was carrying a large sum of money, which was left with his body." Narrow band could burn an inch-wide hole through your body, incinerating flesh. Wide band was for crowd control and could give a sharp burn at two hundred feet. One second and a chicken cluck sound between blasts. We called them *peeps.*

"What?"

"You heard correctly on his call. It was about his uncle, Joshua Rand. He's been kidnapped. We're going public with that soon looking for leads." He pulled out a small blue chip. "Give me your hand." I reached over and he touched the chip to my ring. "Share this with your friends."

"You're lucky I don't expel you now, Spartak," Thragman sneered, "for having sex with another student."

"Actually, Mr. Thragman," the enforcement officer said, "what is important is finding a killer. If you suspend all your sexually active students, there might not be anyone left in school. Mr. Jones has been very cooperative."

He stood and reached out to shake my hand. "I follow sports news about you. Congratulations on the national title. Win gold for all the downers in Vancouver, Spartak. Make us proud."

* * *

"No, I've never seen her before," Rhonda said, looking at the image as we sat in the Burning Bush at the end of the school day. "I'll share it."

"She is one tough and sexy woman," I said, still trying to figure it out. I touched the side of my ring and the screen dissolved.

"Boys should not tell girls they sleep with that other girls are sexy."

I grinned. "You know I love you."

"Yes, but also that you're more hom than het." She scrunched her mouth. "You're about a 70-30. And I'm okay with that. At least I've had a sample." She giggled. "I love making you blush."

"Switching topics," I said, rolling my eyes, "did you see Zinc McClain at the back of the concert room last Friday?"

"Yeah," Rhonda said. "He was with Sonia Washington. Talk about a power couple. She's so classy."

Hearing a grunt, we both turned our heads. An arm's length away, a man dressed in a green page's uniform, his white hair tinged with yellow, climbed stiff-kneed up a two-story wheeled ladder. It was Mr. Pennyworth and it made no sense for him to be doing this. But leather-bound treasures were status symbols in an age of cheap and ephemeral electronics, thanks to Barron Ogden. He'd said e-books were as valuable as the cost to reproduce them. Zero. And he had the money to create a new market. Studies eventually backed him up: comprehension and critical thinking improved with old-fashioned books, so they became a badge of intelligence in fashion circles. The man scanned a shelf and pulled out a brown book with gold letters and slipped it into a pouch clipped to his belt. With another groan, he began his descent and gave me a granddaddy wink as he whispered, "You did good, son." He lowered his voice even further. "I got another one for you. See me later."

"Cosmic. I'll stop by in the morning."

Mr. Pennyworth was a marvel. He was a librarian but got demoted to a page after he shouted at some barronial kid who was cutting pages from an ancient book. I liked him even more after that. He was a regular downer like me, like all the librarians. It was kind of a subversive club and I wanted to learn more about it. Books that gave an alternative view of American history and politics than were taught in the classrooms were here, hidden and circulated covertly to curious students like me. We kept the secret. And this is what I was getting for Kimber. The librarians wanted to preserve what they said was our true history and I was grateful. Another benefit of books. Off the electronic grid, there was no record of what we were reading. Mr. Pennyworth was one of my heroes.

Rhonda took my hand, rolled it over, palm up, and ran a finger along the creases like a fortuneteller.

I told her, "At the concert every time I glanced up he was staring at me then turned away…It made me nervous."

"Sweetie, you were playing a piano solo. Everyone was watching you." She folded my palm. "You have beautiful hands, by the way, and a long life line."

"And they were at gymnastics practice."

"Hmmmm. His jerk brother's on the team. I suspect you know that. More important, the guy was with a woman who likely—no let me rephrase—absolutely brought him so she could ogle you. You said she whistled. And watching hot, muscular, half-naked young men flex big biceps is prime. Oh, sweet honeysuckle! And your tits sizzle. Remember, I've sampled 'em more than once. And a lot lower. Yum!" She stuck out her tongue and licked her thumb.

"Stop it!" I felt myself burn. She was wicked.

"Zinc McClain's a real introvert, I've heard, almost mental about it," she said. "Taciturn. Yes! That's my thousand-dollar word of the day. Read it this morning in my *A Word a Day to a Better Vocabulary.* Withdrawn. Inhibited. Maybe even phobic about crowds. Some kind of illness. Convinced he's ugly, or something. Nobody like us talks to him. I mean, he's a SENIOR. And the first son of the McClains."

"I know, heir to the first of the Twelve Families. And I'm the eldest son of a jewelry repairman and a seamstress."

"And they're fabulous."

"I think so. But I did once talk to Zinc—or do I say Mr. McClain? How do I address somebody like him? He's two years older and trillions of dollars richer. Anyway, he was in a calculus refresher session last summer. I was the TA. He asked me a question and did seem to have a problem talking to me, almost like he stuttered, but he was polite, even a bit shy, and we were friendly. We laughed. I liked him then. Now he just seems pissed off."

"Really? I've never heard of one of us talking to him. There are rumors that he's ruined people who crossed him, students and teachers. Keep your distance."

"You're so reassuring."

"I'm curious. If you call Zinc McClain *mister*, what do you call Connor?"

"Asshole!" We giggled. "One brother conspires to get me expelled and spits on me. Which is progress. The other brother is glaring at me. Maybe I should learn how to sew and leave school."

"Do you want to play with my titties?" Rhonda cupped her hands under her breasts, squeezed and lifted.

"Do you want to play with mine?" I pushed back my jacket and grabbed my pecs.

We began to laugh, holding each other, crying. I fell on the floor. Then we howled until a librarian ordered us to leave.

Outside, we leaned against an ornate brass banister. She took out her handkerchief from its special place and wiped my cheeks.

"Thanks for the offer on your astonishing tits," I said, "but I'm meeting Coach for pizza and need to run."

"Too bad, they could use the workout. You do remember this is the Fourth of July."

"Yeah, I'll be with my family. We're going up on the roof and grill tofu wieners. You're welcome to come."

"Yum. Too bad I'm staying on campus," she said. "My advice is to fill up on sausage calzone with Coach."

I kissed her goodbye and jogged to Bizzo's Pizza Paradise six blocks off campus. I'd eaten there often with other team members. It was perfect even on a downer budget but Coach usually bought. I spotted Coach as I entered the tiny, crowded, garlicky restaurant, sitting alone in a corner booth in front of a red, green, and blue stained glass window of Christopher Columbus on the Santa Maria.

Just like Coach to have already ordered, and my favorite protein froth was waiting for me on the table. We talked strategy and techniques as we ate. "You'll master the quadruple," he reassured me. "Nobody's ever done it at the Olympics. It just takes practice and your level of talent."

The calzone was good and I had a third piece, taking Rhonda's advice. Tofu wieners weren't my favorite. As I looked across the room, my eyes began to lose focus. I concentrated, shaking my head, and they slid back to normal. Minutes later, the room seemed to be moving. I gripped the tabletop.

"Are you okay? Should I find a doctor?"

"No, no. I'm fine, Coach. Really. I'll catch the underground to my parents' house. I promised my little brother, Geo, I'd be there for the pyrotechnics." I wanted to be strong, as Coach taught. Never show weakness. Maybe I ate too fast.

"If you're sure."

"Thanks for everything." I gave him a hug and pushed through the crowd to the door. Somebody wished me "Congratulations." I said "Thanks" not looking at her face.

Outside, the mist was invading—colored fog fireworks again this year—and the air was cool. It helped clear my head. Feeling better, I began jogging through the woods to my train station on the other side. But in the redwood grove I stumbled, trembling, sweating, my feet like weighted workout boots at the gym. The world moved in circles. I hugged a tree to keep from falling. Two men ran up behind me as my eyes lost focus. They grabbed my arms as I dropped to my knees.

Everything faded to black.

CHAPTER 9

I sensed something incoherent in my sleepy fog and shoved it aside, wrapping my arms around the soft pillow. I smiled, remembering Coach's words praising my dominance in the rings and floor exercises.

The room seemed blurry as my eyes opened. The warning in my head refused to hide. Something weird was happening. The ceiling started to tilt. Slowly at first, then twisting faster. I lifted my head and collapsed back into the feathery refuge. My stomach gurgled; a nasty taste sloshed my tongue, my temples thumped. I lifted my hands toward my face but stopped midway, staring at the handcuffs around my wrists.

I bolted upright and swiveled, feet on floor, ignoring the pain. Vomit punched up and pooled on the pillow. Standing, I rubbed my eyes and wiped my mouth as best I could. My crotch felt scratchy and I reached below and felt something crinkly. I was naked except for paper underwear. What was happening?

"Hello!" I said and winced. I tried again, softer. "Where am I?" No answer. I did it a third time. Same result. I must be crazy.

It was a twelve by fifteen cell, walls a light green. No windows, a metal door with a small opening, sealed with a steel plate. The room slowed and came to a halt. I focused again. Better now. The illumination was from recessed lights around the edges of the ceiling. I looked again at my hands. My school ring was gone!

Stay calm. Think. Analyze. Why?

A toilet, sink, and shower were in the corner, all exposed. I was in front of a single bed with a vertical metal-bar frame, tight to the wall. The only other furniture was a steel table with a standard zan-cube and one chair. I noticed a small black half-sphere in the ceiling, likely a surveillance node. Did I get drunk and arrested? No, never happened. I was always too afraid liquor might make me lose control. I'd only had a protein drink and pizza with Coach. I couldn't remember anything else. How long ago?

I had to pee and wobbled to the open toilet, holding the wall to maintain balance. As I did what I had to, the toilet water bubbled purple and smelled like lilac. I started to laugh but cringed; it hurt my head. Moving with caution, I washed my face. Yes, I could see better. Bloodshot blue eyes stared back from the polished circle on the stainless steel wall above the sink that passed for a mirror, my curly blond hair a twisted disaster. There was a bottle of Silburn's aspirin on the counter. Should I use it? Hell, I'd likely already been drugged. I took two.

I tested the door; locked, no give. The room reeked of my vomit. I cautiously took the pillow, dumped its contents down the toilet and rinsed the pillowcase. I found a spray deodorizer under the sink. Lavender scented. *Good for the Environment*, the can claimed. Someone had planned ahead. It helped. Not like any jail cells I saw with Officer Rango. Definitely upscale. In another cabinet I found a dozen protein bars, so I wouldn't starve. And a stack of paper underwear. I'd read somewhere that this was to keep the condemned from hanging themselves with the cloth and elastic in regular shorts. There was a small sliding panel labeled: "Trash and soiled undergarments." I giggled before getting depressed.

Over the next hours I noticed footsteps outside the door seemed to fit a schedule, every half hour, I guessed. No response when I called out or pounded on the wall. I stopped looking at the overhead lumin. I lived a tightly controlled life, the only way to survive at the academy. But this was scary.

I heard voices. The lock buzzed and clicked open. A dark-skinned man, maybe twenty-five, with an ebony braided ponytail, entered the room. He wore a snug black uniform with some kind of starburst insignia on the shoulder, maybe a private military unit. And sergeant stripes. His nametag said Hernandez. And a blue pistol was clipped to his belt. It was one of the new sonics I'd read about, burpers they're called, a round tube with a handle. They could cause eyeball fluctuation and disorientation at low levels and stop the heart or shear flesh at full power. And more deadly than solars carried by enforcers. It took about a half second between blasts to recharge and it burped when ready. This was serious. A woman in a white kitchen outfit walked in behind the guard and placed a tray with something under a glass dome. It smelled spicy. I stepped toward them.

The guard held up his hand. "Stay where you are."

"*Please* tell me what's happening? Have I done something? *I beg you.* Do my parents know I'm here? How about Coach Condar Johanson at the academy? I have contact information."

"I'm sorry, Spartak. I'm not authorized to give information. But I'm told you'll be informed soon. Have some lunch. And the zan cube is working. Incoming only."

"Can you at least take off my handcuffs? Please."

He shrugged, lips pinched. They stepped outside; the door closed and locked. I went to the table and lifted the lid: great looking chicken stir-fry and brown rice with bok choy. It smelled wonderful. Deciding I was hungry, I ate.

As I sat alone, I started trembling, the tension getting to me. Time to exercise and calm my nerves. But the space was tight. Squeezing between the bed and table I began a rapid-paced series of pushups, chins on an overhead pipe, crunches, handstand dips, and isometrics until exhaustion. Exercise was my life; and now, my escape.

The shower was a surprise, a hot geyser for sore muscles, splattering water on the bed if I wasn't careful. I brushed my hair, used an oscillating toothbrush with mint paste, and put on a new pair of paper underwear. So far, paper skivvies and the handcuffs were my entire wardrobe. I crinkled when I walked. Rhonda would laugh, probably think it was a sizzle.

I touched the zan with my fingertip and the screen popped open. Because of the handcuffs, I used a toe at one end and my hands at the other to stretch the display wide and tilt it the way I liked. Being limber had advantages beyond gymnastics and sex.

The Z-ether responded to my voice commands but when I tried to contact friends, a mechanical androgynous voice announced:

"Unauthorized." Still, there was lots of news on what was happening in the world: stories at the academy, even about me, speculating on the Olympics. But no mention I was missing.

Was I a danger to someone? Was I a hostage? It made no sense. I leaned back in my seat, adjusting the handcuffs, imagining how ridiculous I looked, in diapers, hands behind my head, stretching. Had I failed at something? Was I kidnapped? My parents had no money. Could it be some kind of elaborate prank, maybe by friends on the gymnastic team? Vengeance for me winning the individual title? An image of Rhonda and Billy filled my head. Did they know? God I missed them.

Someone was at the door. The lock buzzed and clicked. I jumped to my feet, knocking over the chair. Two security guards entered, Hernandez one of them. The other was muscular and red-haired, dressed in the same kind of uniform. The badge said, Michels. The guy fingered a yellow arc-truncheon on his belt, like an electrified billy club, clearly a warning. I'd never seen one this close. A long, tight row of silver electrodes, like a medieval mace, protruded just above the surface at one end. I must have done something really bad.

"Go over by the bed," Hernandez ordered.

"Please, what's going on?"

"I'm sorry, son, don't talk." He unlocked one of the cuffs. "Turn around. Hands behind your back."

No point in fighting. I eyed the arc and knew the odds. Nothing made sense. The second cuff growled back into place.

"What have I done?"

"Answers later. We can't say more. Orders. For your own protection, please do as you're told. You won't be harmed."

Hernandez took a small black clip from his belt and touched the wall by the sink. A hidden door slid open. He took out a folded piece of clothing and rubber floppers. The sergeant hung a green bathrobe, matching the wall color, around my shoulders and tied it in front. I slipped on the beach sandals and the guards marched me through the door and down a long hall. It was daytime, visible through small windows on my left. There was a view of the Golden Gate Bridge. I was still in San Francisco—somewhere in the central part of the city, looking north! We came to a door marked Medical and stepped inside.

"How are you feeling, Spartak?" a nurse asked. She was about sixty, short and round, dressed in navy blue with a matching cap. Her teeth were oddly uneven but they were almost luminous when she smiled; her demeanor showed her to be friendly, grandmotherly, a fat angel. At least I hoped she was.

"Fine, ma'am, except for being confused...Could you explain... "

"Questions will be answered later," she said sweetly. "Come this way and...congratulations on your title." She wiggled a finger and smiled again.

I was taken to a small room with a table draped in a white sheet. The door was closed behind me and bolted. "Slip off his robe," she said to the guards. "Spartak, lay on your stomach, sweetie."

"Please. I don't want to. Just tell me what's happening?" I backed up.

The guards grabbed my arms, forcing me to the edge of the table.

"Spartak, no trouble," Hernandez warned. "You'll be all right. We'll force you if we have to. Those are orders."

"No hassles, boy!" Michels said, his voice deep and unfriendly.

I pressed my jaw shut to hide the quiver. Holy shit. I leaned over the table. Hernandez took my robe. But with my arms handcuffed behind me, my knees shaky, I couldn't get completely onto the draped surface. The redheaded guy lifted my legs into place. It wasn't reassuring, graceful or dignified. The guards pulled canvas straps over my back and legs, cinching them tight. The nurse wheeled over a small table and brought a box from a cabinet and emptied its contents.

"Ready, doctor." She spoke in her honeyed voice.

The guards stood back against the wall. I tried to move but couldn't. A dark-skinned man in a white lab coat entered. He was balding with sunken eyes and saggy skin. He picked up some utensils from the table. I couldn't see much as he got closer.

"Hold his head to the side, right side down."

"Why won't you tell me what you're doing?" My voice broke. *"Please, tell me!"*

Michels gripped my hair and pressed fingers hard into my jaw, making talking impossible. I was helpless and struggled to control my panic. I'd lived my life trying to manage my emotions. But my knees were shaking; my breathing shallow and fast.

"First things, first, young man." The high register, singsong voice of the doctor was gentle; the guard's hands were not. My left ear was swabbed with a cold liquid. It smelled pungent, nasty. Maybe alcohol mixed with something. I couldn't see anything but a black pant leg. Measurements were taken and discussed. A needle prick.

"Round it carefully," the doctor said.

The whine of a machine. They tested something on the top edge of my ear, then more gyration noise. Something was pressed against my skin. The cinch of a metal clamp. "Perfect fit," the doctor said. "Now polish."

A high-pitched whirring.

"Hold him tight. Take a deep breath, Spartak, and remain still."

Something cold, metallic pushed against the top of my ear. A loud crack. I jerked up into the bindings. It felt like the top of my ear just ripped off.

"Oh God, please..." My jaw was shoved closed. Another pop and they must have cut off whatever was left behind.

"It's working fine," the nurse said, sounding crisp and professional, looking at a small screen. "Vital signs are all showing perfectly." She checked a machine. "And the locator."

"Take him back to his cell," the doctor ordered. The redheaded guard released his grip and unbuckled the straps, helping me to my feet.

"Please. What's happening?"

"I'll stop by later and we'll talk then. It's not easily explained."

I felt dizzy even as the doctor smiled, like he was hiding a terrible secret. He patted my back, looking uptight, and handed Hernandez my bathrobe.

"Thank you, Sergeant." He disappeared through a door.

Walking back down the hallway the guards laughed, not in a mocking way but more like two guys who were uncomfortable, even nervous. Hernandez removed my handcuffs at the door of my cell.

Back inside and alone, I hurried to the polished stainless steel above the sink. An inch long piece of metal, blue enamel in the center, gold at the edges, was wrapped around the top of my ear. There was a tiny starburst insignia in the center, like on the guard uniforms. A piece of jewelry riveted in place. The surrounding skin was red, throbbing and swollen, painful to touch. I took a series of deep breaths to defeat the nausea. I recalled photos of prize livestock with ear tags. Is that what I was now?

CHAPTER 10

I MOVED TO THE CHAIR, TOUCHED my thumb to the cube on the table and the Z-ether popped open.

"Ogden Station, San Francisco, live cam."

Movement on the display, students in their blue blazers headed to class. I remembered my first day of school, riding up the same escalator. I'd felt alien and alone following strangers through the black wrought-iron gates. Many were laughing, some my age but most older, obviously friends.

A clank outside the cell. I bolted upright and turned around, ear to the door hearing a muffled conversation. "Hello! Anyone there?" Silence.

"Barron Ogden," I said, swiveling back, watching the face of America's greatest philanthropist appear on the screen. A man in his eighties, a white goatee, fierce eyes cutting into you from the screen, like a hawk, someone to admire and never cross. The multitrillionaire who built the academy, with his own cash, to showcase what was possible in education, employing thousands of construction workers, building and landscape architects, artists, stonemasons, and designers. It had ignited a massive era of philanthropy by his class to step up and give back. And give the ruling class the talent it needed to run the country.

A mechanical voice announced: "Barron Ogden, archival speech, '*The Challenge.*'"

"I have modeled my life after Lorenzo the Magnificent in Renaissance Florence," Ogden said in an old DIMM1 recording, standing before a black-tie dinner audience. "When you are as rich as I am and as old, you can say things like that. Lorenzo took a humdrum city and made it bloom—the center of art, intellect and power in the world. Tonight, I challenge you. Build academies as I have in San Francisco, hire the greatest talents, fund great architecture, awe-inspiring art, master teachers, and find students of any class to match our dreams of America. Put your own money in public buildings, churches, train stations, schools—God knows we have more than enough. Make America bloom. Don't let the Depression and selfish greed sink our great nation. Forget Wall Street nonsense. How rich do we have to be? Build America!"

I was grinning when it ended, a famous speech we'd all seen many times, played often and a welcome source of familiarity for me now. Most of the top families had accepted his challenge that night, shamed perhaps or seeking glory, and had transformed American education for those showing promise, a competition to greatness but also sometimes ego and excess. But it saved the country by injecting heavy private spending to fuel the economy and rescued its best minds from the dead end of public schools, long starved for adequate funding. The man's first name became synonymous with his class of super rich.

Barron Ogden believed in equality at least for bright kids. He'd decreed that every such student had to live in a dorm on campus during the sixth and seventh grades, and preferably the entire six years.

"Ogden Academy, Dormitory 12, Room 206."

There was the doorway on the screen showing my first room. With help from a uniformed security guard that first day, I'd found it: two beds, separate desks, a view of a vast garden. I'd set my small suitcase in a corner. No one else was there. It was much bigger and nicer than home.

"Dining Commons, live."

There was the food court, overhanging a lake with lily pads, papyrus, ducks, and swans. I pulled my knees to my chest and wrapped my arms around them, feeling relief. I was returning to old friends, no longer alone in a cell.

"Food line, live."

Students pushed trays along a shelf as workers handed them plates of eggs and bacon.

"TESSIE!" I shouted at the screen and started to tear. She was working today. The elderly woman had a bemused look, her face all laugh lines and dimples. The white cap and apron contrasted with her brown skin. I wiped my eyes and remembered my mouth dropping in amazement, that first day, when she plopped a steak on my plate, covering half of the surface area.

"All for me?"

"Surely is, young man." She added broccoli and a baked potato. "You're a scholarship boy, I'll bet."

"Yes, ma'am."

"My name's Tessie. This place can be a bit overwhelming. Come see me if you need help."

I'd carried my tray, looking expectantly at several boys my age, hoping they'd invite me to sit, but they turned, uninterested, back to their friends. I sat alone at the end of a table and wanted to look busy, like there was a reason I was by myself, so I examined my new class ring, a gift of the school for poor kids so everyone had one. It was real gold, the most valuable thing I owned, my initials—SJ—on one side, OA on the other, a minzan inside, and a green synthetic emerald on top. The school colors were green and gold.

"May I join you?" a boy had asked, standing beside me.

"Please."

"I'm Billy. I'm a scholarship guy too, just like you."

"Am I that obvious?"

"Stare less, keep your mouth closed with tongue inside as you walk around."

"Oh, God! Am I that awful?"

We ate all we could before lunch period ended and a kitchen aide, a young woman, obviously pregnant, picked up our plates and dumped the partially eaten steaks into a composter. Eating meat was rare for most Americans, at least beyond small amounts for flavoring or special occasions. We couldn't believe something so valuable was waste.

With just a few pen strokes on a napkin, Billy sketched a three-dimensional eagle and handed it to me with a smile. He was an artist. My first friends: Billy Eagle and Tessie the food server. Maybe things would be okay.

I'd headed back to my dorm room after lunch that day, excited about the future. The door was ajar and I entered. Inside, a student was hanging clothes in a closet.

"You must be my new roommate. I'm Spartak Jones." I held out my hand as the student turned.

The curly black-haired boy, about my age, examined me, ignoring the outstretched hand.

"What the fuck? You're a commoner. They booked me with a fucking pleb. Anyone else would know I'm Connor McClain."

CHAPTER 11

I STOOD AS MY CELL DOOR opened and, thankfully, no longer wore diapers. I had on clean gym pants and a blue knit shirt. The man who bolted the tracker into my ear walked in with Sergeant Hernandez, the one guard who was friendly.

"I should have introduced myself when we met. I am Dr. Sachin Rai and I oversee the medical services in this complex." He put out his hand and we shook. If I expected to get any answers, being hostile wouldn't help. "Please…" He pointed to the bed, not that there was an alternative.

I sat at one end. I could see him better now since I wasn't strapped facedown on an operating table. He was skinny with a big head and black eyes, wearing a white medical tunic. He perched next to me, perfect posture, hands in his lap, professional and a bit delicate. Hernandez picked up a chair, turned it around, legs wrapped around the back legs as I might do.

"Questions?" Dr. Rai asked.

"Thank you. Where am I?"

"In my favorite building, kind of a castle, in San Francisco, plunked high on a hill called Buena Vista." Dr. Rai smiled at me and sounded enthusiastic, like he was sharing a secret. It was a small gesture but felt good. "I am an aficionado of Medieval and Renaissance architecture. This cell is in the basement of a seven-story residential compound but only three are obvious. Above ground is a sixteenth-century Tudor estate from Wales, dismantled stone by stone and reconstructed at this site over a modern foundation, four stories hidden by shrubs, trees and 'electronic obfuscation,' as the architect called it. There are a dozen fireplaces and observation decks that look like battlements.

Henry VIII would have felt at home. And maybe he did." Rai grinned with perfect teeth and fat lips.

"I know the building. Who owns it?"

"The first of the Twelve Families."

"Oh, fuck," I mumbled, dropping my head into my hands and posed the question I somehow dreaded, asking: "Why am I here?"

"You have been…" Rai stopped and rubbed his mouth. "You have been *harvested.* I am using the term of the people in this unfortunate new business. Harvested to make certain you came to this family. Your parents have signed documents making you the property of Sergei McClain."

I just stared one to the other, examining their faces, hoping for a reprieve, that this was some kind of joke before they told me the real reason. The guard's eyes welled. Rai pinched his mouth bloodless, obviously concerned, maybe even revolted, but still dignified and fully in control.

"Breathe deeply, young man," Rai said. "You are strong, a brilliant athlete and student. You will survive. Your family will get a new home in a good neighborhood. You know your father is not well. He will now be taken care of because of your sacrifice."

The word ripped through my head. *"Sacrifice?* And...and…what happens to me?" I felt dizzy and held on to the metal pipe headboard.

"You will serve the McClain family as it wishes. I assume you are familiar with the *Sasser* decision of the Supreme Court. To our knowledge, you are the first person taken under it."

"But…I was drugged…and…and…kidnapped."

"Yes. Apparently multiple buyers were targeting you, just waiting for the decision to make it legal. The McClains acted first. Glenda McClain, the actress and wife of Sergei, picked you out personally from a DIMM4 on vulnerable boys. She also observed you in San Diego at the Faceoff and gave instructions on your handling once you came here. I would have assumed a contract would have been executed first but this is new law and, honestly, laws don't matter much to the Twelve Families. I'm told in your case, there was a need to take you off the market, and then your parents…after some persuasion… agreed to accept the incentives and signed."

"This isn't possible. It can't be legal. Why would someone want to own me? *My parents wouldn't sell me!*"

"Spartak..." His voice trailed off. Then he sighed. "I think you understand the power of the Twelve. The Supreme Court ruled that human ownership is acceptable under contract law, to protect the lender. Humans can be collateral on loans when borrowers have no other assets. And they can be sold outright, the buyer getting clear title and apparently the right of resale. You're the latter. In exchange for money and other considerations you become the personal property of the McClains but if you fail to perform or run off, your family must repay the loan or go to prison. And the law suggests once harvested, you lose any rights as a citizen even if given freedom later on." He exhaled and seemed exasperated. Troubled.

"But they didn't ask for a loan, did they? Or offer me?"

"Not that I'm aware but I was not involved until I got explicit orders about your physical exam and...your ear. I'm sorry." He looked pained.

"I don't understand..." My voice evaporated, my brain short-circuiting.

"Please, think before you act," he said, avoiding eye contact, "co-operate and learn the rules and the opportunities. Use your instincts and swallow your pride for now. Doors may open if you're observant and ready." He stood, presenting a make-believe smile. "I have other duties now but will return if you need me." He exited the cell without looking back, maybe afraid he would lose his professional calm.

"Be strong," Hernandez said, standing and squeezing my shoulder. "I'm...I'm from a downer family too. Now I'm in the orbit of the McClains. It's not a bad life. I'll do what I can to help. Use your wits and follow Dr. Rai's advice. He's a good man. Street smarts and cunning count for a lot. I know your history. You understand how to survive."

At the door he turned back. "It isn't fair. It isn't right. But America is a twisted place. Good luck, Spartak. I hope they allow you to go to the Olympics." The door closed, the lock buzzed.

I sat, rubbing my hands, replaying the conversation. I thought of the discussion in class about the court ruling. It was abstract, just noise, theoretical stuff, Connor getting angry. Now his family owned me; Mrs. McClain had a cow tracker bolted on my ear. How real is that?

My parents, Geo, and Kimber would have a better life. That's what I'd hoped for but not like this. Tears started, I couldn't stop them, my knees trembling, breathing through my mouth, hyperventilating. The McClains would decide if I went to the Olympics? I was afraid. Angry. But had no idea how to fight, or if I could. I felt helpless, the full crush of government and the barronials pressing against me, the fate of my family balanced on my back. I felt myself losing control, some part of my brain consumed with rage, another part trying to pull me back. I ran to the metal door and slammed into it, pounding, punching it, kicking, screaming, my heart hammering. Swallow my pride?

"I'm not a slave!"

I was in a dream, watching myself act crazy. I saw blood, my hand ripped open. I butted my head to the door. More blood. I didn't care; the pain was good, real. I kept pounding, howling, growing weaker, frustrated, losing hope, and dropped to my knees in tears. The door snapped open.

"Stop it!" Corporal Michels screamed.

I saw the flash of the silver glove just before it grabbed my arm. I tumbled onto my back, my body shaking, electricity pulsing through me.

"Please. . . !"

"Get on the bed!" He grabbed me with his other hand, yanking me up.

I was uncoordinated, dazed. He started to handcuff me. I swung my fist at him and it punched into the glove. I screamed, vomited and shook until I couldn't move. He cuffed me to the bed, wiped my mouth with part of the sheet and gagged me.

"You got no right to damage yourself," he said, standing over me. "It's not your property." He swiveled around and left.

* * *

A dark-haired young woman was cleaning my bed as I awoke. I was groggy, the gag off, unsure how much time had passed. I stood, arching my arm over the bed, trying to give her room but still handcuffed to the bedframe. My right hand was bandaged. The room reeked. I'd done more than vomit in my delirium.

"I'm sorry," I said, barely able to open my mouth, humiliated.

"It is nothing," she said, not looking at me as she bundled all the sheets and left.

Hernandez came over from the doorway and removed the cuffs. He got me a glass of water and a wet rag. I drank, grateful, and wiped my face.

"I'm so pissed," he said, giving me an arm's length hug, confirming my odiferous state. "This should never have happened! Michels is cruel and arrogant. I should've been here. With Mrs. McClain's direct involvement, lines of authority are confused. I shouldn't say this but it's a mess."

"You're very kind." He seemed almost like a friend in my new post-America world and I needed one.

The door opened and in walked a massive man, wide as a pro-wrestler, wearing the black uniform and McClain sunrise crest on his shoulder. He carried a blue burper on his belt. He oozed lethal. His long brown hair was pulled behind his head and woven into an intricate braid hanging past his shoulders. His nose was straight and broad, his chin dimpled, eyes dark, making him more menacing than handsome. Hernandez swiveled to him and saluted.

"At ease," the man said. "I'm Ransom Bolt," he said, staring at me and extending his hand, "the head of McClain security and you're Spartak Jones."

"Yes." I accepted his firm grasp and could hardly speak he was so intimidating. I assumed it was obvious who I was, the guy in the jail cell and an embarrassing, smelly mess. "I…I apologize for the way I am…"

"This should not have happened and will not happen again, I assure you. My apologies. We've never dealt with this issue before and different people are reacting in strange ways, orders are being overridden. Please don't hurt yourself. I know you're scared and frustrated. Are you in any pain?"

"No, sir. I'm as good as a slave can be." Mistake. I should not be smart aleck. "I'm sorry, I…I didn't mean to sound impertinent. I'll…I'll learn my place."

"Oh, son," he said, "the world is fucked up. Hernandez, stay close to this boy." Then he smiled. "And make sure the shower is working and there's lots of soap."

"Yes sir," Hernandez said, saluting again.

Bolt turned and left the room and the door lock clicked shut.

"He's impressive," I said.

"And a great man. He's been with Sergei McClain for twenty years. His two sons grew up with Zinc and are close friends. He was furious when I told him what happened to you. He never talks politics but I suspect he's against this slave thing."

"I feel like you're an ally," I said to the guard, hoping it was true, and maybe eventually a friend.

"I brought some food," Hernandez responded with an aw-shucks smile. "Eat, shower, change clothes. A clean pair of pants, shirt, and underclothes are on the table. Dump your soiled stuff down the chute. Let your head clear. Please use the air freshener." He grinned. "I'll be back in twenty minutes. Okay?"

I didn't want him to go but needed to feel human again, smell like one. I thought about what Michels had said: "You got no right…"

That about summed it up.

* * *

With Corporal Michels standing to my right, just out of sight of the lumin, and Sergeant Hernandez to my left, I touched the connector dot. I felt helpless, overwhelmed, waiting for my family to appear on screen.

Somehow I knew what happened here, how I handled it, would impact my life and, for better or worse, theirs. I was grateful they'd given me a few hours to regain my composure, such as it was. My right hand was bandaged and sore, a patch on my forehead, my voice still hoarse from shouting. My self-esteem was a ghost.

The live image popped onto the Z-ether. My family was arranged around a table not in our apartment. I felt like I could reach out and touch them. Mom and Kimber wore matching blue and green calico blouses, likely made by Mom with leftover material from work. These were new, made just for me. She'd do that. Dad had on his old thread-bare gray suit with a red tie like I wore at school. Nice. Geo had on the academy letterman's jacket I'd given him for Christmas. Under it was a black Hawaiian shirt with multicolored tropical fish and florescent green eyes. Clearly the boy would be het. His right hand was clenched around what might be my tank top from the Faceoff. It made me desperate to hold him. He looked up at the screen, his eyes puffy and red, as if his best friend had just died, his lips pressed tight, ready to implode. He held up the cloth in his hands, showing the Ogden crest. I struggled to hold my emotions tight. This was for them. I was acting my part in a sadistic play.

"Hi everybody. I've missed you." They didn't seem able to speak. "Nice shirt, Geo." His face scrunched and he started to cry. Dad pulled him close. Kimber blew her nose on a white handkerchief and glanced at me and away, her face red.

I heard a muffled male voice at their end. Immediately, Mom licked her lips and picked up a folder. Her hands trembled and she put it back down, unable to hold it, pressing her hand against it, fingertips white, trying to present an illusion of calm.

"I...I've signed the contract giving Sergei McClain control of your future, making you...part of the first family." She wiped her eyes, her voice raspy. "It's a great honor. So many new opportunities for you." Mom looked down, her palms pressed against her eyes. Maybe I had to do this for her. After a minute to compose herself, she looked up, staring just past the Z-ether, away from my stare.

"We'll be moving soon," she continued, sitting up again, clearing her throat every few words, "to a high-rise downtown...facing the bay, a safer neighborhood, less rent. Your brother and sister will begin academy prep." She wiped her mouth and attempted to smile. "And... our monthly stipend has increased. And, and we get to keep all of it!"

Dad leaned forward. "You should know, Spartak, that I'll get the... the treatment for my heart. We now have complete medical care. It's because of you." His forehead glistened.

I was a minor; the document signed. And they knew my future. Did they sell me? Had they sacrificed me so they could live better? Didn't they love me? These were terrifying questions maybe best not answered. At least not in this setting. Maybe not ever.

"I'm happy for you all." I tried to be upbeat, to be tough. "Their mansion is… extraordinary."

I still hadn't been out of the detention block except for that one time. Sergeant Hernandez had taken me to a room upstairs. An elegantly dressed middle-aged woman at a desk had swiveled around. The flawless olive skin, the perfect straight nose, full lips and thick black hair—I recognized her. It was Glenda McClain, the famous phantasmagorical cinema actress. A second guard, older, ordered me to remove my robe and underwear, facing forward then back. I hesitated, disbelieving, finding it outrageous, and the man reached for his arc-truncheon. "Please do it," Hernandez had urged me. I'd complied, staring at a wall to minimize my humiliation, feeling like livestock with my riveted ear clip to monitor my location and vital signs. She had smiled but not at my face. With the wave of her hand, I had been returned to my cell.

I saw tears slipping down Mom's face. Father ran a palm across his forehead, offering a wobbly smile. My brother and sister focused on the tabletop. My family was disintegrating and I was the slave. As long as I performed satisfactorily, my family would have a better life. That was the law; the Supreme Court had said so. My dad would survive. I needed to remember the tradeoff.

"We were forced to sign this," Dad shouted with a sob, his face contorted, fists clenched. "I love you son and want you back!"

"We love you, Spartak!" Mom cried out, losing control.

"Spartak!" Geo shouted, arms toward the screen. I could hear Kimber too.

The connection ended. I started to cry but felt only joy. My question had been answered.

Hernandez put his arm around my shoulders and pulled me to his chest. "Go ahead, Spartak, let it out."

CHAPTER 12

"I am Nocturne," announced an older woman's
melodic voice on the all-zan blast.
"O, let my land once again be the home of Liberty.
Where opportunity is real and all men and women are free.
Let us reclaim the America that used to be! Join AR2!"

I READ THE HACK ON MY class ring—they had not taken it away—as I sat on a stool behind two drapes hanging in front of one of several doors in the dining room of the McClain mansion. They'd been put in place for tonight's birthday party. It'd been three days since I had talked with my parents, giving me lots of time to prepare my head for what was about to happen. I was hidden but could see through an open slit where the tapestries came together.

An hour ago my heart had been pounding so hard I couldn't stand and gagged for breath. Dr. Rai had put an inhaler to my nose and my breathing eased. Then he gave me a pill and slipped a sack of them into my pants pocket for later in the night. After a half hour my heart slowed to normal and a sense of serenity subdued my brain, a drugged calm but a welcome one. And my senses seemed normal so it wasn't like I was comatose.

A diminutive, pixie-like woman with bobbed white hair and dressed in a conservative blue pencil-suit was leaning against a stool next to me at the doorway, holding a small briefcase. A large yellow-felt chrysanthemum pin on her chest undulated as she moved. Most odd. I had no idea who she was since she'd arrived after I was already here. And I was all fancy in an emerald-green blazer, cream-colored shirt and yellow lit-glo bow tie. The nicest clothes I'd ever worn.

"Son of a bitch!" Sergei McClain shouted as he punched his

temple to turn off the retVue in his cornea. He must have just gotten the same hack. They were becoming more frequent and security told me they couldn't figure how AR2 was able to do it. The fifty people in the room all looked at the father, some in sympathy, others smirking, likely pleased they'd the sense to turn theirs off.

Glenda McClain arose from her seat, always theatrical, and clapped her hands repeatedly. "May I have your attention?"

Several guests clinked their glasses with knives and forks. More than a few seemed intoxicated as the luncheon reached its climax. Zinc was sitting next to Sonia; they were holding hands. Connor was with some friends at the end of the table. I saw Ransom Bolt with two young men, likely the sons I'd heard about, best friends of Zinc, about his age.

Mrs. McClain looked stunning in a trim, floor-length red silk dress and a shimmering silver lit-glo shawl, the rage in couture fashion, the queen of modern cinema. I'd never seen one of her fantas, way too expensive.

Zinc had opened all his presents from his friends and other guests, but nothing yet from his parents. Sonia kissed Zinc on the cheek and squeezed his arm. She was glorious, her hair twisted into high loops with a white rose slipped in above her right ear. Simple elegance. She had given him a rare 18th century walnut lap desk with real stationery inside.

I glanced at Connor who was gulping another cocktail. He'd given Zinc a sonic rifle with a scope and laughed when Zinc seemed flummoxed about what to do with it. It was apparently the first armament of its class, its beam designed to pulverize enemy eardrums or stop hearts a mile away. Developed by McClain weapons lab, Mr. McClain had explained with pride.

Now it was Zinc's parents turn. My stomach gurgled. The little woman patted my arm, trying to reassure me that it would be okay. For her, no problem.

Glenda floated gracefully into her seat, arms out like a bird, as her husband rose. The room was silent. Sergei McClain was intimidating but also distinguished. The way he moved and with the trim patrician beard of his Russian ancestry he had presence. But his ferocious,

Rasputin-eyes were almost enough to make you soil your pants if you angered him. He wore a golden felt fez with black tassel, a weird touch.

Sergei bowed to his wife and walked to the drape as everyone whispered. The woman beside me slipped out and I was pulled back out of sight by someone behind me. She walked to the end of the dining room table and opened her case, taking out an old-fashioned hand stamp and inkpad.

"And now for your present, my son. First, I will sign the papers giving you ownership." He handed the woman an envelope from his suit pocket. She withdrew a contract and opened it, pointing at a spot where he signed his name.

"Zinc," his father called out.

He went over and signed where he was told and returned to his seat. The woman stamped the contract with the state seal and wrote her name. She took a tiny Z8 from her briefcase and aimed it at the document. The contract was copied, printed, and filed within seconds. Her work as a notary was complete. My ownership was transferred, father to son. Somehow that didn't make me sanguine. She gathered her materials, handed Sergei the notarized contract with receipt and left.

Sergei gestured to Glenda.

"I wanted you to have something beautiful for your birthday," she said, standing, gesturing widely, and looking adoringly at her eldest boy. "And unique, even a bit *shocking*. You know me." She giggled like a little girl getting away with something naughty and loving it.

Her smile made me twitch.

"It is something that is now legal, the very first time it has been done under the new Supreme Court ruling. A first for the first of the first." She grinned, dimples extraordinaire, turning her face to the drapes and back to her son.

Zinc looked nervous, his mouth open and pinched as if in dread and likely ignorant about what was about to happen. I felt woozy again and Dr. Rai squeezed the inhaler up my nose.

"It will be controversial! It is extraordinary, if I say so myself. Your father and I worked hard in making the selection. And, I hope, for you, it will be fun, a new responsibility as a man now that you are eighteen."

Sergei motioned to a guard and the drape was pulled open with me standing there holding on to Dr. Rai. They were originally going to handcuff me but Hernandez intervened and I promised to be obedient. Not a term I liked applying to myself. A second guard moved up behind me, taking my arm, and nudged me into the room.

Zinc stood as I was brought to him. His face twisted and red. He looked like he might pee his pants.

"Happy birthday, son," his mother said, giving him a hug and kiss. "He's yours. A unique gift for a marvelous son; a debt-bond companion. Spartak is a remarkable young man with many talents. Enjoy."

Connor started laughing then taunting. "Downer Boy is now Slave Boy!"

While Zinc stood, listening to Sonia scream something in his ear—she obviously was upset—Connor dashed around the table and punched my shoulder. "He's a Sasser!"

My knees nearly buckled. I felt degraded, a piece of meat, and wheezed then held my breath to stop it, hoping they wouldn't notice.

Don't hyperventilate. Did I need another pill? Connor was hollering inches from my face. I knew many of the people from school.

Samantha Ikes from algebra class.

Mark Kroger from English lit.

Tom Lok and Slade Grendel from gymnastics.

Kids I'd seen in the hallways. It'd taken years to prove myself. Eyes that once showed admiration and respect now suggested a range of reactions—shock, pity, disgust, amusement. I was a joke. My face flamed hot. Total humiliation. I wanted to scream or cry or run away. I clenched my muscles, my whole body, to keep from shaking and desperately wanted to smack something; Connor's mouth would be perfect. And I couldn't do anything. Bury your pride, Dr. Rai had told me. Look for opportunities. I muttered, "Don't let them destroy me. Survive. Protect my family." It was my mantra, a mental cocoon to keep me sane.

Connor grabbed my lapel and tried to yank off my jacket. "Strip the slave," he taunted, ripping off the bow tie. Other classmates around the table took up the call.

"Strip him!"

"Strip him!"

I tried to keep the jacket on but was uncertain what to do, whether I could protect myself. Other academy students—drunk friends, egged on, morphing into a mob—pulled me further from the table, shoving me back and forth, a game. I didn't dare hurt them. Two boys from school held my arms while a girl from math class grabbed my shirt, popping off all the buttons. I pulled loose and crossed my arms over my bare chest to protect myself.

Sally Uris, a buxom brunette from music class, laughed and grasped my belt, pulling at the buckle. I'd thought we were friends.

"Please, no!"

The crowd roared, hyenas at the kill, tossing my coat on the floor. Someone behind was trying to push down my trousers. I was surrounded.

"STOP!" Zinc's voice cut through the spectacle and they turned to him. He walked up to me and gestured for everyone to back off.

"He's m…my present! Mo…move back."

He looked into my eyes and seemed as panicked as I felt.

"Please," I whispered so only Zinc could hear, biting my lip as I glanced down.

He turned to the crowd. "Mom and Dad—for this unexpected and pro...provocative gift—thank you. Total surprise. And let me repeat, he is m…MY birthday present. I shall do the unwrapping… privately. Hands Off!" He threw his head back and gave what sounded like a forced laugh.

The group raised champagne flutes and cheered. Sonia started singing *Happy Birthday*. A cake was immediately brought out from a side door, the server apparently waiting for her cue.

Zinc signaled to Ransom Bolt who came over near me. I listened while Zinc leaned into the man's ear: "Please take him to my suite, make him comfortable, let him get dressed and don't let anyone near him, particularly my brother."

Sonia's eyes were venomous as she stared at Connor and then turned toward Zinc. She strutted past him and up to me, touching my cheek. "I'm sorry," she said. "Somehow we'll end this madness."

Zinc ran up to her. "Trust me," he said as he kissed the side of her face. "I need your help. Okay?"

Her jaw was set hard but she nodded. Zinc returned to the cake and blew out the candles and forced a grin as he addressed his guests. "Cake later! Now let's p...party!" He wiggled his hips and laughed. "Grab your champagne and let's dance!"

The crowd sashayed into the ballroom to the beat of *The Revelers*, America's top grodo band. I stood there and watched. Connor pointed at me and laughed while making an obscene gesture. Others stared until they disappeared out of the room.

Ransom came up and gently touched my shoulder. "Let's go, son."

CHAPTER 13

Two hours later, the door to the bedroom suite opened. I leaped to my feet, trying not to fidget, to maintain some dignity, not that I had much left. I watched Zinc avoid my gaze and step into a house-sized closet and hang up his jacket. The birthday boy sauntered to me, a lanky physique, looking down, hands in his pockets.

"I…I…I'm sorry," Zinc said. His lips were pinched tight, clearly upset, maybe a little scared. *How was that possible?*

Not what I was expecting from the first of the Twelve. His long brown hair was held back behind his neck with a black ribbon, just like I wore. He was masculine, but not mean, his eyes, when he finally glanced up, like a boy, a little anxious and curious. I liked that. As he stood next to me, I admired his beard line, unlike me with just an occasional whisker. And he owned me.

"M…may I take your coat?"

I slipped it off and handed it to him, my other hand holding my shirt together. Kind of silly feeling prudish but I was desperate to hold on to some of my self-esteem, more than a little shaken at the moment.

"D…did they get you re…refreshments?" Zinc carefully folded the garment over the back of a chair.

"I'm fine, thank you. I know why I'm here. It was explained to me. What do you want me to do? Should I take off my clothes?" I asked, holding my head up, hoping I looked strong, maintaining some sense of pride, that I was willing to meet the terms of the contract.

"Oh, my God, no!" Zinc blushed, sounding upset, uncertain, maybe even embarrassed.

Again, not what I expected, given what the doctor, lawyer, and guards graphically, sometimes gleefully, detailed why I was purchased. But it was reassuring, kind of cute.

Zinc put out his hand to shake.

"My name is Zinc Ogden McClain, please call me Zinc. What's y…yours?"

"Spartak Jones. You know that." We clasped hands.

"Yes, but let's pre…pretend we're meeting for the first t…time. Turn back the clock. I'm a…appalled by what just happened." He pointed to the sofa.

Who was this strange man? More than my life was on the line.

Sitting at the other end, Zinc glanced at me and then away, looking at his hands, fingers pressed white against his knees. I sensed he was frightened. That made two of us. Reading the changing expressions on his face wasn't easy; the man was having a war in his head.

"I…I admire your piano playing," Zinc said quietly, breaking the silence. "I've attended several recitals. You're good. Sonia's a fan."

"Thanks. I've seen you in the audience a couple of times and we appreciate your support. I knew who you were. Everyone does. It really helps scholarship boys like me. It tells the school people like you are supportive." I did an awkward grin, the best I could muster. "Why didn't you say something?"

"I guess I c…could have com…complimented your playing or your mastery of the p…parallel bars. And I should have. But I was there to see friends." He spoke very slowly, like he was struggling. "You could have approached me."

"Impossible," I said, shaking my head. "You're older, one of the Twelve. I'm a scholarship kid, a charity boy as your brother calls me. Honestly," I said, taking a risk, "I always assumed the worst about you, that you'd be like Connor. I guess I was wrong."

"I'm not my brother!" His voice was sharp. "Sorry."

I was pleased with his comment; there was something antagonistic between them. Good to know. We sat in silence. I tried to think of how I could endear myself to my owner.

"I haven't seen you in school the last week," he said.

"You don't know?"

"Know what?"

"I was in a jail cell in this building."

"WHAT? How?"

"I was drugged, kidnapped, and woke up there. In the lower basement level, in handcuffs and paper underwear." I shrugged, raised my eyebrows and tried for my most endearing smile to win him over. "I was quite the fashion statement."

"My God! That's horrible. And w...what's in your ear?"

"Nobody told you? Dr. Rai did it as well as other testing to make sure I was healthy and disease free for your use. He was under orders, your mom's I think. It's a tracker, like they use on cows and pigs, giving my location and vital signs, only fancier with your family crest on it. At least they didn't use a branding iron. You'll always know where your property—me—is at."

"I...I..." He slipped to his knees on the floor in front of me and took my hand.

I about fainted, stunned at this turn. Who was this man? His face looked like a pretzel, almost in pain. "Believe me when I say I didn't know."

Was this a sick game?

I was frozen, examining him, his face, his mouth, his hands, searching for clues to the man inside. His eyes were hazel, and inquisitive, without the nightmarish hardness of Sergei's. He was eighteen and hadn't created this legal monstrosity. Zinc seemed in genuine shock. He stood, rubbed his face, walked over to a wet bar and drank a glass of water. "Would you like some?"

"Thank you, no."

"You'll b...be returned to your family. Somehow I'll work it out."

I liked what he was saying but had been warned about the shifting legal issues, "all awaiting clarity," as the attorney put it. I was suddenly afraid again.

"Do you know much about *Sasser*?"

"A little."

"I'm not a lawyer but I know what I've been told and stuff I read. If I go back to my family..." I turned to the wall, my voice strained. I coughed, regaining my poise, such as it was. "If I go back...some lawyer...one of your guys...told me this...if I go back I may have no legal protection, no longer a citizen, maybe not even considered human under the law. The ruling is unclear. My family would lose its health care and home. My brother and sister wouldn't get into the academy. They could be thrown into prison until the debt to your family was repaid. I could too." I exhaled, talking too fast, sounding like a screeching bird protecting my nest. "And…and…I was told someone else could then buy me or take me, my family getting nothing."

I felt a tremor return to my lips and pressed a fist against them. I'd never been this scared, even when kids were beating me up, even waking up in the jail cell. So much depended on this moment.

I continued, "It may be beyond your control, given the legal issues. My father…." I couldn't finish. I tried not to yammer but my head was spiderwebs. I wiped my eyes before making a fist and bringing it to my forehead. *Don't sound pitiful.*

I straightened in the chair and turned to him. "Please don't let my family be hurt. I'll do whatever you want."

The man's face visibly drained of blood, gray with splotches. Zinc pushed his palms under the arms of his shirt. "I…I'll do everything I can to pro…protect them." His voice broke. "And you."

He moved away from the bar. "I guess that means you'll be staying with me until we figure this out. I…I won't force you to do anything. That…that wouldn't be right. Something like that has to be consensual. You may think I'm j…just a…a spoiled and clueless rich teenager but I do have my own set of m…morals and p…pride."

He walked to a set of pocket doors across the room and slid them open. "This is my den but there's a bed as well." He started to move toward the main door to his suite.

I stood and slipped off my torn shirt. It was all I could think of doing to keep him from leaving. The guards said he was hom and I was purchased for his sexual amusement. But that didn't mean he liked me. If he didn't, my future was dim. We needed to connect.

"Do you not find me attractive?"

Zinc grabbed his stomach and bolted from the room.

CHAPTER 14

I JUST STOOD FOR A LONG time, immobilized, in Zinc's bedroom. I was scared. This was the worst day of my life.

He'd rejected me. Why the hell had they bought me, destroyed my life, if he didn't want the gift? Students hit on me every week and I was good at the polite turndown. Here I stood half-naked, offering myself, and he'd run away. He could at least have said, "No thank you, or not now, thank you." Maybe I needed a little humility; maybe my ego was too inflated since the title.

I slipped on my shirt and jacket, making them look as presentable as I could. I walked to the open bedroom door. An armed guard stepped out of the dark.

"I'm sorry, you're not authorized to leave." The man grabbed the knob and pulled the door closed. The click of the lock sounded like my jail cell. And in a sense this room still was, only larger than my parents' entire home. And every inch seemed to be decorated in lavish French antiques and rich fabrics I'd seen only in history books.

The spare bedroom. Zinc said I would use it so I walked to it and left the doors open. No point in closing them. I was supposed to be smart, a great athlete, a musical prodigy, a gifted student. And I had no idea what to do. Rejection was difficult, particularly when it was about survival, not love. I placed my jacket over the back of a chair and pulled off my shirt, examining it to see about emergency repairs. I went into the bathroom. It was like a giant cave, all surfaces covered by rich brown marble with gold veins. I washed my face and wiped up some drops of water I'd splashed on the counter, not wanting to make a mess. In a drawer I found some safety pins and attached them to my shirt to replace the buttons.

The second room had a four-poster draped bed at the far end and a desk with carved eagle legs, overstuffed chairs, and two walls of books and awards. I perused the titles, surprised at their diversity and seriousness. I hadn't taken Zinc as a scholar nor a fan of printed books. Of course, I'd not taken him as much of anything before tonight. And now this stranger controlled my life as if I were a pet gerbil.

I picked up a memoir by Ulysses S. Grant on the Civil War—nothing like a book about fighting slavery—and wandered to a chair at the desk. It could be a long night and reading about the Civil War seemed ironic.

"Well, well, well…"

I looked up just as the young Grant enrolled at West Point. The day just got worse. Connor was leaning on the doorjamb, smirking, hands in his pockets. He moved toward me, more a drunken swagger than a walk.

"Stand up, slave boy!"

I set the book on the desk and rose to my feet, seeing no alternative. I tried to hold my gaze steady, hands at my side, determined to appear strong, like nothing had changed. At least in school there were people who could intervene and stop a fight. Now, it was just the two of us.

"Look at Mr. Muscular, so popular at the academy, so much attention, Mr. Perfect, America's top gymnast. A lot of good it does you. I saw my brother run out of here looking like he just lost his lunch. Guess you didn't pass. Maybe that means you'll belong to me now."

Connor walked around me, conducting an exam. I started to turn and face him again. The thought of being Connor's property made me dizzy. If I didn't fulfill the contract, his parents…

"I didn't give you permission to move, BOY! Face forward."

I did, nearly slicing my tongue as I crunched my jaw.

"Nice ass. I guess my brother didn't like it." He laughed and slapped my butt. I jumped around, facing him.

"What are you doing, Connor?"

"Whatever I want, *Sasser* boy. We own you and you'll do what I tell you. Understand?"

"Connor, please. I don't know why you hate me. If I've ever done something to offend you, I apologize. But don't do this. Wait for Zinc to come back."

"Who said I hated you? I just want you to do what homs like to do to other guys."

"No, don't do this!"

Connor unbuckled his belt, pulled down his zipper and lowered his pants. "Get on your knees."

I backed up. If I was fast enough, I could leap over a chair and get into the bathroom and lock the door. Besting him in a fight wasn't the issue.

"Please, Connor! We're classmates, on the gymnastics team together."

Connor pulled off his knit shirt. "Do me now. I know you want a het boy."

"NO! Leave. I belong to Zinc!" Somehow that horrid new truth sounded better.

Connor lurched for my head, grabbed a fistful of hair and pulled me forward as he yanked the collar of my shirt down my back, popping off the safety pins, to limit my arm movement. I needed both hands to get the shirt off. He punched me once in the gut before I tackled him and we hit the floor. He was no match and I seized both of his wrists, holding them overhead while I pressed a foot against his pants, now below his knees, immobilizing his legs. Fighting with your pants down was bad strategy.

"Stop! Please! I don't want to hurt you!"

"Don't touch me!"

"CONNOR! What are you doing?" Sonia stood in the bedroom doorway, her voice loud and harsh. She crossed her arms. We both froze, Connor pinned to the floor.

"Pull up your pants you spoiled jerk or I'll tell everyone at school you tried to give Spartak a blow job! And maybe get the word out you are tiny where it counts!"

I released him and jumped up, stunned to see her. And grateful. Connor got to his knees and struggled, legs entangled in underwear and trousers.

"Shit," Connor muttered as his penis got caught in the zipper.

"What will Zinc say when I tell him?" She stood over him.

Connor cleared the entanglement with another yelp and stood, putting on his shirt, adjusting his pants, his expression grim as he turned to face her, puffing out his chest, his face flushed and taut, trying to look dignified. He seemed unable to speak.

"Get your ass out of here now!" Her voice was like an ax slicing into a tree.

Connor jumped as he turned away from her, looking at me, curling his lips in contempt, clearly a warning, and stomped from the room.

"Thank you," I said. "You…saved me. The cavalry," I said, thinking of Ulysses Grant. "I had no idea what to do." I smiled and exhaled. "I'm kind of unfamiliar with the rules in my new…capacity." I couldn't stop grinning. She was an angel.

"Close your mouth or you'll catch flies. Please sit," she said. "I'm sorry this happened."

We sat on the edge of the bed.

"I talked briefly to Zinc. I wanted to say goodbye after seeing off the last of his guests. He went looking for his dad to talk about you. I won't lie; he's very upset. And offered no explanation. But he's a good man, honest and genuinely kind. Also shy, quite unlike Connor. I love Zinc. We've been friends since we were toddlers." She smiled at a memory.

"What?"

"We wanted to be girlfriend and boyfriend. We got naked once a few years ago. It was a disaster. We were so embarrassed. So now we're joined by real affection, lovers because we love each other, but not as mates."

"May I put on my shirt? I feel kind of strange."

She laughed. "Sure. You're funny. Did you know your physique is a topic of endless conversation at school?"

I felt myself blush as I put on my shirt and sat back down, fiddling with a safety pin. There was no possible response. She was opening up to me to make me feel safe, like I was important.

"You always like to show it off at practice in the arena."

"Coach makes me."

"Thank you, Coach."

"I saw you whistle at me. Two fingers. It was so funny." I grinned, totally infatuated.

"And with good reason." She laughed.

"What should I do?"

Her face was seductive even to a most-of-the-time hom, kind of like with Rhonda. Sonia had both warmth and hardness, unexpected in a trim, rich, perfectly coiffed high school senior. I was still in shock over her drill sergeant put-down of Connor. I wasn't sure if she was genuine. *Take a risk.*

"Zinc and I were talking about my…contract…my responsibilities…and he got upset and left." I had to be honest. "I…I think he's rejecting me. I don't know what that means for me or my family."

She squeezed my arm. "Reject you? Ridiculous. Take a look in the mirror. He's impressed with you. Please relax. If he doesn't oppose *Sasser* I'll break his neck. I'll talk with him and we'll work this out. I know we've never formally met but we've seen each other at the academy, and I touched your cheek at the party. Know that you're deeply admired. Your concerts, athleticism, and friendliness are important to me. Consider me an ally."

She stood and her expression hardened. "I'm morally offended by the debt-bond abomination! Zinc knows that. Millions of us in this country feel the same. It's the final indignity. Things must change in America. I think you can be important in making that happen."

She motioned for me to stand. "Give me a hug."

The embrace felt sincere. I held tight, soaking up the warmth, desperate for the first friendly gesture since I was harvested as a slave.

"Okay, that's good," she said, pushing me back. Her smile made me realize my loneliness.

"I'm sorry," I said, feeling foolish, "I…it's just…you're so nice… and…"

"I understand." She kissed my cheek. "I'll contact the guard captain about keeping Connor away. Be safe."

Sonia touched my chin and I watched her leave.

CHAPTER 15

I WAS ALONE AFTER A RESTLESS night of thinking about the horror of the birthday party. Stripped of my freedom, my pride, my clothes, mocked by my friends, shunned by my *owner*—now that's a shudder of a noun—humiliated by Connor. Not a night to tell Mom about. Then Sonia had appeared and saved me. This slavery gig was not for the fainthearted.

There was a knock on the door and I jumped up, hands at my sides, chin high, to face whoever was coming for me next. It was ridiculously early in the morning, the sun just rising, but I didn't want to be caught in bed in my underwear, so I was showered and dressed in my ripped birthday party finest, ready for anything, when the skinniest, tallest man I'd ever seen walked in, a living flagpole, holding a tray with breakfast and a small piece of luggage with a shoulder strap. He was dressed in a black suit with a lime-green collar that wrapped a half dozen times around his neck, draped like a stiff scarf, and worse, the ensemble had a faint undulating pattern in gray that floated from his feet to his neck and back again. It made me dizzy but was intriguing, like a train wreck. He was older than my dad. He stopped close in front of me. My nose was even with his chest so I looked up. He was maybe ten inches taller, his face angular, dark, without expression and with ridiculously long eyebrows combed out, maybe waxed. What part of him should I look at first?

"Good morning, young sir," he said with a slight nod, setting down the tray on a nearby table. He placed the suitcase in a chair. "My name is Gunther, Master Zinc's personal valet." His voice was impossibly deep, his tone formal, pronunciation clear, and he had a big and bouncy Adam's apple that I tried to ignore.

"Here is breakfast. But…before you begin, please remove all your clothing for laundry and repair." He pulled a small cloth sack from his coat pocket and flipped it open.

He waited and I stared, tired of taking my clothes off in front of an audience, and hoping he'd reconsider.

"Put them in here." He clicked his tongue, like a warning, wiggled the bag in front of me and stared over my head to a wall to give me some sense of privacy or maybe he found something there more interesting. So I stripped to my underwear and shoved everything in the bag.

"That too."

So he *was* watching. I was embarrassed, a feeling I was getting used to, as I removed my shorts and dropped them in the sack. He drew the string top closed, tossed it by the front door and walked to a closet. He returned with a long, plush blue robe and real leather slippers.

"Wear these for now. New clothes are in the valise and I promise to get others. My apologies in advance." He pushed up his lower lip. "No one planned clothes for you; your appearance was a secret to the butler's staff until last afternoon. We were told a slave *boy* had been purchased, no details, no dimensions and no way to get answers." His eyes tightened as he paused. "And seeing you now, we obviously not only got the age wrong but…uhm…your *abnormal* dimensions." He pointed to my chest and arms.

I wasn't sure how to respond to having my body described as abnormal so I just watched as he left with my old clothes. I slipped on the robe. I'd never felt anything so sumptuous, draping to my ankles. And the slippers were soft, some kind of lambskin inside. This was luxury I'd never experienced. I ate breakfast, blueberry yogurt with rye toast, and continued reading the book by President Grant, rubbing the fabric over my arms and legs. Just as General Grant seized Vicksburg, there was another knock. This time I remained seated, assuming Gunther was back.

A dark young woman, not much older than me, in a starched green uniform with a white apron, walked in and picked up the tray.

"Hello. My name's Spartak," I said, standing and offering my hand. "What's yours?"

She smiled like I was an idiot and said nothing. Why would she care who I was? She was here to get the dishes.

"What's going on?" I put my hand back to my side.

"Put on the clothes in the valise, please, sir, and hang the robe back in the closet." With a tight, irritated smile, she curtsied and walked out with the tray. Curtsied? Charm may not have been part of the training program for all staff.

Today had to be better; that was the prime mantra for optimists. When I opened the little suitcase, I found a dark blue jumpsuit with red stars and white moons, a stretchy fabric. The outfit was ridiculous, alternatively boxy and tight in the wrong places. Maybe it belonged to one of the staff's children. Gunther was right. Was my shape that weird? Why assume a skinny ten-year-old slave? The powder blue underwear ripped as I tugged it on. And there was a pair of color-coordinated deck shoes that only accepted three toes inside. I dressed, looked in a mirror and laughed, throwing up my arms and kicking off the shoes. Crying and beating myself bloody was pointless; maybe I could join a circus.

My mouth tasted nasty, and—clearly someone planned ahead—I found a bottle of antacid liquid in the bathroom. Chalky but effective. I went back to my reading.

A single knock on the door again. I was getting popular. General Grant was just now running for president as the muscular security chief entered.

Oh, shit. I leapt to my feet, the book dropped to the floor and I stood motionless at rigid attention.

"Mr. Bolt, nice to see you again." I struggled to keep my voice under control. The man had unnerved me after my humiliation by the guard. To describe him as menacing was an understatement.

"I doubt that."

"Are you taking me to jail?"

"What?" The big man crossed his arms. His face was hard, intense.

"The contract. Zinc…ah…Mr. McClain…the son, Mr. Zinc McClain…found me repulsive and rejected me." I was jabbering again.

"Shut up, boy. Sit!"

I dropped into the desk chair, a chastened puppy, and folded my hands in my lap. The man stood, looming over me. I couldn't win a fight against him; I was psyched out just looking at him.

"First, good to know. Zinc is special to me. And you may call me Ran in the future; and call him Zinc." He smiled just for a moment before the steel mask returned. "Second, something has happened to Sergei McClain. Zinc's with him now. I'll explain. Third, you're staying here. Zinc insisted." Another micro-smile.

He grabbed a second chair and sat, leaning forward, hands on his knees. He looked at me, pressing his lips together like he was trying to decide something.

"Is Zinc all right?"

Nearly a minute passed before he responded; his mind seemed elsewhere and I thought he'd forgotten my question. "Emotionally, no. His father's unconscious in our medical facility. Dr. Rai is growing new bone and reattaching nerves and muscles aided by robots and brain syncs. We actually have one of the best private hospitals around. And we all use it, including families of people who work for the McClains. I say this just so you will understand this social unit you are now a part of."

I squirmed in my seat. Social unit sounded like an ant colony.

"There was an assassination attempt against Sergei." He stopped and I sensed he was wrestling with his emotions, although his face was a rock. "Somehow terrorists were able to hack into the retVue in his cornea and right temple. The side of his face exploded as he was talking to Zinc about you and he collapsed into his arms. This is not supposed to be possible but it happened."

I stared, unable to respond. They were talking about *me* when the father was attacked. My God! And Ran had spent his career with Mr. McClain and was trying to reassure me or maybe just distract himself from the horror…or he had time to waste before his next appointment and pitied me. He leaned back in the chair. He was Paul Bunyan-sized and while his brown eyes were hard there were friendly crinkles around the edges. I sensed from his tone and body language that he was a good guy. I could certainly use one and I must think positive even in this Alice through the looking glass world.

"The grafting and growing of new nerves and muscles may go on for hours. Rai is advised by experts and the MechDocs are first rate. Zinc and his family are at the medical suite. He won't likely be back for hours."

"I'm sorry." This was more complication than I needed. "You said terrorists. Do you know who did it?"

"No. But it must have been someone wanting to foment trouble or seeking revenge. Sergei is arguably the most powerful private citizen in the world."

"Is he the richest?" I was curious but from his expression I realized I asked the wrong question. I should be showing concern. But I didn't know Sergei McClain, only enough to see him sign my slave papers and his arctic face didn't engender a feeling of warmth. The man looked at me and I twisted a bit, before he responded.

"The term *world* doesn't mean what it used to, Spartak. China has been in a no-prisoners civil war for nearly a generation and the population began declining even earlier." He thought for a moment and grunted, kind of a scoff preceding a smirk. "Some say the death of the last rhinoceros decades ago preceded the slumping population as ground rhino horn was no longer available to men with erectile dysfunction." He cleared his throat and focused on a vase of roses nearby.

What did he say? Mr. Bolt sucked in his cheeks. The man had sense of humor! Maybe it was a momentary escape from the attack on his friend or an effort to bring us closer together.. Of course, it could be true. One way or another the killing the magnificent creatures to grind up their horns was disgusting; ignorance and conceit squashing science and respect for nature. I wondered what it would have been like to see one alive.

He continued, serious again, turning back to me. "The Middle East is mostly tribal fiefdoms since oil ran out and the princes, even heads of state, absconded with the money and abandoned storybook cities to decay in the heat. Religious feuds now near the thousand-year mark in that part of the planet; Russia is bankrupt. So Sergei is the richest in this hemisphere and Europe, no question, but not loved."

"Who are his enemies?"

"The Dominionists hate him and there is AR2. Members of the

Twelve are not always friendly with each other although their fights are normally through hostile corporate takeovers."

He touched his ear and turned over his wrist. "I must go. I wanted to make sure you were safe and talk to you again, to get to know you. I suspect you're lonely and nervous, and that's to be expected. I've asked my boys to visit. And they're great kids. Tripper Bolt you may know from the academy, the same age as Zinc. My other son, Paolo, is two years older and attends Stanford, going to be a doctor. They've been a tight trio all their lives, growing up together." He stood and I did too. "Enjoy the terrace or any place else in this suite." He paused, looking at me. "That's quite the outfit."

I laughed and started to breathe again. Mr. Bolt—Ran—stopped at the door, smiled in a kind of embarrassed way, and left. Thank you, I thought, watching him close the outside door to the suite.

The sons showed up in less than an hour. Paolo was a slender young man, softer looking, taking after his mother, he said, big on hugs. Tripper I'd seen at school but never met. He was a senior with a linebacker build like his dad and the same marine sergeant demeanor. He slammed a fist into my shoulder, a jock's hello; he threw a serious punch. They were appalled by the slave sale, were verbally pummeling Zinc over it, they assured me. They acted like I was a brother, telling stories, sometimes funny and sometimes lewd. Normal young male stuff.

Gunther brought lasagna and salad. We were silent as he did his work.

"Your dinner, young sirs."

"Thank you," we all said in unison as he exited the room.

I giggled as the door clicked shut.

"He's a good man," Tripper said, not an admonition but close.

"Totally loyal to Zinc," Paolo added. "I think he's intentionally outrageous to mask his uniqueness. I adore him and consider him an uncle. In fact, I sometimes call him Uncle Gunther."

"I didn't mean to be rude."

"As you become part of this household, Zinc's household, Gunther will serve you, support and protect you." Paolo's voice was soft and I felt my face flush as if he were yelling. Their message was important and they were gentle teachers.

Tripper grabbed a zan and punched up a Z-ether. *"Cosmic Raiders,"* he shouted and the face of a monster appeared.

We played and talked until late that night. I drank my first ever glass of wine, a zinfandel, and it was sweet. I always turned down any kind of alcohol because I felt a need to always be in control; wine cost money and was only empty calories. But they insisted and I felt safe with them. And somehow, they said nothing about my stretchy outfit with red stars and white moons. I guess it proved that het male teens were oblivious to what other guys were wearing or, maybe, just too embarrassed to comment.

Later, they made me go to bed while they slept one at a time on overstuffed chairs, the other standing guard making sure no one bothered me and forgiving my blunders. My number of friends in this new world seemed to be growing. Of course they all owed their allegiance and income to the McClains.

CHAPTER 16

SAN FRANCISCO, CA (Associated Media)—Mayor Joshua Rand is missing, perhaps kidnapped, according to Harmony Enforcement Chief Greg McIntosh. And the mayor's 18-year-old nephew, Cedric Rand, has been murdered, apparently trying to deliver a ransom for his uncle's release...

It was hard to imagine that I was sitting in a rose garden amid hundreds of yellow, red, and white blooms, the air motionless and fragrant, on the roof just outside Zinc's bedroom and dressed in my freshly rinsed blue moon suit. I was cross-legged on a white calfskin divan, soft as a baby's butt, feeling like royalty, studying my Spanish with an interactive Z-ether program. I rubbed the synthetic emerald on my class ring, so astronomical, as Geo liked to say, a world under the gem, my initials on the outside releasing the power of the zan. But it wouldn't get me out of this muck.

Language gave a deep view of different cultures and I did well but not brilliant. We were expected to be fluent in a least three: English, French and Spanish. Reading literature as originally written was considered critical by OA—at least for scholarship kids and the brighter barronials—to appreciate the subtlety of an author's words in his or her own tongue. We often compared translations to the actual words of the author and there were sometimes huge differences. Of course we weren't all that proficient. Voucher or public schools did nothing like this. I'd wanted to take ancient Greek or even Latin, at least a learner course, to read original biblical texts since Christianity was the official state religion and Dominionist dogma was everywhere in the media. But the year I enrolled a new law dictated only scholars approved by the Dominionist Council could study ancient languages and they would be the sole interpreters of religious history.

Tripper and Paolo talked to their father in the morning. Another guard was now at the door to Zinc's suite, making sure Connor didn't come in again. Gunther brought breakfast and I asked him to sit and we talked as I ate. He was unattached and considered Zinc a son. He gave me some hints on my Spanish before he left. I felt foolish I'd once laughed at him, judging him on his looks not the amazing man he was.

"En un lugar de la Mancha, de cuyo nombre no quiero accordarme," I read aloud, stumbling through the original *Don Quixote, "no ha mucho tiempo que vivia un hidalgo de los de lanza en astillero, adarga antigua, rocin flaco y galgo corredor."* Now what did it mean? "In the village of La Mancha…something, something…has not long ago lived a nobleman of the lance and ancient shield…"

"This tracker works really well," Zinc said, standing over me.

"Ahhh!" I jumped two feet, bumped my shin on the coffee table, and stood. "Oh, wow, ow." I lifted up my right leg and rubbed my knee. "Sorry, I didn't hear you come up."

"I should've announced myself. I was s…searching for you and used the ear tracker. Your heart rate is elevated." He was looking at the SubQ embedded in his forearm. He pointed to the sofa. He was dressed in a dark blue high-collared shirt with a zipper down the front and trim gray cotton pants. His face was drawn, eyes red and puffy.

"For good reason," I said, feeling like a frightened errant cow, putting my leg down but bending over and continuing to rub it before sitting. "I hope this is okay. To be out here, I mean. Ran said I could."

"You call the Chief of Security by his first name?" His voice was gruff and he was pale, clearly upset. I know I would be if my father were attacked. His emotions ripped his face, jaw muscles rippling, lips twisted.

"I'm sorry. When I called him 'Mr. Bolt' he insisted I call him Ran. I…I should have realized my place." I looked down, not at Zinc's face, not sure what to do while he was in this mental hotspot. Normally I was good at reading people.

"Yes, you should have."

The silence went on with him just standing over me, and I stared at my feet, feeling vulnerable. "I'm sorry about your dad. I hope he's doing better. Mr. Bolt told me and Tripper and Paolo shared details. They're worried too. They love your family."

"So now you're talking to my best friends?" He sounded pissed off and shook his head, flustered.

He'd had no sleep; that was obvious. I was just another complication for him, given what just happened to his dad.

"Fuck," he said, swiveling around and crossing his arms. I watched his back for a long time before he turned toward me.

He held my gaze for a moment before rubbing his eyes with his fingertips. He was emotionally spent, lashing out. I didn't know the rules, how far I could go. If it were Billy or Rhonda, we'd hug and cry. And this guy just snapped at me. And could put me back in that jail cell. Or give me to Connor. Or, whatever he wanted.

"Thanks for your concern," Zinc said just above a whisper. "He's unconscious. They removed what was left of his eye socket and the side of his skull." He sat on the lounge, looking at emotion's end, like maybe he didn't want to say anything more. It'd been a very long night and morning for both of us.

I scooted next to him and put my arm around his shoulder.

"He'll be okay."

"How would you know?" His voice was exasperated and hoarse. "That's all I've been hearing for hours, empty bullshit statements! Doctors lying to me, trying to reassure me." Zinc bent down, elbows to knees, face in hands, like he was trying to hold it together. "You don't know my dad. And who said you could touch me?"

I jumped to my feet again. "I'm sorry."

"You say that a lot."

"Well...I don't know what to say. I don't have much practice being a slave." I was flustered and a little defiant, wanting to help but clueless on how to work with a spoiled guy facing a catastrophe. And I was in crisis too.

Zinc looked up and studied my face, his own expression softening. "Look, I'm the one w...who should apologize. I d...didn't mean to be cruel. I'm just upset. C...come, sit by me."

I sat back on the divan next to him, hunched over, hands between my knees, determined not to touch or offend him.

"Do you rem…ember when we met?"

"Yes, that summer math class. We talked and laughed."

Zinc smiled as if pleased I knew. "A friend said he once overheard you say you were mostly *hom* and you even used the old-fashioned term *gay.*"

So he'd been talking about me to his schoolmates. "Your friend is correct, I did say that. I like both sexes but prefer men."

"Me too."

"That's good to know. I kind of assumed it."

"I was talking to my father when the attack came." He spoke in a controlled way, careful with his words. "I…I don't want to talk about his condition in detail, not yet. It's too r…raw. But I do want to d… discuss what we said to each other. I want to be hon...est with you; you deserve that and I feel like I know you." A sheepish smile. "Because of our rather unique rel…ationship I hope I can be…and…I need to think this through with somebody."

"I'm somebody."

He smiled. I hoped that was acceptance.

"I couldn't believe a human being could be p…purchased," he said softly. "Dad said you were a commoner, not of our class. That if we were in my gr…grandmother's country—that would be Russia—you would be a peasant. And I a p…prince." He stopped, shaking his head, looking embarrassed. "So silly." Those must have been his dad's exact words. I wondered how well he knew this man he called father.

"He called you a *re…restavek,* like a slave child in Haiti. He was not mean in the way he talked, just matter of fact. That is his w… world view." He was silent again and I waited, not wanting to upset him more. And I needed to understand. He was trying to help me and maybe himself. Owning a boy must be quite different than getting a dog. I had no experience in either situation. In my neighborhood, we often shared pets between families, a communal dog or cat. Easier to afford.

"I asked him *w…why* the court ruled as it did," he said, his voice rising as he shrugged. "He and the other Twelve could have stopped it.

They have on other decisions. And the answer sur…prised me. In a word, *'More…*is the answer,' he told me. *'The ultra rich crave more, beyond need or common sense; pastors, pol…iticians and thugs, same thing. P…people like to acquire and show off,'* my dad said. You can only have so many yachts or islands or d…iamond necklaces or favorite charities and it becomes ridiculous, unsophisticated. So those con…sumed with the envy game, the hunger to impress, were looking for new toys."

"Thank you for sharing." The man was more complicated than I expected. I was a "new toy."

"He said he didn't know anything about you being k…kidnapped, put in jail or the tracker in your ear. I believe him. He did approve the purchase and watched a short D…DIMM4 of you from headhunters. Or do we call them slavers? Mom did the shopping and worked out the details and gave orders on your…oh God…your prep…preparation. He said you were ex…expensive. I have no idea how a price is determined for a hu…human but one was set by the people who run this new b…business. Your coach is one. I heard he got a major finders' fee."

"Ugggh." It just slipped out. I pushed my palms hard against my eyes, then pressed my fists together as hard as I could to control the stress and keep from getting emotional. I knew it had to be true. My champion had been prepping me for sale, getting me ready for purchase. That's why I had to take off my shirt so often. Maybe that's who those men were in the arena seats last time, checking me out, setting a final sale price.

Zinc just sat for a long time. I watched him wipe away a tear, probably thinking about his dad. He seemed lost.

"Enough of this," he said, startling me, lifting his head high. "He's in re…recovery and will be un…unconscious for hours." Zinc pulled his shoulders back, took a deep breath, exhaled loudly, slapped his palms on his thighs and turned to me with a playful look.

"Where'd you get that hid…eous outfit?"

I grinned and glanced down at the fabric, hoping this was an opening. "It really is dreadful, isn't it?" I felt playful, ready to take a risk. "A disgrace to tasteful homs everywhere. Gunther brought it to me as well as my breakfast and took all my old clothes that were desperate for repair after your friends used me as a piñata. He's undoubtedly het." I bit my lower lip. "And...honestly...my wardrobe is...kind of sparse. You may be surprised to learn that my trip here was a bit... unanticipated, at least by me."

"Gunther." Zinc smiled, then we both did. "He's a very good man, someone I've been able to share secrets with since I was a boy. He'd die to protect me and I'd do the same for him."

I absentmindedly touched Zinc's shoulder and yanked my hand back like I got an electrical shock.

"Sorry."

"And I heard my b...brother paid you a visit last evening. My apologies. He can be a jerk, no, he is a jerk, even a thug. He's been c...cruel to me my whole life. He likes to make people laugh at me because of my face and the way I t...talk. Don't let him touch you." The man looked away embarrassed yet I sensed he was relieved at the revelation. I didn't know why he was telling me this, being so brutally honest to someone like me, almost a stranger.

"I did my best to dissuade him," I told him. "Connor is persistent but stopping him, as you saw at the party, isn't easy since he's part of the family who owns me." I pinched my lips tight as I looked up at him. "Can I punch an owner's brother?"

"Connor was born perfect and handsome," Zinc said quietly, looking across the room, ignoring my question. "I...I guess I'm o... obsessed about my looks, just so you'll know, since I'm different and my parents re...refused to let me change them. It was unmanly, Dad said, and it would build character to give me bal...ance, something to overcome in a world of sycophants." Zinc tightened his lips. I was too stunned to speak. He turned and looked at me, his expression gentle. "Ran said you thought I found you re...pulsive." His face looked like a million upsetting ideas were surging. Given what had happened to his father, he didn't need to stress over me.

"Spartak, I...uh...think...you're...man, this is hard...I think you're the most bea...beautiful, talented, and smartest guy I've ever met."

We looked at each other, both of us uncertain after this declaration. I know I was in shock. I remembered what Zinc had said yesterday, that he would never force me. The initiative had to be mine. Did he want me?

"Thank you…" I started to say.

He held up his palm. "L…let me finish this or I won't h…have the nerve to do it. I've admired you since y…you entered the academy."

He seemed so vulnerable right now. My heart went out to him.

"I've thought a lot a…about this since my parents…I can barely even say it…since my p…parents bought you and gave you to me." He coughed, a nervous one, as he glanced down then back up to my face. "I have w…wondered how it would feel if our pos…itions were reversed. A life shattered after one sp…iked protein drink at a pizza p…parlor from a man you trusted like a father. Then your par…ents sell you into slavery in exchange for a better life." His eyes examined mine. "And you sit here, your head r…raised high, looking right back at me, prepared for whatever is to come. The dignity you d…displayed when my jackal brother and the others tried to hum…iliate you. You have remarkable courage. More than I have."

I gasped, my hands covering my mouth.

"And…it's okay…if you…want…to t..touch me."

"Now?"

"S…so…sounds g…good to me."

* * *

It was the last thing I expected to hear. The man had a crush on me! And he seemed like a nice guy for somebody from another planet. I debated how aggressive I should be at what could be a breakthrough moment. He was obviously shy and insecure. And he stuttered. Hard to imagine for someone in his position but I had met his brother and parents and they could warp anyone. I'd stutter too, or worse, if forced to spend much time with Mrs. McClain, much less call her Mother.

"You said you didn't like this jumpsuit. So I'm going to remove it unless you object."

Zinc just watched as I unzipped and slipped out of it, taking my time, doing a little flexing, and tossed it across the room like a basketball.

"What do you think of this dreadful powder-blue underwear?"

"Dis...distracting."

"Yes, I think you're right."

I took the shorts off an inch at a time, tossed them and did a slow stretch complete with some groans. I stood naked in front of him and did a little pouty twist with my lips. He just stared at my face and then began a slow scan to my feet and back up. Gradually he grinned.

I moved closer, putting my hands on his shoulders, rubbing the tense muscles. He kept his hands in his lap as if intimidated to touch me. I kissed the top of his head. My legs pressed against his knees and I could feel them trembling. The richest teenager on earth was nervous about being naked or soon to be naked with one of the poorest. He was a special man. Everything was upside down. I was in charge of my owner and wanted to protect him, lead him gently into making love.

I dropped to my knees and pulled the zipper down his tunic and helped take it off. I let my fingers lightly dance over his chest, drawing goose bumps. He had a solid body, trim and the dark mottled skin was intriguing not a turnoff. And his weird face was kissable. The world was overstocked with perfect ones.

I sucked a dark nipple; he jumped and let out a yip. So I licked and nibbled more, my hands on his back, pulling him tight before leaning away to see his face.

"Thank you," I said. His expression was curious, a delighted boy, not the taciturn teen Rhonda described. I ran a finger around his lips, slipped past them to his perfect teeth and he sucked it inside. Then I smiled, pulled out my finger and wrapped a hand behind his head, pulling him to me and we kissed. Slow at first, a gentle meeting of tongues. I didn't want to spook him. Then he got into it. Good instincts for a rich guy.

I stood and took his hand.

"Let's go to bed."

"I thought you'd never ask."

CHAPTER 17

"I GUESS I'M *LEGALLY* STILL A virgin," Zinc said, grinning, leaning on an elbow, stretched out next to me on his bed, "assuming I care about Dominionist dogma anymore."

It had now been a week since the birthday party. When he wasn't with his father, he was here with me; Gunther kept us fed. We didn't talk about missing school. I suspect no teacher would complain and I didn't know if school was even in my future.

The tips of Zinc's fingers explored my left bicep before slipping over to my pecs. Zinc confided he'd never had sex before, pushed into chastity by his father. That seemed beyond comprehension.

"A virgin only because of a technicality." I smiled, taking Zinc's hand and leading it lower.

"That's one big tech...nic...al...ity."

The Ninth Circuit Court of Appeals in San Francisco had ruled that virginity was now defined as the condition before vaginal penetration, at least in nine western states. So the President Bill Clinton argument had finally won, anal and oral wasn't sex. Homs got a free pass on the virginity issue.

"May I ask why a guy like you would still be a virgin? I don't understand what you told me about the Dominionists. Lots of guys would be thrilled to be with you." I touched the side of his face. "I am."

"Thank you," he said, sounding pleased and looking a bit discombobulated. "You're a generous and gentle teacher." He finger-combed my hair and I leaned my head back, enjoying it. "Dad wanted me to be different, meeting the Dominionist d...de..demands for purity in case we might someday have an alliance. Kind of silly but it matched my own insecurities and I went along willingly, maybe even relieved. I had a reason to remain chaste." He watched me for a minute. "Such an odd word for a guy."

I touched his shoulder and he kissed my chin. He seemed anxious to make up for lost time.

"I…It's hard to know if someone is after me or my m…money. I wanted to be het and marry Sonia. Her family is wealthy so my m… oney isn't an issue be…tween us. But that is not to be; it would have been unfair to her. I was shy. Hard to believe, I know, and ashamed of my body and the way I talked. The longer I waited the more difficult it became for me to approach anyone or the reverse. It was impossible to be anonymous. I was isolated by choice; only comfortable talking to a few close friends. So I just pretended I was harsh and angry to keep people away. If you're a virgin long enough you get intimidated by the thought of someone knowing." He touched my cheek. "I like talking to you."

I took his palm and brought it to my lips for a kiss.

"So why is Connor not held to the same standard? He's at the Palladium every week, if rumors are true, picking up downer girls for sex. He certainly brags about it."

"Ah yes, my s…spoiled and arrogant brother. One reason is likely rebellion; I will in…inherit one hundred percent of McClain enterprises thanks to the primogeniture laws passed a generation ago to concentrate wealth and power. Connor will have what I want to give him. He knows that and is angry with me. Strategic he's not but cruel, yes, kind of twisted. Dad knows. Mom won't admit it." He rolled a leg over my thighs. "You're very intimidating and so beautiful. Do you know that? I would never have approached you."

"Stop it."

"Your blushing is adorable." He looked like he had just had a revelation. "I stutter less with you."

I pulled him into a deep kiss. As I leaned back I took his left forearm and turned it over, rubbing my fingers over the SubQ implanted just under the skin. It felt and looked normal. It was impossible to see except when the device lit up. It was as creepy as it was irresistible. I would never have an implant; not that I could afford one.

"Could the terrorists do what they did to your father and blow up your arm?"

"Dad had a ten-year-old device and refused to change it out. I think that made it easier to hack with new technology. Mine is switched out every year and upgraded constantly for weaknesses."

A chime sounded and an opaque screen materialized in front of the wall opposite our bed. "Ransom Bolt," a disembodied announcement. Then a familiar voice, "Sorry to disturb you. Please activate with your voice print and code, Zinc, if appropriate."

Zinc pulled up the sheets as I scampered out of bed. "No, stay! Please." I slipped back under the sheets, excited he wanted to include me in something other than sex. "Connect. Authorization 76QZ."

Ran's face filled much of the wall. "Apologies again for the intrusion." He stared for a moment. "Congratulations to you both. I'm pleased. I was hoping this was why I haven't seen much of you the past few days."

I put my arm around Zinc and we sat higher against the headboard. It felt like a validation of my new relationship.

"Not good news. A group of religious zealots accosted Roland Rosenberg, the son of John Rosenberg, at a bar in New York City. His throat was cut and two guards solared. Brutal. The killers were spouting drivel about End Times. They were wearing headbands with a cross at the center. There was also a black woman with them, elegant, beautiful, who engaged him in conversation. We don't know if it was connected. As you may know, John's father is in Congress and has openly opposed the Dominionist agenda. This is a warning. We need to upgrade and reconsider your security, Zinc."

"So it spreads, the rumored religious coup. Just as you predicted." Zinc rubbed both hands over his face. "John was only a few years older than me. And his family?"

"Parents and other siblings survive and are working with their own security forces. We may involve the military, given your father's influence." He pinched his lips together. "I was just up to see him."

Zinc flipped over his forearm and touched it, bringing up a live feed of his father in his room. "He sleeps."

"He's in and out of lucidity, as you know," Ran said. "Per his legal instructions on incapacitation, that makes you the decider."

"Let's meet in thirty minutes, if that works for you."

Zinc put both arms around me. "And security will include my handsome lover."

CHAPTER 18

THE PLANNING SUITE ON THE FIRST floor, known informally as Henry's Room, replicated the main dining hall of the medieval castle Queen Elizabeth I played in as a child. The cherry wood linenfold paneling, square crossbeams in the ceiling, the massive wood table with serpent legs and each high-back chair intricately carved with biblical scenes were deceptive. State-of-the-art electronics were hidden and there were seats and plenty of space for a team of generals. It was a 22nd century war room Henry VIII could appreciate: two suits of fifteenth century English armor, a mural of Alexander the Great defeating King Darius of Persia at the battle of Gaugamela in 331 B.C., and rifles from different centuries displayed on two walls. I gawked and touched the helmet on one of the suits of armor.

"Spartak," Zinc called.

Feeling chastened, I joined them sitting around a rectangle-shaped table, feeling like I'd made a wrong turn somewhere in time. I looked at Zinc, then over to Ran's hard face.

"A red hair was found at the site of Cedric Rand's murder in Oakland," Ran said. Zinc had told me earlier that the security chief had been fastidious in leading the investigation, working with local enforcers, his own team, the FBI, and a military forensics unit.

"Ignite," Ransom said. The tabletop transformed from rough wood to glass. "Brace yourselves. This is gruesome but revelatory."

The image of Cedric Rand appeared at the crime scene as he was found, his handsome young face charred and unrecognizable.

"Ahh!" Zinc flinched and closed his eyes.

"Oh, my God," I said and looked away, "not Cedric!" This beautiful man was charbroil. Just days ago I'd kissed him, enjoying his taste and enthusiasm. I wondered if Zinc knew I'd gone to bed with Cedric the night he died. I knew Ransom would, since he seemed well informed by all security units and that included the enforcers and Lieutenant Mosser. Cedric had been vain and handsome; now it didn't matter. I felt numb.

"Close-up, face. Hair." A bright red hair over burned skin filled the screen. It was horrid.

"It's from a young woman in Cincinnati," Ran explained, "who sold her hair for a wig. All cash. No record of who purchased it. And the hair was placed intentionally, on top of his scorched face."

Zinc swallowed and breathed fitfully. This was his friend and cousin. "Yes, I see what you m…mean. It looks like a cal…calling card," Zinc stated. He raised his eyes to the crossed battle-axes on the wall behind Ran with a shield above them showing the McClain sunburst crest.

Seeing Cedric like this flamed my head. I'd remember him not like this but as he was his last night: excited, passionate, and vulnerable.

"Exactly. Perhaps from one killer or group leaving it to take credit."

"Is it r…related to the murder in New York?"

"If so, certainly a different style."

"So there could be m…more than one person or group involved?"

"That's my assumption." Ransom sat facing Zinc and me at the table. I watched each of them closely, wanting to contribute but overwhelmed. This was not my world.

"It could be N…Nocture and AR2."

"A ploy to frighten the Twelve and distract them. But from what?"

"Maybe it's within the Twelve, divide them, eliminate me…other m…members so the p…pecking order changes."

"Like the Fifth become First?"

Zinc nodded.

"Or just to obliterate us entirely as the religious End Timers want."

I was impressed with how Zinc could move ahead with the discussion and shove his emotions aside. He was more than just a self-absorbed teenager. He could think while looking literally at the face of destruction.

"I'm not sure they're ready to murder," Ran said. "The End Times blather could just be an intended false lead, like the hair. And the Rosenbergs could also be cover. But they've crossed the line, urging a holy war against our government and way of life. That is treason. We must not treat it lightly."

"Crushing them with the military seems morally questionable..."

"...and dangerous," I mumbled. It just tumbled out. "Sorry."

"Say more," Ran urged.

"Okay. Because it would make them martyrs, inspire others. Maybe that's what they want, to provoke a war to recruit an army, spark an uprising."

Zinc touched the back of my neck, squeezing with affection. "Good point."

His puppy did all right. But I was pleased I'd contributed something useful.

"You may be right, Spartak," Ran said.

"Beyond the uber-holy, there may be a personal vendetta we don't know about," Zinc continued. "Certainly there are enough people angry with the Twelve or j...jealous. But to risk a war with us is suicidal."

"Not for thrill killers. Or those anxious to die for their cause. Or those who are mentally impaired."

"And those don't have to be separate categories," I added, feeling a bit more empowered.

We were silent for some time.

"There are at least four p...plausible motives," Zinc said.

"Or more," I added.

Zinc touched my hand. "I know this is new to your life and experience, Spartak. Hell, it's new to me and the sh...sheltered life of privilege I've led, never really thinking about anything life-and-death important."

He was opening up and being honest with me. His other hand was under the table, massaging my thigh. He could contemplate more than one thing at once.

"And I must assume that I'm also a target," he said.

"Unfortunately." Ran tightened his lips.

Zinc rolled his forearm and glanced at his glowing SubQ. "My father's awake. I must go."

* * *

"Zinc."

He turned, touching the carved lion newel post on the stairs to the master bedroom suites. I stood below in the hallway just outside Henry's Room. I gave him a thumbs-up. He did the same back. The unexpected exchange seemed to lift his spirits.

"Come with me," he said, holding out his hand.

"Oh, no, to your parents' rooms?" *That's insane.* "I know what they think of me and don't want to create problems."

"Please."

"I'm afraid; they'll get mad."

"Please. I want you to be part of my life. Trust me."

A week of nonstop sex and his slave boy was part of his life. Okay by me. Being entrepreneurial is part of survival. I walked up the stairs and we held hands. I wondered if I should be pleased or appalled and prayed this wouldn't be a disaster. People don't always want their house slave dropping by unexpectedly.

Looking through the open doors into his mother's room, we saw her asleep, under medication, emotionally drained by the attacks. She was best this way. A dark-haired nurse was in a chair beside her; three others tended blinking machines against a wall. It was kind of like an emergency ward with museum furniture. The bed was a raised platform, like a stage, with a carved wooden crown, echoing the size of the bed, hanging from the ceiling, with angels looking down from the clouds. Zinc had told me his parents kept separate bedrooms.

"I find it sad," he said, walking down the hall. "I hope in my life my lover will always sleep beside me."

My stomach was queasy. I didn't belong and shouldn't be up here.

"As a k…kid, I always felt like I was approaching a throne room, walking through double twelve-foot doors from some ancient French chateau."

Sergei was propped up against a hill of white pillows in the middle of a four-poster bed as we entered. "This once belonged to Peter the Great of Russia," Zinc whispered. It was now draped in red and gold tapestry. Simplicity was not the McClain lifestyle.

Three guards at the door stood at attention. Zinc nodded and acknowledged each, "Thank you, Jerome, Justin, Mercedes." They ignored me.

His father seemed alert and energized compared to the Z-ether images I'd seen earlier. Zinc walked to the edge of the bed. "Hello Father. Is it permissible for Spartak to join me here? He is important to me and I would like him to get to know you better."

"Hmmmm." That was all Sergei said.

Zinc pointed to a chair out of his father's limited sightline and I rushed to it. I knew Sergei's memory was at times lucid, other times fog. Most of his face was bandaged. Experts had calculated that the retVue data channel had been hacked and a reverse power signal had overheated the old implant, causing it to detonate. The manufacturer, the FBI, and the security team claimed it was impossible. But his dad had a hole in his face to prove them wrong.

Sergei lifted a hand and touched Zinc's arm. The man was on stimulants; otherwise he would be lethargic and useless, the doctors had told Zinc. But the drugs carried serious risks of their own. Zinc had been here daily since the attack, often staying for hours. Connor visited once a day for a few minutes, I was told, as if performing an expected duty. Zinc hoped he was wrong. Perhaps it was just too much for him emotionally.

"Have you filed the documents?"

"Yes, Father, yesterday in court. I now have full control of the McClain assets, properties, and companies. And I'm feeling over… overwhelmed."

"My advisory council will help initially. You know the members. Use them to hone your own judgment."

"Yes. I've been talking privately with each member. They call me." I knew Zinc was stressed, as an eighteen-year-old would be being solicited by CEOs of multitrillion dollar companies he now owned. In the past year, his father had included him in his trips and brought key people to the house so Zinc could meet them. That had helped prepare him.

"You're a man now, the head of the family. I will be honest with you because you need nothing less. Your mother will handle minimal household items, and you everything else. Queen of the Phantas. She's focused on glamour and movie scripts, not leading a family or way of life under attack. Give her plenty of money for her nonsense. Candidly, she's not pleased but is totally devoted to you and the law is on our side. But, be watchful. And Connor is peeved but his focus is rebellion and girls. And he has serious emotional problems. Be cautious of everyone."

I couldn't believe I was hearing this private family discussion or what he'd said about Glenda or Connor. I leaned further away from the bed and couldn't see him directly, just a reflection in one of the ornate mirrors, and Zinc's back. I'd read somewhere that servants are invisible to the people they work for. And I was less than that, more like a family beagle but not as loveable.

Sergei coughed and rubbed his face, bandaged and not. I squinted at the reflection and saw that he looked haggard, one eye gone, the other seeing the world through a *rheumy*, as Zinc had described it earlier and I had to look the term up. Disgusting. Poor man. "Ransom is loyal," Sergei continued, "his insights invaluable but in the end, it's your own counsel that is the most useful. While my brain is clear, we need to talk about your preparation. Strategies for remaining first, protecting our financial empire. Recruit friends for their talent but understand they may become enemies. And for money almost anyone can be bought. Fortunately, we have more than anyone." I heard what might have been a coughing laugh from Sergei.

Doctors had been candid with Zinc; any number of complications could take Sergei's life. His father was often formal and dismissive, Zinc had told me, but he knew the man loved him even if he never said it.

"I've finished the portfolio you gave me, Father. I understand the dangers and have a sense for the intrigue. But Machiavelli I'm not."

"You must be, son. You're now in charge of a financial empire bigger than most countries. The essence of *The Prince* is practical advice even if it is over six hundred years old. Don't put your private conscience ahead of what must be done to save our world. Gnashing your teeth is weakness. Understand your enemies. Violence, physical or economic, is only a tool, used judiciously to protect us. Once you realize what must be done, do it. Failure to act is your enemy. If opponents see you as weak and indecisive, they will sense opportunity. Ruthlessness in defense of our world is not one-dimensional; there are degrees of down and dirty, open or clandestine, surgical or a cavalry charge, taking their money or taking their life. Crushing an adversary can preclude future violence. Understood?"

Zinc seemed caught in mid-breath and touched the bed to keep his balance. "We h…have two known enemies of our class," Zinc eventually responded. "One wants government reform and the other our heads."

"Well said. Worry about the liberals and AR2 another time. It's the Christian Dominionists who are the immediate threat. They've infiltrated and run all the main churches and many schools. Worse, they recruit the gullible with gibberish and fear even as they raise an army of fanatics. And politicians owned and operated by the Dominionists who see dithering as a virtue paralyze our government. AR2 is just liberal do-gooders with great communication skills but no balls."

Zinc gave me a quick glance, like he was rubbing an itch on his leg. I sensed he didn't want to remind Sergei I was here.

"What are you thinking?"

"Father, I want to protect our empire but I'm no warrior. Not like you."

"But you're a McClain. Hop on the bed, son, and let's plot. We'll find your inner Machiavelli."

Sergei laughed, Zinc pressed his lips together, and I did my best to remain invisible but with rabbit ears.

CHAPTER 19

Zinc's calm seemed shredded after we got back. His body was twitching, his lips pinching in and pushing out. Sergei's advice and strategy had been harsh and my sense was Zinc was a sweet, nonviolent kind of man despite his demeanor.

"I'm going to have my face changed," he announced as we sat on stools in the small kitchen nook in his suite. "No one can stop me now. If I'm going to be assassinated I might as well have a pretty face." His words raced, the hysteria matching the silliness of the topic.

"Why?" I asked, confused. A panic attack, I decided, a screen between the reality of his new role and his carefree life as a rich teenager. He was floundering, overwhelmed, self-doubting. All understandable. This was not a life either of us wanted. I had to bring him back, build his confidence, make him strong, for all of us to survive.

"I want to be beautiful," Zinc continued in a monotone, "someone people won't wince at when they look at my face."

"Do I wince?"

"No, not that I've noticed."

"May I express my opinion?"

"Stop it, Spartak. I've given you per...mission to be yourself around me."

I touched Zinc's hand. His were the words of someone in power to someone with none. He was clueless about the gulf between our worlds. It wasn't intentional but it was reality. And it cut. Fear and responsibility were new experiences for Zinc but just part of life for downers. You grow up quick when subsistence was your hope and neighbor kids liked to pummel anyone weaker. And he had a personal security squad with pistols.

"You've been very generous with me, Zinc. I also know my legal position, as your property under the law. So, please forgive me if I'm cautious."

Zinc squeezed the back of my neck. "You sure aren't cautious in bed," he said. "A dom slave boy. What would people think?"

"They'd be jealous. So let's not tell 'em." I grinned.

Yeah, I was aggressive. And we both liked it. But this discussion was about curing Zinc's lack of confidence. I thought about the best psychology to use. I needed to be compelling, maybe even eloquent to connect and save us both. *Think before engaging mouth.* Always a good principle. I touched his chin.

"Please don't change your face. You're not a freak; you're just different and different is sexy in this age of cheap perfection. When everyone is beautiful, what defines beauty? A handsome man who looks like a million others? For what it's worth, I like you the way you are. You're masculine, kind of like a boxer who broke his nose in the ring. I love the way it jags and hope you like what you see looking AT me and IN me. We're more than surface. You're making a statement about independence and strength of character. You dare to be different; I admire that. And you're becoming a leader, untested, but you'll be brilliant."

"Do you believe that?" His face looked hungry, almost desperate for the right answer. And it was easy to give.

"Yes. As I've gotten to know you, I glimpse a special power. I even see chivalry within you, rare for your class, hungry to come out. Have confidence in yourself." I leaned close, running my fingers through Zinc's hair. I could sense heat rising between us. But sex right now was less important than talking. Zinc needed self-confidence more than fucking.

"And…and…I s…s…stutter. It's humiliating. I have been with d...doctors my whole life."

This surprised me; I thought we'd been through this.

"I am pretty good at h…iding it, just nod…ding, smiling, looking aloof or mean."

"Zinc, please let me partner with you on this. I don't care about it but if it bothers you, we'll work together."

"You'd do that?"

"Even if I wasn't your slave boy. I'll bet there are exercises you're supposed to follow and you don't. Right?"

"Yes, and I've tried them all. I r…remember in the seventh grade when Mrs. Reilly called on me in his…tory class to read. They all laughed at me. I can't forget it."

"We'll fix it, Zinc."

He ran a finger down my nose then kissed it. Time to move on and not get sidetracked.

"I think I read in a gossip column," I teased, "that there are now twenty-three thousand women who look exactly like your mother—olive-skinned, dark-haired beauties." I hoped Zinc wouldn't be offended.

"Can you imagine if they all got t…together?" Zinc's snicker burst into laughter so hard he slipped off the stool and grabbed me. I gripped the corner of the bar and kept us both from hitting the floor.

"May I touch the object of our discussion?"

"Any time."

I ran fingers around his face, down his crooked nose, slow, teasing with affection, pinching his chin, around his full lips, pushing a finger inside his mouth, as I had that first night together. Zinc bit lightly with his teeth and sucked. I placed a palm against his cheek.

"Stay yourself." I cared for him; a good man for someone born to staggering wealth and likely convinced he'd earned it. But I didn't know how he perceived reality. Zinc remained mostly an unknown. And lively sex between horny teenagers was no test for integrity and honor. He could easily get tired of me or find another boy after he gained confidence. Most anyone would be hot to bed a Twelver, hom or het.

There was a long silence. Zinc seemed to examine me.

"God you're beautiful."

"Stop it, Zinc." I wasn't getting through. Switch directions. "I don't know your religious views, but if we are created in God's image, might he have spent extra time stylizing your face, a unique man, perhaps for a special purpose?"

He began to speak and couldn't, then started laughing. "I feel so idiotic and vain. And you're trying h…hard to make me focus on what's important. Such a HORRID argument! You win!"

He cleared his throat, hands on my shoulders. "Do you want to compete in the Olympics? The trials are in four months."

I blanched, the question unexpected. It was my dream but my current situation seemed more challenging than the games.

"Yes."

"Wonderful. You deserve the glory."

"Thank you." I hadn't realized I'd been holding my breath. "I'll try to make you proud." My eyes watered.

"You already make me proud. Are you ready to return to school?"

"I want to but..."

"But what?"

"I worked hard for three years to establish myself and make friends…so that people didn't just see me as another downer boy. Most eventually treated me as an equal, with respect, at least once they learned that kids from my neighborhood know how to fight and win if they wanted to survive."

"So you beat the crap out of bullies?"

"A few."

"That's solar."

I bit my lip, nervous about what I needed to say. "If I go back to the academy, I don't want to be pitied."

"So being with me makes you an object of pity?"

"No! Please. You know what I mean. High school is all about cliques and the Slave Boy Club has only one member. And…I must face Coach."

"I'll go with you, if you like. My mother made the selection and paid his enormous fee. I guess that gives me some influence. She has fabulous taste. In slaves, not coaches."

Funny, yes, but with a rapier thrust as the punch line. "I need to talk to Coach alone. He was my hero, gave me confidence and skills to survive, before he betrayed me."

"And brought us together." Zinc stood and pulled me to my feet, hands resting on my waist, our faces inches apart. "You take my breath away, Spartak Jones." He kissed me lightly on the tip of my nose. "But enough wallowing in self pity. Be the Spartak I know and admire, s… strong and proud even if your life is a little mix…mixed up right now. You're extraordinary."

We touched foreheads. After a deep sigh, he continued. "And I'll grow up. You're more a m…man, more an adult than I am. I promise to be less self-absorbed and meet your standards, if that's possible. Tell me when I fall short. Pl…ease! I need it. No one else will be honest."

He pulled back, holding me at arm's length. "And I admit I'm s… scared about the future and if I have what's needed. It all seems so big and n…nasty. But we'll be there for each other." He grinned. "And… my face stays unchanged! I listen to my slave boy. You have to look at it, I don't."

I pulled him close, hoping this was past us, not sure why it was even an issue. My world of street fights, petty crime, and getting enough to eat was easier to understand than this odd new universe.

He took me by the hand and pulled me to his room. "I know you like to read. Let's start tonight on *The Prince.* We may need its wisdom."

"I'll bet that's second on your list."

CHAPTER 20

A HOVER-CRUISER TOOK US TO TREASURE Island, an odd name for a parcel of land under water since 2052 because of sea rise. With most buildings removed or abandoned, it was now a giant aqua farm with the best oysters on the west coast.

Sonia squeezed my hand as her driver, a member of her security team, docked at a wooden pier. She led me inside the four-story barge, all glass on the sides and a white nautilus-shaped roof, named after Ayn Rand, a famous libertarian novelist. I'd read a couple of her books—required study items at OA—and didn't care for her views. I knew all too well about the "value of selfishness" she preached. Maybe *Atlas Shrugged* and Rand's other polemics made the rich feel less guilty. Of course, they were fiction. A second craft with five additional security members tied up behind. The guards waited outside.

The middle-aged maître d', his auburn hair twisted into horns, rose from his stool as we approached. He bent at the waist, a formal nod and his blue caftan shimmered like sun on ocean, irresistible to watch.

"We are honored to have you with us, Ms. Washington. Your uncle is in his usual spot."

"Thank you, Mr. Rupert." She shook his hand. "And this is my special friend, Spartak Jones from Ogden Academy."

"I recognize you, young man, from sports stories. Congratulations."

I took the man's warm hand and smiled. "Thank you, sir."

The inside walls were partially covered by flowering and scented vines. I stared up at a magnificent life-size replica of a gray whale, extinct for decades, hanging from the ceiling. Tabletops were beige stone aggregate of assorted seashells and chairs had carved legs, depicting various aquatic life. In a corner was a bronze statue of Poseidon.

Sonia led us across the restaurant to a booth hidden from view until you turned a corner behind a giant potted palm. A seated man smiled and stood as we neared, embracing Sonia.

"Uncle, this is Spartak Jones."

We shook hands; his grip firm, skin dry. Then I recognized him, the craggy face and white dreadlocks. "Oh, OH! You're Justice Washington! He's your uncle?" My heart pounded.

"Please sit." He gestured. "I've been anxious to meet you." He wore an old-fashioned pair of wire-rimmed spectacles and was dressed in a dark business suit with a green silk brocade tie. None of the high Napoleonic collars and neon colors so popular with the gentry.

"Yes, Spartak," Sonia said, "my uncle and role model."

Why would he want to meet a downer boy? "I'm honored and a bit humbled, sir. I've studied many of your opinions on the Court and I know what you did on *Sasser*, one of three no votes. Your arguments were powerful. Thank you."

"And ultimately unpersuasive. If I had carried the day, we likely would never have had this opportunity to meet, young man. I am familiar with your history. Some time ago, Sonia told me about this remarkable young man at school and I have followed your career closely ever since. I hope you will be on the Olympic team. Given what has happened and the increasingly tenuous state of government, you may well become a symbol for freedom."

I stared and eventually realized my mouth was open, something that was happening with increased frequency. Justice Washington seemed to study my reaction.

"Me, sir? I'm just a teenage downer."

"Oh, I think you are far more than that. Let's order and talk."

* * *

As we ate lunch, I observed my hosts in between glances at the graceful San Francisco skyline. The grilled oysters were sublime. I'd never eaten this kind of seafood before or most any seafood since it was rare in the wild due to pollution and overfishing and way beyond anyone's family budget. Once nearly all the fish were gone, fishing bans had been put in place to great publicity. Odd how that worked.

Sonia was nearly my height, slender yet with serious muscle. She came across as an elegant young woman, at times dainty; yet she was a member of the track team so she had to be tough. She wasn't a star, because she didn't put in the time, but she was solid. Her eyes were unusually large, more caramel than brown, more feline than standard issue. And she could swear like a lumberjack and make a snotty teenager flee in panic.

The justice had a grandfatherly countenance that exuded kindness. Yet something about him suggested tensile strength. His eyes were black, piercing at times, and proud. I felt completely inadequate and insignificant sitting between them.

"Uncle," Sonia said, "I want us to be open with Spartak. He's a dear man, smart, and my friend." She patted my forearm. "Let me start by being blunt." She addressed her uncle: "Don't you think the *Sasser* case could be a disaster for the Twelve?"

"Yes. And that was my argument in private with the other justices."

"So, why? Why would they engineer this? Why would they allow it? It's revolting and my Zinc is the first official slave owner since the Civil War. I love him and adore Spartak, but it isn't right."

"I've been a justice for over two decades and it's the worst decision not just in my tenure but in two centuries. So says the great liberal on the court." He leaned back in the booth. He picked up his porcelain coffee cup, pressing it to his lips and blowing the steam. "The barronials always make sure there are six votes. But why they did this is beyond comprehension."

"We're barronials."

"Yes, Sonia, but I'm the outlaw, allowed to sit on the court as a dissenting voice, someone they ignore because I have no real power. Liberals gave up, allowed themselves to be vilified and lost influence long ago. Having me there gives the illusion of democracy and rule of law at work." He set the cup down on its saucer, never taking a sip.

"Ironic, isn't it?" he said. "Two privileged blacks sitting in a restaurant with a gifted and charming white boy, son of poor parents, purchased openly, legally in 2115. And Ginny Sasser, a beautiful but penniless white girl, out there somewhere, her convoluted subjugation made legitimate by the court. Social class, not race, is our reality. And hubris."

I swallowed. People didn't talk like this, not in my world, not to me.

"If a business can own human genes, as the court determined in 2050, why not a person?" the judge asked.

The pain in his voice surprised me. I was now in a world parallel to my own.

"If a corporation is a person," the judge continued, looking at me, "then everything is just a financial transaction. And now we have this crazy decision born from a toxic brew. The debt-bond has roots going all the way back to the Great Recession of 2008 and the Panic of 2040. To a financial community obsessed with the middle class not paying its obligations and applying ever tightening chains. Democracy is on life-support." He touched his lips with the starched white napkin.

"But the Constitution—" she started to interrupt.

"—means whatever five justices say it means," he snapped. "Sorry, I didn't mean to bark. In this case six votes. The Twelve stayed out of it, disinterested, no financial stake. The orignalists on the court led the charge, absurdly quoting parts of the Constitution and even the histories of many Founding Fathers that owned slaves. All irrelevant. The word slave is never mentioned in the decision."

"It's pomposity," she said, looking at me. "Hunger for the next trophy. They did it because they could."

I looked up at the Bay Bridge, feeling like I was an invisible presence, hearing people talk about me. I had a hard time imagining myself as a trophy, particularly when I looked in the mirror in the morning. The view from the window offered little comfort, only a reminder of an America that was.

"It seems antithetical but there can be too much liberty. *Live and let live* is a noble goal until *live* devours everyone else. Until one man's freedom denies someone else of theirs," Washington argued even if no one was disagreeing, "and if there is no effective governmental apparatus to ensure fairness and protect rights. The libertarian philosophy runs deep in America. Let people do their thing, minimal interference by government. And this is the price—liberty run amuck for decades, a slave boy as confirmation."

Washington's expression softened as he looked at Sonia. "We both are a pejorative—liberals. Spartak, I believe an active and powerful government is the only counterbalance against rapacious business interests, unprincipled individuals and groups often all too willing to deceive, poison, and ruin in the name of their own liberty. Without us, the powerful face no limits, no scrutiny, pay no price and never face justice. My life's work is to return integrity and influence to the public sphere. I wear barronial scorn with pride." He shook his head. "Of course most people think I'm a fool."

She reached across me, pulled her uncle's hand to her lips and kissed it. "You're the man I admire most in the world."

"Don't let your father hear you say that."

"I know. He sees government as the enemy, useful for a narrow range of functions like the military so he can sell them no-bid contracts for million dollar toilets."

"Careful." The judge shook his head. He turned to me. "Sorry, son. I can get carried away in political talk and get preachy. Are you treated well? Is your family safe?"

"Yes sir, mostly. Zinc and Sonia are very kind to me. I'm just an object to the rest of the family. Maybe someday it will change. My family seems more secure, for now. Their rent is stable, less than they paid before and they get to keep the stipend for me being what I am. But I do worry about them."

"Do you see yourself remaining a slave?" he asked.

"No sir, at least I hope not. I treasure my freedom even in a downer world…and it seems more precious to me now that I don't have it. Zinc says he wants to give it to me but is afraid his mother or others might retaliate against my family or me. I understand I'm in a legal netherworld if he frees me. I heard you say that in court. It's scary. So he's trying to protect me. He really is a sweet man."

"It pains me to say it but, yes, I think his understanding is correct, you would be at risk. Ironic that slavery is the safer position. For now." He grunted and shook his head, clearly upset. "If I may venture elsewhere, does he force you to..." The judge's voice trailed off.

"No sir. He doesn't have to. I...I care for him."

"Extraordinary," the justice said. "So innocent and appealing. You are perfect for what's to come." He picked up two small volumes sitting on the corner of the table. "Here's a book I'd like you each to read. Sonia knows of my fascination with the real thing, a passion we share with the late Barron Ogden. I think you'll find it remarkably relevant. History has much to teach us."

"What?" I asked, scanning the frayed cover.

"It's called, *The Kidnapping of Edgardo Mortara*, by the historian David Kertzer, written in the early part of the last century about the creation of the Italian state in the 1860s."

I sat upright, spellbound. The man was magnetic and I was dumbfounded someone of his status would treat me so adult, as a barronial insider. Being with them made me want to speak in full sentences.

"In the middle of the 1800s," the judge began, "most of Italy was ruled by the Vatican and policed by a foreign army aligned with the pope. On a night in 1858, in Bologna, armed guards of the Inquisition entered the house of a Jewish merchant family. They seized the six-year-old son, Edgardo Mortara, claiming a former servant girl had seen him baptized. Under Vatican law no Jew could raise a Catholic child. She received a bounty for turning him in. It was a popular way to make money, one encouraged by local church officials who got special points with the pontiff for converting Jews, by force or otherwise. The boy was taken, despite the screaming protestations of the parents, and placed into a special monastery where he stayed for years until his conversion was complete. He eventually became a priest and never saw his parents again."

"That's disgusting," Sonia said.

"Yes, eventually much of Europe thought so too. The anger was fueled by the clever and well-financed campaign of the Rothschild family and other Enlightenment leaders. It keyed into a widespread but nascent movement to form an Italian state without the cruel indignities of the Catholic leadership. Eventually the Church collapsed as a secular power and retreated to where it is now, inside the Vatican walls. One kidnapping ended an empire. The proverbial straw."

"And the book is..." she said, flipping open the cover, "a first edition. I'm amazed." She ran her fingers over a missing corner. I knew that for both of us, real books were treasures not just chic ornaments.

"You don't see many originals," I said.

"Not much demand, I suspect," he said with a chuckle. "Kidnapping is a grotesque crime yet not all kidnappings are equal." He turned in his seat, looming over me. "In 2115, a gymnastic coach betrayed his prize athlete and the boy was kidnapped and sold into slavery."

The man looked directly into my eyes, making me squirm.

"You are Edgardo," he said.

CHAPTER 21

I STEPPED OUT THE SIDE ENTRANCE of the mansion and stared. Floating in front of me, about two feet off the ground, was a semitransparent, sea-green vehicle, undulating, there one second, gone the next, shaped something like an eel I'd seen at the aquarium. I couldn't see inside and touched it, half-expecting my hand to go through. It was hard, like glass. I dropped to my knees and looked underneath; nothing but quiet air and a low-pitched hum.

"Get in, Sherlock," Zinc said, laughing, as he walked up behind me and slapped my butt. As I stood, the top lifted open from the other side revealing six seats and a blinking control panel up front. Zinc hopped his rear end to the edge, swung over his legs, and sat. The vehicle rocked like it was floating on water.

"What is it?" I asked.

Ran walked by me, put one leg over the side, stepped in like it was easy and sat into the front seat. "Countdown," he said. Bright multi-colored screens opened up, hanging in the air. "Jump in, Spartak." He pointed with his thumb. "Let's take this babe for a ride."

"Wait," Zinc said. "He may be tired from our workout. Let this barge curtsey."

Ran laughed and the side of the machine tilted toward me. I put one foot inside, determined to look cool, and it suddenly lifted straight.

I caught my toe on the edge, landing across Zinc's lap, facedown.

"Not now, sweet lips," Zinc said, helping me sit up and strap in. The seats were deep and firm. The glass top closed and locked. I could see out. No obstruction in view, and utter silence. And no Connor or Mrs. McClain.

"Engage," Ran said, wrapping his right hand around something that looked like a human palm on a stick, only red in color. It seemed to mold about Ran's fingers. Two traditional uni-wheeled armored security vehicles were with us. "We've developed agile warships for land and space," Ran continued, looking ahead. As he pushed the machine into gear, it seemed to glide over the roadway. "This is a new class of El-Stat-Lev transport, a battle cruiser, and a distant cousin to the old maglev trains that connect San Francisco to LA, with the ability to go invisible to the eye or any kind of detector. A new toy from McClain Enterprises."

"What's it stand for?"

"Electrostatic levitation, using an electric field to lift a charged object. It can easily reach 400 mph, go over water or land, and take direct hits from solar cannons while delivering enough sonic blast to incapacitate an army."

"Okay," I said, not really wanting to consider the kill capacity. "Sounds useful. But you need to find a better name. An actual door would be nice."

"I'll tell the engineers," Ran said with a chuckle.

We floated over the Golden Gate Bridge, about twenty feet above the roadway, and rose into the Marin Headlands, pulling over the road barriers at one point and floating up and over scrub brush hills, all in silence. We approached a series of World War II concrete bunkers and lookout posts atop the cliffs facing the Pacific Ocean. They appeared abandoned, broken columns and walls covered in graffiti from generations of campfires, sex parties, and reaper encampments. Roads were now blocked and no-trespassing signs warned of unstable soil, landslides, lethal contamination, and private property.

The cruiser pulled into what appeared to be an abandoned concrete stall. But it opened on command revealing a garage. Other vehicles were inside as well. Ransom parked, led us to the elevator, down ten floors and through a hallway into a large well-lit laboratory. Ceilings were twelve feet tall, all concrete, just like the floor.

"This was an underground staging area, heavily reconstructed, that most people never knew about or, if they did, assumed it was lost to erosion and decay a century ago," Ran explained and nodded to several workers in white lab coats as we walked past. Zinc reached down and took my hand as we moved toward a rack of clothing.

"Spartak, this is our finishing school for new weapons technology," Ran continued. "We have numerous labs and testing sites around the world. The most interesting results are brought here in secret. Not everything is sold or shared. It gives us an advantage if we need one."

A raven-haired woman in a skintight, flesh-colored suit walked up to us, a severe grandma face atop a teenage body. "This is Dr. Sally Merkel, chief of our protective gear unit."

"Young men, good to meet you," she said with a slight east European accent. "You," she commanded, pointing at me, "lift this box. Now."

I blinked but walked over to the three-foot square plastic container. Inside was broken concrete and iron bars. I tested one side; maybe my weight plus a few pounds. Given the audience, I had to do this…and maybe show off a little. I slid the box to my thigh, braced myself and lifted. It came a few inches off the tabletop. I groaned and hoisted it to my chest.

"You may place it down again, young man."

"That's serious dead weight."

"And yet you hoisted it. Few men could. Impressive."

I looked to see if Zinc heard the compliment. His eyes were on her. She walked to the side of the box and lifted it effortless with both hands, then moved it to one forearm. "Easy, no?" Dr. Merkel laughed, watching our expressions.

"Sally is wearing a multipurpose garment, a full body, two piece, top and bottom plus gloves, exoskeleton that gives her strength. We call them XOs. And it also does this…Ready?"

She rubbed her leather-soled boots on the floor and gripped a nearby pipe. "Proceed."

Ran lifted a red-orange solar pistol from the table, pointed it and a sunshine blast hit her midsection.

She swayed but remained standing, her smile unchanged throughout.

"How?" Zinc asked.

"The second XO function is deflection, a type of thin nano-silk armor," Ran explained. "It also gives her that fabulous physique."

"What I like most." Her lips curled modestly while hands slinked over her hips. "No bulges in the wrong places."

"It carried the current to the pipe and the boots, like an old-fashioned Ben Franklin lightning rod. She remains unharmed," Ran explained. "Solar pistols are what the military and most private enforcer groups use. The XOs also work with our sonics should an enemy grab one of our pistols."

"Sir," I asked, "how likely is the wearer to be near a ground?"

"The boots alone are an effective conduit. She used the pipe as a backup. Always play it safe." He pointed to her boot.

She lifted her foot and a thick, three-inch spike with a knife-edge popped from the back of the heel at ninety degrees. "You can deploy just by training your calf muscle to move in a certain way," she said. "It offers insurance and an unexpected weapon in a fight. A range of other useful equipment is embedded within the boot lining. To help distract attention from their purpose, they're designed to look like the current teenage fashion craze."

She turned her boots sideways. "You have to learn to walk in these. The sole is quite thick and hardened to withstand the kickback from the blade into a hard surface such as concrete. And it adds over two inches to your height."

"Yes!" I shouted, pumping a fist in the air. "I'll be almost as tall as my lord and master." I grinned up at Zinc.

"Do you have an XO gag for his mouth?" Zinc wrapped his arms around me and I leaned back into him. Zinc rubbed his knuckles into my scalp.

"Stop it!"

"There are also gloves," Ransom continued, shaking his head, "... pay attention guys...socks and a pullover hood with a Liteon type mask to drape over your face. You can be fully shielded." Ran tossed a small bundle to me. "Strip down and put this on. With normal clothes on top, no one would know you're wearing it. It feels much like a standard undergarment."

I caught it, placed in on the table and began to disrobe. I wondered if he was doing this for Zinc's amusement. "Everything off?"

"Everything."

Naked again. I turned around for a little privacy. I assumed they could handle some boy butt. The fabric felt like skin, flexible, comfortable. Satisfied, I faced the group.

"Oh, my," Dr. Merkel said, bringing a hand to her mouth.

"Check yourself in the mirror," Zinc said, presenting the full brilliance of his perfect white teeth.

I turned. "Nooo!" I used both hands to cover my crotch, mortified. I reached inside the tights and adjusted myself as best I could, given there was nowhere to hide anything.

"Hot! Hot! Hot!" Zinc applauded.

"Notice how the color of the XO suddenly shifts to match Spartak's new reddish skin pigment," Ran pointed out with a straight face. "Some models have this chameleon feature for camouflage."

"Pick up the box now," Merkel ordered.

Turning around, I lifted the box with ease, like it was a carton of milk. "Astounding. Will it repel a lead or plastic bullet?" I set the box down.

"For the untrained," Ran answered, "it could leave a welt or knock you down but no real damage. I'll teach you how to dissipate the force of a bullet."

"Look who's here!" Connor McClain said mockingly as he and his mother sauntered up to us. "Our hunky slave boy in a bad ballet costume."

"Shut up," Zinc snapped.

"Hello son," Mrs. McClain cooed, allowing the eldest to kiss her cheek. Her expression, as she glanced at me, suggested roadkill. "So this is what you want us to wear? You expect me to look like a circus freak?"

"Mother, please be respectful." Zinc's voice had an edge.

"Why? He's just a trinket."

"A low-life charity boy," Connor said with a smirk.

I felt heat as I looked away, one part humiliation, ten parts anger. This was getting more difficult to suppress with each encounter. At some point I'd ignite which was what Connor wanted. Stay calm, stay calm, be numb, Rhonda's mantra.

Connor walked over and pushed me. "Ballerina boy." I fell back and Connor shoved again. "Is your butt sore?"

"Spartak," Zinc commanded in a loud voice, "let's test the equipment. My l…loving brother wants you to lift him overhead and go for a jog."

"Yes, Master," I shouted, stern-voiced to hide the jubilation, "as you order!"

"Mother…!" Connor's eyes were wide, panicked.

I swiveled Connor around and entwined one hand in his belt the other in his shirt collar, and flipped him overhead, his face to the ceiling. I ran between workbenches with Connor raised high, pumping my arms up and down every few yards like I was holding a foam barbell. I sprinted around the lab, Connor screaming, arms and legs flailing, a helpless rag doll.

"Mother…!"

When I brought him back, standing him on his feet, the front of the guy's pants were wet. Connor stomped away, tears welling.

"You horrible boy!" Glenda screamed at me. I winced, closing my eyes, waiting to be punished. I really hated her. Nothing went right with them. But revenge was sweet even at a price.

Zinc jumped between us, grabbing her hand midway to my face.

"Mother, I ordered him to do it. Blame me if you are unhappy. Connor is a bully and, frankly, a real jerk. Warn him. I will NOT accept him abusing my friend. I've had it with him."

He turned and glared at his brother who was standing behind a nearby bench. "I need to start standing tall because of what's happened to Father. We are under attack. And this is my first effort. We will NOT have fights within the family. And Spartak is NOW family!"

Connor was wide-eyed and silent, turning away, clearly intimidated. Glenda seemed shocked, stunned by the ferocity of her son's put-down. It felt fabulous. She touched his face, snarling toward me.

"Mother, I mean it. Don't push me!"

"Okay," Ran said after a long silence, "Zinc, Spartak, let's do weapons and combat training at the west end while Dr. Merkel works with Mrs. McClain and Connor."

I grabbed my clothes, Zinc took his XO, and the three of us jogged away.

"Spartak, did you play with swords as a kid?" Ransom asked lightly.

"Yes." Just a piece of wood.

"I suspected you had and have something extraordinary to show you. And both of you be warned. We'll start doing an intense workout every afternoon going forward followed by combat training."

"I thought we just did combat," I teased.

Zinc gave me a shove.

CHAPTER 22

"Cowards!" Ransom Bolt said, spraying spittle. "The unthinkable has happened. Minutes ago, forty members of the US Senate and 120 members of the House filed a joint resolution calling for the US government to cede control to the Dominionist Council to prepare for the return of Jesus next year."

"Insane," Zinc said. "It's treason."

We were in Henry's Room. Most of Ran's top security people, about a dozen, were seated around us.

"It shows the extent of Dominionist influence over key legislators," Sonia said. "This is who they own. That may prove useful. And we can't say we didn't know it was coming or something like it."

"Consider this as we watch this live stream from the Danville Coliseum in East Bay," Ran said, turning to the screen.

A blurry image, moving as we watched, a bit shaky, showed hundreds of young men chanting, shirtless, jumping up with arms raised in fists. Audio was intermittent. Zinc, Sonia, and I leaned forward. I was more comfortable in such settings but feared any miscalculation on my part could bring disaster.

"We have four agents inside," Ransom continued in his no-nonsense, impossibly deep baritone. "We've infiltrated the Dominionist youth brigade and they're surreptitiously sending these images with SubQs and eye-cams, and transmitting through various options. The leadership and, worse, the young militants, are brutal. A young FBI agent was found beaten up and mutilated two weeks ago in Florida. He attended a training camp."

"There are those headbands again," I said, looking at dark blue strips of cloth wrapped around their heads with an oval crest at the center—a gold cross over silver stars.

"Yes," Ran responded. "It's like the Nazi Storm Trooper uniform being unveiled, the council coming out of the closet, ready for the takeover."

"Liberation theology," Sonia said, turning to me, "claims the anointed ones are to take over the powers of Darkness from Satan and his demons on earth. An elite new breed will subdue all the enemies of Christ as they gain power. All secular authorities must submit to them or be destroyed."

"And these are their shock troops?" I shivered as I watched their faces, angry one moment, ready to kill, then their eyes rolling back in their heads, entranced but still bouncing up and down.

"It appears that way," Ran answered.

"Oh my God!" blurted one of the women against the wall as young men in the arena took whips, dozens of tiny weighted strands, from their belts and started flaying their backs. Over and over, blood splattering, faces uplifted, joyous.

"Perhaps some kind of hallucinogen," an older man suggested.

We watched in horror until the image disappeared.

"Damn," Ran snapped. "I hope they didn't catch one of our guys. We're now convinced the Jesusistas committed the murder of the young man in New York City."

"Bastards!" Zinc muttered.

"The FBI agent in Florida," Ran went on, "before he was captured, transmitted some interesting material, taken in a smaller meeting room, just a few hundred people. Here it is. It's shot from the side. Note the American flag with the golden crucifix sewn over the stars. That appears to be what's on the headbands."

"Frightening," Sonia said. "No, sad. What happened to religion?"

"Here is Bishop Perry, the iron man of the movement, one of three leaders, giving a pep talk," Ran said. "For decades some conservative religious types denied man-made climate change. Now that disaster is here, it's a sign from God. Flexibility is important in politics. Here's the Bishop."

"Everything points to the final days of man on Earth—rising sea levels, a melted ice cap, droughts, floods, ferocious storms, polluted waters, dead oceans, epidemics, wars over scarce food resources, millions starving and collapsing governments. For decades, fools talked about humans creating the problem. Those close to God know the truth. It is time to act. The Old Testament offers many creative means to smite enemies of God. Social norms and taboos must give way when the prize is Heaven itself. All is Prophesized! The Lord returns next year!"

"Halleluiah! Halleluiah! Halleluiah!"

"It certainly makes it clear who was behind Cedric's murder," Zinc snapped. "Fucking hypocrites."

"Hints, yes, but doesn't confirm," Sonia said, looking firm and touched Zinc's arm. "I'm shocked at the brazenness. At first some claimed AR2 was behind the murder. But that was a ruse, I suspect."

"This looks like a photo op," I suggested, hoping I had something to contribute. "If this group has the technical skill to try and assassinate Mr. McClain, it has the means to hide this kind of show from its enemies. This looks like they wanted it seen, a staged event, like theater, transmitted to send a message. And fear. And it ties in with what you just told us about the members of Congress announcing their treason. It's like a package. To scare government into more concessions or provoke them to attack to ignite a mass religious insurrection."

"Actually, even if the government wanted to put them down, there's some doubt the military would support the president," Ran said.

"Our own military?" Zinc said, astonished.

"There's backstory starting a century ago, fundamentalist religious groups proselytizing the military. Unit cohesion in many cases was built around belief in Jesus. If you didn't believe—say you were a Jew, Muslim, Buddhist or even an atheist—you kept your mouth shut.

Four-star generals and admirals, in clear violation of military rules, went around to religious events in uniform claiming America was a Christian country and calling for a Christian military. The military peacocks were out in full display when Congress named Christianity as the official religion. Two generals, one marine, the other army, sit on the Dominionist Council. It's unclear what the military would do if the president ordered military intervention against the Jesusistas."

"Amazing," I said, touching the edge of the XO sleeve under my shirt. "Is this one of the reasons you don't share all developments at McClain weapons labs?"

"Not all work is done for the military," Zinc explained. "We fund much of it ourselves and have no obligations to share."

"If the military were to abandon the nation it's sworn to defend, a straightforward fight might not easily succeed." Ran leaned back in his chair. "Saving democracy might require unconventional tactics."

I was struggling and wanted to understand. "Or maybe unconventional alliances."

"Say more," Ran said, turning to me and leaning his elbows on the table.

Opening my mouth was often a problem and I knew some would be upset. "I'm likely the only one of my social class in the room. If my experience with downers in the Bay Area is true nationwide, I don't believe more than a small percentage support the End Timers. But AR2's message resonates, we are not equal and our lives can be harsh. And we are the vast majority of Americans, even if now powerless. Basically we just want to survive and be treated fairly, to have hope for a better life. I suspect most downers think the Dominionists are even more predatory than the barronials."

I heard a gasp. I looked around the room, not sure who editorialized. People were staring and it was hard to read the reactions. They were probably not ready to elect me prom king.

"Continue," Ran said, leaning back against a wall and folding his arms.

"AR2 says democracy doesn't exist in America. And my experience suggests they're correct. My life is quite different from what they teach in school, what's taught is not reality. We may be poor but we're not stupid." I noticed some scowls from security officials. Zinc was watching me closely. "I know I'm still not a legal adult and I'm not trying to offend anyone but if you had to intervene against the Dominionists, would you be seeking to preserve what we have or create something new? Maybe, like the legend suggests, what once was? An America that used to be. Can you offer us a better life?"

Expressions around the room were hard to read, lots of squints. I knew they were all comfortable with the status quo. Sonia had a tight little smile.

"Spartak," she said, "don't be silenced by scowls. I want to hear what you have to say."

I was quiet, trying to think about how far I should go. I thought of my brother and sister. "If you have no power, it gives you a different experience. Enforcers don't protect downers, they exploit them, rape them, steal from them." People seemed startled, twisting in their seats. "I've been handcuffed by a female cop and…" My voice got a little shaky. "And…raped…more than once. To refuse would mean being put in jail and maybe my family harmed." There was total silence. "Barronial thugs raid our neighborhoods for much the same reason, beat us up for sport. We have no justice. They almost kidnapped my nine-year-old brother." I stopped just ahead of tears and breathed deep, not wanting to get even more emotional. I needed to tell our story like an adult. This was important. "Knowing that a war would bring equal treatment under the law, that fairness would return, might make a big difference in support if people believed it was real and not just public relations bullshit." I decided I'd likely hung myself and shrugged as I slid back into my seat. I was afraid to look at Zinc.

Ransom nodded. "Well stated! You are a remarkable young man. I value your opinion and want you to give it to me without syrup even if you think it runs counter to my thinking. Don't worry about offending anyone here. I like being challenged by people who think deep. You have a good mind. And, frankly, you're right, you've had a different life experience than anyone at this table. And that's valuable." He grinned. "Hard to believe you're only sixteen. And," he paused, his face dark, "we need to deal with the enforcer issue. I want the name of the officer. That's intolerable. Let's talk privately."

"Nicely done," Sonia said loudly enough so everyone in the room could hear. I could see dampness in her eyes.

Zinc squeezed my knee. I guess I'd gotten through this session in a favorable way or he was horny.

* * *

"Zinc, please, must I go?"

"Yes." He looked a little contrite. "Please, as a favor to me." He put his arms around me. "You need to build a relationship with my mother. It's not impossible. This new circle theater in the Civic Center was made for *phantas* cinema and is extraordinary. It will mean a lot to her, an opening for you. If she knew you, she'd love you."

Incredulous, I looked at Zinc's face and then down at the floor. The man was oblivious, an innocent. The volume of bile in my throat seemed directly proportionate to the proximity of Zinc's mother and brother. But slaves needed to pick their battles.

"Please don't leave me alone with them."

"They're already headed to the theater for a pre-show party. We'll wear the XOs under our tuxedoes and you'll take a weapon of your choice from the armory." He grinned. "An adventure. And we need to get used to it."

"Don't guards stop people armed for war from public events?"

"Not me. Besides, we'll only take prototypes that aren't visible or detectible with their scanners. Just ours."

It was hard to imagine this would turn out well. I suspected Zinc's machismo act was to protect himself emotionally from what had happened to his father and friends. He needed to have peace in his household. And he'd been spending countless hours meeting with his dad whenever Sergei was lucid, then studying material from the cube his dad gave him, coming back to our room wound tight. At first Zinc kept the contents to himself then invited me to study with him. It made me hope I was becoming more a confidant and less a slave. Everything depended on Zinc.

We looked through the weapons room in the basement and selected some small stun grenades. "Good choice," Zinc said, laughing, like it was amusing. "Let's go."

It only took a few minutes in an armored uni, driving past the gold-domed City Hall, to reach an underground garage. Inside, the theater ceiling was forty-feet high with Corinthian stone columns every twenty feet around the walls in a perfect circle.

A raised stage was at the center with luxury contour seats surrounding it. The ceiling was in the style of the Sistine Chapel except scenes from California history were featured, not biblical stories. In the center was a glass circle with silver tubes and black squares inside, some kind of projection and enhancement equipment. A similar circle was directly underneath at the center of the stage, and a dozen special projectors dotted the walls. Phantasmagorical cinema, 360-degree projectors, created a virtual image almost touchable.

With Zinc beside me, we walked through a door framed with thousands of red roses into a private party room. Glenda McClain was surrounded by dozens of friends, well-wishers and gossip columnists. I saw Connor in a corner with other teens, some from school.

We walked up to Mrs. McClain. She ignored me and kissed her son.

"Mother!" he chastised her.

"Hello, Spartak," she said with a raised eyebrow, pursed lips, and a brusque tone. "Thanks for coming." The actress turned and walked away.

"Ohhh, Tarley Rose," she said with enthusiasm, pointing at a nearby woman, "the star of the *Times.*"

The *Times* reporter, a middle-aged brunette dressed to black sequined perfection, watched Zinc and me. After Glenda moved on, she whispered into her wrist zan, then pointed it in our direction. A moment later she alerted her assistant. He raised a DIMM4 at us and began to move closer, capturing our image.

"Glenda," Tarley Rose asked in a loud voice, a few feet from the actress. "Is this the Sasser boy, the slave you purchased for your son? Did you buy Spartak Jones, the beautiful Olympic contender as a birthday gift?"

Glenda swung around, her shock obvious. And intense irritation.

Zinc had told me earlier she planned to leak the story next week, about the family owning one of the world's premier athletes. This could spoil her premier coverage. Lumins focused on us from a dozen lapel patches, eyes, and wrists.

"Spartak! Spartak!" shouted three reporters. The crowd turned and faced us.

Zinc put his arm around me. "Smile!" We mugged. "Let's go!" Holding hands, we fled the room, laughing.

An hour later, Glenda Ogden McClain graciously acknowledged the ovation from the overflow crowd, stepping up to the round platform. She blew kisses and thanked them humbly for attending. This phantas was a love story, she explained, set in Paris during the First World War.

I had never seen a complete phantas cinema before, just snippets. The oversized figures projected onto the platform seemed as real as Mrs. McClain had been, standing in the same space just minutes before. You felt like you were part of the action, inside each scene, next to the actors, sensing their emotions, participating. Zinc said there were stunning new advancements in technology coming out in a year or two, exclusive to McClain Enterprises, that would make this comparable to an old-time newsreel. I lost myself in the tale, focusing on the story, not the actress. And she did well; it was a good show.

"Selfish boy!" she snapped at me as we got in our separate armored vans to return home.

"Mother!" was Zinc's unrepentant reply.

CHAPTER 23

SAN FRANCISCO, (Chronicle-Guardian)—
The first human being bought and sold since the controversial Sasser v Peabody decision of the US Supreme Court is a 16-year-old athlete in San Francisco. The world's richest family signed a debt-bond agreement with a downer family and took its son, Spartak Jones, a student at Ogden Academy and the national champion in high school gymnastics, as an eighteenth birthday gift for Zinc Ogden McClain. Mrs. Glenda McClain, the noted stage and phantas actress, confirmed the purchase through a spokesman.

Our faces were on every news program, gossip sheet, and political channel in the western world. I scanned one site after another and was appalled.

Everyone, it seemed, was curious about the "handsome slave boy" and his wealthy owner. Many commentators were angry, often disgusted, and criticized the transaction openly, such was the level of repulsion. Others, just as venomous, felt it was proper, giving a poor boy a new life, the wealthy showing social responsibility toward the disadvantaged, offering opportunities. A few said it was the natural progression of God's design: the wealthy are favored and must control those who are not. They were talking about me.

Most of it was just pointless gossip, focused on the "sexy, hunky gymnast" and his trillionaire owner, often showing Zinc in unflattering photos and me with my shirt off. I'd never thought of myself this way. I knew Zinc was both proud and hurt. It was like it was about some other Spartak Jones. But it wasn't and the slave-owner dynamic didn't really exist between us. At times I thought I was Zinc's only confidant, bringing him emotional release amidst the anguish from his long-held insecurities and the stresses within his family. His life was not easy.

Old DIMMs of me at tournaments in my gym outfits including my sweat-popping high-bar poster, one showing me in a shower with my butt hanging out, seemed omnipresent. Where did they get this? I felt exposed, almost raw with humiliation. I never imagined I would receive this kind of sleazy attention.

I worked out with Zinc at the gym this morning, neither of us mentioning the publicity, maybe too embarrassed, before going our separate ways. Zinc to his father and me to my piano. He'd purchased a concert grand for me and set it up in a small soundproof room in the second basement, not far from the security rooms.

I had a performance set at week's end at the OA recital hall featuring a piece I loved although not my favorite. Chopin's *Masurkas, Opus 6*—lyrical, soothing, deep—the music filled my head. I also had to work on two other Nocturnes for possible encore performances. It didn't always happen, but it was thrilling and scary when it did. My family would attend as well as Zinc, Sonia, and friends. Everything had to be perfect. I wondered, sometimes, what Frederick Chopin was like, the personality he was to create such beauty. All I did was play his music.

When alone, I used circuitous routes around the compound to evade Connor and Mrs. McClain. As I jogged into a back hallway, I stopped. Connor and two of his thug friends from school, Tony and Marco, were waiting. They circled around me, mocking with the usual names.

"Hey dick lips."

I'd only defended myself that once, when Connor tried to rape me. Not counting what happened at the weapons lab. So, maybe twice. And the first day of school in our dorm room. Okay so three times. But Zinc told me yesterday—no, ordered me—to fight back if provoked and use all force necessary. "Connor must be brought in line," he'd said. "He needs to respect you."

"How's our little hom slave?" Connor shoved me against the wall. "Take him."

"Please, no, Connor!"

Tony and Marco, both big guys, grabbed my arms and held me.

"You're so clever sneaking around the back hallways but security lumins are everywhere, smart boy. And you wear your cow tracker." Connor and his friends laughed. He punched me in the gut with little impact. I thought about my last fight with Dalix and friends. Those guys were tougher and there were four of them. This was almost too easy.

When Connor stepped back, pissed off, ready for another assault, I used the two holding me as levers and whipped my legs up and around Connor's neck, capturing his head, pulling him to the floor on his back as I smashed both guys' heads together before shoving them away. I squeezed Connor's neck with my thighs, watching his face turn crimson as he struggled. Damn this was fun. But I shouldn't be feeling good about hurting someone. Still, this was Connor.

The other two were no threat. Tony seemed disoriented, having difficulty moving. Marco had his arms around his head, whimpering. Thugs aren't used to their victims hitting back.

"Three rich kids against one pathetic downer-boy? Should I let you go or do you want to choke?" Connor thrashed, fists pounding into me with no effect. I pulled his arms around my thighs and held them with one hand. With the other I covered Connor's mouth and pinched his nostrils while tightening my legs around his neck.

It was now clear, even to a psycho brat like Connor, that this classmate he hated could destroy him without breaking a sweat. He arched his back, eyes bulging. The anger drained, replaced with what looked like fear, maybe even defeat. Grateful I didn't have to hurt him, a bit disappointed I didn't have to do more, I removed my hand. Connor gasped for breath.

"IF I let you go, we will talk. Understand? Talk respectfully. I am not your enemy!"

Something came out of Connor's mouth but it was muffled. I unwrapped my legs from around his neck. He tried to stand and collapsed to the floor. I leaned over and lifted him upright.

Connor coughed and wheezed, offering no resistance, and crashed against the wall. Tony was still prostrate. Marco struggled to his feet. I gave him a push and he went down. They would never survive on the street. I hoped I wasn't too rough. I'd been strategic, holding back, focusing on defense as Ran had taught me. And Zinc would support me, I was certain. And if not, I probably wouldn't ever have children of my own.

I tightened my arm around Connor and walked him into a nearby room, closing the door behind us. I let him flop into a seat and went over to a beverage tap and punched in two glasses of cold water, no ice. I handed the glass to Connor and sat next to him, waiting for his breathing to stabilize, and took a sip of my own drink. He picked up his glass, looking at it suspiciously, took a long swallow and set it down. We stared at each other for what seemed like minutes.

"How dare you touch me! You're just a fucki—"

"Don't!" I held a finger an inch from his nose.

Connor tried to stand. I pushed him back down.

"We're going to talk. Then you can tell your mother and Zinc that this pushy slave abused you. Maybe later the guards will hold me while you cut off my balls because I defended myself. But right now we will figure this out." I knew my situation was precarious but tried to hide my misgivings. Being pissed off and scared was not an easy combo.

"Okay," Connor said. He wiped his face and folded his hands. "Are you wearing your XO?"

"No. You know I can fight."

"Yes."

"Is this about what happened in the dorm room three years ago?"

"You humiliated me."

"So that's it. How? You—one of the richest boys on the planet—were stealing what little money I had from my desk drawer. When I confronted you, you swore at me and slugged me on the chin. I bloodied your nose. You ran out and we never talked again except when you screamed obscenities at me in the halls while you and your friends hit me." We'd lived in the dorm room in angry silence for a full semester. The Burning Bush had been my sanctuary away from him.

Connor looked away. I sensed embarrassment, an improvement over hate.

"Why? Please tell me. What did I do to offend you?"

He cleared his throat and turned to face me. "I guess...because I thought I could do whatever I wanted and get away with it. You took my abuse and never said anything. I thought you were afraid of me."

"I was."

Connor looked surprised. "I was irritated Dad didn't back me up and let me change dorm rooms. I wanted to be with one of my friends. My father said I needed to man up and follow the rules of the academy my grandfather founded. I felt rejected, like my dad abandoned me, didn't care..." He stopped and fidgeted with his hands.

"Please...go on."

"And you are so fucking handsome. Even in freshman gymnastics you were amazing and I was a loser. Only my family money kept me on the team. I knew it. So did everyone. And you had musical talent, were good in math. I guess I couldn't stand it. And you always tried to be so helpful, offering me advice. It pissed me off. I didn't need your money but you did. I wanted to hurt you."

I was silent; we both were.

"I know that wasn't easy. Thank you."

Connor squirmed. And I felt sorry for him, or as sorry as one can feel for a rich predatory kid who just got a spanking.

"I don't know if we can not be enemies," I said, hoping to build on this breakthrough. I had to find a way to get along with him.

"That's a double negative."

"What?" I stared at him for a beat and then started laughing.

Connor burped. "Oops!" Then he joined in.

Eventually we both wiped our eyes and were still.

"You're good in English class," I said, "I've always admired your writing." I wasn't sure how to continue. The hostility seemed diminished, the opportunity real. "That was really funny. I didn't know that about you. And I like it. We're both just people, Connor. Maybe someone from your social class can't be close to someone like me. A few months ago I was a free boy. Now I'm a slave in your family. And it's legal. But I'm not a bad guy, just a poor one. And there are real bad guys who tried to kill your father and did kill your cousin. Maybe they'll want to murder Zinc or you. Your mom. Maybe me. Whether you accept me as an equal or something less, I think I'm at least a tiny part of your family. I didn't ask to be but I am. That makes it my family too. And I'd like to protect it." I took a deep breath. "Do you still hate me?"

"No. I don't think I ever did." His voice dropped to a whisper. "I was...envious."

"And I really was afraid of you. I still am."

I held out an open palm. "Peace?"

Connor took it. "Peace."

"Now let's go check on the guys outside."

CHAPTER 24

It was like the first day walking through the arched stone doorways of Ogden Academy, the hallway a crush of students headed to classes. As I stepped inside with Zinc and two armed guards, the sea parted. People, many friends and classmates, pressed against the walls, staring. Based on all the publicity, they were afraid of me or repulsed. Hard to tell. Curious, mostly, I guessed.

Under our regular clothes, we wore our XOs with hoods and gloves in our pockets. Ran had ordered us to be always prepared in public.

Connor had arrived earlier. Nothing had happened after the fight. Tony and Marco, embarrassed at being pulverized by a downer, had told the nurse they slipped and banged their heads horsing around. "Good," was all Zinc said after I told him about what I'd done to his brother; obviously he was preoccupied. I wished we'd talked it through.

I smiled awkwardly at people I knew. They just watched, examining me anew. Billy Eagle ran up, arms wide. "Spartak!"

Sergeant Hernandez grabbed him, dropping him to his knees. Damn, the guy was fast. The crowd jumped back, talking excitedly. I stooped down, prying myself between the two.

"Please, Hernandez, let him go. He's my friend."

"You don't know who your friends are anymore," he said, lifting Billy up and scanning him for weapons. "I hope you're right."

I wrapped my arms around my dorm-mate. "I'm sorry." We walked together. "Can we talk later?"

"I'd like that, so would Rhonda."

"Hey slave boy," someone taunted.

"On your knees, boy!" a male voice shouted along with numerous whistles and disgusting sound effects.

As the hallway reached an intersection, Zinc stopped and embraced me. "My class is this way. See you after school." Our affection seemed freakish in this setting. The last time I was here, I was free and we were strangers. "I'll be in the bleachers watching at gymnastics practice." Zinc grinned. "Coach better treat you right."

I nodded, holding him tight. "Thanks Zinc." As I turned down the hall to my first class, students continued to keep a wide berth, like they were shunning me. Life had changed.

"*Sasser* boy," another male voice mocked.

Two girls whistled, classic wolf.

Billy was tight to my side. He'd gotten a tattoo on the shaved side of his head. His parents would be upset.

"Cool phoenix," I told him.

* * *

"Coach, we need to talk."

Condar Johanson swiveled his chair around and faced the front door to his office. I saw the man's shoulders stiffen when he heard my voice. His open mouth and stare confirmed his discomfort. That was good.

Coach stood and offered his hand. I merely looked at him and sat down uninvited. He was middle-aged but somehow looked older, pale. He slowly slumped back into his chair.

"I thought you were my friend, a second father. I worshipped you." It just kind of shot out of me. "And all that time, all those years, you were just preparing me not for the Olympics but for the slave market. And you sold me for a big fee. You get rich and I lose my freedom. You drugged me that night."

"Look, Spartak, I really had no choice. It was expected of me. And…" He leaned forward, his face anguished, his voice emphatic, "I WAS preparing you to be a great gymnast. AND YOU ARE!" He flopped back, rubbing his eyes. "The slave apparatus has been in place for years," he said, "but controversial. Headhunters were always on the hunt. But most elites waited for the safety of a high-court blessing.

You were in play only then, a high status target. The school protected you, the headmaster wanted his cut."

So that was why Headmaster Thragman didn't expel me.

I said coldly, "I don't believe you. You wanted to muscle me up, a pig for slaughter, to bring a good price. You made me take my shirt off at practice so prospective buyers could check out the merchandise. I've read that lots of people knew what the court would do. You sold me out!" I didn't shout but knew my words were tough. I hated being emotional. Slow and soft was more effective than screaming, although less satisfying. "I'm a human being, Coach, an American, and you made me a piece of meat." I closed my eyes and held my breath, on the edge of tears. I needed to calm down. What he did to me hurt. He was my friend once. I hoped.

"No, the US Supreme Court opened the door." He said defensively, "I admit I had my eye on you. Yes, I made money on you. But so did the school. And your family. It's the way of the world. Accept it."

"Easy for you to say as a free man with my bounty money in your pocket."

Coach was sweating, his hands clenched tight. Not the usual confident teacher, always in charge. There was nothing I could do to him other than make him squirm. And while satisfying, it served no other purpose. No laws were broken. That was the real crime. And now I had other needs.

"By the way, I saw your written report on me. Zinc shared it. It seems I'm a great match for an organ transplant if Glenda McClain or her kids need one and other sources aren't available. So having my heart cut out of my body was something you were okay with given the size of your commission? I saw the amount by the way. My dad won't make that in two lifetimes."

"I…I'm sorry."

"I like your gold bracelet. New?"

He did not reply.

Enough, time to get to business.

"Zinc McClain wants me in the Olympics." It was all so ridiculous. I couldn't help but curl my lips into a tiny grin. "If I make it, I'll be the first slave to compete since ancient Greece invented the games.

You're set to be an Olympic team coach. I'm in good shape, maybe in even better condition than when I won the national championship. Exercise was about all I had to do in my jail cell. My...*master*...said you need to get me competitive to win a spot on the US team. And his granddaddy founded this school."

I stood up. "So let's get to work." I walked out.

CHAPTER 25

The auditorium seated over a thousand people on the first floor and about that number in the two large balconies. The three of us, Sonia, Zinc, and myself, walked down the aisle on the mezzanine level to our reserved seats next to the railing. Armed McClain security, hidden in the crowd, were scattered around the room.

I'd never been in the First Christian Pentecostal Church, just south of Market, a huge three-story stone complex with square twin towers at the entrance, one of the oldest buildings in the city, dating to the 1850s. And I'd never seen Bishop Damone "Halleluiah" Perry in person.

In media clips of the man, he seemed intense, too certain about topics it was impossible to be certain about. Indeed the charm of religion, I always thought, was accepting the unknowns with an open heart. Perry spoke about absolutes with a focus on Old Testament cruelty rather than the uplifting messages from the Gospels. Sin and punishment were his favorite themes. It seemed to me that forcing Christianity down people's throats was not the way to win converts. But what did I know? He was popular and seemed to be building an army of angry young people. And there were certainly lots of reasons to be angry.

Sergei said his son needed to be seen and this was the church to attend. Even though they knew Perry was plotting to end the power of the Twelve, it was important to be here, to show confidence. I was in the middle with Sonia and Zinc on either side.

She put her arm around me. "Maybe he'll suggest people attack us with hatchets while shouting hosannas," she whispered to Zinc, waving at others across the balcony. Her smile was dazzling and people responded. If we were the enemy, not everyone here had gotten the message.

"Best not to make such statements in public," Zinc warned as he stood to shake hands with people behind him.

I noticed parishioners turning and looking at us, some pointing wrists, pushing their temples, twisting pieces of cloth at us that I assume contained lumins. I tried to look away and heard a few references to myself, not by name, but my new status.

"Is that the slave?"

"The *Sasser* kid is a heart-stopper."

"Sad the McClains had to buy their child a sex boy."

I assumed if I could hear it, so could Zinc and Sonia. I raised my palms in front of my companions and they each took one, a trio against the world. The look on Zinc's face was blank and suggested his usual aloof exterior, hiding the shyness and embarrassment. I squeezed his hand and Zinc squeezed back. Little things were important.

"You're a sweet man," Sonia whispered in my ear.

She had become close over the past weeks. We were strangers at school before, a face in the audience, but now she sought me out, wanted to know what I was doing, introduced me to friends, let them know I was important to her. She was clearly protective, like an older sister.

A massive pipe organ, the biggest I'd ever seen, vibrated the walls and audience, starting the Sunday program. The organist was riveting and I wanted to meet her. She was a small woman in a sky-blue suit with silver trim and ratted out white hair. She kept turning her face toward the audience and grinning. Her fingers were covered with sparkling diamonds and rubies. Hard to say if they were real or electric. Religion was still a big moneymaker.

Then he came out in a black Puritan-style suit.

Perry spread his arms wide and addressed his flock from center stage. "Sodom and Gomorrah were damned by God not because of homosexuality, a difference we now know God created—but because of dark angels cavorting with humans," Bishop Perry thundered. "The all-powerful defiling the poor and helpless, a pit of debauchery unacceptable to our creator."

I wondered if this was for our benefit, so he couldn't be seen as prejudiced by his parishioners when he attacked us.

Perry stepped back, pursing his lips, as if deep in thought, recharging his venom. Then he stormed the podium. "And what does it mean for us in this time when the all-powerful, the angels of darkness, the super rich, demons of Satan, take what they want of economic and terrestrial resources, even buying human beings as slaves? And waiting in heaven is Jesus, on standby, anxious to return—but the existing hierarchy must tumble so God can rise again."

"Halleluiah!" shouted hundreds of voices.

"We are entering the beginning of the end, the final days…this Sodom world will perish…"

I felt Zinc tightening his grip on my hand at the blistering attack. I squeezed back and leaned my head toward him, offering what I hoped was reassurance. I had a hard time imagining an omnipotent God needing a revolution to make an appearance. But theology was not my topic. Zinc was.

"I love you," I said softly.

"Thank you." Zinc's voice was all but lost in the noise.

I stopped listening. No subtlety here. Let the organ lady play again. It was hard to imagine people actually buying this stuff but millions did, according to polls. It was a war. Eventually the preacher was silent and the singing rebooted, loud and infectious even if the songs seemed bizarre.

"In that old rugged cross, stained with blood so divine, a wondrous beauty I see…"

Behind the altar, in a large open space, a three-dimensional, larger-than-life image materialized of a gray-haired man carrying a wooden cross over his shoulder and dragging behind him, the end mounted on a wheel.

"My great-grandfather carried an oaken cross across this great nation over a century ago, from California to Washington, D.C., to proclaim America as a Christian nation," Perry said, more matter-of-factly this time. "How proud he would be to see the federal government has made it happen: Christianity, the official religion of America. Savor it! And next year, this cross will be placed permanently behind this podium in honor of that noble quest. It will complete our remodeling program in this cathedral, just in time for the return of the Son of God."

They seemed to believe it.

There was an interlude of hands-on healing, people shouting "miracle," but hard to tell if it was planned, spontaneous, real or fake. Then holy laughter, something I'd never experienced and it made me laugh, but not in the way I was supposed to. I had no idea if Satan was in the room but I loved the idea of laughing at, rather than fearing, evil. Of course in my world, if you laughed at a thug you got a worse beating than if you just submitted or beat him up first. Everything at the church seemed upbeat and fun, except all the talk of sin and hell and the need of Christian sovereignty. Or, dictatorship, depending on your view.

"God appreciates your attendance," Perry said afterward, standing rigid and cold, shaking hands with Zinc and Sonia as we passed in the receiving line. I was surprised the minister would even speak to a Twelver but Zinc was determined to return the hellfire with dignity and confidence. I stepped out of the way.

"And this is my special friend, Spartak Jones," Sonia said, excitement in her voice, pulling me forward. "He's trying out for the Olympics next month and is the state champion in gymnastics. I know you'll pray for him."

Bishop Perry looked like he smelled a sewer leak and turned away to other congregants, talking about the remodeling that would take place before the new cross was installed. He knew how to make you feel insignificant.

"Good day, sir," Zinc said with frost as we turned and exited the church, holding hands. "I suspect we will talk again."

"But not soon," Sonia said as we skipped down the front steps. "What a jerk."

"But a powerful and dangerous jerk," Zinc reminded us.

* * *

Our armored limo pulled up in front of a new high-rise residential tower on the east side of the city facing the Bay. Our security van parked behind. We both dressed fancy at Zinc's insistence, high-collar Napoleonic style jackets and tight black pants with knee boots. Kind of a snort and I felt glamorous. He was in dark green and I wore a shimmering blue. We were meeting some friends of his, "to show you off," he'd said, but declined to divulge names. I was pleased he was proud of me but didn't like feeling like I was a prize poodle at a dog show. We rode up to the hundred and first floor in silence, holding hands, enjoying the stunning Bay view.

"Mother!" I tripped on the doormat when I saw Mom's pale face in the doorway, her long blond hair puffed and draped to her shoulders with a curl. Zinc grabbed me to break the fall. "Mother..." I tried to be dignified but as we hugged and she squeezed I was helpless.

"Son! " Dad stepped up and wrapped his arms around us both.

"Dad!" I squawked, my throat frozen, my old world crashing into the new, embarrassed to be what I was in front of my family, embarrassed how it happened, how it humiliated them as well as me, yet humbled and grateful that I was here. Zinc handed out a pocketful of white handkerchiefs with the McClain crest. For an owner, he could be a sweetheart.

"Spartak!" Geo and Kimber joined the hug.

Tissue boxes were omnipresent as we drank and ate and talked. There was a pot roast, something we'd never had before, and lots of mac 'n' cheese. Obviously they were doing dramatically better and this was a special occasion. My dad looked healthier, a relief. I talked about school and the Olympic trials in a few weeks at Stanford.

The topic of slavery was never mentioned nor what life was like at Buena Vista, the McClain compound. Clearly everyone wanted to avoid the elephant. I'd ached to visit but was afraid to push Zinc given all the other complications as I learned my role in a new reality, one that could be glamorous, often cruel and sometimes lethal.

"Have more spinach," Mom said, handing Zinc a bowl.

"Thank you, Mrs. Jones, you're a fine cook."

"Please call me Barbel."

We'd talked twice since they'd signed the papers but the relationship was awkward and I was always under surveillance at the mansion. Hell, everyone was under surveillance everywhere, sight and scent. Tonight we inched closer to normal and I welcomed back a sense of calm and family.

Their new apartment was stately compared with where we'd lived before but the whole space was about half the size of Zinc's bedroom. My brother and sister had their own rooms with walls and doors, not just drapes, actual privacy, and were full of news about preparation for entering the academy.

"Spartak," Mom said, "Zinc contacted me personally to set up tonight's dinner as a surprise." She looked happy, younger with her family together.

"Thank you," I said an hour later, as I kissed Zinc on the cheek, sitting in the backseat of the armored limo headed home. "That was so thoughtful. Absolutely phantasmagorical!"

Zinc kissed my hair and rubbed my temples as I leaned into his chest.

A flash and blast behind us.

The security vehicle exploded in flames, the engine lifting up and crashing onto our trunk, knocking us sideways. All four of us were screaming and our driver accelerated and fishtailed. We'd sped less than a block when a pair of dump trucks, coming from two directions, smashed into us. The side of the armored car ripped open.

Zinc and I slammed hard against the roof, dazed as we crumpled onto the seat. I thought I saw masked men rush up, firing solars at the guard and driver in the front. There was a smell of fried meat.

"Surrender!"

I couldn't focus or think, my vision blurred, my body limp, non-functioning. The top of my skull felt like it had been sheared.

"Zinc!" I yelled. Then collapsed.

I was kicked in the balls. Someone yanked my hands behind my back and tied them, a noose slipped around my neck.

I thought I saw Zinc but my senses were at five percent, everything was hazy. Then I was in a dark tunnel—a bag had been yanked over my head. The rope cinched tight on my neck as I was pulled out of the limo and inside another vehicle.

My face was shoved into a carpet, two men on top of me. Breathing was impossible as the truck bounced over rough pavement, moving at high speed. My lungs felt like they'd explode. I heard a clasp open next to my ear and something slammed into my neck with a hiss.

"Zinc?"

Then nothing.

CHAPTER 26

I AWOKE WITH COLD OATMEAL BRAIN, arms tied behind the back of a chair. A sound snapped me out of the haze.

"Please...mercy..." The sounds of fists hitting flesh. A scream. Zinc's voice! He was being pummeled.

"Leave him alone!" I yelled, my mouth sticky, words sounding twisted. "You have no right to hurt him, murderers!"

"Well, well," a metallic, artificial voice responded. Zinc was silent, the thug apparently distracted. "The slave is worried about his owner."

My hood was yanked off. It took a moment for my eyes to adjust. Two figures stood a few feet away, faces covered with Liteon cloth sacks. I saw a luminous shape. They could see me clearly through the fabric. I noticed my jacket, shirt, and XO top had been tossed in the corner. They likely didn't know what it was.

"And you are pretty," one said, coming up and squeezing my mouth open until it hurt. Then I was slapped hard.

"A shame to kill you. The Twelve deserve death for suppressing the rights of the majority. Suppressing the number of people who can vote to stay in power. Using global economics to impoverish Americans. We die so they can have bigger yachts. And own beautiful boys and girls as human trophies."

I glanced at Zinc, not interested in a lecture. His face was bloody, one eye swollen shut. But he tried to smile at me through ripped lips.

The thug grabbed me by the hair, snapping my head back. "Listen when I speak, *Sasser* boy!"

Zinc started to yell, more a croak, but coughed blood. A guard came over and slammed a fist into his gut. Zinc vomited foamy slime.

"Zinc!"

"Thirsty, slave boy?"

My head was yanked back, a bottle of water poured over my face. I opened my mouth and drank what I could, hoping it wasn't poison. I wondered why they were being generous with the water.

"Thank you," I said. My mouth moved, no longer sticky.

The chairs were turned so I faced him just a few feet apart. Zinc looked even worse head-on. They'd cut a design on his bare chest, a cross, with a knife. I couldn't stop the tears. Then hot anger I worked hard to suppress. But couldn't.

"Bastards! Yes, I'm a slave and hate it. I despise what the Twelve have done. But I don't hate Zinc. He's a good man, still a teenager and has nothing to do with politics. For the love of God, I beg you, leave him alone."

"Don't tell me about God!" A fist hit me in the mouth, slamming my head sideways. "Speak when given permission. If you want your friend to live, tell him to give us access codes to some of his fortune. He won't miss a few trillion but it will fund the revolution."

I could taste warm fluid in my mouth. The thick plastic ropes around my feet and across my chest were tight and my legs felt numb. With all my strength I couldn't stretch what was around my wrists behind my back. Better luck with my feet; I still had on the XO pants and could feel the rope stretch as I tested my strength. But I couldn't move enough to get momentum to break the rope. Even if I did, I needed my hands. Best to wait for an opportunity.

"I think McClain loves his slave, judging by the panic in his good eye." They both laughed. "Do you love this boy? Do you want to see him die in front of you?"

Zinc twisted in his chair, grunting, vomit covering his chin and chest.

The shorter one unhooked an arc-truncheon from his belt clip, holding the elegant and brutal weapon in front of me, letting us both see it up close. I heard it buzz and saw a spark at the head.

"I don't like slaves who support the Twelve. Judas!"

The club slammed into my abs. The thin rows of electrodes at the end bit into my skin, latching on while injecting an electrical jolt. My face quaked, mouth open, back arched, my body pulling against the plastic straps, ripping skin, every cell ablaze, exploding.

I waited for my eyes to clear after it unhooked. Zinc was screaming. I could just make out their figures when it hit me again. And again.

Then darkness.

* * *

As I regained consciousness, I sensed being alone. Unsure how much time had passed, I was waiting to make certain there was silence before I opened my eyes or moved. The only light was a faint glow at the bottom of the door. Maybe this was a holding cell. I could hear voices somewhere distant and laughter. There was music, faint, some kind of Goth revival rock.

My stomach was slashed and crusted with blood. I felt for my ring but it was gone so I worked my right hand upward to my belt, not easy given the plastic rope entwined around my wrists and looped through the back of a chair. With great effort, I managed to pry open the hidden slit on the inside, acting as a sheath. If the captors were present, I couldn't have pulled out the ultra thin band of plasteel, a handle at the beginning of a long blade, wrapping completely around my waist, so sharp it could sever a finger, even my hand, if not careful.

Straining, a centimeter at a time, I got it out far enough for the cutting edge to touch the plastic band around my wrists. It sliced easily. My hands free, I kicked my calves but the ropes held.

I stood, slowly pulling out the floppy sword from the belt and bent over, using it to cut the ropes on my feet and chest. It was a silver flaccid razor, useful but not optimum in a fight.

I touched a raised bump, waiting for it to read my thumb and gene prints. There was a green flash and the sword lengthened, thickened, erect, hard, and lethal.

I stretched my arms, bending over, dizzy, moving my legs up and down to bring blood into my limbs. I touched my stomach. It was raw, parts of it still oozing. It hurt so bad I had to stop and hold onto my chair, teeth clenched. "Wooowwww." Coach had taught me to concentrate when hurt and I needed to finish a routine, compartmentalize, lock away the pain, focus on the task ahead.

I found a case of bottled water and drank, then flooded my wounds. No antiseptic but my stomach looked better, or maybe scarier. Zinc's shirt and XO and my own clothes were in the corner. I tore the shirts into a thick bandage and tied it around my waist. Then I slipped on the tight-fitting XO top to hold it in place. I rubbed the bulge in my abs. Looking pregnant was okay for now.

I pulled a hood, facemask and gloves from a slot in my boot and put them on. My boots! Yes! So many gadgets to remember. Slugging a guy was so much simpler than all this technology.

The door was locked. I squeezed with my XO glove and the knob shattered. Peeking out, I spotted an old granite block and brick wall at the end of a hallway. Given the water stains and dampness, we were likely underground. The bricks were in a wave pattern and looked familiar.

I heard a thug's electrified voice.

"I'll check on the princess, go ahead and deal."

I closed the door and moved further back into the dark room, remembering the training with Ran. This was the one that hit me with the arc-truncheon. Mercy seemed inappropriate given what they'd done. And I needed to save Zinc. Time was critical. I turned so the glowing sword was hidden behind me.

The guard partially opened the door and stopped, examining the broken lock. He pulled out his sonic and I heard it power up. He bent low and turned, aiming the weapon into the darkness and reached for the light switch. I swung the shimmering sword, severing the head, still covered in a Liteon hood. The only sound was the thud of the corpse on the concrete floor.

I listened and only heard music. I turned on the light.

Stepping across the body I pulled up the hood, freeing its contents. I rolled it face up with my foot. As I started to gag, I closed my eyes, took a deep breath and puffed it out. Compartmentalize. Then I looked at the face.

Not a he. A young woman, maybe middle twenties. Who'd she work for? One of the End Timers of Bishop Perry? Who would so boldly challenge a Twelve? Was it another group? At this point, none of it mattered. I had to find Zinc.

I set down the sword and removed her belt with a solar pistol in the holster and an arc-truncheon and put it around my waist. I pulled out the orange weapon and adapted it to narrow band for maximum damage. No games here. I picked up my sword.

Closing the door behind me, and turning out the light, I snooped down the hall and turned right, toward the music. Through an arch, I found myself in a stone passageway. Yes, I'd seen the wall before, above ground near the old sewer plant across the highway from the ocean, closed years ago. The air smelled of mildew, rot, and salt.

I saw an open door in the distance, apparently where the others were, judging from the light and noise. There was one door before it. I twisted the knob. It moved then jammed. I gripped harder. The knob broke loose. I slipped inside the dark room.

It had a high concrete ceiling, some kind of small storage facility full of boxes. There was another door, hopefully into the room where Zinc was, letting in a blade of light. I moved a slice of ripped leather on the tongue of my boot and pulled out a hidden thin pencil wide coil. I hooked it to the micro hidden in my bootlace tip. I slid the other end under the door.

Ransom had so many fun military toys. This one had a weird name, Justice Rod, no idea why. A small Z-ether appeared, transmitting a live image of what was inside the room.

There was Zinc, still tied up in a chair. Even bloodier, head forward. He wasn't moving. My teeth clenched. Control the rage. Use it.

There was a makeshift kitchen and beds. This was their living area. And there was a cage with someone in it. I had no idea who it might be. There were six thugs. Everyone was deep in the room, far from the door. One stood by Zinc, holding a solar, screaming at my lover. Fuck. There might not be enough time. Next to him was a tall woman, black and strikingly beautiful. She seemed to be asking Zinc questions, but in a more subdued way. I could make out the slow, deep resonance of her voice but not the words. She was not armed. I remembered the DIMM surveillance inside the Palladium. Kinuba Steele. Could this be her?

The others seemed to be eating, some playing cards. Maybe it was just a game of intimidation. But I couldn't take the chance and go for help. I needed to do it myself.

All had their masks off. One older man, a woman, and four in their twenties or thirties. All had solars in their holsters. Two wore blue Jesusista headbands.

I thought of Ran's training and tried to compute a plan. The odds were against me. So do the unexpected and do it fast.

I returned to the hallway, let my eyes adjust, and moved to their doorway. Stooping down, I ran the Justice Rod around the corner. No one had moved. No wait. I didn't see the woman. Had she gone?

That left five. A challenge. These weapons took a second to recharge between blasts. But I was unexpected, quick, strong, and limber. I replaced the device, reviewing strategy. Kind of like a gymnastics event, floor exercises, only with weapons and people would die.

I moved back down the corridor, took a breath and ran full speed, pivoting into the room, through the door and leaping, catapulted by the XO, slicing the sword through the back of the closest one as I landed almost on top of him, severing his spine. Pulling it out, I did an easy forward roll—one, two, three—before popping up and embedding the sword in the other thug's chest as he tried to run. Tumbling again—four, five, six—then up, firing the solar, frying the guts of the third man near Zinc, a deer in headlights. Tumbling was one of my best events.

The fourth guy, a brown-skinned man with bleached white hair, raised his pistol. I stood, defiant, and heard mine peep, ready to fire again. I flexed my right calf muscle and the boot knife in my heel punched into the concrete floor.

"Kill him!" an older man next to him screamed.

White light. I turned my head and took the full blast. When it finished, I looked at the stunned terrorist. Laughing, looking for vengeance, pumped, I slipped my pistol into its holster and unhooked the arc-truncheon from my belt, flipped it on, waited for the hum and hurled it—XO enhanced, punching deep into the man's gut, electrifying his intestines. The terrorist screamed, collapsed to the floor, twisting, twitching and then was motionless as the club continued to purr and cook. I pulled the blade back into my heel.

The fifth man ran to Zinc and grabbed him, holding an old-fashioned lead pistol to his head. I looked around the room for the woman. She wasn't here.

"Back off or I'll kill him!" The man had a well-trimmed gray beard, chicken-feet brown eyes. Dressed better than the others, a dark traditional business suit and red clerical collar.

I dropped my voice, wanting to sound more adult and deadly even though the guy knew who I was. "Freak 'em out," Ran had told me when confronting an enemy.

"Interesting threat. I cut off the head of the woman you sent to check on me." I chuckled, hoping to goad him into anger. "What will your head look like when it's disconnected?" I moved slowly forward, already set on a plan. "Shall we find out?"

"I'll kill him!"

"Hear me, pimple. My justice will be worse than you'll face in Hell." I needed to draw the gun to me. "Kill him and you will die. It won't be pretty."

"Satan!" the minister swung the pistol.

I put out my hand as the man fired.

The force of the bullet hit my padded XO glove, and I twisted, as Ransom taught me, my arm thrusting sideways and back, taking the force, almost knocking me over, down on one knee, then regaining my balance, standing. I held up the bullet.

"Superman," I said. "You lose."

The man stared, stumbling back in shock, open-mouthed, pale, the gun aimed at me. I leaped and spun, flexing my calf again as the heel knife connected with the man's chin. The terrorist slammed back into a wall, much of his face skidding across the floor, as he collapsed.

I retracted the blade and approached. No more trouble. But he was still alive, barely, for questioning. My XO hood and mask made it seem more like a game and less like real life. That helped manage the horror. I swiveled around, kneeling by Zinc, wrapping an arm around him. Eyes welling while I examined his wounds and cut the ropes.

"Are you okay?"

Zinc moaned, his head down, barely able to respond.

"Are there any more?"

A grunt.

"I think you said no."

I pulled the micro from my bootstrap and contacted Ransom. I was crisp with details and described where I thought we were. Ran reminded me of a GPS transmitter in my belt. I slapped my forehead with my palm. Dumb! I pushed it on, then touched the transmitter riveted to my ear. Too bad it was now only linked to Zinc's SubQ. Given the new reality, maybe it needed to be hooked into the system.

I yanked a mattress from one of the beds and gently lifted Zinc on top, kissing his forehead. He groaned and cried out as I straightened him on the cushions. With effort, Zinc touched my arm with his fingers. I pulled back my facemask and hood. I had to stay strong and alert. It wasn't over.

The man in the cage called for help.

CHAPTER 27

"Holy shit!"

Ransom always had a good way with words. He arrived with a medical team, local enforcers, and a large McClain security detail. Two surgeons and three medics floated a gurney laden with equipment and surrounded Zinc. The McClains didn't mess around.

Ran pulled me away. "Please let them do their work."

"Let me out!" The man in the cage again demanded release. I'd asked him earlier if he was injured. "Not badly," he'd answered. I'd asked him to wait patiently until help arrived for Zinc. I didn't need any more distractions or trouble.

Ran blasted off the lock on the cage and helped the man out. He was about thirty, disheveled, hair matted, a filthy beard, a badly swollen face and bare feet, one encrusted with blood, missing a toe. One arm appeared to be broken.

"Are you all right, Mayor?" Ran grabbed a chair and called a medic.

"Thanks to this young man." He pointed to me. "That was fucking amazing!"

"Spartak, this is Joshua Rand, Sergei's younger half-brother, Mayor of San Francisco, kidnapped some weeks back."

The mayor put out his left hand to shake and I took it. "You're the slave boy, aren't you? They let me watch some news feeds."

I didn't respond. My legs were suddenly weak. A crime unit began attending the dead. The older terrorist was still alive, someone yelled. I backed away and leaned against a wall, sliding slowly to the floor. I watched Zinc, helpless, surrounded by men in white coats. The bodies, the carnage seemed everywhere. I'd done it all. The sword, a few feet away, glowing, covered in blood, the arc-truncheon still humming. The world was insane. My stomach throbbed, roadkill, red now seeping generously through the XO. Leaning my head on my knees, I began to roll sideways.

"Doctor! Over here!" It was Ran's voice.

* * *

"There's the bastard!"

I was sitting on the edge of a bed in my hospital room when Glenda stomped toward me down the hall, arms flailing. I leaned away as she neared.

I'd regained consciousness about midday after two days and two operations; doctors had finally left about thirty minutes ago. Mark, a swarthy male nurse, told me Billy and Rhonda had waited for hours but finally had to return to school. She'd left a heart-shaped note that said: "Get well, sweet honeysuckle."

Mrs. McClain charged right up to my face.

"You saved my son but if it hadn't been for you he'd never have been kidnapped!" I could smell her sweet perfume and feel her spittle. She slapped me, knocking me back onto my side and I grabbed my abs hoping they wouldn't rupture.

"He felt sorry for you and took you to see your parents," she snarled. "And it nearly cost him his life!" Glenda's face was directly across from me.

I scooted back, holding myself with one arm over my stomach, the other on the bed as a brace. Connor was watching, his expression blank. I knew Zinc was semiconscious in a suite down the hall. A nurse told me a few minutes earlier that Joshua Rand was holding a press conference in his hospital room a floor below. Glenda raised her arm to hit me again. I closed my eyes; not much I could do. Ransom ran up and put an arm between us, pulling her back.

"Please ma'am. Not now. You're upset. Zinc is alive because of him."

"Watch yourself, Ransom! You failed my husband and now my son. This boy is bad news." She pressed against the security chief, hissing as she pointed at me. "You will be punished."

She swiveled and stomped away, taking Connor by the arm. They stepped into an elevator just outside the room. Ran helped me sit up. I touched my stomach, wrapped in med-foam, the rips cleaned and glued tight. And pain meds made it feel sort of normal.

"Are you all right, son?"

"Yes, sir," I replied, looking through the semitransparent goo on my stomach to the jagged cuts below. It wasn't pretty. I leaned back into the pillows and watched him, feeling cursed. "What do I do?" I couldn't appease her no matter what I did.

"Can you walk?"

"I think so."

"We're going to visit the mayor." He straightened my hair with his fingers and helped me stand. "Hold on to me. You don't have to be pretty and it's best you're not. Let's hurry."

"Is my butt covered?"

CHAPTER 28

"I am Nocturne," said a teenage boy, his voice emotional, then breaking, on the all-zan blast. "These are the times that try men's souls. When did liberty die? Every citizen should be able to vote. We are all slaves of the elite. Join AR2!"

I WAS BACK IN MY CELL. It was the same color-coordinated hellhole with no windows or outgoing communications. I was told a dampening field blocked any outbound transmission. At least I had my clothes and my class ring back. Ran found it in a sack of personal items taken by the End Timers. I twisted it around my finger, the ring giving me a sense of normalcy. After Ran took me to the press conference and was mobbed by the media, including having the mayor hugging and crying about me being a hero, we'd returned directly home on Glenda's orders. She'd met us as we entered the McClain house.

"Ransom, you shall take this slave immediately to his old holding cell in the basement."

"Madam, please reconsid—"

"Don't fuck with me, Ransom!" She was out of control. "My husband is unconscious, maybe dying. My eldest son is in serious condition at the hospital. I RUN THIS FAMILY! Understood?"

"Yes, ma'am."

"And you will not contact Zinc about this. Understood?"

"Yes, ma'am."

He personally escorted me to my cell. I was in shock.

"Please forgive me. I work for the family. But I also do what's right. She's upset and tends toward the dramatic. Zinc needs to know and he will. He and I have certain understandings I don't want to reveal at this time unless necessary. I'll make certain Dr. Rai keeps an eye on your wounds."

"Could someone contact my parents?"

"Absolutely, son." He squeezed my shoulder. It was comforting. "And I'll post a guard outside. You will not be moved without me knowing."

Somehow, that sounded ominous, Glenda or Connor coming for me in the night. The jail door hummed into place.

* * *

I pulled a book from my shoulder pack, a serendipitous discovery in the OA library. The first line grabbed me: *"Take away all of someone's freedom and you have a slave."* I stared at the steel door to my cage and set the book down. Greed, self-righteousness, vanity, lack of empathy, willful self-delusion, a compliant and not always bright political class gradually brought America to this place. The book's author, James Oakes, had written *Slavery and Freedom* over a century ago about a time in the old South. I felt the steel tracker in my ear and ran a finger around the raised McClain crest. My brand.

I couldn't sink into self-pity or I was finished. I went to the zan and scanned the news. There were endless repeats about what I did and that Zinc was in and out of consciousness in the hospital. Some commentators said I was a hero, but someone with no freedom is still a slave, hero or not. I rubbed my eyes and looked up, ready to howl.

The door buzzed and I stood. Mrs. McClain and Connor stepped inside. I saw two of her personal guards outside the door.

She pointed at me, her mouth twisted. "You will be sold. I will not have you dividing this family." Her voice was a growl, angry. Connor glanced at me then down, pursing his lips. I couldn't tell if he was gloating or embarrassed. "Today is your last here. Arrangements are being made." She turned around, he followed; the door slammed shut, the lock buzzing into place, proof of their power and mine.

I exhaled, realizing I'd been holding my breath. Could she do this? Maybe if she acted before Zinc was here. My knees were weak and I sat, holding my head in my hands. At least she didn't hit me.

After a few minutes of wallowing, I sat up, ready to wrap myself in the only protection I had, Chopin. "Create a piano keyboard," I told the cube and a small one appeared. I stretched it out with my hands to regulation size and pulled it low in front of me. I'd never played like this before and needed a light touch. The sound wasn't bad for air keys; it was the solid texture that was missing, the clunk of the ivory. I played and was surrounded by music, reuniting me with old friends, a nocturne, a waltz, a concerto.

I heard the door lock open again and kept playing.

"Spartak." It was Sonia's voice.

I swiveled around. She was standing there with Tripper Bolt. I let out a scream and dropped to my knees, holding their legs, sobbing. Sometimes I was not a stud fighter.

He pulled me back up and she wiped my face with a handkerchief then pushed it into my hand.

"We're going to the hospital," Tripper said. "We need to get you to Zinc and away from here. Now!" He put his arm around me and walked me out the door with Sonia right behind, touching my shoulder. Hernandez was holding the door.

"Thank you," I told him. His eyes were wet.

We reached Sonia's armored limo in minutes and raced to the hospital, my three saviors sitting around me. At the door to Zinc's room we stopped and Sonia and Tripper hugged me.

Hernandez started to shake my hand. "To hell with it," he said, and pulled me tight.

"Take your time," Sonia said, "we'll be in the restaurant. Your ring and ear tracker are working here. We'll be close."

"And I'll be here," Hernandez said. He nodded to two other guards who stood aside. He opened the door and I went in.

Zinc was sitting up in his bed, waiting with sparkly, perfect white teeth, his face and chest not so good.

I hobbled to him as fast as I could, my abdominals still screaming, and we both cried, holding each other. Our hands were running over each other's broken bodies, examining wounds, kissing gently, seeking reassurance.

"I am so, so sorry," Zinc said over and over. "My mother lied about where you were. You're amazing."

I noticed not everything on Zinc was damaged. We'd discuss his mother later. I smiled at him and went to the door, whispering my plans to Hernandez. He laughed and closed the door behind me. I immediately slipped the lock, returned to the bed and pulled back the top sheet.

"Yeah?" Zinc asked.

"Oh, yeah!" I replied.

* * *

Zinc was released the next day. I let Sonia and Tripper tell him what happened and I wasn't allowed nor did I want to be with him when he met with his mother. When he returned, his face was contorted and he was incoherently furious. I'd never seen him so mad. He refused to give details and I knew it was wise not to press.

I tried to hide my abs from Zinc, now mostly concealed by a plastic wrap, not wanting him to see the jagged rips only partially healed. Maybe I'd have them cosmetically fixed; or, maybe not. They were badges of honor and the doctor, while gluing the wounds tight, said it would take at least a month to mend internally. No esthetic repairs until then. Still, I wanted to be perfect for him.

Attended by team of doctors, I exercised those parts of my body that I could, gradually increasing focus on my abs. I'd never felt so pampered. Doctors, nurses, physical therapists, massage therapists, estheticians, five-star chefs, and dieticians. I would never be a barronial but I could get used to this. After ten days of recovery, I started formal training. Coach Johanson was tough for the next three weeks, not cutting me any slack.

Working until exhaustion, I was perfecting my moves, mastering a quadruple twist on my release from the high bar, at least two of four times, developing new swings on the pommel horse—not easy with arms so big—holding motionless on the rings. And the dreaded vault, my worst event. I fell several times trying to do a triple twist dismount, never mind a quadruple. If only I could wear my XOs. The floor events were cathartic—running, tumbling, circling and handstands—letting me compartmentalize, focusing on form and movements instead of the horror of the kidnapping. And the tank top at least hid my scars and scabs.

I ripped one wound on a high bar dismount and one of the doctors was able to patch it. A stern-looking woman, black hair in a bun, forbade me from continuing and going to the trials. I talked with Coach and he intervened.

A week later, the competition to make the US Olympic gymnastic team began. "You should not compete. Your wounds could rip," Dr. Rai had warned at the McClain clinic when we were alone together. Zinc only trusted the family physician and wanted his opinion to make sure I was safe.

"I must do this. I beg you not to tell Zinc. I'll be careful."

After what seemed like endless haggling, the doctor had agreed only if he attended. I gave him a hug and he smiled.

Sonia, Ran, Dr. Rai, and a large security detail accompanied me to Stanford Stadium where the trials were held. Zinc was home but still recuperating in bed.

The athletes were mostly friendly. "Could I have a DIMM with you for my mom?" David Chon asked with a grin, a sweet Penn State student holding a small lumin. I ran to him and we both shouted, "Hi Mom!"

"Hey, slave boy," taunted some guy from UCLA, "I hear you lost your nerve and can't win."

I bulldogged my lips and rubbed my crotch. Negative comments were a game, to freak out your competition, to throw them off. Winners would be determined by a fraction of a point. Then I remembered the ever-present lumins. I knew Zinc was watching—but hopefully not that, the event was being carried live on a dozen national media sources.

"You're the reason," Marcus Wing, an AP reporter had told me.

It gave me energy, a need to show off. But it was also hard to believe the level of notoriety I had reached. I felt electric on the floor tumbles, still rings, and high bar, sticking a quadruple, something not planned. All tens. Each win made me hungry for the next.

"Hey slave butt," a guy yelled from another school, laughing.

"Want to kiss it?" I hollered back.

The uneven bars were last. I completed my first pass, getting a lousy stick on the landing. The second time on a triple high flip, my arms pounded hard on the bars. I felt my stomach rip.

Searing pain. I lost my grip, grunted, and fell helpless on my back. I opened my eyes on the mat, blood on my hands as I touched my gut and felt a gash an inch above my groin. Dr. Rai and the team doctor were on me seconds ahead of the media DIMM crews and worried athletes.

After ten minutes of emergency work in a stadium that had gone silent, I begged, "Please, let me walk off the floor."

"You are impossible," Dr. Rai snapped. He watched me, tightened his lips and looked away. "All right," he conceded, "but carefully."

I tried to sit up but collapsed back to the mat. Rai shook his head as he kneeled, slipping an arm behind my back and sitting me up.

Ransom was there too and put an arm under mine and around my shoulders. "Take a deep breath," he said and lifted me to my feet like I was a rag doll. He held me steady.

I glanced down at my bloody tank covering the medfoam. Both Rai and Ran were holding me. "Let me try." They let go but kept within inches. I started to collapse and they had me, keeping me vertical and steady. I looked at the crowd as I waited for the pain medication to take hold and my legs to stop wobbling. Every face seemed to be staring at me. I took several deep breaths. "Let me try again." They let go and I stood. I nodded once and they stepped away.

I slowly lifted my arm, struggling with my balance. I started to stumble; Ran grabbed me then moved back. "Do it, Spartak," he said, squeezing my shoulder.

I scanned the crowd, waved, and smiled, apparently the signal because everyone leaped to their feet, thousands of open palms skyward, whistling, screeching, applauding, and assorted foot stomping. It sounded like the stadium announcer was crying when he screamed my name.

I paused at the gym door, saluted, energized by the reaction, then turned and walked inside. I took two steps, collapsed and was immediately lifted onto a gurney and raced to an air ambulance. Sonia was with me, rubbing my forehead and giving me a kiss on my cheek. I understood why Zinc loved her. She contacted him to offer reassurance that I would recover and used the Z-ether from her class ring to let him have a look.

"Zinc, Zinc, he's okay," she insisted. "Please calm yourself." I couldn't hear what he said but could read it on her face.

"Zinc," I said, slurring his name, barely able to talk because of the pain medication.

"I'll call from the hospital. Yes, I will." She disconnected. "He was…a little upset. Hysterical, actually." She smiled and touched my cheek. "And he sends his love."

I learned in the recovery room that my first pass on the uneven bars was accepted. I'd lost points on the last event, no leeway for torture victims, nor should there be—but still made the team.

Tripper came to visit and told me the Z-ether universe was alive with unending reports about me—the kidnap, rescue of Mayor Rand, the dramatic reinjury at the trials and my status as the first slave to compete in three thousand years. And there were lots of DIMMs of my face, torso, and popping sweat at earlier matches. He thought it was funny but made no sense to me. Why was so much attention focused on a 16-year-old downer-boy?

The next morning, after the med-foam and meds stabilized the wound, Paolo took me back to Buena Vista House and wheeled me into the bedroom. Zinc was waiting.

CHAPTER 29

HAND IN HAND, WE WALKED INTO the ornate Beaux-Arts San Francisco City Hall, built in the early 20th century after the great earthquake, and just slightly taller than the capital building in Washington, D.C. Zinc loved the design, atmosphere, and audacity of the builders.

We were attending a fundraiser for the Chang Foundation, raising money for millions of refugees from the Chinese civil war. It was a stellar turnout of the super wealthy and political classes. And more diamonds and emeralds than perhaps were ever in one place in history. My presence had been announced as an additional draw.

Zinc was pleased people were anxious to meet me, even forming a queue at one point as if it were a reception. I tried to be warm and polite, but after an hour I gave him a look and he rescued me, making excuses and we headed to the men's room and bar. He handed me a glass of Hetch Hetchy water—I refused to break training—and chatted with Sonia, stunning in a floor-length, slinky aubergine silk dress.

"Hello, Spartak Jones," said a voice behind me. "I've been looking forward to meeting you. It's one of the reasons I'm here tonight."

I turned and faced a handsome Chinese woman, dressed conservatively in black with lots of pearls.

"Thank you, ma'am. I…it's always nice to meet new people." I stuttered, unsure what to say. "Beautiful necklace." I'd complained earlier that they didn't do name tags. Zinc stepped up. She put her arms around him and they exchanged a social kiss. "Wonderful to see you, Zinc. How is your father?"

I looked at Sonia and others while they talked, zoning out. When there was a pause I looked back and realized they were looking at me. I had to say something. "You know, you look amazingly like President Chiu."

She smiled and Zinc laughed.

"Spartak," he said with flourish, "may I present the President of the United States, Ali Chiu."

I dropped my glass.

* * *

"I want you to interrogate the prisoner," Ransom said in the small security room in the second basement of the mansion. "We've been trying to break him for two weeks."

"Why me?" I asked, glancing to Sonia and Zinc, then over to Ran's two sons, hoping they'd disapprove. I'd stayed with Ran while Zinc was recovering, grateful to be away from the McClain household. Tripper and Paolo also took part in the daily workouts and defense training. "Shouldn't the enforcers be doing this?"

"We've been working together, but they give me the nod when it concerns the McClains. I know this is not your kind of assignment but we need you."

Petre Martin, the man we were discussing, was a Russian Orthodox priest, a prominent End Timer. Missing most of his lower jaw, thanks to my boot knife.

"He's too delicate to use brain pumps or chemical extracts. But fear could get us what we need. Fear of you." He touched a finger into my chest. "The man denies any relationship to Bishop Perry," Ran continued. "Claims they acted alone. We don't believe it. The others were students at Claremont Christian Institute. All hard-core Christ-is-about-to-return-so-give-us-power types, determined to overthrow the government and Twelvers. The girl you decapitated was nineteen-year-old Molly Zoefeld of Modesto, a real sadist. She did much of the torture of Zinc, cut off one of the mayor's toes, and used the arc-truncheon on your stomach. The other woman who was there and disappeared is Kinuba Steele, a hired executioner."

I winced but others looked at me with what seemed like admiration. The world was fucked. I skimmed the bios of those I killed and mutilated. It was personal knowing names, seeing photos with family.

Dreams and lives ended. But it was necessary, I repeated endlessly in my head. Sixteen-year-olds shouldn't be doing this.

"Martin is terrified of you, with good reason," Ran said with a hard grin.

A little unnerving to see someone smile about it. But Ransom Bolt was hard, like a general in war.

"Dress like you did during the attack, including the boots. Leap and threaten. He froze when I told him you'd visit. Don't be gentle. Cut him again if useful. You'll be alone with him. Intel could save hundreds of lives, maybe thousands, and stop a war. Did they murder Cedric Rand? Any connection to the murder in New York? What else is planned?"

I didn't want to do this so I let my mind hunt for distractions. My geometry test was tomorrow afternoon, a paper in English lit about Shakespeare's love sonnets due in two days and I was horny, the perfect diversion. I gave Zinc a look, running a finger over my lips, and the man blushed. Setting priorities was critical.

* * *

Before me was the man who murdered two guards, kidnapped the mayor, and tortured the man I loved. I was undecided on God, but certain on my view of this self-righteous hypocrite who broke all the commandments in the name of his faith and ambition. Petre Martin watched me as I entered the hospital room and the guard exited, closing the door behind us.

I clicked the lock as loudly as I could. Sadism wasn't my thing but Zinc's favorite new book from his father suggested it might have a purpose.

Martin's eyes were wide, frightened as he tried to scoot to the side of his bed. His face was heavily bandaged with the bottom section of his jaw missing, a brain implant protruded from the base of his skull. Wearing my XOs and boots seemed like overkill but my orders were to be theatrical and in theater everything is make-believe. I saw no point in jumping on him or cutting him, as Ransom suggested.

Despite the disgusting things I'd done, that was not me. You don't have to torture people to get information. Hadn't we learned that long ago? He was no longer a threat but I could play with his head. I gave a full-tooth grin in spite of my queasy stomach. We stared at each other until he looked away.

"I only cut off part of your head when last we met. I hope you're not disappointed." I let him ponder the question, staring at him until he closed his eyes. He was trembling. "I think you have much to tell me. If not, I'm told you serve no purpose except as *'food for worms.'* That's on Ben Franklin's tomb. Maybe it can be on yours." I remembered the quote from history class. School stuff could be useful. Perhaps I'd tell my teacher. No, probably not. "Are we ready to talk?"

The word "YES" appeared immediately on the Z-ether at the end of the bed. I touched my ring and began asking a list of questions Ran had given me. I exhaled quietly, thrilled my approach worked.

* * *

Ransom gave me a bear hug when I left the room. "An inspired performance. You're exceptional, a reluctant warrior with remarkable instincts. I was ready to hurt him. You proved we didn't need to. Ben Franklin?" He laughed, folding his arms. "It won't be admissible but we have the names and confirmation on Bishop Perry. We don't need more to take action."

"What about Kinuba Steele?" He'd admitted they worked together but said he had no idea where she was.

"The FBI has the lead." Ran was wearing his black military-style shirt, stretched tight to accommodate his chest and arms, towering over me. He was my friend now and despite his size, I felt protected not threatened.

"Thanks for being my friend, Ran. You help me keep my sanity."

"No problem. I know things are rough on you sometimes." He touched my shoulder. "I admire you and will help anyway I can. You know my sons are fans too. Same offer."

"I feel totally overwhelmed at times. I'm a teenager who knows street fighting. I met the President yesterday…"

"I heard."

"I guess I looked pretty stupid."

"I've done worse. Zinc said she was charmed."

I stepped into the hallway and was surrounded by my ever-present security detail and went back to the mansion. I assumed they were to protect me, not hold me prisoner. Likely both. At least I liked Hernandez. Of course he worked for the McClains too.

CHAPTER 30

"I am Nocturne," a young woman's
urgent voice announced on the all-zan hack.
"America the beautiful, land of the free.
If only it could be.
Free Spartak. Freedom to vote.
Join the Second American Revolution, AR2"

"LEAVE HIM ALONE, MOTHER. HE'S MY lover and I care for him."

"He's not of our class. We are the chosen that is why we are so rich. He's beautiful but he's nothing, just something to use, a pretty bauble to enjoy and discard."

"I love him."

"You do not! You are infatuated because of the sex. It will fade, trust me, then what will you have?"

"A caring, smart a—"

"Enough. I bought him because I could. A gewgaw. Now he's famous, an even bigger prize. He is cunning, just using you, using us now that he's here, trying to break apart the family. Be wary."

"You are so full of shit, Glenda!"

They turned as Joshua Rand limped into Zinc's bedroom suite.

"Why are you so packed with venom?" His voice was harsh, his face still showing signs of the beatings. "Spartak is a hero. The Jesusistas are out to kill people like you, Glenda, and me and Zinc and Sergei. This boy you denigrate may have eliminated thugs who'd have detached your head from your body."

The mayor shook his head in disgust. "Zinc, don't let her poison you toward this young man."

I just stood there in Zinc's bathroom, the door partially open, listening.

* * *

"Just how big are you?"

"What?" I felt myself blush. Zinc was on his elbow on the bed, a few inches away, watching me read, stroking my arm. "It's not something we measure at the gym."

Zinc laughed and squeezed. "Your biceps, stud. They're huge."

"When pumped, eighteen inches."

"And when not pumped?"

"Then I don't measure."

"They look almost the size of your waist."

"Get glasses. My waist is twenty-seven inches."

"And your height and weight?"

"It's all in the purchase receipt when your mother bought me."

"Humor me, slave boy." He leaned forward and bit my shoulder.

"Yes, master. Almost five foot ten and growing. *Don't you leave a mark!* One hundred seventy-five pounds. Naked." I closed the book and rolled over, rubbing the inside of Zinc's ear.

"Oh wow, unfair." He took my hand and kissed it. "I think you need a new measuring tape. You're barely past five-nine. And naked is how I like you best."

"What's an inch or two? I thought you kept me for my music."

"I do as long as you play naked." I smiled as he continued, "It reminds me of perfection."

I rolled my eyes, sat up and pinched Zinc's stomach. "Actually you could use some tightening."

"Bunghole. You don't like me the way I am?" Zinc pinched himself. "Okay. Maybe you're right. But your just-outa-bed exercise regimen is insane. We already do the afternoon session and then combat training. How many sit-ups every morning before breakfast?"

"Crunches, not sit-ups. I do three hundred. Then two hundred push-ups and a hundred chins. Then I do stretches. Flexibility is important. Want to join me?"

"No way! But I do enjoy your flexibility. Maybe you can set up a program I might do just before we get out of bed."

"Hire a trainer."

"I have you under contract."

"Somehow I don't think what we do is training."

"What're you reading?"

"It's from Sonia's uncle, Justice Washington, about Italian history. It has much in common with *The Prince*."

"Tell me about it." Zinc sat crossed-legged on the bed.

I gave a brief synopsis.

"Really? Give some examples."

As I talked and read excerpts, Zinc's expression changed from love-sick teen to someone more distant, analytical and focused. He turned and looked at me, into me. I squirmed. "It's just ancient history," I said, closing the book, hoping I'd not made a mistake in sharing it.

"Not so ancient," he said, touching my leg before standing. "I'd like to read it. Want a black fizz?"

CHAPTER 31

I NEVER EXPECTED TO SEE THE nation's Capitol. The majestic domed building was iridescent at night, still glorious and making my heart pound. It was the focus of a major architectural preservation campaign. I thought about how many generations must have done the same thing, determined to keep it standing. As we passed the Lincoln Memorial, I had to remember to breathe. The statue inside wasn't a myth; it really existed. It was also my first trip in a plane—a posh 15-passenger sapphire blue bullet that took just over an hour. I'd expected some loud whoosh from the engines but they were silent. Zinc loaned it to Sonia; her family jet was in use by her dad. My family had three old bicycles.

There were five security guards including Hernandez. I wore my XO at Zinc's insistence but no one was to know. Surprise had already proven its value.

Sonia and I were hacked simultaneously on our minzans, and we both watched the young girl talk about America being America again.

"The hacks are actually quite intriguing," I said. "Some from *America the Beautiful*."

"Yes, from the original 1893 version. My favorite line is, *'till selfish gain no longer stain, the banner of the free.'* Other pieces come from different sources. Have you ever read Langston Hughes' poem, *Let America Be America Again?* "

"Yes. I discovered it when my poetry class assignment was to dig up a long-forgotten poem and perform it dramatically. And I came across Hughes. An anthem on freedom from the 1930s. I got goose bumps. The teacher was not pleased when I started reading and cut me off before I could finish. Connor applauded and called me a jerk."

"It is seditious if you are on the uptight, self-righteous receiving end. I suspect the teacher was just afraid. And we both have the same opinion on Connor."

We rode on in silence and I watched her in the shadows. She was a complex woman with depth and independence, not a spoiled baronial princess.

* * *

A bill on striking down impediments to voting and returning to a paper ballot was up again in the Senate. I remembered it from civics class. "S.B. 112 is always the first bill introduced by the liberals and always dies in committee," Sonia explained. "Until this year. Now public demonstrations, street fighting, and AR2 hacks have applied enough pressure and insecurity to cut a deal. There will be debate on the floor before it's killed."

"And this is progress?"

Our limo was flanked by two security pods and a dozen enforcers on black raptors. Sonia's family was clearly important. As we pulled into a private entrance at Congress, a phalanx of reporters surged forward barking my name, pressing hard against the barricades manned by capitol enforcers.

Sonia and I waved and ignored questions shouted about the rescue, being a slave, about voting rights. "Just smile and look beautiful," she had instructed. Ridiculous but fun. I was a good waver.

She'd given me bios on some of the players. In the Senate gallery, from a private box, I watched the senators from Mississippi and New Hampshire in a verbal duel.

"Thanks for bringing me here," I whispered to her.

"You're welcome. All part of my plan."

I had no idea what that meant but turned back to the action on the floor. Somehow the chamber seemed smaller than I expected but the sense of history made the hair rise on the arm of this downer-boy.

"Mr. President, I stand in support of S.B. 112," United States Senator Slade Greufew stated in a sweet tenor. The sixty-five-year-old politician ran a hand over his shoulder-length black hair streaked with gray, tied neatly behind his neck like one of the Founders, and adjusted his high-collared morning coat. He took a sip of water and checked the time on his gold pocket watch before tucking it into his glimmering red vest.

I'd met the senator in his office earlier, filled with photos of New Hampshire and famous politicians. When asked about his wardrobe, he had straightened, running a thumb under his lapel, telling me he loved the early 19th-century inspired look now in vogue with 22nd century touches. "Perfect for a senator, reminding me of John Calhoun or Henry Clay. Maybe even my oratorical hero, Daniel Webster." He was a member of the newly rechristened Democratic Freedom Party, stretching back to founder Thomas Jefferson. And he was used to losing. "Sometime," he admitted, "I'm not sure it matters."

The senator had asked me to autograph a photo. I signed it, "To My Dearest Friend, With Affection, Spartak Jones." The man seemed pleased. In return he had given me a copy of the new *Wild Elephant Protection Treaty of 2115* just approved by the Senate.

"I thought poachers killed the last wild elephant thirty years ago?" I'd asked.

"True but compromise takes time."

"It is time to eliminate the ever-changing, farcical requirements to receive a voter ID card," Greufew now thundered from the Senate floor. "The mandate is complex and can cost up to a week's wages of an average American to pay the fees to obtain the certificates. It seriously diminishes the number of Americans who can vote, thereby making it easier for a minority to rule. Eighty percent of adult Americans are not able to register. This is not democracy." He gestured with open arms. "And fraud in election returns is rampant. Electronic ballot counting is like having your competitor compile the tally. This must change for a return to freedom."

Eventually, he sat down. Even though I agreed with him, I thought time limits were a good idea.

"Senator Boatwright of Mississippi," droned the President Pro Tempore without looking up. The man looked like he'd died the week before. I was convinced his lips weren't moving.

"My distinguished friend and dear and respected colleague, Senator Greufew, fellow members of this august body. I rise in opposition." Barely fifty, Boatwright glanced around the chamber, gesturing as if there were a crowd, his long brown hair parted in the middle, hanging straight and touching his shoulders. Dressed in a black cutaway coat and high collar with glo-lite seams, he was the epitome of an antebellum and 2116 upper-class gentleman.

"What we have now IS real democracy," Boatwright said, already on a roll. "Our voting rate in the last national election was nearly eighty-five percent of those registered, the highest in history. Our campaigns are robust. I believe every self-supporting American should have the obligation to vote. And they do. The voter ID card is free. No barrier. There is no proof of fraud using the electronic ballot. I am fatigued by this nonsensical bill every year."

As his voice reached a crescendo, the Senator seemed to lose his place on his small Z-ether, uttered a profanity, barely audible, before continuing without notes. "Remember the advice of the late great President, Calvin Hodel, who warned that when the financially challenged vote, they seek more benefits by electing redistributionist politicians, better known as lib-er-als. *'Registering them to vote,'* he told this body in this chamber, *'is like handing out burglary tools to criminals.'* Enough!"

I agreed only with his final point. Enough.

My parents couldn't vote. It could take a week to visit all the necessary places and stand in line, pay fees to get approval. If you got that far, there were often challenges and appeals that could extend for months, even years. After that, the voting card was free. Most people were too stressed with survival to do this dance. And a constant barrage of media discouraged the vote. I'd hoped for more from such august and powerful men. Passage of S.B. 112 wouldn't solve all our problems but it was a first step. And maybe people would appreciate what it meant to vote. A dozen other members spoke, none enlightening. When I looked away and around the gallery, I noticed more eyes were on me than the senators. I leaned back and folded my hands in front of my face. Eventually the session ended, no action. Up next, a bill on hog futures. We left.

A reception later that evening included dozens of senators, congressmen, wives and a surprising number of children, many of them teenage girls. I lost count of how often my photo was taken with cheeky girls and boys who giggled, chomped gum, and occasionally touched my butt, which the shower room photo had made a popular point of interest.

"How do you think people might react if a DIMM of Senator Boatwright's tantrum found its way to Nocturne?" Greufew asked Sonia.

"It would make for interesting viewing," she replied, noncommittal.

Later that night, at my request, she took me to the Lincoln Memorial, the white marble radiant under the lights. I asked if I could just stand there, at the president's feet, in this Greek temple, and read his *Second Inaugural* and the *Gettysburg Address.*

"...American slavery is one of those offenses...God...wills to remove..." I said aloud, absorbing the power and relevance of the words, a slave, before Lincoln. I hadn't noticed any Lincolns in the senate.

"...a new nation, conceived in Liberty, and dedicated to the proposition that all men are created equal..."

As I read, I listened for Lincoln's voice, as my English lit teacher urged in class. I was convinced I heard it. "Martin Luther King stood here," I said, awestruck, turning toward the capitol at the far end of the mall.

I jumped. There were a dozen reporters with DIMM4s pointed at me. I wasn't sure why, but I felt a need to pose, looking into the distance, Lincoln behind me, proud even if I was not a free man. I walked to the nearby free black woman and offered my arm. She put her hand on it and we moved in silence down the white marble stairs, lumins recording our short journey to the waiting motorcade.

Moments later inside the limo, Sonia's eyes were moist as she wrapped her arms around my shoulders. "I'm so proud of you. You're a natural. Now we need to let you rest for tomorrow."

"What're we doing?"

"You'll be asked your views. Be honest but cautious. You'll be reaching a national audience via multiple channels. For nearly everyone, this will be the first time they've heard you talk and seen you outside of a sports or news DIMM." She took my hand. "Frankly, details are less important than image. A big smile right into the lumins, always upbeat, humble and boyish. Never say anything bad about anyone. Be the young man mothers love."

* * *

There was a live audience for the Dennis Claudius Myers Show. I spent a few minutes in a makeup chair where they focused on a stubborn shine on my forehead, and afterward met the host briefly, a short man with a light brown face, bulbous nose, and a gravity-defying swirl of sand-colored hair. He smelled like bourbon.

I was taken under the stage before he started and was told to sit in a steel chair with blood-red upholstery and safety fingers ready to encircle my chest and thighs. Remembering the cannon ride, I hesitated.

"Hurry," the assistant ordered, snapping her fingers, glaring at me. She was a young woman with a massive knot of green hair. I sat, squirming when the metallic straps snaked around me and tightened. On a Z-ether, I listened to Myers, or D. Claudius as he liked to be called, give my history and play clips from the rescue as well as shots of me in the Olympic trials, my collapse, even the photo of my butt in the shower. Myers claimed the student who took the shot made a fortune. The audience guffawed.

"Get ready," the woman said. "And hold on." I grabbed the chair arms and held my breath. My seat spiked up just as the ceiling slid open. I popped up on stage, bouncing a few inches above my seat, feeling like a carnival act. The area under my chair melded into the floor. My harness automatically retracted.

The light-washed set sounded like Ogden Stadium at capacity with applause and cheers, some of it real. It took a moment for my eyes to adjust and realize Myers was waiting for me to shake his hand. I did. It was limp and damp. He asked a series of questions and I talked about the horror of the car being ripped apart, being knocked senseless against the roof and dragged from the limo and beaten. I tried not to be a total wimp recounting how I regained consciousness hearing someone pounding Zinc.

The audience shrieked in horror when a photograph of my stomach hit the screen, taken when I was in surgery. I winced, appalled. Talk show hosts apparently had no limits on sensationalism.

A clip was played showing the explosion and attack, captured by street lumins, an avatar reenactment of the rescue, Zinc on a stretcher, a couple of corpses, the face of the chinless minister as he was being patched up, Mayor Rand hugging me and recounting my prowess and bravery. Totally gross. I looked away from the monitors.

"I had to save Zinc," I whispered at one point as a DIMM of his puffed and bloody face came on screen. Then Myers just sat there, watching me, eventually offering an inappropriate and disconcerting grin. He spoke slowly, emphasizing each syllable in an almost accusatory tone.

"You were in Washington to watch the debate on S.B. 112. What do you think? Should it pass?"

This was the knife.

"I think all citizens over eighteen should be able to vote. It's the American way. Voting is the heart of a democracy." It seemed elementary. There was scattered laughter, no applause. This was likely an all barronial audience.

"How about dumping the electronic, computerized counting of ballots, a process used successfully for over a century? Do you distrust it?"

I was at a total loss. Senator Greufew flashed in my head. "I was impressed by the kind of clothes popular in the Senate, old-fashioned jackets and high collars," I said, trying to sound thoughtful. "Like George Washington wore. I guess in terms of voting, if paper ballots were good enough for Madison and Jefferson, who am I to disagree?" I tried to look innocent, remembering Sonia's advice.

The audience whistled and laughed. Myers seemed shocked, his mouth open, and then joined in with the crowd.

"Tell me about the night you were kidnapped in the park near the academy, when you were captured and made a slave."

Another dagger. I couldn't answer directly. Criticizing your owners, even if you wanted to throttle them, was not recommended for long-term survival.

"I admit it was a surprise. I'm not sure why it was done...before the paperwork, I mean." I blathered as my mind searched for a way out. "My parents have a better life now, and my brother and sister. I'm proud of my role in helping the people I love most. So often one doesn't have the opportunity to give back to your family."

I took a drink of water to buy time while the audience applauded and whistled. "And while I don't want to be a slave, never thought of myself as one, I willingly give myself every day to the man who now owns me, the man I now love, Zinc Ogden McClain."

I was surprised when the audience jumped up, making more noise than seemed possible. I blushed and tried to smile as a tear slid down my cheek. This was fun.

Soon it was over. "You were brilliant on the voting questions, Spartak," Sonia told me later. "I wasn't surprised." She was upbeat as our convoy headed to the airport. "And you may now be the fantasy heartthrob of anyone with a pulse. Every mother in America will want to hug you or get in your pants."

"I hope not."

CHAPTER 32

ZINC MET US AT A PRIVATE airport in Marin. Beside him was a tall olive-skinned man, striking, with curly black hair, dark eyes. His biceps stretched the sleeves of his white knit shirt. He looked familiar. Zinc grabbed me, kissed me, his tongue on overdrive. Sonia kissed her man with considerably less drama. Zinc had told me before I left that she had a love interest.

"Spartak," Sonia said, shaking her head as she watched Zinc, "this is my new special friend, Adi Aban. He goes to Cal and is quarterback on the football team."

I managed to pull one arm free. "That's where I've seen you, sir," I responded, unsure how I should address the man, Zinc licking my neck. "Nice to meet you." We shook hands.

"Hey, just call me Adi. No 'sir' shit. I'm just a guy crazy about Sonia."

"Get in line," I responded, "we're all crazy about Sonia."

"Thank you," I told her as she prepared to leave with her own security team. "It made government real, for better or worse. You're very kind."

"Treat him well," Sonia admonished Zinc before leaving.

"I wept when you said you loved me and surrendered to me each day," Zinc said as we walked up to the metallic gray limo. It made me giggle when the door opened, the side of the vehicle sliding with a swish to the underside of the chassis for maximum room in getting in and out. He pushed me inside with a laugh. "That was so romantic." Zinc was all over me in the backseat, activating the privacy shield only after I begged, as my pants were unbuckled and pulled down.

"We only have thirty minutes."

"Plenty of time," Zinc whispered, leaning in for a kiss, unbuttoning my shirt. I enjoyed the sex, was deeply fond of Zinc, and knew that as long as Zinc wanted me, my family was safe. It was an odd reality for an honest relationship.

"We'll have your abs repaired before the Olympics." Zinc ran his fingertips over the scars. "The guy who does my mother will make you perfect again."

And thirty minutes wasn't enough. The security detail waited quietly outside the limo that rocked in a familiar rhythm until we exited, red-faced, and straightened our hair and clothes.

* * *

School settled down, closer to normal. I had to convince Hernandez and Zinc to keep security guards in the control room and give me freedom to interact with friends. "As teens like to do," Hernandez agreed. The man who helped prep me for the transition into slavery now fussed over me like a brother, not a jailer. We were after all only about ten years apart.

I had regular contact with my family, even having them over for a tour of the McClain mansion when Connor and his mother were traveling. They were intimidated, awestruck. Zinc showed a surprising interest in learning details of their life. He had no idea how downers lived.

I headed back to class after lunch period, leaving the cafeteria with Rhonda. We heard a yell. Someone was being beaten. I recognized the voice.

"Billy!" I shouted, running into a storage area behind the kitchen, hoping my bearings were right. Students swarmed behind me, anxious to see a fight. I leapt over a line of trash cans into a large pantry. Two barronial toughs were holding Billy, a third pounding his gut.

"ENOUGH!" I commanded, tensing my arms and legs for a takedown. *"Let him go! NOW!"*

"Shut up, slave boy," Duncan Spike snarled. "You gonna make me?"

"No problem," I said, stepping toward him. "This time it's personal, picking on my friend." Payback time. This would be sweet.

"Fight, fight, fight," the crowd behind us chanted, maybe thirty students. An audience seemed good; witnesses were useful.

"You can take the first swing. I figure you'll need some kind of advantage to stand a chance against a downer boy."

"Punk!" Spike snarled and swung a fist at my head.

I ducked and jumped back. "Is that the best you can do, big boy?"

He charged, screaming, arms wide, at my midsection. I dodged to the side and grabbed one of his wrists, yanked it behind his back and slammed the edge of my outstretched hand between his shoulder blades. He hit the floor face first and hard. You could hear a crunch. I flipped him over, like a sack of potatoes. He swung a fist and I grabbed it, squeezing until he yelped.

"Do it, Spartak!" A familiar voice in the crowd shouted a few feet away. I glanced over. It was Pablo, the seventh grader Spike and his goons beat up in front of the music department and I'd abandoned to keep from being expelled. Since then I'd discovered peach was his favorite flavor of ice cream.

"This is for Pablo." I hammered my fist into Spike's gut. He bolted up, gagging like he was about to vomit, like Pablo did that day. "Step back!" I yelled to the crowd and I grabbed an arm and ankle and did an airplane twirl, faster and faster, then let go. He flew across the room, hitting a wall and collapsing into a stack of boxes. The thug disappeared with screams under jars of strawberry preserves and peanut butter. XOs were so cool. The other two jerks, jaws open in shock, still held Billy.

The double doors from the kitchen entrance banged open. Tessie and a half dozen kitchen helpers, armed with rolling pins and pots, charged them, making contact, knocking them to the floor as the boys screamed. She held up her hand, the general in command. The room was silent except for the string of Spike's obscenities from under the boxes and the whimpering of his friends.

"Billy's a friend of ours," she warned the two staring up, her upper lip drawing back to show teeth as the boys cringed. "Don't fuck with him! Understand?"

Both barronials nodded.

"Get out before we get really pissed!"

They ran off just as Spike stood. The thug looked at Tessie and the students. Regaining his balance, he straightened his clothes, rubbed his head and tried to walk out with dignity, spitting on the floor by me. "You'll pay for this," he snarled. Tessie hit him in the back of his head with the pin. He fell to the floor with a scream and she prepared for another swing. Never mess with Tessie. He did a fast crawl through the laughing students until he could get up and run.

"Are you okay?" I asked Billy, holding him.

"Yeah, I'm fine. Just my pride. Another wimp-boy who can't hit worth a shit."

"I promise you this won't happen to you again. I'm going to give you some training and get you a special addition to your wardrobe."

"What?"

"I'll explain later." I ran to Tessie and embraced her. "Thank you and thanks everyone." I raised an arm and shouted: *"The cafeteria crew is number one!"* There was a loud cheer and then the crowd started to break up, the fight over, students talking excitedly about what they'd seen. It was unprecedented, taking on barronials, downers fighting back. There would be consequences. But at this moment, it felt great.

"Did you see Spartak fuckin' toss that asshole like he was a pack a wieners?"

"And the way he jumped!"

"You are amazing," Pablo said, coming up to me. "Thanks for being my friend." We hugged and he walked away, turned and grinned. We exchanged thumbs-up.

I turned back around. "Billy, what happened?"

"They grabbed me when I left the cafeteria and pulled me in here. Then started hitting me. But I don't think it was me they wanted. They wanted to coax you here, to rescue me. Not sure why."

"Makes no sense."

"Spike mentioned your name as he punched me, making sure you were close before he started pounding. At least I didn't fall down or vomit like I sometimes do."

I put my arm around him, proud I could help my friend.

CHAPTER 33

Duncan Spike, his two friends, and their parents filed a formal complaint of hooliganism and assault against Billy and me, with the school and enforcers, demanding we be expelled and arrested. It was all over the news. A major San Francisco law firm, Browner and Dean, submitted the charges. There were demands that Tessie and the kitchen help be fired and blacklisted.

Zinc examined the paperwork, explaining our options as we sat in his office. He seemed like a new man, a grown-up one. "This is a direct attack on my lover and family," he pronounced. He saw it as his first challenge as head of McClain Enterprises, a test of leadership. People would be watching. And he needed more than a passing grade.

"I'll do with my power, money, and my dad's connections what you do with your sword," he said, full of bravado. "These barronials are just billionaires, their total net worth a rounding error for the McClains." He reached over and took my hand. I sensed he wanted me to be proud of him.

Zinc collected his financial, political, and legal teams and conferred with Sergei, using Henry's Place as his war room. His lawyers interviewed all witnesses and prepared notarized statements, coordinating with the DA and enforcers. Politicians met with his lobbyists, donations were made to upcoming campaigns. There were people from the Justice Department, bank examiners, the mayor's office and a couple of judges. It seemed like a small army, some looking less savory than others.

"You're going to enjoy this," Zinc said as he pulled me into the grand offices of Headmaster Thragman.

I knew Thragman rarely acknowledged Zinc in the hallways and was sometimes dismissive, seeing Zinc as a stuttering loser. And yet the guy was afraid of Connor. Big mistake. I had shared the story of what happened outside the music department involving Spike, Connor, the freshman boy and the Headmaster. Also the enforcer interview about Cedric's murder and Thragman's threats. And it fit with what he'd witnessed many times, he said, the double standard on justice. Zinc swung open the main door and we walked in.

"We're here to see Headmaster Thragman."

"He's busy, make an appointment," Mrs. Buttersworth mumbled, sounding bored, touching her hair. I decided her head looked like a wedding cake today, the long creamy hair braided around, flat on top just lacking a plastic bride and groom.

Zinc marched past her, swaggering just a little, and opened the door to his office. I followed, wishing I were somewhere else but excited to see his expression. Scholarship boys did not challenge the headmaster.

"What are you doing here?" Thragman growled. "See my secretary. Leave!"

"I am here to discuss the incident involving Duncan Spike and Spartak. First, you will do nothing against any of the cafeteria staff."

Thragman stood and snarled: "You do not walk into this office uninvited with him and order me to do anything. You are both students."

"A student who is the grandson of the founder of Ogden Academy, heir to the McClain fortune, and the main benefactor of this school."

"Get out!"

"Listen closely, Headmaster, I will only say this once. The academy *will* host a face-to-face with everyone in the assault case—including you, top administrators, the enforcer chief and district attorney. Plus all student witnesses."

"I will do no such thing! This is a private matter, not the school's fight." Thragman fumed, "Settle it in court!"

"You need to understand, sir, this is not a request. There are consequences should you choose to oppose me. Your contract is up early next year and could be terminated earlier. Do you control more votes than I do? You may want to query the board. I have."

Zinc bowed formally, like some European prince and exited the room with me trailing. It was delicious. I could see he burned with an intensity I'd never before witnessed, a new calling, controlling his anger, making himself stronger, more like his Dad. He was being trained as a businessman and "an operator," as his father liked to say, so this was his public debut, a small venue preparing him for the big stage. And people would judge his performance.

We worked overtime on his stuttering. When he was engaged mentally, driven, the stuttering disappeared. It was present mostly in awkward social situations or when he wasn't concentrating. The things that most embarrassed him in life, he openly shared with me. "You are my sanity," he told me.

The opposition lawyer sent a snooty electronic response declining to meet. Zinc sent a succinct handwritten note by courier.

Dear Mr. Browner:

If you believe your firm serves no purpose, that the case is beyond your capacity, then by all means boycott the meeting and save yourself public humiliation.

Zinc Ogden McClain
CEO, McLain Enterprises

The meeting was held in an old-world conference room at the academy. Nothing unusual there, the oak table had carved lion legs, the high backed chairs embossed with the ornate OA crest. All players were there, including the student witnesses.

Dr. Thragman welcomed everyone with lofty condescension. This would be a slam-dunk, the outcome a certainty. "I am delighted all parties were willing to come together today. Let us start with the plaintiff's attorney, William Browner." He gestured to the attorney, a short, balding man, who rose to speak.

Zinc jumped to his feet and raised his arms. "I will begin this meeting. My name…is *Zinc…Ogden…McClain!*"

"What?" Browner said, looking shocked. Then angry.

"I am certain that it was an *unintentional* procedural mistake on the part of our *current* headmaster to call on the plaintiff's attorney rather than the person who filed for this meeting. We shall discuss this later, Dr. Thragman." He turned to Browner. "And you may sit down now. When I am done, you will have your turn." His expression was stone, like his dad when angry.

If Zinc were anyone other than one of the most powerful teenagers on the planet, I suspected the lawyer would have huffed off. But the man was uneasy, I could tell from his expression. This was not the Zinc he expected. Everyone seemed nervous. I knew I was. Browner sat uttering a curse under his breath and pinched lips. He was beyond pissed. People twisted in their seats, exchanging glances. Zinc seemed satisfied.

"I introduce myself because it's important as the new head of McClain Enterprises to give you a sense of how I will handle my responsibilities in this case." He picked up a soft-cover binder.

"First, here is a copy of all statements by witnesses proving beyond a reasonable doubt that there is no case and, further, that this was a staged confrontation to do physical, criminal harm to Spartak Jones and Billy Eagle."

"That's improper!" Browner shouted, rising.

"DOWN!" Zinc commanded, more like father than son, more predator than cub, the hungry expression of a powerful man ready to devour.

Browner stood, red-faced and with curled fists. Then he dropped into his seat, scribbling notes at a furious pace to distract from his humiliation.

Zinc turned to the three students who filed the complaint then to their parents and pointed at them. They stared back at him, nonplussed. He spoke in a slow cadence, taking each sentence in short segments, concentrating on his pronunciation. It just made his nonstuttering delivery more dramatic, like he was controlling his fury.

"Since you have challenged a member of my household and his friend with false allegations, I will leave it to the enforcer chief and district attorney to determine your criminal liabilities. I believe there should be repercussions but the law will be followed. Beyond that, there will be serious financial ones. Your lives will change this hour."

He touched the yellow zan-cube he brought and had preset the Z-ether on the sidewall. On Zinc's command, it showed a list of companies, banks, and figures.

"Note the column on the left," he said, trying to sound like an accountant with attitude, not an arrogant rich teenager. "The plaintiffs have their funds managed by these financial service companies. As of nine p.m. last Wednesday night, McClain Enterprises took control of all the corporations in question. What stock we didn't already own we bought.

"As of ten a.m. this morning, administrators froze all assets of the plaintiffs until certain irregularities in their accounts are addressed. It appears there may be criminal abuses. We are working with the Attorney General and federal prosecutors. A federal grand jury will investigate and an indictment is possible."

The parents looked shocked, disbelieving, numb, exchanging incredulous glances. They erupted, spouting obscenities, denying the coup.

"It was Connor's idea!" Spike screamed, red-faced.

Zinc held up his arms. I could read his face. Suspicions confirmed. Deal with it later.

"Further…further…" He waited for the room to quiet, his voice commanding, arms still raised. "Tomorrow my lawyers will notify all barronials, the national Chamber of Commerce, and all businesses associated with McClain Enterprises, that Browner and Barnes or any attorney on its staff will never do business with my companies nor will my companies work with any business that uses their services." He looked directly at the president of the firm.

"That's illegal and unethical!" Browner barked, indignant, stunned, his face crimson. "We'll sue!"

"Interesting threat," Zinc said, resting a finger on his lips, considering his point. "If you're not in jail or disbarred, then I guess the question is whether your financial resources can outlast mine. There are consequences, Mr. Browner, when you assist those bearing false witness against my family or any family. Integrity applies to lawyers above all. Perhaps you can plead ignorance at disbarment proceedings. I suspect every attorney in California will understand if the plaintiffs seek new legal help."

He interlaced his fingers, touching them to his nose, like his father did, as he looked at the plaintiffs, all pale as ghosts.

"These are my terms." He picked up a written list from the table and handed it to Browner. "An immediate apology, verbally, today before witnesses and in writing tomorrow, properly notarized, accompanied by a statement on DIMM, appropriately humble. There will be an admission of filing knowingly false and reckless accusations and a conspiracy to harm the accused by the three students. The three plaintiffs will be immediately expelled from the academy. That means this afternoon. A declaration from the law firm admitting criminal bad judgment in taking a case it knew was false. And all of this goes public."

"That would ruin us." Browner's voice dropped to a whisper. "And make the boys liable for criminal action."

"Yes," Zinc said. "Oh, one more thing. Tessie and her friends will face no reprimands or problems of any kind. Indeed," he said, looking at the stunned headmaster, "she will be promoted two grade levels and all will receive substantial raises. Letters of commendation will be put in their records, signed personally by you, Mr. Thragman, in your most florid prose. And the size of the raises—fifty percent seems reasonable. If there is not enough money from the kitchen budget, take it from the Office of the Headmaster. I will so notify the McClain representative on the OA board who will make it a priority item at the meeting next week when we discuss your contract."

Billy and I stared at him. It felt fabulous, energizing, and no stuttering. Finally, finally, the bullies knew exactly how it felt to feel helpless, to be themselves bullied. Applause started, one person, two, until all the student witnesses were on their feet. Tessie was gleaming. The headmaster looked like he just birthed a porpoise. Spike and his two accomplices hurried toward the exit with their distraught parents.

Ransom and five San Francisco enforcer officers stepped into the doorway. Ran, who looked even more imposing than normal with twin sonics on his belt, held up his hand. "You are not done."

"Just a little more, I promise," Zinc said, smiling as if this were a pleasant chat. The families turned to him, far more panic than anger now in their faces, the taste of unconditional surrender bitter on their barronial tongues. "I will have notarized reports on your confessions before sunset or you will be on the street tonight or asking friends for charity. Assuming you have friends after word spreads. And the rest of my demands tomorrow. Your credit and all bank accounts were frozen as you sat here. Even the secret ones in the Caymans and Zurich. It will likely take a decade to untangle your finances, if you have the money and if you can find legal help. I wouldn't be too hopeful. So you may want to cooperate."

One of the parents started to yell and Zinc help up his hand. "This is really a contest of zeros," he said. He leaned on the edge of the table, a teacher lecturing students. "You should learn to count before you pick a fight. And you should have taught your children to be responsible and honest." Zinc crossed his arms. "Do what I've requested. This afternoon. The deadline is absolute. Your homes are now padlocked with enforcers in front. Mr. Bolt, let them go."

They stumbled away, parents shrieking at their sons.

I ran over and embraced Zinc. "You're amazing. My hero." We kissed.

"Let the word go forth," he said to a round of applause.

I knew for Zinc this was about more than just this event. He was using it to establish himself as unassailable, ruthless, not to be crossed on pain of destruction. I was thrilled but something also made me apprehensive. This whole thing wasn't right no matter how giddy I felt. He did to middling barronial families what they did to downers, no process for justice just force, bending judges, a district attorney, even a governor to the will of the most powerful. It was retribution, vengeance, and perhaps deserved. Maybe there was no other way in this America and this was a legitimate platform to prove his might. But justice should not come at the hands of the aggrieved and most powerful. That was thugocracy. Schoolbooks explained the theoretical process of the courts in a fair trial. That should be the goal, not this, no matter how giddy I felt, and proud. I knew I was dealing in the hypothetical, dreamy liberal ideals about American fairness, but that was just me, overthinking my Zinc telling the world I was his Spartak and don't mess with me, us. For that I had to love him even more.

Back at Buena Vista, he left me inside the living room as he stomped out onto a patio overlooking downtown. Connor and Glenda were there enjoying drinks and the sunset. If they'd heard word of the proceeding, they didn't show it. Or perhaps they felt immune.

"Connor, you're behind the attack on Spartak and his friend at school," Zinc charged in a low roar. "That is unacceptable."

Connor looked calmly at his brother. "I deny it. You can't prove it. And Spartak's a bully." Glenda nodded.

"Duncan confessed to me in front of dozens of witnesses, including enforcers and the DA. And I have destroyed his family and two others to make my point. They are ruined because of you, beggared. Don't fuck with me. Not anymore. Connor, you think there are no consequences for your foolishness. Your allowance and lines of credit are forfeit until you show signs of maturity."

"Fucker! Who are you—"

"I'm the man who now controls your entire trust fund, all your bank accounts, all disbursements, all property, all credit. All are now frozen. Don't mess with me. Don't tempt me!"

"Boys! Please…" Mother said, rising to her feet.

Zinc turned his back on her and left the room.

CHAPTER 34

"We're going to heaven?" I wasn't sure I heard it right. "Are you going to kill me or are you going to join the Jesusistas?"

We were in Zinc's obscenely large closet suite, sated, showered, and picking out a wardrobe. Until now, Zinc refused to say what we were doing tonight, rejecting my ideas, and it was already eleven. Something was happening. Even Paolo and Tripper had been secretive and largely absent the past week.

"Yes, we are." Zinc tossed me a sleeveless green crew neck, open on the sides, narrow on the front. "Put this on, and...wear these Clingers."

"Those pants are too tight and don't cover my rear if I bend over."

"True, but they move well on you. Or do you prefer the paper underwear that adorned your bubble butt in the holding cell?"

I pulled them on. "I look like I'm advertising. Will angels care?"

"Very much. Try on the shirt."

I pulled it over my head. "No way!" It was threadbare and holey. "I can't believe St. Peter wants to see me in this."

"You'd be surprised. As your owner, I command it."

"This *'I command it'* shit is getting old, Master." I tried to sound serious, a bit miffed. "You own my body, but not all my body parts may obey you in the way you like best if you're mean to me."

He touched my hair and kissed my forehead. "I love your sassy mouth." Zinc lifted the front of my shirt and ran fingertips over my abs. "Mom's surgeon did wonders on the scars. They're almost gone."

He moved behind me, turning me toward the mirror, his chin on my shoulder. Heaven was stamped across my chest in a glowing rainbow of colors. My arms and pecs bulged; every curve on my abs was obvious. He was grinning as his fingers danced over my stomach. "One, two, three, four, five, six, seven, eight. I thought an eight-pack was just legend. And here it is. Perfect for Heaven."

"Please be serious."

"It's the name of Paolo and Tripper's new dance club. It opens tonight in previews and we…that means you…are going to give them the sexy sparkle to make it the place to wiggle and sweat. My role is to show the paparazzi that rich kids love Heaven too."

"I knew they were up to something. When I asked they kept putting me off. Heaven." I watched him buckle the top of his favorite boots. They were hideous and no way would I let him go out wearing them. "Hold on! Is this in the old Episcopal Church building you bought on Nob Hill?" As I waited for an answer I pointed to his feet and shook my head. Two can play the wardrobe game.

"Yes," he said with an indulgent smile. "I'm leasing it to them for a dollar a year." He sat on the sofa, took off his boots and shrugged his shoulders, waiting for my suggestion.

A sofa in his closet! I pointed to a pair of party shoes, shiners, I called them. They lit up like purple lightning when you tapped the toe. He nodded, grinned and put them on. I rubbed his hair. We were good together. "We can thank the blood feud between the US church and the egomaniacal archbishop in Nigeria," he said, ignoring our mutual teasing, "now officially the Archbishop of Canterbury, who detests anything American. And still hates homs even though rumor is that he is one."

"They're competing with the Palladium." We'd gone there once with Tripper and Paolo. This explained the visit, my second one. I liked this guy, Zinc McClain, and ownership did imply more than a one-night stand if I could survive.

"That's one reason we wanted to keep it under wraps until we were ready for a private preopening that will launch a major media campaign. Oh, and there will be signs announcing it is a San Francisco sendoff for our own Olympic athlete and hero, Spartak Jones."

"What? That's embarrassing."

"More embarrassing than the outfit?"

"About the same. Why didn't you just ask?"

"I thought you'd want to help them."

I thought about the brothers, there for me when Zinc was hospitalized. I remembered being locked in the cell and Tripper getting me out. "I'd do anything for them."

"Thank you." He nodded, smiled. "I knew that."

"The name's funny." I tried a puppy face. "Please let me wear a larger shirt like yours, asshole."

He laughed. "Nobody wants to see my body."

"I look like I need a bra." I enjoyed giving him a hard time and he loved it.

Being embarrassed was nothing new; it seemed to be part of my job description. I looked back in the mirror and shook my head. "Dreadful. Undignified. But kinda hot." I thrust out my butt. "The slave does as commanded."

* * *

"You're triumph!" Tripper shouted, running to us as we entered a side door to Heaven, my name on a big sign outside. He hugged Zinc and held on to me, squeezing tight. "Thank you."

"Thank you for the invitation," I said. "But please don't ask me to bare my butt."

Tripper laughed.

"No need," Paolo said, walking up and slapping my rear, "not with you in those pants."

I sensed their affection was real; it was for me. We were brothers by choice.

The music was tactile, throbbing from the floor, down from the stone vaulted ceiling, blasting from the sidewalls. The dance platform was crystal shards of light, pulsing, shifting, wrapping around the sea of sweaty dancers as they thumped each other reaching for the magic. It was all in counterpoint to the building, an old Episcopal cathedral on Nob Hill with dramatic flying buttresses and Renaissance era bronze doors.

Zinc took me by the hand as we oscillated to the heavy beat of a six-member band on the apse, a curved stage at the east end. I'd never experienced anything like this. A dozen male and female dancers were gyrating on six-foot columns spaced evenly down the long nave of the old church. They were naked except for glowing blue collars and minimal coverage in strategic places. It was classier than the Palladium and with no lines of mostly naked poor kids offering themselves to spoiled rich ones. I saw several downers from school and waved. They just wanted to have fun.

Outside lights shot through the stained glass windows, moving to the beat. I watched closely. No, it was a clever phantasmagorical projection. The holy figures seemed to vibrate, Mary, Joseph, and Jesus alive, floating in the vault over the dancers. Maybe Tripper should invite Bishop Perry.

People pointed at me as we danced to the center of the floor. I felt lost in the sensation: I swayed, pounded, and jumped, grinding into my master, making love to the slivers of light, reaching toward an archangel high overhead. I wanted to give a good show. Zinc swung to me and away. He looked a little overwhelmed by the sexual energy. The crowd circled around but left us plenty of space. I waved at the gawkers and cams, holding on to Zinc's belt. I let go, turned and landed a series of somersaults, as people shouted. The band transitioned to another song, a female singer stepped up, her long pink hair swirled high, the sparkles on her dress like fireflies.

"Shadows in the dark, yearning to be free
Waiting for the sun, desperate to be part of day...
Let me find love...Let me be free..."

I swiveled back toward the stage. It was her song with a heavy dance track.

"Rhonda!" I was ecstatic, jumping up and down, arms overhead, grabbing Zinc. *"My God, it's Rhonda!* Did you do all this? Thank you, I love you!" Zinc was helping my friend, an opportunity she would not likely have without him. And obviously he could spot talent.

I pulled him close and kissed his ear. We danced our way to the base of the stage. Rhonda pointed at us, bent down and touched fingers. "Sweet honeysuckle!" I screamed and she blew me another kiss. Billy Eagle, wearing a red bead headband with a real eagle feather dangling over his ear, pushed through from the side. We hollered and hugged.

"How?"

"Tripper and Paolo invited me!" The rest was lost to noise.

I saluted Zinc and rubbed butts as we three danced, song after song, drenched, taking off our shirts, watching Rhonda seduce the crowd.

Then, suddenly, Zinc turned over his forearm, looking at his SubQ. He touched my shoulder. "An emergency. We must leave now."

CHAPTER 35

"I am Nocturne," an old man's wise
voice announced on the all-zan hack.
"We are all slaves of a corrupt system.
Return the vote to all Americans.
We are all Spartak! Join AR2."

The funeral was held at City Hall, rather modest for such a rich man, because Sergei apparently didn't want anything to do with the churches. I got my family invited to experience the spectacle and Zinc insisted they sit with us. Neither Connor nor Mrs. McClain said a thing to me, just looked away, perhaps nervous in the face of this new reality that the geologic plates in their lives might be shifting. Glenda sat white-faced in genuine grief.

Sergei's death had shocked even those close to him despite the doctor's warning that it was probable. A stroke had ended his life within minutes. Zinc wasn't able to get back in time to say goodbye.

President Ali Chiu delivered a moving eulogy about the role Sergei had played in her career as the first Asian American woman to reach the highest office. My parents, brother, and sister were startled when she walked over, gave me a hug and introduced herself, saying what great parents and siblings they must be to have such a sensational son and brother. One of the few times I've ever seen Geo or Kimber speechless. I remembered dropping my glass when I'd made a fool of myself over her in this same space.

Sonia sat next to Zinc, holding his hand. Justice Washington attended as well as the governor, members of Congress, major entertainers and other faces I didn't recognize but knew they were rich by their clothes, jewels, and pushed up noses. Ransom, looking grim, his family and most members of the household staff were there.

I knew Sergei had, at best, been an emotionally cold father but pushed his eldest son to do well in school and provided special tutors in economics, business, and practical politics. But hugs and love seemed absent. Just the opposite in my family; no money but constant encouragement and affection.

Glenda McClain was dramatic, emotional, as if a scene from a play and she were awaiting applause. Zinc had rehearsed his eulogy with me, helping craft a loving tribute from a grieving son and leaving no doubt who was now in charge. Some of it had been worked on weeks earlier by Sergei himself and a top speechwriter. The man was always looking three steps ahead, ghoulish and ever ready.

"...After the assassination attempt, my father and I spent many hours together, reviewing the future of the McClain family and McClain Enterprises, exploring and firming all legal, financial, and political issues, laying long-term plans as my father knew so well how to do. While heavy with grief at the passing of a great man, my loving father, I feel empowered and anxious to step forward and lead my family and our business empire through the 22nd century."

It was not exactly weepy but it left no doubt about the transition. Women took a secondary position in inheritance, a nod back to the 19th century, a product of religious and conservative forces pressing federal and state governments decades ago. I hoped that meant Glenda would keep her distance. But I was nervous; she was devious and relentless. As always, Zinc was my protection.

Connor simply stared at me through the crowd.

* * *

I dressed quietly before dawn while Zinc slept, and slipped out of the bedroom.

"Hi Malcolm," I told the thin, serious-looking robo-guard near the front door. "Early rehearsal." I'd told Zinc last night that I was going to the music department but not that I was including a side trip to my old neighborhood. Or, that I'd ditch security. I didn't want to get Hernandez in trouble by asking him to lie. The robot could sense deception so I was the epitome of calm.

I walked midway down Boehner Lane, took off my school blazer and hung it on a corner of a green compost container. The alley still smelled like disinfectant and mulch. Some things didn't change: the apartments still needed paint; the red geraniums were brown; the dumpster smell hopefully gave the Sniffers stuffed noses; the same tiny flag with my name on it still hung from a second-story window. Now I just needed to wait. I'd sent word that I'd be here. More than a little nervous, I sat on an old metal bench and concentrated on my breathing to keep my knees from twitching. I was crazy to do this. I saw a calico cat run down the alley. No other life could be seen but I heard plenty on nearby streets; a couple groaning near an open window. Hets did some odd things in bed.

No fog. Strange. There was always fog.

"Hey, pretty boy."

It was Dalix, same bass voice. Jason, Mark, and Onzi were with him, all standing in a line. When last we were here, I was lucky and walloped them before they could do it to me. I knew what was coming. I broke the code and showed disrespect. Dalix looked smug, dressed in a black tank that highlighted his biceps and shoulders. His hair was still in the Samurai topknot, a good look. Jason rubbed his hands together, always anxious, all brawny with pumped legs, dark with long black hair pulled behind his head. Horse was the perfect nickname. Mark, the thin man of the pack, with a bulky green sweater, wore his standard snarly grin. Onzi with the massive kinky orange hair. We loved each other. Now they wanted to hammer me.

"I want to talk," I said, standing up and moving closer, arms open. "If you want to hit me, I'll just stand here. I'm sorry for what happened before."

"You got your security goons hiding?" Onzi asked.

"No. I'm here alone to see you and take my punishment if that's what you want. I want to be your friend again. I need to talk. I think you'll be interested in what I have to say."

They circled me. I stood, lowering my arms. Dalix grabbed my tie, yanking me forward, face-to-face, and punched me in the gut. I staggered back, into the others who started a game of it, shoving me and battering my midsection and back.

"Don't hit his face!" Dalix yelled.

After three rounds, I folded over, gagging, one arm holding myself from the pavement, then to my knees, letting the pain and breathing even out. I looked up, arms again at my sides, waiting for more.

"Enough!" Dalix ordered. Jason helped me stand. "Despite proof to the contrary, we really don't want to hurt you," Dalix said. "Much. Never did really. It's no fun if you don't fight back. Even when you beat the crap out of us." He laughed. "What a war last time. You were magnificent!"

"You guys punch hard." I tried to smile while rubbing my gut. It held up just fine, considering.

"You too, bro," Jason replied.

"So, you're not going to obliterate me?"

"No," four voices in unison.

"If that disappoints you," Dalix said, a voice like thunder, "we can change our minds."

"No, no, I'm good." I tried to smile but my gut was doing somersaults.

"Why are you here?"

"I want to talk. I know I've not been a good friend, even as a kid. Too busy with school or trying to get into the academy. I understand why you're angry."

I kept turning around, trying to talk to each of them. "I don't want to turn my back on anyone. Would it be okay if I stood in front of you guys so I don't have to twirl?"

"Yeah," Dalix said, hands on his hips, chin up, appraising me. The others nodded; too street butch to smile. They formed a line in front of me.

"I just found out you were picked up breaking into the McClain mansion a few weeks back." Which was why I was here. "A guy in the security team, a friend, came across a report in the records. You were trying to hop a fence, claimed you wanted to rescue me. Why?"

"You're an asshole for shutting us out, leaving our gang," Mark said, his hands knotted into fists. "We're family. Could've done big things together." I could hear disappointment in his voice more than anger.

"But you're still one of us," Onzi said, his chin pushing out, sounding hurt. "We were pissed when you were bought like a horse. The rich bastards got no right!"

"We wanted to break you out," Jason said, looking at my face with pinched lips, then down.

"And were a little drunk," Onzi admitted, grinning. "I think that's why they let us go."

"Thank you," I said, starting to well up. They did care for me, were still my brothers.

"Do they hurt you?" Mark asked.

"No, my owner—sounds pretty strange, I admit—is really a great guy. Our relationship is not what you may think, master and slave. It's more like awkward friends becoming lovers. By choice, actually, because he refused to force me to do anything. I initiated the intimacy. I really like him. And my family is taken care of for the moment. It's not easy at school. His family is psycho and dangerous which could mean a disaster down the road. Honestly, I don't know about my future," I confessed. "The Olympic trials gave me some publicity and the mayor's kidnapping but I'm still a slave. I have no money or power. I don't even own my underwear."

The guys just stared at me. I hoped it wasn't pity in their faces. Finally Dalix spoke: "We were proud of you at Stanford. That kidnapping and rescue—my God it was butt-kick fun! All the net interviews. Seeing you with the president!"

"The whole neighborhood went crazy," Onzi said. "People were screaming from every window, thousands of 'em."

"It's all anyone talked about," Mark added. "Made us proud someone from Castlemont could do something important. We all cried. Bragged to everyone we were friends."

I tried to compose myself. "Let's go to Max's Coffee Bean." I came prepared and held out a spare handkerchief. Onzi took it then passed it around. We all laughed. "I'd like to catch up," I said. "And I have a proposition."

* * *

"Why are you called Zinc?" I asked, holding his hand as we shared a plate of macaroni and cheese at the small counter in the kitchen nook.

"It's a romantic story, actually. I was born the same day Dad bought his first zinc mine. Why are you called Spartak? Certainly unusual."

"It's the name of a Russian relative."

"You're Russian, like my father?"

"It was long ago. Never met him nor been in Russia. Yeah. The guy was a Cossack and a horse thief. A noble profession in some areas, I'm told."

"I have a ranch in Southern California with lots of thoroughbreds if you yearn to put your butt on a hard saddle."

"Groaner. Have I thanked you for rescuing me from Spike and his thugs?"

"About sixty times."

"So make this sixty-one. You were alpha." I lifted his hand and kissed it. "I'm so proud of you."

"No one messes with my beautiful slave boy. And it's had side benefits. Crushing three baronial families gets noticed. I'm told they now live on the charity of friends and many say I'm like my father. And that's useful externally. But here, I'm not him."

"Thank you for that. What do I do about Connor? He looks angry all the time."

"He is."

"I thought we'd worked it out, made peace. We even shook hands."

"Some people aren't rational, Spartak. And he's one. He doesn't think he has limits and is jealous of you. He thinks you're shouldering him out of his place in the family. So does my mother."

"I don't think I was doing much shouldering in the seventh grade when he started pounding on me with his friends."

"Just so you know, I've had reports that he has tried to use credit and was turned down. Apparently there were some embarrassing scenes. He'll have no access to money until he grows up."

I held a fork of pasta midway to my mouth, then set it back down. I couldn't imagine the size of Connor's allowance or even the concept. "What about your mom?"

"I've told her not to interfere or I'll talk to the DA about charges against him. Spike's confession to the enforcers implicates Connor in a criminal act. She didn't believe me. I told her I'd no problem sending him to prison if he doesn't straighten up, that it might be good for him. She was really shocked. I don't love him or even like him. Brother or not."

"Connor's complex, I think. Some guys at school say he's fun at parties and the Palladium. He does well in class then gets with his friends and they hunt down and beat up poor kids."

"He has two personalities."

"I don't think he's evil, Zinc, deep down. Just scared, insecure, overwhelmed with his abundance, and spoiled. If I may venture an opinion, you all enabled him by not enforcing rules. Having a few hundred trillion dollars can mess a guy up. A lot of people born rich think they have God's blessing." I turned to Zinc and touched the side of his face. "But you're not like that. You're real. I admit to not understanding Connor and I don't like the way he's treated others and me. He's a bully. But I couldn't handle it if Geo or Kimber were angry with me. Please don't give up—he's your brother."

"A guy has his goons try to beat the crap out of you and your buddy. You argue his good side. No wonder I love you. I'm in awe. I don't deserve you."

"But you've got me. I've seen the ownership papers."

CHAPTER 36

ZINC PUT HIS PALM ON THE silver square and the lock buzzed, opening the door to Henry's Room. Inside there were five people around the table. Everyone was here.

I'd made the introductions to Ransom weeks before and, although scoffing, he'd agreed to follow up as a personal favor. Looking hopeful with puppy eyes and begging terrier-like seemed to be my major talent.

"I wasn't expecting guests," Zinc said. "I thought we had a lead. Who are they?"

"Zinc, these are guys I grew up with in the Avenues," I said, then my tongue went inoperable, stunned at the way they looked. Hair perfectly combed back and ribboned, like founding fathers, except for Onzi's wild orange steel wool tied on top of his head with tips dyed scarlet. He looked like an erupting volcano. And all were wearing the latest high-collar, neon-colored Napoleonic jackets and lit-glo ascots.

"The ones who tried to beat you up? The ones with enforcer records?"

"Please, Zinc, I have a record too."

"Do you think I didn't know?" Zinc grinned. "Got rid of it long ago."

I stared at him, not expecting this revelation, and introduced him to each of my friends. They each stood, shook hands and sat, all very formal.

"Hear him out," Ransom said.

Zinc sat next to me, looking with suspicion at my gang across the table. Under the table, Zinc reached over just as I did. We entwined our fingers.

"A while back, Spartak came to me," Ransom explained, "and asked me to meet with four of his…associates…from his neighborhood. It seems they have unique talents in *Crackin' da Zan,* as the not quite legal experts call it."

"You mean stealing money through clever hacking."

"Only rich folks," Dalix clarified.

"Comforting," Zinc said, glancing at me, an eyebrow raised.

"Spartak had briefed them on your father and some of the miniscule leads. They took the sketchy info and ran with it. I must say, I was skeptical at first but impressed as we started kibitzing about techno-sleuthing. I assigned some of our best talent to assist them, taking their direction." He pointed at me.

"And they found the breakthrough lead," I said, grinning. "And Ran followed up."

"Spartak did the math work on codes. Couldn't a done it without his brain," Onzi said. "He's a real cracker." The others nodded.

I held up my hand with my index finger an inch from my thumb. Not a talent I wanted to brag about in front of Zinc.

"I wanted you to meet them," Ransom said. "Now, guys, I'd like to discuss findings and strategy with just Zinc and Spartak. I think it best you're not here for the next discussion. Your work is appreciated. I'll be in touch."

"Me too," I said as I stood, and rubbed open palms with each as they passed.

"Thanks, Spartak." Dalix embraced me and kissed my cheek. "Those robots love your newest codes," he whispered, rubbing a hand down his fancy coat. "You should see what else we got."

After they left, we moved to the other side of the table, facing the large Z-ether screen.

"I don't think we could have solved this—or at least solved it as fast without Spartak and his friends." Ran gave me thumbs-up.

"I think it would be nice…" I started to say, fumbling my words.

"He thinks we could use guys like these in our operation," Ran said. "And with some training and proper supervision, actually a lot of supervision, very close supervision, I agree."

Zinc turned and kissed me on the cheek. "Thank you for so many things in my life. Now this. If you want 'em in and Ransom agrees, they're in. Now what about the killer?"

I beamed. Debts being repaid.

"It's a group of god-nut technos living in Silicon Valley, enmeshed inside a legitimate business." Ransom pointed to an aerial map with a three-story concrete block building in Cupertino painted Pepto Bismol pink. "I guess even geeks can murder for prophecy."

"And have bad taste," I stated.

"How many?" Zinc asked.

"The entire company has about ninety employees. They work in shifts round the clock, about thirty at any given time. The management often meets with Dominionist leaders, usually at nearby restaurants."

"Part of Bishop Perry's group?"

"Yes, mostly. And aligned with Cardinal Iglesias. Some say he's the real monster. The firm is Tartronics. They make surveillance equipment and sell to the military. But last year, that stopped. Not even bidding on contracts."

"Funding?"

"Lots of cash deposits, impossible to trace. Now let me drop the next bomb. Tartronics is owned by Tarlon Timko."

"IT CAN'T BE!" Zinc exclaimed, swinging out of his chair. He turned to me. "He's the eldest son of Sherilyn Timko, my mother's social rival. About six years older than me. I knew the animosity was deep—but…"

"May I ask what?" It didn't make sense to me.

"Her grandfather was a zealot, funded efforts to keep what he considered 'unacceptable' Americans from registering to vote. My grandfather and Dad called him a fool—committing dangerous overreach that'd backfire. They all had too much to drink at some function one night and got into a fistfight. Grandpa Ogden had a quick temper. And Dad did some serious damage to their fortune. So there are two generations of bad blood but I'd not expected this."

"And you've ruled out AR2?" I asked.

"Correct," Ransom responded. "All the pieces fit. Tarlon went Jesus a few years back, a fanatic. And his first love is technology. His mother may or may not be aware. Not sure yet. And Bishop Perry is a regular visitor."

"So, you're confident?" Zinc asked Ransom, his hands pressed together, fingertips white.

Ransom nodded gravely. "We did our own surveillance once we developed the lead from Dalix, Spartak, and the group. Two of Tarlon's engineers were singled out for praise in the attack. We have it on tape."

"Unbelievable!" Zinc mumbled, clenching his fist.

"DA and the courts or…?"

Zinc was silent, considering the options. "Let's get the FBI and local enforcers involved. I'd like the government to go in with us so we can layer on public humiliation while we dismantle the Timko fortune. Dad would approve. And Grandfather. Let's develop strategy and a timeline. Sooner is better but absolute victory is the goal."

CHAPTER 37

"AMERICA IS THE NEW SODOM," BISHOP Perry fumed on his nationwide multichannel network with an audience of forty million. "The dark angels of Satan are in power and they have many puppets in elective office. All must submit to us, the true followers of Jesus Christ, his anointed, or be eliminated. This is the word of God."

He was dressed in black with a red clerical collar, addressing two thousand parishioners in his San Francisco church. His parents must have beaten him daily and kept him locked in the basement. How else could a man get so mean-spirited and demented?

"Must be nice to speak for God," Ransom commented as we sat in his office, watching the preacher's rant. "It's a little hard to verify his source."

Ran was never shy about expressing his perspective and Zinc told me he found it reassuring that the man was comfortable, even sassy in his descriptions. An honest man was the most valuable member of any team. Sycophants were overpaid at any price and dangerous. "Notice the guy behind him, to his right? That's Cardinal Iglesias, about as unscrupulous a man as you'll find."

I'd seen him in photos but this gave me a chance to watch him, live, smug, sitting behind the Bishop in full view. The cardinal looked like a Spanish conquistador getting ready to slaughter Aztec children. He had a gaunt face, mean, sunken black eyes with dark smudges underneath, thin lips on the cusp of a snarl, long hair, black with gray, and curling perfectly to his shoulders. I suspected he spent a lot of time with a stylist.

"This church, and those who believe as we do, must gain control of earth's governmental and social institutions, and establish HIS holy Kingdom on earth," the Bishop proclaimed. "Jesus will not return until we do our work. We must deliver for the sake of our God and our place in Heaven."

"Too much," Ran added. "He wants to be king of the planet."

"I think he believes it," I said. "If he didn't he wouldn't be risking treason and war."

"Or, he's simply crazy. Religious extremists don't have a good track record on delivering anything but misery."

"Twelve dark angels stand behind the drapes and manipulate," Perry went on. "One demon recently died, the leader of the jackals, and was replaced by a boy king, untested and vain. Beside him is a slave, a human being held in bondage. As repugnant as that is, I have little sympathy. For this boy, this handsome and charming boy, has become Judas, a tool in support of the hegemony of the Twelve."

All three of us were on our feet. I was light-headed, shocked at so personal an attack by one of the most influential men in America. What had I done to offend him? What would my parents and friends think? Is that what I was?

"The bastard will pay," Zinc snarled.

I did my quick breathe-in, breathe-out routine from gymnastics competition, trying to focus. Zinc wanted to protect me, but we needed a plan, not just lash out. I wasn't sure how important this was, being pilloried by the leader of a massive religious movement. I didn't think I was smarter than Zinc and I assumed he'd dealt with his share of scrounges. But I had to use my wits to survive, while he used his money. Beating Jesusistas was not just about money. I didn't want him to miscalculate.

"Halleluiah, Halleluiah, Halleluiah!" The shouting by the congregation was deafening. Ran turned down the sound.

"Zinc, may I say something?"

"You don't need to ask."

"I'm upset too. But let's be measured. Like you, I'm really angry. My heart's pounding. But let's make plans to stop him, not aid his cause. He's trying to provoke us into doing something stupid. He knows we're watching. This is calculated, I'm sure of it."

"The fuck! He called you an enemy. We will NOT turn the other cheek. He's going down." Zinc went to the weapons rack and picked up the sonic rifle Connor had given him for his birthday.

"Spartak is right, Zinc," Ran said. "Let's do it our way, in our own time, strategically. And be lethal if we must. Perhaps the government can act first, but likely not. Many politicians are either in his pocket or frightened. It'll be tricky. We have the mixed loyalty issues with the military and he'll hide behind the First Amendment, claim he's being persecuted even while he murders." He swiveled his chair toward Zinc. "I have an idea."

"In three months," Bishop Perry preached in a soaring voice, "we will consecrate an oak cross in this temple symbolizing the death and life everlasting of Jesus Christ. It will be the beginning of the end, when we must be prepared. God and heaven await."

Cardinal Iglesias was grinning. Perry's eyes seemed to turn up in his head, enraptured.

"Mark your calendar," Zinc said, adjusting the scope.

CHAPTER 38

Zinc squirmed in his seat, visibly uncomfortable, and I tried to keep a Zen face as Sonia and her uncle lobbied him on federal legislation. The two were outspoken in expressing views diametrically opposed by their own class. Sonia had invited us to Justice Washington's Pacific Heights mansion, the judge's home away from the nation's capital and its scorching temperatures, thick as sweat humidity, and the politics. I knew Zinc admired the judge for standing tall on his convictions even if he thought the man was a pathetic dreamer, a liberal.

"Let me make one more point," the justice said. He sat on a green and white striped sofa with palm leaves arching overhead. The back porch, with a view of Alcatraz, was a garden, flowers and shrubs everywhere, smelling of jasmine. Zinc listened, likely feeling apprehensive that they might ask him to do some particular political act. He didn't want to offend Sonia.

"Over the next year, the Dominionists pose a greater threat to the barronial way of life and to American democracy than actually letting citizens vote and having that vote count." The judge paused and sipped his Campari and soda.

Zinc crunched a handful of Spanish *Marcona* almonds, one of the gastronomic passions he shared with Sonia. I was sitting to the side, not wanting to intrude or pressure him, glancing at sailboat races on the bay. I was most effective as a private sounding board.

"Many of us believe that expanding the voter base would be an effective way to diminish the power of the churches gone mad with Dominionist nonsense. Most Americans are skeptical of their *'let us run the world'* mantra but get drawn in because of social services the churches provide and the tough lives most people live. Government does little to help or build loyalty and often harasses the poor."

Zinc turned and looked at me as if to confirm the truth. I bit my lower lip and nodded. The lower lip bite was always effective with him.

"It's also true," the judge continued, "that most adult Americans cannot vote, thus depriving them of any role in government. Most barronials are happy with the status quo but that reality is breaking apart; the bubble will burst. To transition peacefully to a new actuality, we must take the first step, this piece of legislation. The idea of an honest count of the ballot when everyone has the opportunity to vote and feel part of the system, well, that just goes to the heart of what America is about and offers an alternative to the Jesusistas."

It was exciting to hear this from someone important, not just quiet rumblings in Castlemont. It sounded like my dad and likely was what got him purged.

They watched Zinc. Me too, the silence making him respond. "I understand your pos…ition on S.B. 112. I don't think I've ever be… been lobbied before…"

"You've never been the head of McClain Enterprises before," Sonia said. "We're not asking you to make a decision today but to consider it. I know you have many pressures."

That was true. I watched the poor man dealing with the McClain Enterprises board, armies of financial leaders, lobbyists, corporate CEOs, military officials, accountants, elected leaders, suck-ups and advisors of every sort, all of them wanting his help as the heir to an empire that touched every business. He was always standoffish, imperious if you didn't know him, and did a lot of nodding, keeping his cards and words tight to his chest. He trusted some of his father's close advisors but was leery of others. Zinc had told me he'd make changes as he gained confidence. And all this happened between his working on homework for English lit, art history, and geometry. I thought it was important he finish high school although it wasn't as if the degree would get him a better job or into college. I worried that he might break.

Of course some of it was sweet. The headmaster had looked like he was birthing a manatee when Zinc strode into the last academy board meeting with me in tow to personally reclaim the family's seat. Thragman's contract discussion was tabled for a month to keep him twisting.

Sometimes, in the midst of the pressures, Zinc retreated to the nearest bathroom, where he could be alone, to wonder if he was a financial king or lanky, vain, and insecure teen. And now Sonia and her uncle were on him. How taut the wire before it snaps?

"I'm curious, Zinc, if you think allowing people like Spartak and his family to vote would be bad for America."

He looked like he got sucker punched. "No, ob…obviously not. Spartak is extraordinarily intelligent as are his parents. They should be allowed to vote."

"But the rules make it impossible."

Sonia stood and took Zinc's hand. "Let's go for a walk. This is a perfect sunny day." Zinc looked elated to leave as they skipped down stone steps deeper into the garden.

"Spartak," the justice said, "let's go into my den."

* * *

"I was hoping to have another chance to chat with you," the judge said as we walked into a small room with a fourteen-foot ceiling and walls lined with shelves filled with leather-bound books and a collection of tortoise shell boxes. A brass telescope stood on a wooden tripod before a round leaded-glass window, a marble bust of Socrates sat on a square marble column and a life-size oil painting of the judge as a young man hung behind his desk. We sat in facing, high-back, green sharkskin chairs with an ornately carved walnut Victorian coffee table in between. It was a bit overwhelming. The absolute silence surprised me, plus the faint aroma of lemon polish. I wish my brother could see this.

"May I ask you something, sir?" Start with something small and test how far I can go with a semi-mythic figure.

"Of course, anything." He leaned back and crossed his legs.

"Where are your glasses? You always wear those wire-rimmed frames."

He laughed. "Just for show. I don't need them but I do think they make me look more judicious. Do you agree?" He grinned. "Any other questions?"

I never thought judges did costumes. But why not? "Thanks. Yes... and yes." How do I take advantage of this moment without being naïve or offensive? "I've read America was once...different, not like what we read in school textbooks. Nocturne talks about an America that used to be."

He watched me, his expression flat, like a judge, then his lips spread into a smile. "It *was* different. There was a time when all adults had the right to vote, even if many didn't bother, and there were few barriers to register, when average people had enough income to fuel a vibrant consumer-based economy, when there were enough jobs for full-time employment, when public schools were excellent and government actually worked in championing the less fortunate, leveling the field, giving everyone an equal chance of success."

The judge pulled a cigar from his jacket, holding the long odiferous brown tube under his nose. He leaned forward, slid a silver tray across the table and picked up two vintage Steuben crystal glasses. "For a serious talk with my friend Spartak, we need a serious man's drink." Using silver tongs, he dropped in ice cubes from a bucket and then poured in his favorite brand of scotch. He handed one to me. I sipped it and didn't like the nasty taste but hoped the ice melted fast so I could drink it and not grimace. Parking his cigar in his scotch, the judge folded his hands in front of his nose, elbows on his chair armrests. This was such an odd sensation, talking privately with a justice of the United States Supreme Court.

"While media platforms proliferated, ownership concentrated. And public relations experts kept the average voter angry that government no longer seemed to offer much value or hope. And antigovernment people were elected to government making sure it didn't. As the world became a single workforce, wages collapsed in America and so did the middle class. Everything became part-time, contract work, with competition working against workers, desperation driving down wages. No benefits of any kind, a longtime business goal. Workers had to make enough to purchase products, something Henry

Ford knew two hundred years ago. With most people stuck in survival mode, contingency work, there wasn't a mass market for goods. The wealthy had what they needed, the poor shifted partly into a barter system, the historical fallback of more primitive societies. And our rich history in the arts, literature, and science was dissolving although, one good thing, a vibrant art culture sprang up in many communities like Castlemont. I actually have one of your father's woodcarvings of nymphs perched on a ram in the forest, a gift from a friend. Magnificent work."

It made me grin. "Thank you. I think he's pretty magnificent myself."

He nodded. "Indeed. To continue, labor unions, traditional champions of the working class, were often their own worst enemy, arrogant and abusing their power when they could, losing public confidence, not much different from corporations. And now no longer exist." He shook his head and paused for a sip. I watched the man, convinced I was being subversive just listening to him.

"All funding for long-term scientific research was eliminated and the responsibility passed off to private industry. That was always the solution. And the drug companies did nothing, refusing to invest long-term, content to just make money on drugs they had or ones easy to bring to market. That decision eventually forced the barronials to directly intervene. When new pathogens emerged years later, America was unprepared. It killed rich as well as poor—self-righteous Congressmen, barronials, drug makers, pastors, and the innocent. Hundreds of thousands. Money couldn't save you. Amazing how death can give you focus or motivation." He leaned back in his chair and watched me.

"How, sir?"

"Barron Ogden was ruthless, impassioned by the death of his wife. He brought together the richest people controlling eighty percent of all wealth, then about two hundred families, grabbed the steering wheel and made a U-turn. As a first step he forced a dramatic increase in federal basic research funding."

"But you said the politicians hated government."

"Some of the biggest critics of long-term research died in the pandemic. Not a bad thing, actually." He laughed deep in his throat. Not particularly funny but I understood. More like justice. Reap what ye sow.

"When democracy is a phantom," he continued in a soft voice, "people feel it's not important. Many of us felt that all adults should be able to vote if only as a safety valve. But others, including Sergei, cynically believed that political power didn't rest with those who cast their votes but with those who count them. Personally, I find that idea repugnant. Electronic voting was omnipresent. And barronials, McClain Enterprises, actually, made the machines. A few hundred votes in a close election, your guy wins and nobody can prove otherwise. The worst radicals were eliminated. They elected a safe majority of conservative, pro-business people, never considering character or capacity, and made sure we had a compliant president and stacked the Supreme Court. It stopped the dysfunction. Government did things again, passed legislation without much disagreement, but not in a way that helped the average American. Fealty was always to the financial elites."

He took another sip and I tried to do the same. How did people drink this?

"Ogden challenged, shamed, and led by example in creating his academy and spent a vast fortune on public works projects, creating jobs, and bringing art and quality education back to life, at least for the talented few. Many followed his example across the country, Europe, and South America." He shifted in his seat, never breaking eye contact. It made me feel special. "Just so you're not totally depressed, some good things happened. Crime had been rampant, fueled by drug money. Zinc's father, backed by Barron Ogden, what we used to call police associations, and the pharmaceutical industry, led the effort to legalize narcotics and take control of the production and distribution channels. And crime collapsed within a year. Drug use declined and Mexico had democracy restored. That's part of barronial history that's good. It also made Sergei and Barron staggeringly wealthy."

As he talked, I noticed the sun came through the leaded glass window behind him and suggested a halo. Naw. I looked back at his craggy face.

"When Ogden died, the barronials turned away again, letting their experiment do its thing while they counted their money. And that was a mistake. If you already owned everything, as the barronials did, life was good. Just wall yourself off from the masses and hire bodyguards or private armies. Millions of people were hungry, sick, and hurting, out of sight of media and the rich. The opposition was easily demoralized and lacked the viciousness of its opponents. The federal government was not only dysfunctional it became puritanical, just plain mean-spirited post-Ogden." His delivery was matter of fact, his voice soft yet confident.

"We were all caught flat-footed by the sudden emergence of Dominionist Christians as leaders of nearly all religious denominations. The End Timers had been quietly working into positions of power, masquerading their harsh views until they had control then started converting their dispirited flocks, and claimed revelations from God. It was all well orchestrated. And, to our horror, the government we put in office caved in, including key leaders in the military. Many members of Congress put their religious faith above obligations to serve everyone—not that they ever did. In their narrow vision, they saw science, particularly biology, as a threat rather than the hope of civilization. Basic research was reluctantly funded but much of its work remained hidden outside the scientific community. Dissent was unacceptable to the new government elites and a purge began. Social media and the government's anti-terrorist obsession offered decades of collected data. It was easy for them to find their enemies and networks. And the targets had no idea why careers tanked, campaigns fizzled, and they became marginalized."

As he said this, I thought of my parents, crushed because my dad dared to criticize. The judge pulled his cigar out of the scotch and tapped it on the side of the glass. "Don't watch," he said, arching his eyebrows. "Sonia thinks it's disgusting and I only do it in private. Also note that I never actually light one up." He sucked the end of it. I took his advice and admired Socrates. Another slurp and he set down the glass. I had a hard time not staring at him and took a tiny taste of the scotch, pretending it was my favorite root beer. But it was more like poison.

"It's all right if you don't like it," he said with a wink, "but it is an affectation of the self-important barronial male."

"Thank you." I tried not to grimace. "Can that kind of economy come back?"

"First we start with election reform, then economic and education come next."

"Deal," I said. Somehow I felt safe saying it since he was suggesting far more subversive ideas.

"Back to the topic." He looked amused. "The Dominionist social program was a reversion to Neolithic times, putting a biblical view to women's rights, making Christianity the official state religion, and denigrating other faiths and nonbelievers as well. Demanding proof of virginity to marry, the death penalty for anyone having or assisting an abortion. Now they've added this nonsense about the end of the world. Eventually, some of us realized that being fantastically rich, hiding in gated communities or on private islands, doesn't mean much if the world is crumbling from stupidity. The planet is headed toward catastrophe, polluted groundwater, dying oceans, the North Pole open water, and wars over food shortages spawned by climate shifts. The Dominionists claimed it was God's sign of the end of the world and the return of Jesus. And worse, many believe them."

Justice Washington stretched his arms and looked up, like he was staring back in time. "Wealth has concentrated over the years; the two hundred are now *The Twelve*. Sergei picked the number so it would sound biblical. Dominionists called them dark angels."

I thought of Bishop Perry and his ranting. All a bit wooly to me, surreal.

"And that is where we are now," he said, rubbing his lips, "kind of a calm before the storm. AR2 arose from the grassroots urging a return to democracy and the End Timers demand a dictatorship of believers. Now, astoundingly, slavery is sanctioned in America."

I winced at the word and changed topics. I didn't like to talk about my status. "Is S.B. 112 really important?"

"Yes, but just as a tiny first step. Voter suppression has been the obsession of both parties at different times, a disease of fearful politicians, disenfranchising any voter block that might be in opposition.

After a while, there are not a lot of voters, or, almost as bad, thoughtful candidates. Not good for a democracy. Not that we have one now. The bill also returns the vote count to systems less subject to secret manipulation."

"I don't think Zinc knows what to think on the bill."

"Sonia will help him on that. I know he's uncomfortable in his new position, but he needs to learn to handle multiple demands. And I think he'll do fine."

"Everything seems so depressing."

"Hmmmm. Often, yes, unfortunately." His eyes seemed to twinkle. "But let me offer you something positive on a totally different topic." He looked down, concentrating, then back at my face with a mischievous smile. "Look what we're doing for science fiction writers."

"You got me. How about a hint?"

"Why are skyscrapers possible?"

"Elevators?" I had no idea what he meant.

"Keep going. Look up, high into the sky."

"You mean the Space Elevator?" We both laughed. I never thought of a Supreme Court justice having a sense of humor.

"Indeed. The Elevator has cost over twelve trillion dollars with profits for Sergei's consortium somewhere in the future mostly from mining asteroids. Our emaciated, unimaginative government could never have done it. And, of course, the benefits and power go to the funders." He bent forward. "Enough of this, young man. How are you handling your well-deserved fame and glory? I suspect you are confused?"

"Uhmm, yes, I don't really understand why people are so interested in me."

"You're a genuine hero, Spartak, your national gymnastic title, saving Zinc and Mayor Rand in a battle scene that was thrilling. You were brilliant at the US Olympic trials. The whole country was rooting for you, even more so when you fell with an open wound. I know I was holding my breath. You're humble, a very fine, rare quality, and deeply admired. And that's good for both of us."

"How so?" Downers aren't supposed to be anything. I sensed he wanted to give me answers, that this was why he invited me here.

"You personify the injustice that is America today. Slavery is so repugnant to millions that your bondage becomes a flash point of anger and political organization. You also have a great demographic—Caucasian, blond, clean-cut, handsome, wholesome, athletic, musical. For many in the twenty percent the Twelve Families allow to vote, you are their all-American poster boy. It confuses the hell out of 'em." He laughed. "I called you Edgardo at lunch that day, and you are like him, a symbol of both what is good and what is wrong, the center of a revolution."

I stared, not sure he could be talking about me. It sounded almost silly. "Is that what we're in, a revolution?"

"Yes. I don't believe the oligarchy we have now is sustainable. My goal is to return real democracy and the rule of law. And the religious zealots want a theocracy, a religious dictatorship. So a three-way."

"And if Zinc gave me my freedom?"

"We would lose our symbol and legally you would be abandoned property, not free in the proper sense of the word, given the court decision."

So I needed to remain a slave for the good of the revolution? Should I laugh? He was serious. I coughed, remembering I needed to breathe.

"Sonia says you're magnificent with the classics on piano," he said casually, giving me time to recover and think. "Would you honor me with some Chopin? The music room is just down the hall."

"Of course, sir, I'd be honored."

"Do you by chance know the *Nocturne in C Sharp Minor?* A delicate piece."

"One of my favorites."

CHAPTER 39

It took the Director of the FBI and the local enforcer chief to give consent but Zinc, Ransom, and I were part of the fifty-member SWAT team sent to secure Tartronics. We wore the standard bodysuits and headgear, but underneath were our XOs.

When he was first briefed on the raid, Zinc demanded to be part of it, to avenge the killing of his cousin and especially the attack on his father. I insisted on being with him, to keep him safe. After a screaming match, Zinc agreed. Ran demanded that neither of us go. A foolish risk, he argued and we rejected. "Kids!" he mocked. So he too went, to look after us.

Forensics labs had finally found a direct link to Tarlon Timko in the murder of Cedric Rand, although Ran questioned it. It was a piece of Tarlon's DNA on the red strand of hair. His hubris betrayed him. The Timkos all had red hair. Zinc figured it was a one-fingered salute to the McClains, using red hair to draw attention to themselves but then, proving a false match, sending enforcers elsewhere. He wondered if they found it amusing.

"I know it looks like a slam dunk, but I've my doubts," Ransom said. "It's too cute, like a game someone is playing on the Cedric murder."

"But we have proof of the lab being the source of my father's murder," Zinc replied. "And that's enough."

Scanners detecting bomb-making material in the Pepto Bismol structure prompted the FBI to intercede in force, not just arrest him. Timko had been seen entering the building that afternoon. The team took up positions in a nearby warehouse.

Two agents in gray business suits walked into the building. While having tiny lumins planted in their eyes gave me the creeps, we could see what they saw, approaching a reception desk, identifying themselves to a young woman with brown and green striped hair curled under at the ends.

They held up badges embedded in their palms. "May we speak with Mr. Timko?"

She touched her ear and talked quietly. I couldn't hear. We waited. Several minutes later a red-haired man came out along with a half dozen security forces, including two Jesusistas in headbands.

"It's Tarlon," Zinc confirmed, watching our Z-ether.

"Mr. Timko," the older agent said in a respectful tone, "we'd like to ask you some questions regarding the murder of Cedric Rand."

The guards rushed. Shouting. A white blast. The images went dark.

The black troop carriers stormed out of the garage and encircled the building within minutes. Timko's SubQ was dialed. No response. Same for the agents. A low-tech loudspeaker shattered the calm in the Cupertino warehouse district, effective and intimidating. Enforcers evacuated nearby buildings. The young woman from the reception desk stumbled out, shaking, struggling to hold it together. She handed a note to senior agent Malvo Lynx:

Attack and we will kill the agents.

There were about thirty workers, security guards, an unknown number of Jesusistas, and Timko inside. A message ball was lobbed into the building shrieking orders to come out with their hands up. No response.

We heard screams from inside, someone being tortured.

"Now!" Lynx ordered.

Troops fired nerve-freeze into the building followed by solar rifle blasts. The front door splintered. Solar fire from a top window. A white light shattered a windshield near where I stood behind a troop carrier. Zinc yanked me down. An old-fashioned machine gun sprayed lead bullets from a first-floor slit in the wall, pinging off the roof of our armored car. Agents returned fire. Even with the special ear protectors in the helmets, the sound was intolerable.

"Bullcrap!" Lynx mumbled into his mouthpiece. "Bring up Sally!"

A solar cannon rose with a mechanical whine from the roof of the carrier in front of us. Sally hummed, louder and louder, building its charge, then fired a white heat ball into the building like the fist of an invisible giant, ripping out windows, collapsing walls, the entire entrance instantly rubble and smoke.

"Go!" Lynx commanded.

Three agents were in front of us as we charged, jumping over debris. Zinc had insisted being in the first wave. I was scared and excited, unused to the bulky armor and a helmet that let me see on all sides at once and easily cut through the thick dust and poison. Zinc was to my right, Ransom to my left, all of us carrying McClain sonics with at least double the firepower on the old solars.

Blood on the floor near the reception desk. We headed down the hallway, two agents kicking in a door to the left. We followed the other guy into an open room on the right.

Two solar rifle blasts hit the agent, a hurricane of light, almost cutting him in half. Ran slammed his arms back hard, moving faster than I thought possible, knocking Zinc and myself backward, out of the doorway. He leaped over the dead agent and twisted around, firing a sonic blast into one Jesusista, dodging a blast from another while throwing a knife into the man's neck. He went into a shoulder roll and onto his feet, swiveling around, grabbing his second weapon from his belt, scanning the room, both sonics burping, ready to kill again.

"Sorry guys," he said as he walked past us into the hall and ran ahead toward the sound of more fighting.

Zinc and I looked at each other. He knocked us out of danger and took on the killers to keep us safe. We ran after him. In another room, Ran and the two other agents stood over the bodies of two Tartronics security guards. In the next area were the two dead agents, heads bashed in and throats vaporized.

Another wave of agents ran up the stairway and we followed. On the second floor we found Tarlon. He was hanging, an electrical wire around his neck, both eyes gouged out. A red wig was on his head. No one else was in the building. Agents found a tunnel in the basement leading under the street to a boarded-up structure. Tarlon had prepared for the escape long ago. Agents reported the other building abandoned.

On the car ride home, Ran gave his interpretation: "I'm guessing that once he was under suspicion for Cedric's murder, he was a liability and no further value to the true believers."

"They seduced him into their sect and used his money and technology," I offered. "The cheap red wig will likely match the hair at Cedric's murder scene." I could still see his handsome body when we made love; then the image of his charred face. It left me queasy.

"I'm having difficulty believing Tarlon did the murder himself," Ransom said. "He wasn't the type. And why make an amateur mistake on the DNA? Makes no sense. Someone is playing games, maybe even someone bigger than the bishop."

Zinc was quiet, listening to the conversation. As I watched him stare into the distance, I could see a hint of the man emerging in his features, the growing hardness, and less of the teen. He was getting tougher, more determined, at the edge of embracing his father's worldview. Could I still help shape it? I wasn't sure I knew.

Zinc rubbed his eyes. "Poor Tarlon," he said. "In the end, he was a Twelver. A demon; a dark angel. A traitor to his class and they killed him anyway. What a twisted sense of justice and God."

* * *

The President of the US Olympic Committee, Preston Gibron, sat on a sofa in the Buena Vista second-floor living room. He was nestled deep in the plush oversized couch, soft enough to take a nap; on the walls a dozen surreal paintings of goldfish and an elaborate Victorian ceiling of molded tin squares. Not my favorite room. I'd met him and his parents at the trials; he was all business, fortyish, formal, the Arabic look of his mother, the pointed French nose of his father, impeccably dressed in a blue jacket with green trim and a carpenter's grip when he shook hands.

I was surprised to see Judy LeVene with him, dressed in a clingy cotton body suit that showed her figure to perfection and a pink color that matched her complexion. Her black hair was draped over her shoulders, a striking woman. She was a pole-vaulter from Vermont, a barronial, and we'd become friends as our teams competed around the country and we partied afterward. She loved to dance.

"Welcome," Zinc said, shaking Gibron's hand. I did the same and hugged Judy. She kissed my cheek.

"So fun to see you, Spartak."

"And you."

Gunther entered with a silver tray filled with crystal glasses, my favorite black fizz in a pitcher and lots of tiny crustless sandwiches that rich people seemed to like. He served everyone, winked at me, and departed with a bow.

"I asked for this meeting in person because it is important and there are implications." Gibron's voice was cold, as usual.

"Go on," Zinc said, leaning back in his seat and draping a hand over my thigh, sounding older than his age or trying to.

"As Spartak knows, all members of the team voted by private ballot on who should carry the American flag as we enter the Olympic stadium in Vancouver. Spartak won in a close vote, Judy was second."

I felt my jaw open and I coughed, not certain what I heard. "Me?"

"Yes, Spartak, you. But we have made no announcements until I talked to you both."

Zinc looked at me and grinned, squeezing my leg, then over at Gibron, his face flat. "Go on," he said, an old man voice again.

"As an athlete," Gibron continued, looking a little uncomfortable, "we consider Spartak an equal. Yet legally he is your property. So there are two issues. First the political implications and second your permission or refusal."

I felt like a pair of socks, a thing. He was painfully blunt. At the same time my heart pounded for the honor, doing this in front of my friends and hopefully my parents. It was humiliating having someone go to Zinc to tell me to do something, not my family or me directly. I did my best to stay calm and not explode.

"If he won, he should carry the flag," Zinc said, sounding irritated. "Why wouldn't he?"

"There are political issues." He stopped there and took a sip of the fizz, like he was stalling. "He is…a slave and a symbol for many of what is wrong with America. I'm sorry, there is no other way to state this. As the first slave to compete since ancient Greece, as the boy carrying the flag of America, this would spotlight the *Sasser* decision on a world stage, give him enormous publicity and prestige and validate the opposition. Many barronials will be deeply offended. My board voted to reject the team vote and offer it to Judy. Following their orders, I contacted her—"

"And I said no, Spartak," Judy interrupted. "That's why I had to come today. No way would I do this. This is your honor and fuck the board. We want you!" Her eyes welled up. So did mine. We both stood at the same time and held each other.

"Wow, Judy." I pulled back, holding her at arm's length. "But I think you *should* do it. You're such a special woman. The games are supposed to be nonpolitical. I don't want to spoil it."

"Pretend I won?" She pinched my nose and grinned. "No!" She sat down and crossed her arms, looking pleased and defiant all at once. My head buzzing, I sat next to Zinc.

"Your decision?" Gibron said, letting it hang in the air.

Zinc was quiet, looking at each of us, myself last. He moved his arm around my shoulders and pulled me tight.

"Spartak will look very handsome in those hot blue and gold Revolutionary War jackets you're using."

CHAPTER 40

Civic Center was tightly packed, everyone oiled for the sunny day, bright colors, bare chests, men, women, trans, het, and hom, tens of thousands. Harvey Milk scanned the crowd, his giant head smiling from a hologram encasing the dome on City Hall. A dozen dancers from San Francisco Ballet dashed off the stage and Mayor Rand came to the podium.

I squeezed my hands together and took a deep breath from behind a curtain at stage right. Sonia had insisted I do this and convinced Zinc to make me. I didn't want to and argued I was too embarrassed and had nothing to say at this national holiday celebration of a great civil rights symbol of the old gay rights movement. Sonia won; no surprise. We'd worked on a short speech, a kind of homage to Milk and freedom. It was weird considering my situation but I was ready. The man was a long-ago hero. The mayor told Zinc I was the most famous hom in America and would be a big draw and the event was mostly just an excuse to party. I felt foolish, just a teenager, good at somersaults, sex, complex equations and Frederic Chopin. Not this, not public speaking.

Mayor Rand became emotional describing the courage "of this young man who saved my life despite grievous injuries. A hero for the hom world, our world, for any world, any community. And soon to be an Olympic champion."

I wondered if Zinc was watching at home. He was busy with his mother and a troop of advisors. He was increasingly stressed, so many pressures winding him ever tighter. I worried about him. His face was drawn with dark patches under his eyes. He was not doing well and could snap under the pressure.

There was scattered applause but mostly silence as I walked to the podium. It seemed so eerie I stopped midway, convinced I stepped out too soon.

"Spartak!" the mayor said, motioning me to hurry.

I looked down at thousands of faces staring at me in silence. My gut juices started gurgling. Movement. First one, then ten, then hundreds and thousands slipped on masks of my face. Within a minute, it was a sea of Spartaks, every person I could see. I stared, unsure what it meant or what to do. It seemed preposterous. They were making fun of me. I glanced at the mayor, now wearing one too. Sonia had one, my parents, Geo and Kimber. So did Rhonda and Billy.

"I am Spartak!" a woman yelled from somewhere distant in the crowd.

"I am Spartak!" answered a man's voice, closer.

"WE ARE SPARTAK!" A dozen voices, then a thousand, then tens of thousands. My name reverberated off the granite walls of the buildings forming the square and down the side streets, stretching for blocks, over and over.

The mayor stepped to my side, his arm over my shoulder.

"What do I do, sir?"

"Smile and wave."

"Why are they doing this?"

"You are the symbol of hope for a free America."

Mayor Rand held up his arms and lowered them slowly. The chanting subsided but the masks remained. A series of giant floating Z-ethers materialized and carried close-ups of the two of us at the podium. It was also being carried live on several channels.

"Everybody wants your beautiful face," he teased.

I flushed and the audience roared.

"Marry me!" A woman's voice. More laughter. More blushing.

"You're adorable." A man near the stage.

"My friends," Rand began in a rich baritone. "The time has come for America to return to democracy, away from unbridled libertarianism, not the hollowed-out government we have now where voting is suppressed and vote counting rigged. Globalization has resulted in Americans barely getting by. Government has abandoned the poor. We must prove virginity if we want to be married in a church. Mandatory child bearing. Death to the mother and doctor in an abortion, no matter the need. Churches gone mad and God forgotten in the hunger for power. A planet dying. Wealth consolidation unimagined in human history. Every word, every action seems to have someone listening, watching. Make a misstep and your life can be ruined. It's my shame to be of the Twelve Families and yet the money has given me opportunities too. I can afford to speak truth. Most people cannot."

"Yes!" hundreds shouted. "Speak!" Applause.

I rarely heard this kind of political rant from the left. Media always carried the ministers or conservatives talking about how fabulous America was and how affluent the people. I knew Joshua Rand was popular in the nation's most liberal city yet the Bay Area was also the heart of the Twelve Families, drawn by good weather and beautiful geography. New York was sweltering or freezing, no middle ground, spring and fall lost, and a frequent target for hurricanes. The South and Southwest, even much of the Midwest, were plagued with tornadoes, 125-degree temperatures or extended freezing rain. No one lived there unless they had no place else to go. Greenland, the Pacific Northwest and northern California were paradise.

"I look at this handsome teenager beside me, a free man sold into slavery, in America, in 2115."

The crowd hissed. "As bad as that is, there is a love story. Spartak told me he now loves his master, Zinc McClain, my nephew. Zinc told me too, and seeing them together, it is obvious. Still, the Supreme Court was morally reprehensible in what it did, legitimizing the purchase of people as trophies. It must be repealed. The court must be changed. We must stand together and spread the word."

"I am Spartak!" The high-pitched voice of a boy. I spotted him a few yards distant, slipping off his mask. I pointed at him. The boy pointed back, grabbing his dad to share the moment.

"I think our hero is a little overwhelmed by your love and support. So no speeches," Rand promised.

I looked at him. "Thank you," I mouthed.

"But…I am going to ask him some questions. Do you want to hear from him?"

"Yes!" from hundreds in the audience and applause.

"Take off your shirt!" a woman screamed.

"Recently in Washington, D.C., you watched some of the debate on S.B. 112, to standardize voting requirements and allow all citizens their rights. It also returns America closer to a paper ballot to reduce rigged counting. Do you support the bill?"

I had already done this and survived, so answer like Billy Eagle. "I believe the right to vote is fundamental in a democracy. What I've seen in my neighborhood as I grew up convinces me that this right is denied to the poor if..." I felt my voice get shaky..."if they have opinions unpopular with the people who make the decisions."

Lots of applause, a handful of boos, a vocal wave of "We are Spartak." I didn't know how to read it.

"One more question. You are the first human legally purchased since the Civil War. In fact, you were kidnapped and taken to a jail cell just days after the Court announced its decision. Estimates are that as many as five thousand others have been sold, and so far kept hidden. How do you feel about this?"

I looked at him hoping I wasn't hearing it. I couldn't offend the McClains. I glanced over the crowd, hoping for inspiration, and saw the sign on a granite building: *San Francisco Public Library*. The books inside, one of my favorite places, a sanctuary, history books.

"Slavery..." I began, trying to remain composed. "Slavery...has existed in America since its founding." Talk history, move it away from Zinc and me. "The Civil War freed the Negro slaves, but the southern whites held them in economic bondage and kept them from voting. But there was also another kind of slavery, more recent. Long before the debt-bond started, every year twenty thousand people disappeared, vanished, and enforcers believe most were kidnapped and made slaves, often for prostitution or forced labor."

I took a breath, forcing myself not to think about getting in trouble. "I was stunned when I was...taken. *Harvested* is actually the term the bounty hunters use...I was *harvested*."

There was what seemed like a collective gasp mixed with "My God!" from the crowd.

"Strange things happen in an economy like ours. And I'm no expert. But I'm a lucky guy. I've come to love my master, an extraordinary man as the mayor said, and accept my fate. This is where America is now for a lot of reasons. My Zinc has been good and generous with my family and me. Others may not be bonded to men or women as fine and honorable as mine." And this was the truth. I thought about what else to say, if I would plunge to the heart of it. I wasn't exactly in a position of strength. The crowd seemed to like me but they wouldn't be there to help if I got in trouble.

"And what about those less fortunate, Spartak? I suspect you have views about poverty."

He answered my question. Yes, I did. I was no Judas to my class. I thought of the Tabors. "We need to not only abolish debt-bond slavery but the reasons it exists, people so poor they can't raise their children and make the wrenching decision to sell them to someone better off, hoping for a better life."

"Go Spartak!" screamed a woman in the crowd, openly weeping near the front of the stage, the mask pushed back on her head. She was middle-aged, like my mom.

"Thank you," I said, looking at her, feeling my own eyes well. "I'm sorry I'm so nervous. I'm much better on the pommel horse. I've never done anything like this."

Applause. Whistles.

"We are Spartak," one person then thousands, an ongoing chant.

Mayor Rand put his arm around me and told me to hold up my right fist in triumph, like I just won a meet. I did and the crowd roared.

A fluttering American flag filled the Z-ether screens and music emerged, first low then building, one of the greatest spiritual songs ever written, one that always gave me chills. A female vocalist began singing "Amazing Grace," written by a slave trader in the late 1700s as he sought forgiveness and used as the anthem for outlawing slavery in the British Empire. The mayor had this choreographed. Waving, he escorted me to the stairs at the back of the stage. Two high security mono-tracks and an aircart were waiting. Reporters swarmed as I pushed through, overwhelmed, wiping my nose with my palm, doing my best to smile and say thank you, trying to answer questions.

My parents, Geo and Kimber hurried to me and embraced me, holding their masks. “I am so, so proud of you, son,” Dad said.

“Where did you get the masks?”

“Sonia.”

Before I became a hopeless, slobbering mess, Sonia touched my shoulder and leaned in to kiss my cheek, slipping a handkerchief in my hand.

I felt a tingle and touched my ear. “Spartak,” Hernandez said quickly, “I need to speak with you in person. South entrance.” He disconnected.

CHAPTER 41

GEO WAS SO EXCITED ABOUT THE new security carriers he wouldn't stop giggling and asking questions. Hernandez would have to wait.

My family came here by the PT but would go home in style. The pair of pale blue monos were fun to ride, a single oval tread underneath at the center, they could turn three hundred sixty degrees at high speed, angle corners like an old-time motorcycle and withstand heavy grenade and rifle assaults. Plus they were silent and luxurious inside.

I felt a muscular grip on my shoulder. "We should go." I knew who it was without turning around. It was Michels, my least favorite security guard.

"Okay," I said, not sure who was in charge. Was he protecting me or keeping me a prisoner? "Give me a minute."

"In here," I told my family and helped them inside a mono. Geo was giggling.

Rhonda and Billy hugged me. "We can say we knew you back when" she said, kissing my cheek. "We must dash, a train in seven minutes."

"Please. Ride with my parents," I suggested and looked into the cabin at the driver. I raised my eyebrows and he nodded. I wanted them to experience more of my new world.

"Scorchin'," Billy said, climbing inside. Rhonda just laughed and entered.

As their mono moved out, away from the crowd, the driver banked it into a three-sixty. I could see Geo's arms go up, and Billy's, both screaming in delight. Sonia took the second one with considerably less drama.

I waved goodbye and turned to Zinc's green buzzard. I was shocked when I first learned he had one. Several actually, play toys for rich teenage males. He swore he'd never buzzed Castlemont. The triangular-shaped, vertical takeoff aircart knocked you backward when it accelerated. I slipped into the front seat, Michels into the next one, the top closed and the harness wrapped around me.

"Home base," I said and the craft rose and snapped toward the mansion. Within seconds it landed on the roof. We went to the back chute, dropped to the basement entrance as Hernandez said in his message and rushed into his office.

Hernandez waved Michels off so we'd be alone. "Secure the door," he said, standing up.

I turned and pushed my palm against a screen and a whomp sound indicated the room was sealed from entry and eavesdropping.

"What?"

"I may be overstepping my bounds and hopefully wrong about what I'm going to say. But we're friends, I care about you." He put his arms over my shoulder then hugged me. Somehow this sweet gesture made me more upset.

"Please?" I pushed back to look at his face. My heart was going crazy.

He pointed to a chair by him. We both sat. He started to speak and stopped, collecting his thoughts.

"I wanted to talk with you privately before you see Zinc," he said cautiously. "Something is happening and I don't know specifics or the timeline. One of the maids—please you can't tell anyone you know or it's immediate dismissal and…I think you understand what happens if you get blacklisted."

I nodded. "I'd never betray you or anyone. Please!"

"This friend who works for Mrs. McClain warned me she's plotting with Connor to get rid of you. And they have a plan. They're afraid you'll convince Zinc to disinherit them or at least his brother. He's been quite harsh with Connor and her. They fear you're making Zinc too independent, beyond her influence."

"What? I haven't done anything Zinc doesn't know about."

"They want to disintegrate your relationship, destroy you. Zinc is vulnerable now, exhausted and confused by his new duties and they may see this as the time."

"Zinc loves me and I love him!" I could barely talk. How could they break us up?

"They're clever, vicious, and determined. I just want you to prepare yourself."

"For what?"

"I don't know."

* * *

I opened our bedroom door and looked in. Zinc was sitting in the same spot I was on the night of the birthday party, leaning forward, elbows on his knees, hands covering his eyes. He was crying.

I walked to him, my legs shaky; my steps tentative. "Zinc…are you okay? What's wrong?"

He turned to me, his eyes red, his face twisted in pain. I moved a chair next to him and sat, putting my hands on his shoulders.

"Don't!" he snapped, pushing them away.

"Please, Zinc, is something the matter?" I was stunned.

"Did you fuck Cedric for money?"

"Oh, God. No, he paid me for tutoring and pushed me into having sex."

"You admitted getting ten times your tutoring rate in the enforcer report."

"He pressured me. A downer can't easily say no to a barronial, there are consequences. He could have ruined me or my family. I told him no but he kept insisting. Downers have no legal rights or money." I touched a hand on his thigh. He glared and I moved it away.

"You claimed he was giving you the big increase because he wanted to help your family. Certainly not like the self-absorbed Cedric I knew. That's not true, is it?"

"No." I couldn't lie to him. "It was the only way I could get out of his demand."

"Get out of it? You fucked him for cash. And you lied to the enforcers. And you just lied to me."

"Zinc, it's more complicated than that!" He still had no idea what life was like to those with no power. Unless you experienced the helplessness, it made no sense. To a barronial, even a good man like Zinc, it was incomprehensible.

"My brother swore he fucked you several times for money. He paid you and you went to his bed."

I gasped, stumbling out of my chair, facing him. *"What?"* This was incomprehensible. I dropped down on my knees next to him, again touching his legs. "That's a lie! Connor hates me, he's physically attacked me! You know that. Please, it's not true. It's a scheme to break us up." I wiped my eyes. "He's not even hom!"

"Neither was Cedric. Connor says you're a whore, that you do it with lots of students. And the Headmaster says he thinks your tutoring is a cover. It's in the enforcer report on Cedric's death."

"No, no, Zinc! Please! I'm a top student, you know that, kids want me to help them, teachers recommend me. You took a summer course I taught. It's how I raise money for my family."

"My mother said Connor recommended you for my birthday gift because you were...you were such grr...reat s...sex and would be a...a...fun t...toy for me."

"NO!" I bellowed. "She's lying. They're afraid we're getting too close. It's about Connor's inheritance!"

"You're calling *my mother* a liar?" He pinched his lips and his nostrils flared. He was angry, losing it. All the staggering pressures he was under and now this. He was breaking apart, the real Zinc locked away. "She may be vain and r...ridiculous but she wouldn't lie to me about this. She swore to God it was true, looked me in the eye. She said she saw Connor...Connor... fucking you." His voice broke, tears in his eyes.

"No...no, NO!" I backed up, hands over my face. This was a horror.

"*Fucking my brother!*" He screamed at my face then looked down. A sob. "You were my love, the first person I ever had sex with, my salvation. You betrayed me! I adored you and you were hiding this. You were mocking me behind my back. MY BROTHER!" He covered his mouth with the back of his hand, breathing rapidly.

"Please, I beg you. Think this through, you know they hate me—"

"Two of my mother's guards con…firmed it. You were even n… naked once in front of my mother. MY MOTHER!"

My brain was frozen. He can't believe this. "I love you, Zinc. I would never betray you. You know me." He could check with Hernandez but I just promised the man I wouldn't involve him. "I…I was humiliated. It was before your birthday party. Guards marched me into her office and ordered me to strip. I didn't want to. They threatened. I was in handcuffs."

"You're lying. That's not how it happened."

"I'm not lying…Zinc…" He wasn't listening and seemed to be hyperventilating, shaken to his core, irrational like the time he came back from his father obsessed with his face. Zinc stood and walked to the door, opening it. "How could you?" His face twisted in agony. "I loved you. I opened my heart to you. My brother? That's beyond forgiveness. *Get out…!*"

"Zinc, please, I beg you…" I kneeled and grabbed his leg. This couldn't be happening.

He slapped my face, knocking me to the floor.

I looked up at him, stunned. He'd never hurt me before. I slowly stood, holding onto the doorjamb, trying to maintain eye contact through my tears.

"It's not true," I whispered. "I love you." I ran with no idea where to go.

CHAPTER 42

I SPRINTED DOWN THE CORRIDOR TO the servants' stairs in the back, jumping two steps at a time, toward the second basement level, not sure why, adrift, frightened. I just needed to move. There was no way Zinc could believe this if he were rational but there was enough truth to make it seem real. I remembered the day, before I was given to Zinc, when his mother had guards bring me to her office and forced me to disrobe. Now it was me being lewd. Sex with Connor was impossible. I didn't want to have sex with Cedric. The headmaster was getting his revenge.

The stairway stopped at the first floor and I wanted the lower levels because they were rarely used. I cut through a hallway to get to a second set of stairs that went deeper into the building. I noticed blood on my hand. I'd been biting my knuckle.

"Spartak!" Connor called from behind me. I turned to face him, wiping my eyes. He smirked. "Maybe he'll give you to me after all, slave boy. Think about that. You can be my servant." He began to laugh.

I pivoted, desperate, panicked, my chest heaving and ran to the stairway then down two levels. I hurried to the small office Hernandez used, hoping he was still here, not knowing where else to go, to hide. Maybe I could stay with him or Ransom and his boys. But they all worked for the McClains. Why would they endanger their careers for a slave, particularly when my owner thinks I betrayed him? How could I prove it was a con? Old Faithful was back at work in my gut. Why couldn't I have just been an average student in a downer school?

Hernandez was gone, the room empty, but I noticed a pocketknife on the desk. Maybe I should just end it now. Zinc was my protector.

* * *

I heard footsteps. Someone came into the room. There was a grunt and a click. "He's in Security, Basement 2!" It was Gunther's voice. He bent down. "Please come out, Spartak. Trust me."

I was crouched under the desk, my head over my knees, the knife in one hand, my knuckles white from squeezing the handle. I felt dead, my skin clammy, my brain adrift, afraid to reengage on the wreckage.

He kneeled beside me. "Are you all right?" He pushed back my head and it bumped into the wooden drawer above. "Look at me! Please."

I opened my eyes and closed them again, feeling humiliated in front of a man I admired. Someone who considered Zinc a son.

More footsteps.

"Under here," Gunther said.

"Spartak!" It was Ransom. "Oh, son, pull yourself together." Gunther moved aside. Ran reached in with both hands and pried the knife from my fingers. He held it in front of my face. "Were you going to use this?"

"I can't win. My Zinc thinks I'm a whore." I turned my head toward the back of the knee space under the desk.

Ran growled and grabbed my arms, dragging me out, my legs stiff and tingly. He forced me to stand and wrapped his massive arms around me. "Spartak, don't do this to yourself. We'll figure this out."

Gunther touched my arm and I looked at the floor.

Panting at the door. "Thank God! He's here and okay." It was Tripper followed by Paolo sprinting into the room, out of breath. "We've been looking everywhere for you. Your ear tracker signal is blocked."

My face was wet and slimy. I turned away as best I could, not wanting them to see me like this but I was surrounded.

"We heard," Paolo said. "Sonia told us after talking to Zinc. People care about you, knucklehead. Hernandez is secretly talking to staff. He told Sonia how Glenda's guards threatened you, made you strip for her."

"He believes his mother and Connor over me." I felt defeated.

"He'll understand eventually. He's in a meltdown now, overwhelmed by many issues, and this has crushed him. Give him time," Gunther said. "I'll talk to him."

"Their lies are clever. How do I prove I didn't..." I rubbed my face. "I can't even say it, what Connor said we did. It's so...so..." I couldn't find the words, remembering how he and his thug buddies used to beat me, how I stood up to him. My head filled with Justice Washington's righteous voice saying a freed slave was like a piece of furniture left on a sidewalk for anyone to take. And I was discarded, a piece of junk. What would happen to my family? To me?

"Enough, Spartak," Tripper interrupted. "We'll find a way to make this right."

"Don't be a dickhead," Paolo scolded. "No self-pity. Not with us. We're your brothers. We know you got an A in drama."

"We love you," Tripper said, mussing my hair.

"Yes we do," Gunther added. He was smiling with tears in his eyes.

I laughed, blowing out snot. "Oh fuck." I opened the handkerchief for another round.

"Zinc needs more time on this," Ransom said. "Glenda has bet everything she can control Zinc. She is formidable. But that's my problem. For you, young man, focus on the Olympics. It starts in two weeks. You'll stay with us while this gets sorted through. Paolo, Tripper, get him out of here—NOW!"

* * *

Ransom's kitchen was a safe haven. No McClains.

"He hates me," I said. "I'd hate me too if I had sex with Connor." I rubbed my eyes. "Zinc doesn't believe me. That's what hurts."

Sonia pressed her lips tight as she watched me.

"Sorry if I'm babbling..."

We sat at a long chrome bar in Ransom's kitchen, drinking *macha* tea, one of her favorites. The bitter taste seemed appropriate.

"It's ripping Zinc apart," she said. "And with all the other decisions he has to make about McClain Enterprises, he's physically and mentally exhausted. I think Sergei's death impacted him more than we thought. He held it inside. He doesn't trust anything Connor says but he doesn't believe his mother would lie. She's adamant her story is true. If he doubts her, then he has no family." She stopped and started to speak but couldn't.

"Are you all right?" she asked after a long silence.

"He ordered me to leave. He hit me. He's never done that before." Sonia looked out the window and took a sip of tea, then back at me. Her eyes were red.

"It wasn't him."

I just sat, drained, my puffy eyes cried out.

She said, "He's alone, angry, sickened you would betray him—"

"But I didn't!"

"I know but he doesn't. With his father gone, he's closing himself off, just focusing on the business, trying to remain sane. Glenda wants to break the bond you share with Zinc. And it's a strong one."

"Do you really think there's a bond?"

"Yes, and powerful. His love for you is sincere." She leaned closer. "Is yours?"

I started to speak and stopped, focused on my hands twisting on the counter. "I was frightened when I was kidnapped and woke up in a jail cell, all the medical tests to make sure I was healthy. This dehumanizing tracker bolted into my ear. And what I was told I had to do. I didn't know him and was trained to recognize my place in school, to walk the line. On the street it's different; I know how to survive. Or did. Two worlds. And sometimes it wasn't pretty. Here, in this reality, I felt helpless. Connor and the other kids that night at the party were monsters."

She squeezed my hand. I noticed strands of her hair sticking out where they shouldn't; obviously she came here in a hurry. She was always perfect in public but not here with me, like a friend or sister. I hoped that wasn't a mirage.

"But Zinc wasn't what I expected," I continued, thinking about him. "He was kind, nervous around me. It was...cute. I might even say precious, endearing. I sensed he needed me to confirm he was worthy. It was bizarre, crazy, I know. A poor teenager giving validation to a guy so rich I can't even comprehend it. He was obsessed with his face. And I think he's great looking, different. He was hot. We started having fun in bed as friends. I began caring for him more and more as I saw what kind of man he was and could be. He needed me and I needed him. And I liked what I found. Do I love him? Yeah, I think I do."

"I know it's true. Now, get yourself together. Tomorrow I'm taking you to the Olympic training camp. I have my dad's jet."

I began to laugh. "Of course you do."

CHAPTER 43

RANSOM FLEW US TO THE MARIN jetport in a McClain buzzard and walked with us into Sonia's plane. I sensed he had something to tell me and wanted privacy.

"Spartak," he said, "you need to know that the Dominionists have posted a bounty on your head. We intercepted coded messages between the Cardinal and Bishop Perry. They want you dead for killing their soldiers and defacing Bishop Martin. You're also apparently too popular, a media hero, a distraction from their focus on Jesus and End Times. There're even insane comments that you look like a young blond, blue-eyed Jesus." He snorted, shaking his head. "They're turning their loyalists on you."

Not much to say.

"Ran," Sonia asked, "do you have verifiable proof?"

"Voices of their discussions and messages out to Dominionist churches. Good stuff. Plus the attacks on Zinc and Spartak in Perry's sermons. We have recordings."

"Excellent. Let's get it packaged. People must see this as a follow-up to the kidnappings and rescue. Bishop Martin was not a rogue as they're trying to claim. He was acting in concert. We need to make Perry a pariah, build public disgust and separate him from his flock."

I watched Sonia in amazement, morphing from sweet high school senior into a conspirator.

"I like it." Ran held up a small valise he'd been carrying. "Here are a variety of special armaments you will take with you into the Olympic Village. We're also finalizing a new one for close-in fighting, a real cherry. I'll send it along later."

"They don't allow weapons," I said. This was crazy.

"Security won't know you have them. If Dominionists decide to strike, you must be prepared. And I won't be there the whole time. You know why. It could save your life and those of other athletes."

"So it's still going to happen?" I knew the plan laid out three months ago after Perry attacked us in his sermon.

"Yes, Zinc and I will carry it out."

"Carry what out?" Sonia asked.

"I'm sorry, Sonia, please trust me. It's best you don't know what Zinc and I have planned."

"Please let me go with you!" I was panicked. The plan was insane.

Ran put his arms around me and sighed. "You have an important task to do, son, and only you can do it. Be a great athlete, a proud young man, standing up for downers, their hero. My hero." He let me go and looked into my face. "I believe Zinc wants you in Vancouver. Trust me on the rest. Please son."

"All right but I don't like it."

Sonia's expression was tight. She was used to getting her way. "Don't I have a right to know what you're planning? Zinc is my closest friend." Her eyes turned wide and hopeful as she stared at me.

"You'll have to get it from him," I said, struggling to look at her face, afraid she would hate me. "I can't break a confidence. You'd think less of me if I did."

She looked irritated but nodded that she understood.

"And the weapons are just in case something happens at the games," Ran said. "Bishop Perry doesn't care if innocents are murdered."

"I know. What I don't understand is why people follow such transparently evil human beings."

"People see what they want to see and are sometimes hungry for deception, avoiding what should be obvious. Welcome to the real world."

* * *

The weather in Vancouver, British Columbia, was tank top perfect, wispy white clouds in the morning giving way to full sun by noon, ideal for pummeling your body to get in shape. Training was a relief. But what Zinc and Ran were planning in a few nights was haunting my head.

The American team was in superb shape. I knew all the guys from Stanford and other competitions. Hinkins and Matt were there from the national championships almost a year ago. They both grabbed me and did knuckle supremes on my head and it felt good, like everything was normal. The other team members treated me like a comrade, lots of arm punches and comments about my abs; I did my share of teasing back. We were here for a purpose, each depending on the other. Coach Johanson was one of three men assigned to us. And he pushed us hard during four-hour practices followed by two hours of rest preceding two more hours of training. Every third day was jogging, massages and whatever else we wanted to do with any leftover energy remaining to us.

No leaving the site. A dozen guards, including Hernandez, patrolled the gymnasium and apartments assigned to the US team just outside the city. Ransom had also brought in new sensors and fitted them around the buildings.

My birthday passed unnoticed by my comrades and I didn't mention it. I had a dynamo talk with Geo and my family. Rhonda and Billy sang "Happy Birthday." He should stick with his art. It was wonderful. And I was seventeen.

The next day, the team moved ten miles from our training complex into the Olympic Village, a series of remodeled old and new apartment buildings connected with lounge areas and meeting spaces. And lots of perimeter guards.

* * *

Built specifically for the Olympic Games, the O-Dome seated sixty thousand in downtown Vancouver. The US team uniforms were snappy Revolutionary War coats giving everyone a magic V-shaped figure, dark blue with gold trim. I liked the design, something Congressmen wore, only ours were trimmer and less ostentatious. After a heated discussion with the clothing manufacturers, the entire American contingent—all different sports—voted not to wear tri-corner hats. I enjoyed mine but supported the team. Instead everyone pulled their hair back and tied it with black ribbons, boys and girls, like Thomas Jefferson or maybe Betsy Ross. At least those with long hair, which was most of us.

The opening ceremony was at dusk. The sunset seemed part of the drama, scattered white clouds turned orange, the azure sky slowly became sapphire. The temperature was shirtsleeve, perfect for a parade.

When the United States was announced, I hoisted the American flag, putting the pole-butt in the belt holder around my waist and led my team through the high stone gate onto the field. I knew my parents, Geo, and Kimber were here, thanks to Sonia. Rhonda and Billy too.

The crowd was on its feet. The applause boomed so loud it sounded amped. I heard my name mentioned by the stadium announcer. And an ear receiver also let me hear the comments of the major sportscaster. The woman was talking more about me than the team.

In the stadium I noticed people pointing at me and there seemed to be hundreds of Spartak masks. I pushed it all away and enjoyed the thrill of being in the Olympics representing America. Judy LeVene, the Vermont pole-vaulter, hurried to my side, putting a hand under my arm. Matt and Hinkins ran up on either side. Others came up as well. It was glorious, the proudest day of my life.

Athletes handed off the official torch, one to another, as it was carried around the stadium and up a circular ramp to an eighty-foot tower in the center. This time I'd slipped a handkerchief in my sleeve to be ready for the inevitable, sort of like one of the frilly French kings, one of the Louies. But mine was absorbent cotton, not lace.

I couldn't make out faces in the official box. When President Chiu was introduced and I saw her on a series of giant floating Z-ethers, I looked to where my family and friends must be but it was too far to make out faces. Today was July 4th, a year to the day since I was drugged by my coach and sold. Tonight I didn't feel like a slave.

Tomorrow I'd train again. The gymnastics competition was four days away. The constant question I asked myself was if I could have made this on my own.

Yeah. Being a slave of the elite had nothing to do with my skills as an athlete. Everyone around me was free, as far as I knew. I was good, maybe the best in the world in my sport, confirmed by my coaches and some team members. That was also the media speculation. It felt good, a bit surreal to hear reporters gossip about me, but it added to the pressure. It was also calming to be on a gymnastic team without Connor.

The final torch ignited the gas in the golden bucket high atop where I stood. The Olympic flame shot to the stars and I pulled out my handkerchief.

CHAPTER 44

"I am Nocturne," a young woman announced.
"Bishop Perry vows to kill Spartak Jones.
Watch and hear his call for murder!
Visit any of our sites."
She slipped a Spartak mask over her face.
"WE are Spartak! Join AR2!"

I WAS NERVOUS ABOUT WHAT ZINC might or might not be doing tonight and had had no contact with him or Ransom. Sonia, her hunk boyfriend, Adi Aban, and Justice Washington surprised me by walking into the cafeteria. She said they were thrilled watching me carry the flag in the opening and would attend the gymnastics meet.

Adi was solar, great muscles and a hard demeanor, fierce might be a better way to describe him. And so very sexy. I was happy for Sonia. People were staring, hopefully at them. I had mac 'n' cheese and some steamed broccoli on my tray plus a large glass of milk. They each had a small salad with dressing on the side. Downers ate differently. They asked about training and my teammates. Nice small talk.

"We have news regarding the *Sasser* case," Sonia said, turning to her uncle.

Justice Washington pursed his lips. "Three of my fellow justices have been caught in a delicate situation and I suspect will resign."

"What?" I could not have been more shocked.

"You tell him," the judge said to his niece.

"Well," Sonia began with relish, "the three Dominionists on the court, including the Chief Justice, are known to gamble and drink heavily, particularly on boys' night out each third Friday. They're often indiscreet, figuring people are too fearful to say anything."

"But people know this?"

"People who are insiders to the court. And they keep their lips tight." The judge showed a hint of a smile.

"Their electro-cruiser, a Kiron46 no less, splashed into the tidal basin near the capital," Sonia explained. "They nearly drowned. They were drunk and had three young women with them in the car. All on date-rape drugs."

"Unreal." I had to smile. Some people deserved bad things for what they did, kind of like the inverse Golden Rule.

"Yes," she gloated. "And the story is exploding. Since they were smug Dominionists—pious, married, and scornful—you can imagine how this is awkward. Plus pedophilia is an added complication. One of the girls was eleven." She scrunched her lips to block a smile.

"It's a Wilbur Mills moment," Washington added.

"Who?"

"Sorry. I've a fondness for useless bits of history like Egardo Mortara." His smile widened. "The twist to a popular maxim is that the more you know history the greater your proven options. Some lessons of history are worth repeating. Mills was a powerful congressman from Arkansas over a century ago. He ran his car into the basin at the same exact spot. He had a stripper with him. Ended his career."

"So, how does this help on *Sasser*?"

"The vote was six-to-three. These were the hardcore members of the majority. You need six justices voting at a minimum if the three are gone we have a three-to-three tie. So a fourth vote is crucial. And I believe one of the remaining judges is persuadable to switch his vote. It will take a month for pressure and humiliation to force the three to resign and a year to find a case and get it on the docket. Or maybe Zinc could file suit on your behalf, when he is willing, athough that might stretch out the timeline. There are enough votes in the Senate to stall any new appointments unless they are favorable."

"Isn't President Chiu on our side?" I realized how silly that sounded. What was my side?

"Depends on the definition of 'our'," he said. "The main problem is the likely fourth vote will probably insist on no retroactivity, he would only outlaw them after the date of the appeal. So existing debtbonders would be permanent. His brother has a slave girl and wants to keep her. Outrageous but he's a judge appointed for life and politics is what it is. If his position holds, you'd remain in your current situation. But the *Sasser* decision would be repealed."

A question seemed irresistible but could get me in trouble. "Did you make this happen with the judges?" I glanced at each and waited.

"We were all hundreds of miles removed from the site when it took place," Sonia said, touching my arm.

"Between us, young man," the justice said with a wink, "we suspected something would eventually happen. They were reckless and arrogant."

"Who is Nocturne?" I asked.

"I suspect Nocturne is a catch phrase much like AR2," the judge said as he stood. "Here is something to ponder, Spartak, just conjecture on my part. Words are important in politics. Nocturne has certain magic. With minor tweaks in spelling it can mean a romantic musical melody full of joy and hope as you are known to play. Or, a prayer, perhaps for freedom. And it can refer to the night, maybe revolutionaries hiding their identities while pursuing a new, more just America." He shrugged his shoulders and grinned. "But what do I know?" He extended a hand and I took it. "Make us proud, Spartak. We believe in you."

* * *

As soon as they left, I sat back down at the empty table and gave a command into my Z-ether, turning my back to the crowd. I enjoyed the small talk but this was important. "Find me a channel for Bishop Perry, San Francisco, live."

It popped onto the screen in full DIMM4 and I touched the speaker implant in my ear. I expanded the screen. It was live at the church. The organist worked her magic, the music thundered, the chorus, dazzling in red and blue robes, sounded celestial. The lights dimmed. The drape dropped. Silence. Then shrieking, wailing. Pandemonium. It was everything the bishop wanted. Almost.

Perry was naked, crucified on the cross. His body twitched; he howled. His eyes, terrified, searched the room, then up to the left, looking at the spike in his forearm. Then the other way. He screamed and his head dropped, dead or unconscious, a man defeated.

Ransom's plan was to don Jesusista drag, complete with liteon veils, and slip in as final preparations were made, joining a thousand others dressed just the same, make their way into Perry's office, lock his office door and launch a sound and telecom bubble. With the XOs, they could easily overcome most resistance but didn't want to. This was a stealth operation. If the hidden passageway existed as 1860's plans suggested, the captured Perry could easily be secreted through the building and taken to the cross, cordoned off and hidden by floor-to-ceiling drapes.

It was revolting. But so were the murders of the guards. The torture. The plotting to foment a war. Ran was ex-military and had no issues. Zinc had to steel himself. They were to drug Perry to make him easier to manage through the hidden passageway and to lessen his pain until he regained consciousness. A cruel theatrical death for the bishop but justice for those he murdered and for those his movement would have destroyed if allowed to continue. Odd how I was able to rationalize this; my head in a different place than a year ago. Yet the court system and government were corrupt, justice a slogan, not reality. What would Jesus do? He sacrificed his own life to save mankind. Perry was willing to sacrifice mankind so he could be king. Or was I just rationalizing because I loved Zinc and admired Ransom Bolt?

I watched the screen as the cross slowly turned on its stand—front, side, back, front, side, back. It was on automatic. And the DIMM4s kept sending out the signal to the world.

I saw an envelope tacked below Perry's feet. I knew the contents. A handwritten confession and it was to be posted to media sites around the globe. The final lines would indicate Satan, his master, was recalling him.

"Confession, Bishop Perry," came an announcement.

It popped up on the official church website, hacked by Ransom.

His crucifixion was "symbolic of the thieves," said an announcer with the face and voice of God, "not the son of the creator." He was a criminal, "stealing Christianity, an anti-Christ, as is the Dominionist movement itself."

Gruesome but effective, I thought, revolted but relieved. The guy was implacable and remorseless, a murderer who wanted to control the world. Government couldn't or wouldn't touch him. But a poetic end. Two down, one to go.

I remembered Zinc saying in our planning meeting that Cardinal Iglesias would demand vengeance. A martyr to his cause who would have the full resources of the Catholic Church. "We should find a way to help him," Zinc had said. I thought about my Zinc and Ran. Had they survived?

* * *

"Amigo! Spartak—come play." Miguel Torros, my roommate, a sprinter from Mexico, called to me as I stood and flipped off the screen. The twenty-year-old held the world record in the hundred-meter dash. I joined a group of athletes playing foosball. I knew I'd lose but they were fun and this was distracting. Partway though the first game, Hernandez called my name.

"Here you are. Thank goodness your ear tracker is working again." He pulled me aside.

"We'll be right back, guys."

"Have you heard what happened to Bishop Perry?" Hernandez asked as we walked to a private corner.

"Yes."

"Are you wearing...?"

"Yes."

"It's unlikely but conceivable they'll come after you here. The war is underway, focused on a handful of people. Your sword?"

"In my belt."

Hernandez, already wearing twin standard sonics on his hips, reached into his jacket and pulled out a small, oddly shaped weapon sent by Ran. It looked like a pair of brass knuckles with a stub barrel on top. "Boy Scouts are always prepared."

"I'm no Boy Scout," I assured him.

"This is a sonic knuckle, perfect for close quarter combat. Wear it as brass knuckles in a fight, push here to send a blast. Accurate to a hundred feet, depending on your aim. Explosive up close." He held it in front of my right hand. "Touch a fingertip here." I did. "Hold. I'll set it to your gene print." A minute later he finished. "And here are a few flash balls and a dispenser. Slip it inside your jacket sleeve. It'll hold them in reserve and drop them into your palm as needed."

"Thanks."

"I've got to relieve a man patrolling the perimeter. Be safe. I suspect you want to hang with your new friends but please consider returning to your quarters."

I slipped the flash balls, tube, and knuckles into my jacket pocket.

The floor shook, an explosion nearby. A siren. Dishes fell from a cabinet. People jumped, looked around, unsure what to do.

Hernandez listened to his earpiece. "A bomb at one of the luxury apartments immediately outside the Village. A baronial family."

"ZINC?" I was panicked.

"No. He's not here. I'm being called. Please! Go to your room!"

Miguel jogged over to me. The cafeteria was full, people jammed at the lone doorway to get out.

"I just heard the Dominionists have a reward on you." Miguel looked and sounded concerned.

"Yeah. I'm a popular guy."

We made it through the doors and ran down the hall. I needed a good night's sleep, if that was possible. But I had pills. Too many distractions.

* * *

"Catch me if you can!" Miguel yelled as he raced ahead for our room.

"No fair," I hollered, sprinting behind him, "you're track and field." I didn't want to use my XO advantage. He was a likely medalist and it was exciting to be sharing a tiny room with him.

Miguel pushed a finger into the lock. The door exploded, lifting him into the opposite wall. Two Jesusistas emerged from a door down the hall and fired, hitting Miguel.

I twisted, my back to them, bent over, head down, while I pulled out the brass knuckles. A solar blast hit my rump, piercing my jacket and pants, all the way to the XO. Better than my head until I could get my hood up. I could smell the burn, leather and cotton, but thankfully not my butt. I heard the peep; it was ready again.

I swiveled and leaped, twisting my calf to extend the boot blade. I kicked one leg up as I landed, ripping the front of one Jesusista from his crotch to his jaw. I swiveled, leading with my fist. The force of the XO and brass knuckles punched deep into the other guy's skull. I pulled out my hand, a disgusting mess, and wiped the drippings on the guy's shirt.

Seeing no one else, I dashed back to Miguel. My friend was cut in half by the blasts.

"Bastards!" I slipped into an open room, washed my hands, and decided my pants were wearable, just a small burn hole. I put on the hood, gloves, and face shield, then inserted the flash ball tube down my sleeve and made sure it was working. I wanted my favorite weapon. It took several minutes to withdraw the plasteel sword from my belt and get it rigid and glowing.

I looked into the hallway. It was empty, except for the smell and Miguel's body. My ring pinged, a small Z-ether projected above it.

"Hernandez here. Are you all right?"

"Yeah. They blew up my room and murdered Miguel. I killed them both and am now in full gear."

"Apparently several members of the Iranian team are in league with the Jesusistas. They let them pass security. We think there could be a dozen killers loose inside. Stay put."

"No way. They killed Miguel." I punched off and headed down the hall as I heard guards racing behind me, headed to my room. People closed doors as I ran past. They had no idea who I was and even if they did, I was obviously trouble. Smart people would run the other way.

The Village was a warren of cobbled together apartment buildings done on the cheap. I jogged down a hall toward a meeting room, hearing voices. No one there. I began a more systematic search. There were six levels in this part of the complex. On the third floor, a Jesusista jumped from a room, almost as if he was waiting to ambush me, and fired. I dodged the solar beam and threw my sword. It split the terrorist's chest, pinning him into a doorjamb. The guy was maybe twenty. I pulled his transmitter, listening to voices. They were searching for me. One mentioned my tracker.

"He's on three," someone said, "near 345."

I withdrew my sword, leaving the body as a greeting, and ran to the stairs. There was a storage room on the fifth floor where our team held meetings. Big enough to maneuver in if I could get there and entice them to follow.

I sidetracked into a bathroom, faced a mirror and twisted my ear, stretched it and angled the edge of the sword just under the tracker. I held my breath and cut it out.

"Ahhhh!"

I wiped up the blood and tracker with a towel. Looking in the mirror, I examined what was left.

I ran up another level to the meeting room and banged open the double doors. It had rows of piled boxes and stacked chairs at one end and a big walk-in cabinet nearby. I tossed in the bloody tracker, still riveted around an excised part of my ear, and closed the closet. Then I stepped back, rearranging some of the boxes to conceal myself with enough space to leap and twist. Floor exercises were coming early.

I sensed noise in the hallway, then an attempt to enforce silence. I saw a figure dart past the door and look in. He held a small device, likely locking onto my ear tracker. The Jesusista used hand signals to give orders.

First one came in, stepping on his toes to one corner, perhaps to provide cover, focused on the closet, within inches of where I was hiding. I moved my arm and a flash grenade dropped into my hand. I squeezed its side. Armed. Then three more entered and charged, their orange-red solars firing on full charge.

I grabbed the man nearest me and shoved a flashball down his throat. As it exploded, I was in the air, my heel blade out and sword in my right hand. The blade pierced one man's head then sliced out as my sword cut off the arm of another. They both collapsed, one dead and one screaming. I pulled in the blade and marched toward the remaining killer, enjoying the moment. The man fired. I kept moving closer.

"No. You have to be dead!"

I twisted away his pistol, crushed it in my hand and tossed it across the room. As he looked at me, open-mouthed, I grabbed him and slammed him into a far wall. He collapsed. I returned to the terrorist with one arm, sprawled on the floor, red with blood and angry.

"You need a tourniquet."

"Don't touch me!" The bearded young Jesusista gripped the stump. "Ahhhh. Next time we'll kill you AND your rich lover!"

"Are all religious terrorists stupid? Stop the blood or you die!"

"And if I do, it's straight to heaven!" He butted me with his head, trying to keep me away. I put a knee to his chest.

"Naawww. Islamist fanatics get the virgins. Christian fanatics just end up as rotted corpses."

"You know nothing!" He kicked with his legs and good arm.

"You're making this difficult." I stood, picked up the guy's severed arm and slammed it across his face. He lay flat, apparently unconscious. I untied his headband and wrapped it tight around the stump. "Disgusting." But it stopped the bleeding. This seemed like something I should do even though he'd tried to kill me. I finished with a square knot in Boy Scout fashion, wiped my hands on the terrorist's shirt and stood, picking up my sword.

As I started for the door, four Jesusistas entered the room and spread out. They had some kind of solar rifles. I wasn't sure if my suit would protect me or not. Not much I could do about it.

"You made quite a mess, slave boy." The man had a short beard, grayish skin.

"Payback is tough."

"You're an enemy of Jesus, seeking to stop His return."

"And you are deluded nutcases, conned by a lying and very dead bishop."

I flexed my wrist silently releasing another flash grenade into my palm. I pressed each side, armed and ready. They began to move around me.

I did a forward roll as I tossed the grenade, XO propelled, into one guy's gut. A white beam fired over my shoulder. A terrorist exploded. I leaped and came down on another man with my sword.

The solar rifle pointed at me. A double flash from the doorway. The leader was incinerated and the rifle dropped. The remaining terrorist put up his arms. I looked at my rescuers. We all took off our masks. Zinc and Ransom. Ran handcuffed the Dominionist to a pipe.

"Pig!" the prisoner yelled.

Ran slugged him in the jaw. The terrorist collapsed to the floor. Ran was not subtle.

Zinc ran to me, arms enveloping me, kissing me all over my face. "Thank God, thank God. I panicked when I heard the explosion."

"You're safe! I was worried about you both tonight!" I squeezed him, not wanting to let go.

"And you should have been worried." A man's voice behind us, coming in the double doors. There were five, four with rifles. "Aim all weapons at Spartak. He's the one we want dead. You're all good fighters and you may kill one or two of us, but not before he is destroyed."

"Why?" Zinc asked.

"I will answer that," a woman's voice replied. She took off her hood. It was a black woman, tall, with sculpted wavy hair, her head back, haughty. She had no weapon.

I said, "Kinuba Steele, I presume."

She nodded, an appreciative smile. "Yes, you have done your homework. Too bad I left just before your entrance at the sewer plant. A remarkable feat." Her diction was slow and precise. She stared at me as she walked over and touched the side of my face and chin. "Oh, you are so beautiful. This is really a tragedy because…I admire you. I have never told anyone that before. You are quite a special young man. But my employer resists your charms."

"You work for Bishop Perry?" I asked as she finger-combed my hair. I wasn't sure what to do.

"I work for money and many people have it. Fortunately I was paid before Bishop Hallelujah had those mysterious visitors." She erased her smile. "A very stylish execution."

"So why kill Spartak?" Zinc said again.

"Personally, I don't want to hurt him. My employers think he is too popular," she said in exaggerated perfection, looking at Zinc, "too sympathetic and dangerous to those into the true cause. I'm not a believer myself, all fantasy, but these men are. Your PR campaign building him up has been too successful, they fear. The masses identify with him. I identify with him." She laughed.

"Did you kill Cedric Rand?" I asked.

"Kinuba did meet him at the Palladium. A handsome boy. And a foolish one."

The man with a rifle spat on the floor. "You were hailed as a downer hero after mutilating one of our trinity," he said, curling his lips. Then he turned to Zinc. "There's a price to pay when you interfere with God's work. Jesus must return. This boy's an impediment."

It was hard to imagine adults talking this way. But I didn't spend much time with Dominionists or the certifiably insane.

A flash from the hallway and the leader dropped to the floor, his chest ablaze. The other three turned as two hooded figures ran into the room, a zigzag pattern, firing. Two Jesusistas took direct hits to the face, one swung his rifle looking for the attackers and had a foot shot off. Kinuba just stood there, an amused look on her lips and raised her arms. "Great timing," she said.

"Can I borrow your cuffs?" one of the hooded men asked, walking to Ransom.

He handed him a pair. "Who are you?" Ran asked.

There was a deep-throated laugh. The first hood pulled back. It was Ali. He cuffed Kinuba and kicked the rifle away from the footless assassin, who was thrashing and screaming.

"Shouldn't we help him?" I stooped down, yanked off the man's headband. He was about my age, clean-shaven, and used it as a tourniquet. It was grotesque and bloody. He seemed frightened, grateful, and in serious pain. I wiped my hands on his clothes and looked up as everyone circled around me.

The head covering on the second hero was removed. It was Sonia. "We were here anyway, just in case and thought you could use the help."

"Oh, Sonia!" I jumped up and we embraced. "Thank you. I had no idea, how…"

She put her hand over my mouth. "Later."

Olympic security and the FBI arrived within moments.

"I am impressed," Kinuba said as they took her into custody. "We will meet again."

CHAPTER 45

NEWS ABOUT THE ATTACK WAS WORLDWIDE and the commentary impassioned. Many analysts and elected officials demanded the arrest and prosecution of much of the American clergy caught up in the Dominionist nonsense. Others shouted it was a fabrication by the Twelve Families and we were the aggressors. But mostly, I found myself again hailed as a "lionheart" and with fewer photos of my butt in the shower. Zinc was called a hero too. I was so proud of him. Ransom, Sonia, and Ali, by their choice, were never identified by name, only part of the security team.

Surveillance lumins were everywhere in the building, it turned out, and almost everything was captured, played, and replayed, even events on the fifth floor.

Two days later, walking into the gymnasium with my team, the actual Olympic competition seemed almost anticlimactic. The viewing stands were packed. Other athletes stopped and watched as I walked amidst the American gymnasts. All activity on the floor ceased.

"Way to go, Spartak!" an athlete from Britain hollered. I pointed at the guy.

I heard my name and comments in other languages. People waved. I smiled, proud but not sure if smiling was appropriate after all the killing. The brutality of it all left me depressed and I had to keep reminding myself I had no choice. Spectators in one section of the bleachers rose and started to applaud. People called my name, then the entire auditorium was on its feet, even the coaches, athletes, and journalists.

"Take a bow and wave, Spartak," Coach told me. "You deserve it." He struggled not to laugh. "And you can keep your shirt on this time."

I raised an arm and gave them my best toothy grin, then bowed repeatedly and somehow the noise increased its decibel level. I continued to walk and wave, my energy building. Spartak masks appeared on dozens, then hundreds of faces in the stands. My life back, my future more secure, the crowd—I was perked.

I searched for a handkerchief and settled for my warm-up jacket sleeve. Matt Dowell and Hinkins Martinez were on either side of me and put their arms over my shoulders. Just a year ago we were stuffed in a cannon ball. Now at the Olympics. It felt surreal but genuine. "If you have any female groupies you want to send my way," Hinkins whispered into my ear, "my dance card is open." And Zinc was here, somewhere in the VIP stand along with my family, together, watching.

My team was inspired judging by their performance on the mats and bars. A year ago all this had started with a single gold medal. Now I had seven more.

* * *

"So you believe me?" I just needed to hear it again. We were sitting on the tan baby-butt soft leather sofa in Zinc's favorite jet, headed back to San Francisco. And he needed to show some humility and remorse. Ransom was across from us doing something on his Z-ether. My focus was all on Zinc.

"Yes. Yes. Yes. I was wrong to ever question you. You would never lie to me." He picked up my hand and kissed it. "I am so ashamed I had doubts and even worse, I slapped you." His eyes welled. "I was so confused. Can you forgive me?"

"Oh, Zinc!" I pulled him into a hug. Much better.

Afterward, we sat there, looking at each other.

"I should explain how I knew for certain you were telling me the truth and…and my mother was l…lying." He struggled, biting his lip. "Think about that. My…my mother deceiving me, swearing to God it was the truth." His voice became a whisper, sheepish. "I…I want you to hear it from me."

I touched his cheek and smiled. He was pale and shamefaced.

"Ran caught them on surveillance, gloating. While we have widespread security lumins, they may not be turned on except in case of an incursion." Zinc looked over to Ran. "And this man broke the rules and brought me the truth and I'm grateful he did. I showed it to my mother and Connor. They started to protest it was a fake. Then my brother snarled, spitting at me, and said it was true. '*We did it to save the family from a parasite.*' I left the room and haven't talked to them since. I was such a fool." His eyes welled as he picked up my hand. "You are my family." He began to cry softly and I pulled him tight, looking at Ransom and mouthing a silent "thank you."

* * *

Back in Henry's Room, Ran touched his zan and a DIMM4 image of Officer Imogene Rango popped onto the screen.

"Ahhhh," I screamed and jumped from my seat. He'd called us down to show me something.

"I take that as confirmation." He almost looked amused at my non-stud boy reaction, then the hardness returned. "But let me get this on the record. Is this the enforcement officer who raped you multiple times?"

"Yes." It was humiliation to admit it.

Two more images came onto the screen. Officer Christine Reilly, Rango's patrol partner, and the duty sergeant.

"And this woman was with Rango and this man was at the desk in the station and knew what was happening?" Ran donned his full war mask expression.

"Yes."

"Spartak, Zinc and I have met with Mayor Rand and explained what happened and how downer families are exploited. He is going to revoke the contract for Harmony Enforcers and make the enforcement of laws up to a local government-run police force with a civilian review panel, including downers, and a mayoral appointed police chief. This will set a national precedent. It will mean a fight with another barronial family that owns the company." He smiled. "But given what Zinc did to the three families that tried to hurt you plus the Timkos, I suspect there will be little opposition."

I just looked at him then over to Zinc who nodded. "Honestly?" I opened my arms and Ran gave me a hug. Zinc joined in too. This was big, so big for my neighborhood and downers everywhere. "Thank you. I…I almost can't believe it. This is so important." I looked back at the images, eyes watering. "What happens to them?"

"With your ID they will face prosecution and years in prison. They'll be an example of how enforcers do *not* do their job."

She was a horrible woman and yet prison alone did not seem enough. She could do something useful. "Ran, how about if she had to go out with members of this new government agency, meeting with the public, my downer public, and confess over and over how evil she was and what the new public enforcers will be like?"

He laughed. "Maybe you should be a judge. I like the idea."

"Do you think we could ever come up with a name better than enforcers? Harmony Enforcement seems pretty bizarre. How about something that has to do with justice?"

CHAPTER 46

"MAY I ASK EVERYONE TO JOIN me at the center of the gondola?" Zinc's voice was commanding. Everyone turned from side conversations, white wine, and hors d'oeuvres. He waved us closer. He wore a goatee now, much like his father, but lacked the hardness of his dad's eyes. I'd told him I didn't like to kiss whiskers; he promised to shave it after this trip. Whether I shaved or not, nobody could tell the difference.

It was a stellar group, sitting in this immense red disk high above the earth. Nearby stood the President, Justice Washington, the Majority Leader of the US Senate, the Speaker of the House, the Governor of California, a general, the president's security team, a handful of famous entertainers and trillionaires. And real people: my family, Sonia and Ali, Billy Eagle, Rhonda Van Deen, Ransom, Tripper, and Paolo. And I spotted Dalix in the back, dressed fancy, all cleaned up and looking nervous. I'd asked Sonia to find a young lady to keep him company. Of my old gang members, only Dalix accepted. He was into girls now. Sonia's younger sister, Moisha, was beside him. Hopefully she liked bad boys.

Mr. Pennyworth, my school librarian and secret source of alternative history books, was standing to the side with my piano teacher, Miss Maisey Hedwick. Her hand was draped over his arm. That looked promising. On his other side was Tessie, my cafeteria heroine. I wanted them to come. They were shocked and embarrassed when I asked. "Why?" they wanted to know. "Because you three are very special to me," I'd told them, "and because I can." Who cared if three senators or governors or rich barronials got bumped? Zinc knew Miss Hedwick but was blank faced on the pudgy Mr. Pennyworth. "Who's he?" he'd asked. "A very special friend, a librarian from school," I'd told him. There was no way I could explain about the underground society. I would not endanger the brave librarians who risked so much. Zinc had grinned and shook his head. "Whatever you want. And Tessie too. You are so amazing. And now I have to explain to some very rich and powerful people why they're getting dumped." He laughed and hugged me. "I like your friends better."

Thirty people including security was max cargo on regular gondolas. This one, used for big loads and special occasions, could handle twice that number. Generally the cars only carried a few miners and equipment. Accommodating the president and her security team took some reconfiguring of rooms and she and her staff had boarded early.

Five gondolas were headed up the space elevator, about a quarter mile apart, each with the maximum load, wrapped around different sides of the circular nano-steel tubes, anchored in a supership at the equator and stretching 22,000 miles to a circular space station, like a giant plumb bob, in geosynchronous orbit with Earth. The climbers, as they were officially called, practically floated up the tether, powered by beams of light projected down from the massive solar power units on the station.

Because the president was aboard, a US Naval armada surrounded the McClain anchor ship and military planes circled fifty miles up. The anchor ship and cabling was also heavily armed to repel saboteurs and terrorists.

It was a four-day trip and this was nearly day three. Sleeping accommodations were spartan, even for the president, but the view made the difference. This was the official ribbon cutting ceremony. Everyone wanted to be a part of history. Mankind was in space in a big way, funded largely by the McClains.

"Spartak Jones," Zinc began, "come here!"

"Is that a command, Master?" Don't give him an inch.

"It is, so don't test my patience." If Zinc had not been grinning from ear to ear, I might have been irritated. And the way he was talking told me he was watching his syllables. This was not a place to stutter.

I stood before him. Zinc bit his lip, my old trick. It worked for him too.

"First, let me reset the stage." He touched his thumb on top of his ring. The ebony floor dissolved.

"My God!" someone yelled. Others shrieked and jumped back. We were on glass, floating above the earth. I could see the cabling and the other gondolas below. People regained their nerve and inched back to the center, laughing, talking excitedly about the view and the sensation of floating. Some moved gingerly as if the next step could send them tumbling into space.

"Ladies and gentlemen," Zinc said in a commanding voice, "may I present Mr. Spartak Jones, winner of seven gold medals at the Olympics Games, the man who saved my life, a hero in so many ways." People applauded, a few whistled. "You are all witnesses," he continued. "I have two propositions for Mr. Jones, two opportunities, should he see them as such. And I invite him to select ONE of them. Or, neither. And let me emphasize, you must hear BOTH before making a decision."

"What is this?" I asked, feeling weird already in a partially weightless environment, the earth's curvature obvious miles below, and surrounded by some seriously powerful and famous people. Not my element.

"Right here, on this spot, slave boy." Zinc's smile seemed wicked, pointing directly in front of him. Even so, I always winced inside when I was reminded of what I was, camouflaging the hurt by making a game of it. Smiles and good humor were expected of downers in a rich man's world. On the other hand, I really did love the guy. Zinc put his arm around me, kissed my cheek and stepped back a pace. He seemed more than a little nervous.

"Here is proposition Number One."

Tripper Bolt walked over and handed him a data cube and moved back into the audience next to his dad and brother. Zinc punched it on. "This is a legal document I have signed. If you co-sign it, you will be a free man, the debt-bond fulfilled, and your family will maintain its benefits and you will all be protected."

There was a gasp in the audience. I stood motionless, not sure what I heard. This was not expected.

Sonia just watched; perhaps she knew what this was about. Of course she did. I hated being called a slave, now I didn't have to be. I remembered Justice Washington's warning.

"And now option Number Two." Zinc swiped his tongue over his lips and dried his palms on his pants. He pulled out a small black leather box from his coat pocket. My master dropped to one knee as the crowd tightened around us.

"I, Zinc Ogden McClain, ask if you, Spartak Jones, will marry me and become my husband this night." His voice faltered. Another gasp, a few whistles from the crowd and applause. I could see Zinc's face acquiring sheen. The guy was nervous and desperate to hide it. How I loved this crazy, fabulously rich, insecure, neurotic, lovely man with a weird nose and splotchy skin.

"I love you," Zinc said. "You have captured my heart, bewitched me, and made me a much better man in the time we have been together. I feel whole when I am with you, happy, fulfilled. I know our courtship…has been a little unorthodox." There was laughter, even I found myself grinning and humbled. Zinc seemed to forget what came next. "Damn." He lifted the box and opened the top. Two gold bands were nestled in white silk. "The rings are thin strands of gold, like your remarkable straw-colored hair, twisted and molded together, strong, like you. And the metal is a mixture of gold and zinc, taken from the mine that gave me my name. They are forged together, an alloy that will last forever." He grinned sheepishly. "I hope like our love."

My heart went to him; the man was so vulnerable, opening his feelings in front of so many friends and important people.

"Do I really have to pick just one?" It kind of slipped out, maybe because I was suddenly so nervous.

"Really. You do. That's the offer." Zinc raised an eyebrow. "Don't push it."

I dropped to my knees. I put a hand around the box and Zinc's hand, turning both toward his face. "So beautiful, so creative, just like my Zinc." I looked directly at my lover's loopy grin. "This offer, this opportunity is not something someone like me would expect. Or even have the capacity to dream about." I set the box on the floor and put both hands on Zinc's waist.

"I, Spartak Jones, do accept your offer, Zinc Ogden McClain, and will become your husband and love you forever, forged by the magic of these rings and our special bond, two men who cherish and respect each other." I wrapped my hands behind Zinc's head and pulled him into a kiss. The audience applauded and shrieked. The president whistled using both fingers in her mouth. So did Sonia.

* * *

"So, that's your preference, to keep our own names?"

"Yes," I said, holding Zinc's hand in a private room before the ceremony.

"I like it," he said, "showing equality."

"Hmmmm. Equality. One of us is a downer, the other beyond rich. One an athlete who plays piano, the other beyond rich; one is legally a slave, the other legally the owner. Equality."

He grabbed my head and gave me a knuckle burn. "Owww!" I didn't resist, knowing I deserved it. He let go and slobbered on my cheek. "Yuck!" I slapped his butt.

"I'll bet that doesn't happen too often before a wedding. But I would like to make one change," I said. "I don't have a middle name like you. Would it be agreeable if I was known as Spartak McClain Jones?"

"Thank you," he said with a gulp. "An honor." He rubbed my arm. "Hmmm, nice triceps."

"Later," I said with my best beguiling eye-fluttering smile.

"Count on it." He put his hands on my shoulders and pulled me in front of him. "I want to be clear on the slavery issue," he said. "The law is unsettled and I don't want you vulnerable. Wait until after the Supreme Court overturns it. That's Justice Washington's advice. If something happened to me, and you had your freedom, there might be trouble. Connor and my mother and their allies are still around. Even if the chance is remote, you're safer married to me. We both have enemies." He looked down, considering his next words. "If I die, you head McClain Enterprises."

"Please live forever," I whispered, turned to him and we held each other.

The ceremony itself seemed almost pro forma after that excitement. We stood together. People were seated on thin, lightweight titanium chairs and elaborate inflatable couches. The president officiated; Justice Washington was the official witness. Tripper, Billy, and Dalix were at my side. Sonia, Ran and Paolo stood by Zinc.

Gloria and Connor watched from a link in the second and third gondolas. His brother and mother blamed each other for the fraud and weren't talking. They had a right to be here, he told me. This was his dad's pet project. But they didn't need to be with us. In the third gondola were Mr. and Mrs. Tabor and little Amy. Months ago when Zinc asked me what I wanted for my belated seventeenth birthday, I told him about the family. With security and a medical team, we found them. Amy's teeth were now perfect. Mr. Tabor had a real job in a McClain business and they all had an apartment. How could I not love Zinc?

"And do you, Zinc, promise to love, cherish and obey, this man, Spartak, for as long as you both shall live?"

"I do, with all my heart."

"Could you repeat that part about obey? I want to make sure we both heard that. And do I have to promise that too?"

Zinc reached over and touched a finger to my mouth, shaking his head. He glanced at my ear then reached over and lightly squeezed the top, all restored to normal. The slave tracker was history, never to be seen again. In two more minutes, we were husband and husband. We kissed, probably too long and deeply judging by the coughing and giggles from the audience.

"Get a room!" Tripper yelled.

Zinc asked me to play a song "my slave boy once mentioned with great affection, one he said his father sang to his mother at their wedding." I was surprised, irritated, touched, almost emotional. We walked hand in hand to a grand piano revealed when a curtain was moved and the instrument floated to the center of the room on airborne feet.

"But first," Zinc said to the room, "I believe we have a special request. Madam President."

"Spartak," President Chiu said as she walked to the side of the piano, "I've heard many wonderful reviews of your private performance of Chopin's *Fantasie Impromptu* at the academy. Two standing ovations, I've heard. Would you honor me, honor us in this room with another performance?"

Play here? I didn't even have sheet music. Notes on a Z-ether in DIMM4 were ridiculous. I hadn't practiced this or the others in weeks. My mouth felt like I was chewing on a tar ball, my response a squawk. Zinc opened a folder on the piano with paper sheet music, my preference.

"Madam President," Zinc said, "I believe he is trying to say he would be delighted."

He would be punished later, I thought, sitting on the bench, adjusting the height. And that might make it all worthwhile if I messed up. Certainly it could distract me if I was humiliated. And bringing the music was sweet.

I closed my eyes, adjusted my sleeves, retrieved the notes from my head, lined them up and began to play, lilting, racing, rich, the music filling the gondola as the sun seemed to rise from behind the earth, filtering up through the glass floor, suffusing the room with light, as in the beginning. I was floating in space. At the end, applause and "bravos!" Sonia, Tripper, and that crew were turning it on. I stood and bowed, the blue earth now occupying the entire window below us.

"Encore," the Speaker of the House shouted.

"Please," Zinc said quietly.

Several members of the audience gathered around the piano.

"Play a Chopin *Nocturne,*" Sonia asked, now standing between Zinc and her uncle.

"Yes, Edgardo, a nocturne would be nice." Justice Washington suppressed a smile. His eyes glistened gold in the light.

"*Opus 9, Number 2,*" I said to him. "Thank you for everything." I turned my eyes back to the keyboard. "Let me collect the notes in my head." My hands started to feel it. "This is for Justice Washington," I said in a loud voice. "A brave and thoughtful champion of human rights." It was a magical piece, relaxing, crisp. My mind drifted as I played, lost in the heavens.

"Thank you so much," I said, standing and taking a bow after I finished. "Now my final piece, I promise. This is for you, Mom and Dad, from your wedding. And for my husband, on the first day of our marriage. It is beautiful, like you both, like my Zinc. Written by Franz Schubert. *Ave Maria*. And because I love you all, I will not sing." I sat.

Zinc stepped behind me, touching my shoulder.

Ave Maria, about the Virgin Mary, about redemption, but mostly an emotional high, a prayer for sinners. I never cared about the words, only the melding of voice and music, irresistible, passionate, ethereal, even divine. And what more perfect setting than hovering above the earth like the angels?

As I finished the opening bars and began the melody, an otherworldly soprano arose from some hidden place.

"A…ve…Mar…i…i..a……"

Expecting an angel I turned my head and saw one. Rhonda Van Deen walked languidly from behind a curtain toward me, dressed in a floor-length pink silk gown, matching her hair and the necklace around her throat, a rope of pink diamonds tied into a knot, sparkling like fire in the earth light. Then a man's voice joined in; my father walked to Rhonda's side. He'd grown one of his periodic beards, all blond and trim, making him look older and triggered my own anxiety if I'd ever even have serious stubble. Dad looked at me, almost radiant with love, then turned his head and sang to Mom. Obviously they'd rehearsed.

I'd planned ahead too and had a handkerchief for this kind of occasion but it'd have to wait, both hands were busy. I let my tears and my nose just drip on my lap. Mom walked over and stood beside me at the keyboard and held hands with Dad. I was crying so hard I couldn't see the ivories. At the end, I stood, pretended I was wiping my eyes with the handkerchief. But I had to blow my nose before I could speak. Not elegant but practical.

"May I introduce my special friend at the academy, the fabulous Rhonda Van Deen! And the equally amazing Stuart Jones, my father. He also plays virtuoso violin if any orchestras are in the market." We hugged and kissed as the audience applauded.

A high decibel alarm sounded. A security guard stepped to a command panel at the side of the gondola. Ransom did a quick step to his side.

"Jesusistas," Ran announced after a brief discussion, his voice measured, "headed toward us in spacesuits up the ladder from the lowest gondola."

CHAPTER 47

"There are five white suits," Ransom said. He turned to the huge Z-ether behind us; it was revealed in detail, even some close-ups of their helmets. "They're climbing," he said, "using what workers call a Spoker, a small motor with handle, held in place magnetically, with sprockets for climbing using small inset holes embedded in each of the score of nano-steel tethers. They're for repair work and climb faster than a gondola."

Zinc pointed behind him. "Here's a scene inside the fifth gondola," he said. "That's Cardinal Iglesias in his red robe and hat, with two dozen young men in headbands, chanting death to those who did not submit to the will of God. He dressed a little different coming on board." The man didn't seem to know he was being watched. "We provided no staff on this gondola, letting them use their own team after some training on the food services and equipment." Zinc touched another button on the control.

"Those are explosives," Zinc said to the crowd now in a half circle around him near the wall, "in the cabinet at the back corner. They're on a suicide mission for Christian martyrdom, determined to blow up the platform and ladder and murder all of us after appropriate publicity announcing the arrival of Jesus. Maybe that's where he's supposed to disembark."

The speaker and majority leader stood on either side of the president. I loved films from the early days of cinema and told Zinc earlier that I thought the congressional leaders were much like a silent movie comedy pair but I couldn't recall their names.

"What do we do?" Speaker O'Mally asked.

"Can they get inside?" Majority Leader Druid inquired.

"Give me a moment." Zinc turned to the crowd. "By their actions here, the Dominionists again prove that they are the major threat we face for the continuation of America as a government of the people. These are madmen who want to seize power and kill each of you who does not submit to their fantasy."

I walked over beside him and slipped a thumb inside Zinc's belt. He seemed to be taking this in a strange direction.

"The solution is more democracy, involve more people, dilute the Dominionists. Odd, I know, coming from me and someone of my class. My husband has told me about how our current laws keep people like his parents from voting. I have considered this and the obsession of a majority in Congress and in many state legislatures with voter disqualification to maintain a lock on power. I think passage of S.B. 112 is a way to dilute the power of the Dominionists and return government to the heart of what democracy is about…the right of the people, all the people to participate freely. It's the first of many steps we must take."

"But what about the terrorists?" O'Mally howled, pointing toward earth. "They're nearly here."

The screen showed the fanatics were passing the third gondola. They were also visible through the floor.

"First, let me say that my support for S.B. 112 is a gift for my husband. We are all equal in the new America and in our marriage. I think the legislation could use a name to build public support. Perhaps *Spartak's Law*. Yes, I rather like that." He smiled at the nervous guests. "Don't you agree?"

"Have you gone mad?" O'Mally blasted. "Yes, I'll agree." Others nodded, looking upset. "Do something!"

The figures in white neared the fourth gondola.

"My voice is being transmitted into their helmets as well as all of the gondolas. We are nearing 20,000 miles above the equator. A long way down. Since this ladder is attached to one of McClain Enterprise's ships in international waters, it is beyond the jurisdiction of any country, as was established in our United Nations charter. Justice here, as in a ship at sea, is meted out by the captain. Essentially that is my role here. I state this as context for what is about to happen."

Zinc typed a code into the device in his hand.

All four figures were pulling up just below us. You could just make out faces in the clear fronts of the helmets. Ransom took a position beside Zinc, the terrorists below, the political leaders before him.

"Cardinal Iglesias. You and your brethren have delighted in calling our world Sodom. If that is so, then know this, *I am Sodom's son!* We made certain your supporters knew of opportunities to take part in this celebration. I think your application was as a young adult education program. We allowed you to mislead us and flaunt the rules, knowing you thought us fools. We tapped your communications weeks ago and our private scanners revealed your explosives when you boarded…and disabled them."

The Cardinal screamed a Latin epithet everyone could hear.

"We decided the interests of the American people, and perhaps restoring human faith in religion, might be better served by having you as our guest and allowing you to respond to our hospitality. As Bishop Perry faced his end, crucified in his own church by Satan himself, your demise comes this hour."

I watched Zinc and he turned his face to me. He did look like a younger version of his father. There was no stuttering. He punched in a second code. There was a hum. The four figures stopped their advance. Their Spokers disengaged and the terrorists began floating away, tumbling, arms flailing. One grabbed at a cable and ripped off his glove. He was lifeless within seconds.

Zinc transmitted the image from exterior lumins on the big screen. He turned up the volume on the shrieks and prayers. People were staring and cringing. It was hard to watch but impossible to turn away.

"Cardinal, here are your astronauts in free fall, one already dead. Enjoy the view and contemplate their final words. They scream for you. Since we assumed you would use the spacesuits in the emergency locker, we added a surprise, some special modifications. The magnetic foot and hand pads and Spokers could be demagnetized on my signal. Jesusistas in the suits—you are gradually falling back to earth faster and faster. The outsides of your suits are beginning to heat and, like the fires of hell where you will spend eternity, you will slowly cook." His voice was matter-of-fact and that made it riveting.

Everyone remained fixated on the screen or looking below his or her feet as the figures disappeared. One bounced off the corner of a gondola further down and spun off.

"Cardinal. This is your fault. Your hubris and greed for power brought this about. You are a partner with Satan himself, your Dominionist cause a fraud. Your astronaut friends have about four minutes of life. We will transmit the visuals—flames, then embers, then dust."

Zinc watched the Jesusistas screaming in the car far below, their faces in living color on the big screen. The people around my husband looked stunned. He awaited the flames. His calm, bravura, ruthless performance established his new image for the world.

"My God!" President Chiu muttered, clutching Jim Diamond, her plump, middle-aged security director.

"Gentlemen in gondola five." Zinc punched in a new command. "You should be noticing movement in your cabin. You are no longer climbing higher but slipping out. I just decoupled the car from the elevator. You are floating in space. Within seconds you will begin to plunge. As you roast your reactions will be recorded, perhaps as a warning to others and for justice."

Zinc's face was hard. I'd never seen him like this.

"You placed a bounty on the head of my husband. Your people, in league with the Timko family, murdered my father. Before that you murdered others: my cousin, Cedric Rand; a fine young athlete at the Olympics named Miguel Torros; two FBI agents, the son of a congressman, two of my guards, among others. And you planned the murder of everyone in this room who would not submit to your madness. And here is your penance."

The president and other dignitaries and crew, their faces twisting in horror, watched the screen as the gondola's passengers screamed, some getting into fistfights, one man pummeling the Cardinal, ripping off his cap, his bloody face matched his collar, until the interior exploded in flames.

"Ladies and gentlemen," Zinc said, raising his arms. "America has survived this crisis. Hopefully we will learn that sleeping with Satan for some temporary reward is not worth the price. Those senators and members of congress proposing to turn over the government to such murderers, to the Dominonist Council, will soon add a new word to their titles: *former.* Their actions are little short of treason and they should be prosecuted and imprisoned. The Dominionists are defeated for now. But they are still there, biding their time. And others like them." He coughed and looked back up. Everyone was staring at him, some gawking; my husband, the new center of the universe.

"It is time to build a new America, a more democratic one, a nation where men and women can earn an honest wage, a livable wage. Where everyone over eighteen can vote. No more games. I admit to my own grievous shortcomings in this, my class and family were blinded by greed, hubris, and indifferent to anyone below their status. The trauma of the last months has taught me that we are all humans with short lives." He stepped over and put his arm around my waist.

"I hope to use the power of my fortune to turn things around. I would be honored if we can work together in redefining our goals and…*let America be America again.* Dinner will be served in thirty minutes. Please enjoy the view."

* * *

Zinc was besieged by admirers, everyone in the room asking questions, thanking him for saving their lives, desperate to touch him, pledging support. Wanting DIMMs with him. A single pool reporter, representing thousands of media outlets on Earth, giddy with this career-changing scoop, interviewed Zinc, the president and dozens of people. I got interviewed as well, including about the first marriage in space. Suddenly being an Olympian didn't seem so important. I was so proud of him, my partner, my husband.

"I cried," Dalix confessed to me. "A lot. The wedding was so beautiful. Your husband has a downer soul. Honestly, getting in this machine was the scariest thing I've ever done. The other guys refused but send their love." He gave me a crunching hug. "Thank you for changing my life."

At dinner the Congressional leaders formally announced they

would support S.B.112. "Spartak's Law" they called it. I giggled with Rhonda. And the speeches seemed unending, like in the US Senate. Maybe there should be a talk limitation on Space Elevator trips. An eternity later, it ended.

CHAPTER 48

THE NEXT MORNING, OUR GONDOLA DOCKED at the circular space platform, bigger than a dozen football fields, sixty feet tall, more a cargo bay and docking site for space miners than a tourist hotel. The earth from space, 22,000 miles up, was a dumbfounding panorama as seen before only by astronauts. Everyone gawked. It was a spectacle that demanded humility, like the temple of Zeus. The other gondolas followed over the next hour.

After a simple lunch and congratulatory speeches, we stood before an undulating blue drape that covered the entire back wall of the docking station. When I got closer I discovered it was not an actual drape but a fanta projection. Behind it, the sight every passenger in decades to come would see exiting his or her gondola, an icon.

As Zinc went to the life-like rope projection to reveal the artwork, Glenda McClain walked up next to me. I sensed her before she spoke.

"Hello, Spartak. Congratulations on the wedding. Zinc obviously loves you. I'm happy for you both."

"Mrs. McClain..."

She put up her hand. "No. Let me finish. I've not been nice to you and I know it. Maybe I'm not a nice person. But you are. And I've seen what a difference you have made in my Zinc. He is a man now. You helped him grow up. For that, I am truly grateful."

She walked back into the crowd. I watched, not sure what to think. Maybe there was hope. She hadn't apologized. Perhaps it wasn't in her DNA. It was likely just a ploy to get back in Zinc's good graces and free up her finances. I saw Connor in the distance, watching me. He was standing alone.

Trust but verify, came to mind, a term used in old-time nuclear arms negotiations between the US and old Soviet Union. It might be my new motto for dealing with them. We were now family. And nothing would happen against either of them. I started having a panic attack.

Connor was now my brother-in-law!

GLENDA was my mother-in-law!

Fuck.

Compartmentalize.

I turned back to my husband, taking a series of breaths to calm myself. There he was, looking handsome, masculine, and in command, calling for attention. Maybe I'd have a Zinc mask made.

"My father wanted a mural," he explained to the crowd, "but didn't make arrangements due to his injury and demise, so I took charge just a few months back. It was done by an emerging art talent, a soon-to-be star. He designed the mural and led a brilliant team to bring it to completion in a short time. Let me introduce you to Billy Eagle, a student at Ogden Academy."

I screeched and immediately brought both hands to my mouth. Studly gymnasts shouldn't do girly screams in public. Billy had never told me he was doing this. This would make his career. I thought of his parents on the reservation and how proud they must be. My Zinc had done this for me again.

Billy wore a high-collared ruby red jacket and a lacy silver scarf with sparkling highlights around his neck. So…so…artistic. And half his hair was a twisted black nest, matching his lipstick and eye shadow.

The drape appeared to flutter down and dissolved. Titled *Freedom.* The mural was a montage, the Revolutionary War, Lincoln, Suffragettes in England and America, some in prison, the 1960s civil rights marches, Martin Luther King, Sheriff Bull Connor and his dogs attacking black marchers, Nelson Mandela in South Africa just released from prison, Gandhi, the first moon landing, mining on asteroids, Susan Combs the first transgender president, General Elise Zoltan who ended the big Middle East war in 2070 saving millions of Muslim lives, and at the center, people standing in line to vote framed by the view of Earth as seen from the station.

I did a double take, spotting my face in one small section with people behind me holding a sign, "Spartak's Law." Zinc was next to me, clutching my hand. Clearly he'd planned this months ago or Billy was a damn fast painter. To be included with such giants was an honor I didn't want or deserve. I hoped no one thought I'd asked for it.

The eyes in the painting, in every face, they moved, following whoever looked in their direction. How did he do this?

The palette was intense, a cornucopia of color, everything painted in hues you would not expect—orange babies, green faces, blue trees, lemon oceans. Yet somehow it all worked, almost intoxicating—from a distance it was an abstract swirl of color twisting into a twinkling vortex at the center, the Milky Way at full brilliance above the Earth. Get closer and it was the individual dramatic scenes.

"Like Rembrandt in Oz," commented President Chiu.

"While on mushrooms," Speaker O'Mally offered.

"Do you think there is any way we can take some credit?" inquired Majority Leader Druid.

* * *

"I want to thank you, Zinc, for so thoroughly taking care of some difficult problems." President Chiu spoke as we were sitting in the secondary utility room after dinner, waiting for her assistant, Jim Diamond. She'd said earlier she wanted to talk privately, just Zinc, Ransom, and me. And her staff suggested this utilitarian space, a small table and chairs, banks of controls for electrical and communications. There was even the station trash chute and an elevator for all levels. She said she wanted privacy and this was the place.

"You mean saving us all from the Cardinal?" Zinc asked, stretching back in his chair. "You're welcome." His smile was broad and warm.

There was a bing as the elevator moved down to our level.

"Here's Jim," Chiu said, turning to the door beside her.

But it was Kinuba Steele who stepped out, holding solar pistols in each hand.

All three of us jumped to our feet. She wore knee-high boots, a black one-piece cling, high collar and open to her breasts in front. Her face was stern, her expression haughty, even amused.

"How?" I blurted out. "The FBI took you." None of us had brought weapons or wore our XOs. No need.

"Sweet boy," Kinuba said, "I told you I would see you again. The FBI took me and the FBI let me go. President's orders."

"I trust you all know my associate, Ms. Steele," President Chiu said. "If everyone is going to stand, then I will too." She leaned against a counter, three feet from Kinuba, looking satisfied.

"Not possible," Zinc said, tilting his head, incredulous. "My father made your career."

Chiu snarled, "And he reminded me of that every time we met. I was not his doll nor am I yours."

"No, no!" Kinuba said, raising a pistol at Ransom as he moved.

There were three of us and she had two weapons. One of us would get to her and I remembered how easily she handled Connor. The president didn't appear to be armed. I was the fastest and in a direct line to her.

"Actually, so you will know, I have been told to eliminate Zinc with my first shot." Kinuba looked at him and shrugged. "I just follow the script, not write it."

"NO!" I said, touching his shoulder, stepping in front of him. He tried to push me back but I was stronger.

"Please respect my wishes," my husband said quietly. We looked at each other and I stepped to his side.

"What's this about, Madam President?" Zinc asked, his tone bitter.

"You were very useful to me. Although everything didn't work out as I planned, most things did. The Twelve Families are overbearing, destroying America, and I'm tired of being attached to their harness. The Dominionists wanted to kill anyone in government who wasn't as crazy as they were. But I couldn't go after them. The military likely would rebel. I figured you could with the right incentives. And you did. The End Timer threat has been neutralized and my prints aren't on it."

Her face was smug, fully enjoying her advantage. I wondered if I should go after her first.

"And public sentiment will likely be so energized that I can clear out the traitors in the military."

We stood in silence, unsure what to do. If Zinc was killed, Kinuba and the president would find out just how lethal I could be. The president almost seemed to snicker, looking down, pursing her lips, then back at us with a smile. "We tried to start a war within the Twelve. That's why Cedric was murdered. But you didn't bite. I really thought you'd be more impulsive, Zinc, but maybe your slave or Ransom Bolt tempered you—I'm guessing. We planted the red hair as a distraction knowing you would find Tarlon Timko's DNA. A bit amateurish but it worked. Tarlon's murder was not planned. The Jesusistas just went a little unhinged, sort of their natural state."

"Stay still, Spartak!" Kinuba warned. I was trying to edge closer so I could jump in front of her pistol. There were lots of piano players in the world, but only one Zinc.

"Okay," I said. "I'm an obedient downer slave boy." But my leg was bent, ready to leap.

"So one threat is gone," President Chiu continued with an approving nod to Kinuba, "but my other problem remains. The Twelve. With some suggestions to Sherilyn Timko—she is a friend too, you know, we go way back—she arranged for the murder of your father. Through her son, the Dominionists became allies in that escapade. Odd, isn't it, how politics works? The Timko family really does hate the McClains. And Zinc, you really made a mistake calling for voting reform. I don't care what the general public wants. So you're an even greater irritation."

"You do realize this is being recorded, don't you?" Ransom asked, lifting his head to a box in the ceiling.

I wondered if it was true.

"Clever but no," she said. "My guys read the schematics. And why have lumins in a secondary utility room?" She reached into her purse and pulled out an electro-slug derringer, a lady's weapon with a pearl handle. "I know you've done the arithmetic. Now there are three."

"Put up the gun, Madam President," Kinuba said, turning to her. "You will murder no one up here where the gods live."

Chiu swung her pistol around and Kinuba fired into the president's shoulder, slamming her back against a wall before she dropped to her knees and slid to the floor. We stood there, not sure what to do, gaping in shock, even Ran. Zinc moved first. "Let's get the first aid kit and call the station surgeon."

"A word first," Kinuba said. She stepped over and kicked away the derringer. "She asked me to kill you all and shove your bodies down the trash chute. Then I suspect she was going to shoot me and proclaim herself a heroine, stopping a stowaway killer. I realized that just now when she pulled the derringer. Consider whether you want her to survive. She is not a nice lady." She lowered her pistols and set them on the table.

Zinc pushed an emergency com line. "Emergency medical unit to utility room two!" Then he grabbed a first aid box and kneeled beside Chiu. Ran stood over him, keeping watch on Ms. Steel.

"Why did you hesitate?" I asked Kinuba.

"Bitch!" President Chiu yelled.

Kinuba tossed her a kiss and walked up to me, planting her hands on my shoulders. She was about five inches taller; her grip hard. "Like I told you before, because I admire you, Spartak. I am a downer too, who did good being bad. You are virtuous—maybe with an occasional deviation. And you have made Zinc a better man. There is now hope for the first time in generations."

"And that IS a surveillance with audio," Ran told the president in grim satisfaction. "We intentionally don't show lots of things in nonencrypted schematics as a precaution against saboteurs. Lots of bad things can happen in utility rooms. You'll look glorious when it's broadcast."

Chiu closed her eyes in resignation, in complete defeat. Maybe. It could be an act for now. She was still president.

Kinuba laughed. "I think I will sleep in the president's suite tonight. I understand there is a vacancy."

CHAPTER 49

Hours later, taking a micro-lift, we found our "honeymoon suite." Obviously the builders had a sense of humor. It was one of two hundred tiny metal cubicles stacked in rows for maximum utility. But it did have its own bathroom and near-normal gravity.

Designed for astronauts, miners, and space haulers, the room had a bed and storage locker. A massive curved translucent wall covered the backsides of the cubicles. It felt like we were sitting amongst the stars. The quarters were so small I could barely stand and Zinc had to bend over. He sat on the bed, stretched, took off his clothes, slipped under a sheet and watched the view, more me as I stripped than the stars.

"So what happens to President Chiu?" I asked.

"Impeachment, prosecution, and prison. Or, maybe she just resigns for health reasons and we all say nothing, pretend it didn't happen. The Dominionist generals running the military won't exit their posts easily. She may save her neck in a deal with us. Many unknowns."

"And Kinuba Steele?"

"I've a guard outside her door, not that she couldn't get past him. But we are 22,000 miles up. If the president tells what Kinuba was hired to do, she incriminates herself. Do we press charges or forget about it? She may go free."

"Did she kill Cedric?"

"I don't know."

We were silent for a long time, turning our eyes into the white pricked blackness. My nerves were shot.

"Enough of this," I commanded. "We have other business to address."

"Oh, I hope so," Zinc agreed, tossing the sheet aside and reaching out.

An hour later, still naked, I leaned against the wall behind the tiny bed, Zinc scooted in front of me and we held each other, watching the Milky Way.

"We see what few have ever witnessed. Who'd ever think a downer would be allowed such an honor while sharing it with a vain, sexy, insecure, ridiculously rich, and pampered spouse?"

"You are no downer-boy, Spartak. The term never fit."

"Easy to say, from one who has so much to one who has so little."

"Trust me. Little is not how anyone would describe your gifts. But let me ask, is that how you view our relationship? As so little?"

"Oh, Twelver, enough of this minuet." I flipped Zinc on his back and held his arms tight overhead. My master pulled and twisted, grunting, unable to break free. Then we started laughing, holding each other, side to side on the bed.

"So, tell me slave boy, do ye love me?"

"More than a kitten loves milk, my mollycoddled master."

"Not quite what I was hoping for."

"Let me ask you, my liege, will you ever grant this vassal his freedom?"

"I think not, husband. Given all the accolades that have swollen your head, it's the only way I can hope to win at least a few arguments as a married couple. Otherwise, I don't stand a chance."

I bit the end of my master's crooked nose. "Actually, I think I'm okay with that for now. A slave with benefits."

Acknowledgments

KATHERINE V. FORREST, A WISE MENTOR and friend. Your warmth, wisdom and encouragement kept me writing. Thank you.

Bravo to the Lambda Literary Foundation, dedicated to nurturing LGBT writers, and its fabulous Writers Workshop. I took this book there in 2013 and the talented students and teacher/best selling science fiction writer Samuel R. Delany offered tough love advice. Thank you.

A special acknowledgment to Dennis Myers, the always insightful and brilliant reporter I met in army boot camp, offering ideas and astounding research. Then there is Loa Semrau, always encouraging, a special friend who makes me laugh. Barbara O'Connor, a cheerleader, sage and advocate for all her many friends. And Rebecca Chekouras, a Lambda Fellow from 2013, always ready with insightful and calming commentary.

Did you like this book?

If so, please post online reviews and tell your friends. Do you want to discuss any of the characters or assumptions about life in the 22nd century? Visit our website: www.stevenacoulter.com

Discussion Questions

The *Chronicles of Spartak* presents a cautionary tale, bleak at times, full of action, ruthlessness, betrayal, valor and hope. Here are some questions you may want to explore.

1. Spartak makes difficult choices in regard to his family and his own future. What were they and would you have done anything different? Why?

2. Do you think the world Spartak lives in could ever become reality in the United States? What forces are moving America in that direction? What forces might save it? How do you see the future?

3. Is there anything you could do today to give Spartak a better life in 2115?

4. Various media sources are mentioned in the book. Do you think they were staffed with independent journalists who could pursue a story wherever it led or were they propagandists? What are the trends today on news media?

5. Do you see Justice Washington and Sonia as justified in what they did behind the scenes? Are they good, bad or something else? What else might they have done?

6. If the government and media are not looking out for the little guy, who is?

7. Should Spartak have forgiven Zinc after he was slapped and thrown out of the mansion? What were his options?

8. What should Zinc do about his mother and Connor? What if they were your family?

9. Zinc ruthlessly destroyed three wealthy families to protect his lover and also to flaunt his own power as a mess-with-me-at-your-peril warning. Given that it was a dispute between barronials, all beyond the power of government, was it a necessary choice and/or a moral one, given his reality?

10. Zinc and Ransom Bolt crucified the leading religious insurrectionist, believing the dramatic act would thwart a civil war that could kill millions as well as protect their own power and privilege. Was it an acceptable choice given the state of America? Are they good guys or bad?

11. What would you do if you saw your religion, your local church, hijacked by extremists? Is it inconceivable? Who would you go to if you saw it happening?

12. When government and the courts are weak, corrupt and/or politicized, is vigilantism encouraged?

13. Because of barronial contempt for government, police departments were privatized, the contract held by one of the Twelve Families. The focus of Harmony Enforcers was managing the poor, not justice. Is this farfetched for America?

14. Spartak disdained violence but was prolific in its use. He saw America increasingly as a thug-ocracy, the powerful doing what they wanted. Yet he readily supported the most powerful and often ruthless family. The downers saw him as a hero. Was he?

What questions or answers do you have?
Were these the right questions?

What would you like to see happen in Book 2?
Offer suggestions at
www.stevenacoulter.com

Coming Soon...

Here is a preview:

October 15, 2116

"Spartak! Get up! Suit up!"

"Huh?" I skidded off the edge of my bed, knees banging on the metal floor. It took a moment for my brain to clear as I stood and looked around the tiny room, a metal box with one wall offering a front row seat of the universe. The face of Ransom Bolt popped out of my class com-ring and floated before me on the Z-ether screen, his gaze hard. As head of McClain weaponry and security he was the most imposing man I'd ever encountered, massive and muscular, a granite face and persona that unnerved me and made me submissive the first time we'd met, after a guard beat me when I was in a holding cell being prepped as a slave. But he was now my friend and protector just like his two grown sons.

"What, Sir?" I was only in my undershorts and as I tried to adjust the fabric, I realized I had been thinking about Zinc and what we did this morning. I did my best not to draw attention to the issue in case the Z-ether captured more than my face.

"I need your special talents."

"Could you be more specific?" It was out of my mouth before I could think. Zinc used that exact statement in bed earlier as he woke me up and I cooed this question as I kissed his cheek. Now I just hoped my inflection was more professional. I often had a problem coordinating my brain and mouth.

"Warrior talents."

My least favorite. I did my best not to flinch. He knew I disliked combat. No, I detested it. He seemed to study my expression before continuing. He was good at explaining, not just giving orders, helping you understand the context. It was one reason he was such a great soldier.

"The president's twelve-member security team broke into the medical unit and took her, killing two of our guards, before stealing provisions and retreating to one of the large bunk rooms. They also signaled the military on earth for intervention. We only have six guards left up here, not counting you, Zinc, and my boys. Bring your sword ready to use. Just seeing you, they may hesitate and surrender or we destroy them."

"Where?"

"Second level. I'll be at the climber gate and meet you. Zinc is with me."

"Is my family safe and my friends?"

"Yes. So far they're just protecting President Chiu."

"Three minutes."

His image dissolved. Being mostly naked saved time. I grabbed my ultra thin exoskeleton, XOs we called them, giving me the strength of ten men and able to deflect most weapons, a secret product of McClain Enterprises, not sold to the military or anyone else. It felt like silk as I pulled it on, then my black stretch clinger pants and thick-soled knee boots with the retractable heel knife. I picked a red long-sleeved crew neck with shimmering silver lightning bolts and attached the flash grenade tube down my right arm. I tested it by twisting my wrist and a round ball dropped into my palm. I cinched my belt into place and pulled on my old black leather jacket, still showing a small solar burn from when Dominionists attacked us at the Olympics.

Slowly I extracted the floppy plasteel sword from its hiding place in my belt, a flaccid silver razor, useful but not yet optimum in a fight. Few knew where I hid it, always with me at Ran's insistence, a secret weapon that had saved my life more than once. It had also become a symbol, although of what depended on who was talking. I touched a raised bump, waiting for it to read my thumb and gene print. It would only work for me. There was a green flash and the sword lengthened, thickened, erect, hard, glowing and lethal, a cross between a rapier and a medieval short sword, almost weightless but exquisitely balanced with an elaborate swept hilt covering the grip. It was a glitzy upgrade from the simpler weapon I'd used earlier in the year when I was battling the Jesusistas. Ransom said this one better matched my personality. "It grows the legend of Spartak," he told me more than once, to "help you win by intimidation not slaughter." He was a master of psychological warfare and my image was part of my value as a fighter. And I loved it as much as the wooden pirate cutlass I played with as a boy. This was my signature weapon, the only one of its kind in the world and my battle exploits had made it famous, captured on four-dimensional DIMM4s and projected to billions of Z-ethers around the world and repeated endlessly as news and entertainment.

I pulled up my XO hood, slipped on my gloves, attached my facemask and snapped a blue sonic pistol to my belt, another McClain exclusive, a disarmingly short tube with handle packing twice the power of solar weapons. I set it to wide-band to stun, not kill. I dashed from the room, down the narrow hallway and grabbed a climber strap.

"Level two."

In seconds the transporter stopped and I stepped into a small crowd. I removed my veil and smiled at my husband, dressed like me but without the sword.

"Love you," Zinc said, taking a moment to press his lips to mine. I kissed back and held him tight, hoping I didn't have morning breath. Technically we were still on our honeymoon, day two.

"Enough, guys!" Ransom barked, more amused than angry, towering over me, big as a pro-wrestler with the rough chiseled features of a marine drill instructor, his black hair in an elaborate braid down his back.

"I love you too," I mouthed to Zinc and turned to Ran for orders. He was in his black uniform with the McClain golden starburst insignia on his shoulder. His sons were behind him and we nodded and smiled. No more was needed. They were like brothers and had saved me and helped me survive in so many ways. Paolo Bolt was now twenty-two, slender, studying to be a doctor at Stanford University and a trained fighter. Tripper was Zinc's age, a school companion, and built like his dad, huge and imposing, bigger than a football lineman. There are also three guards in uniform, faces covered.

"Spartak," the trio shouted in unison as they stiffened in a mock salute. I nodded, surprised and a bit embarrassed. One pulled back his mask. It was Hernandez, my personal security guard and now friend; dark-skinned, ten years my senior with an ebony ponytail. We grinned at each other for an instant. Teasing could help cut the tension in war.

"They're in bunk suite three down corridor twelve," Ransom continued. "Security lumins indicate two guards outside behind a solar shield. President Chiu is inside, still on a gurney, with her aide, Jim Diamond, and ten of her guards, equipped with solar pistols and rifles."

"And other weapons?" Zinc asked.

"We must assume they're heavily armed. We gave them total leeway when they boarded ahead of us five days ago." Ran touched a finger behind his right ear and watched a small Z-ether screen pop out and deliver a message we could not see or hear. "Confirmed," he said and it disappeared. He looked at us and announced: "One more will join us."

"I thought this was the crew?" I asked.

"Kinuba Steele," he said, slowly, rolling out the syllables in his bass voice, knowing we'd be shocked.

"She tried to murder us last night," Zinc said, his voice taut, stating the obvious, "on the president's orders." He'd been working hard to always sound calm and serious so he seemed more leader than schoolboy.

"But she didn't," Ran responded, just as obvious, "and she shot President Chiu instead. She is a lethal warrior and our army is a little thin."

"A mercenary is no soldier." Zinc looked and sounded angry.

The woman was indeed a hired killer, recruited by the president to murder Zinc, Ransom and myself last night and also involved when Zinc and I were kidnapped and tortured last year by Dominionists and later at the Olympics. But last night Kinuba figured the president was about to double-cross her and shot the woman. And she was likely right. Kinuba had shifting loyalties and I wondered if she had a moral center. She'd said she admired me, that what I'd done in sports, beating barronials, saving lives in battle, becoming a symbol and hero, gave downers hope and pride. The tape of the whole episode with the president was dispatched to everyone on board the space station and through media around the world.

In her own way, Kinuba Steele was as imposing as Ransom. She was six-foot-three, lithe, ebony skin, hair cut in short rows like undulating waves over her head, with small hoop earrings shifting from gold to blue to red. She moved with attitude, magnetic, high cheekbones, big golden eyes, her head often tilted back, a woman in charge. I found her exquisite. She was a downer too she'd told me and used assassinations as a way to break out of our class. Who she killed didn't matter, she'd explained, "they are just self-absorbed barronials as clients and targets." She'd put down her twin pistols last night after wounding the president and said she would not harm us—not exactly surrender but better than being shot. I would not want to face her in combat.

Moments later the lift groaned, we turned and Kinuba stepped off the foothold. She was in a midnight blue body suit, twin orange-red solars on her belt and a long curved knife in a zebra-striped scabbard. She made me want to run to her and run away at the same time. The lady warrior winked at me, walked to my side, put an arm over my shoulder and kissed my ear.

"Hello precious," she whispered and squeezed me. I just stared ahead.

About the Author

STEVEN A. COULTER uses fast paced fiction to explore a future shaped by today's reality. His work is enriched by his varied careers—soldier, teacher, journalist, state legislator, businessman and library commissioner. He has a BA and MA in Journalism and was a Lambda Literary Fellow in 2008 and 2013. He lives in San Francisco.

CPSIA information can be obtained
at www.ICGtesting.com
Printed in the USA
LVOW07s0130251116
514309LV00001B/62/P